PRAISE FOR GERALD EVERETT JONES

2020 New York City Big Book Awards WINNER in Mystery
2020 Independent Press Awards Distinguished Favorite in Mystery
2020 Eric Hoffer Award Finalist - Mystery

Early Reviews of *Preacher*:

This is literature masquerading as a mystery. Carefully yet powerfully, Gerald Jones creates a small, stunning world in a tiny midwestern town, infusing each character with not just life but wit, charm, and occasionally menace. This is the kind of writing one expects from John Irving or Jane Smiley.

— MARVIN J. WOLF, AUTHOR OF THE RABBI BEN MYSTERIES, INCLUDING *A SCRIBE DIES IN BROOKLYN*

This is an excellent read. Such an engaging storyteller! It really sucked me in. That last page did cause a triple-take, quadruple-take, and whatever comes after, up to about eight. Jones is definitely one of my favorite authors.

— JOHN RACHEL, AUTHOR OF *BLINDERS KEEPERS* AND *THE MAN WHO LOVED TOO MUCH*

A smart, thoroughly entertaining, and suspenseful mystery novel, which is not so much a who-done-it as a how-and-why. The characters are universally well-drawn and quirky, and the relationship between Evan and Naomi is fresh and romantic.

I loved it.

— ROBERTA EDGAR, CO-AUTHOR OF *THE PERFECT PLAY: THE DAY WE BROKE THE BANK IN ATLANTIC CITY*

The constant shifts in trust and tidbits of new information kept me guessing until the end who was friend or foe and the 'need' to find out kept the pages turning.

Many of the common stigmas, questions, and feelings suicide deaths leave in their wake were also addressed in a responsible way, which will help the conversation around suicide in general.

— RUTH GOLDEN, WRITER-PRODUCER, *THE SILENT GOLDENS: A DOCUMENTARY ABOUT SUICIDE* AND *TALKING ABOUT SUICIDE WITH MARIETTE HARTLEY*

Preacher Finds a Corpse is an absolute pleasure to read. Reminiscent of Charlaine Harris's mysteries and Barbara Kingsolver's early novels like *Animal Dreams* and *The Bean Trees*, it's full of quirky characters who animate the small town in which they live. Evan Wycliff is a complex and compelling protagonist, conflicted and lost in his own life but nevertheless fiercely dedicated to uncovering the truth about his friend Bob Taggart's death.

Jones manages to infuse a deceptively simple story with suspense, angst, and whimsy, as well as surprise. His command of setting, history, and behavior is beyond exceptional. I can't wait for the next book in the series.

— PAULA BERINSTEIN, AUTHOR OF THE AMANDA LESTER DETECTIVE SERIES AND HOST OF "THE WRITING SHOW" PODCAST

From the secret contents in a rusty tin fishing box to clues that lead Evan further into danger, Gerald Everett Jones weaves a tense thriller peppered with references to Evan's ongoing relationship to God and prayer.

When the clues boil down to a final surprise, will forgiveness be possible?

Jones does an outstanding job of crafting a murder mystery that romps through a small town's secrets and various lives. His main protagonist is realistic and believable in every step of his investigative actions and setbacks; but so are characters he interacts with; from his boss Zip to a final service which holds some big surprises.

With its roots firmly grounded in an exceptional sense of place and purpose, Jones has created a murder mystery that lingers in the mind long after events have built to an unexpected crescendo.

Murder mystery fans will find it more than a cut above the ordinary.

— D. DONOVAN, *DONOVAN'S BOOKSHELF*

PREACHER FINDS A CORPSE

AN EVAN WYCLIFF MYSTERY

GERALD EVERETT JONES

LaPuerta
Books and Media
www.lapuerta.tv

LaPuerta Books and Media www.lapuerta.tv Email: bookstore@lapuerta.tv

The novel in this book is a work of fiction. Names, characters, places, and incidents either are products of the author's imagination or are used fictitiously. Any resemblance to actual events or locales or persons, living or dead, is entirely coincidental.

The author has attempted throughout this book to distinguish proprietary trademarks from descriptive terms by following the capitalization style used by the manufacturer.

ISBN: 978-09965438-8-0

EPUB ISBN: 978-0-9965438-9-7

Kindle ASIN: B07QLHQGZX

Library of Congress Control Number: 2019904247

Cover and interior design by La Puerta Productions

LaPuerta is an imprint of La Puerta Productions www.lapuerta.tv

Cover photo by Jose de Jesus Cervantes Gallegos © 123RF.com

Cover and interior design by La Puerta Productions

Author photo by Gabriella Muttone Photography, Hollywood

"Amazing Grace" hymn lyrics by John Newton (1725-1807) [PD]

Holy Bible verses quoted from the King James Version [PD]

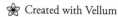 Created with Vellum

In Loving Memory of William L. Kamm

1

WEDNESDAY DAWN
EMMETT'S PASTURE

Preacher Evan Wycliff found his friend Bob Taggart's body in the early light, about a half-hour after dawn, on the frigid morning of February 29. The light snow from last week had all but disappeared in a brief thaw, leaving a frozen crust on the loamy farmland. The wind was brisk, with a bite. It was a bright day to be glad the roads were safe, salted, and dry. There was no good reason for anyone to get hurt today.

Evan had been on his way to a turkey shoot. But he didn't have a gun and he had no intention of borrowing one. He was going to sit with his friends in the woods, learn how to blow silly, warbling sounds on a reed-whistle turkey call, take greedy gulps of strong coffee laced with whiskey, and — most important in his role as compassionate counselor — make a mighty effort to make sure his friends didn't get so drunk they'd shoot each other accidentally. The others liked him because he told good stories and because he'd laugh at theirs even when they knew their jokes were lame.

Now it had all suddenly gone bad. If only the dreadful event having occurred in a leap year would mean he'd have fewer times to acknowledge its anniversary. The mathematical side of his brain worked that way.

Evan had an analytical mind, which, despite his efforts to the contrary, had drawn him away from his studies of theology and into science. Unanswered questions, whether metaphysical or worldly, would get stuck in his head and plague his thoughts.

Cause of death wouldn't take a forensic expert to explain. Bob had shot himself in the chest. He was wearing his Sunday suit, which was probably his only suit. His starched white shirt had a blood stain about the size of a softball in the center of that once burly but now deflated chest. Here was the entry wound, and Evan didn't need anyone to tell him the big damage would be at the back. When he came upon Bob's motionless, curled-up form resting there in the deserted pasture, he took one look, turned, and promptly retched up the biscuits and redeye gravy he'd had with his morning coffee.

Bob's death probably wasn't the act of a demented man. Evan was sure his friend had been sane. But they had argued recently, which would cause the young preacher recurring pangs of regret.

To this point in his life, Evan's loss of loved ones had occurred at a distance. Those events had been wrenching in their suddenness, but this one was in his face. He didn't have to flip a mental switch to cut off his emotions — he'd already learned the response. He'd never been in combat, never seen a friend fall beside him, but on seeing Bob, the analytical side of the preacher's brain took over. Evan wasn't aware of it, but in this moment he became battle-hardened. As if taking a bullet on the run and not falling, he'd feel the pain much later.

Look, then look harder. And remember.

Looking back at the corpse, Evan rested his hands on his knees as he strained to see and remember details. Bob must have pressed the muzzle of the Sig Sauer pistol to his chest as he fired, nudging his rep tie to the side. The tie was undamaged, knotted with a full Windsor at the neck, and otherwise neatly fixed with his gold Masonic tie tack above the ample tummy, except for a small burn mark on one side of the fabric. There were other stains, gravy spills that predated the incident. Like the suit, his patriotic Navy tie with the red-and-white stripes was the only neckwear Bob owned.

Because of the angle of the torso on the ground, listing over on its left side, the corpse had bled out the back. Other than the neat, circular stain in the chest, the body looked whole and restful. Bob's eyes were gazing upward and his mouth was open slightly.

Was he trying to say something?

Bob wouldn't have needed both hands to point the pistol at himself, holding the butt in the palm of his hand and squeezing the trigger with his thumb.

But Evan figured most likely Bob would have wanted to use both hands — to steady his resolve. Maybe because holding them together like that in front of him might feel more like praying, a prayer for forgiveness? Or, maybe Bob feared the kick of the powerful weapon would make it fly up, and he'd take it in the face. Yes, Evan decided, Bob's last gesture had been a prayerful pose. The knees of his pinstriped, polyester pants were wet where, as he knelt, the last of his warmth had thawed the icy soil.

It took him a while to decide.

A neatly folded piece of white paper protruded from the breast pocket of the suit's jacket. Evan was sorely tempted to pluck it out and study what he assumed would be the suicide note. But he had enough presence of mind to realize, despite his close relationship to the deceased, that he'd better not disturb the scene.

Evan's priority should be to call the cops, at least officially. But considering the early hour and the apparent fact that he'd been the first to stumble upon his dead friend, he had a personal duty to call Bob's wife Edie first.

In the few moments for the call to be connected and for her to pick up, he mentally rehearsed what he would say. All he could think of was

"Edie, I have some bad news." But she answered on the first ring, and seeing his caller ID, she simply said, "Evan, I know."

Evan hadn't known Edie Taggart all that long, only since he'd returned home from back East a year ago. From her pleasant greetings, he'd assumed she was a sweet, kind-hearted person. After all, mild-mannered Bob, who had all but given up on getting married again, had committed to her three years ago, and he'd never shared any serious complaints with Evan. But Edie's was not what you'd call a warm personality. Evan had learned she'd been an accountant by training and trade, presumably now retired. She was a local from the nearby town of Montrose, her maiden name being Clark, which was the name affixed to the town's premier tourist attraction, a renovated Victorian house on the national list of historic places. Evan never knew the family connection, but probably some influential townspeople did — stuffed shirts at the Rotary and the city council. Anyhow, she always expected she'd get the best table at any fine-dining restaurant in the area, of which there were exactly two. Fine dining if you wanted steak or chops in the one place and ribs, dry or wet, in the other.

"I found him" was all Evan managed to say. "There's a note."

"I got a note too," she said. "And it says stay away, don't come looking for him. It says tell the sheriff he's in Emmett's east pasture. So I called it in. You should be seeing them any minute."

"What can I say?" Evan asked her.

"What is there to say? You know how he's been. I'll put some coffee on. Come by when you've told them whatever you saw. I'll need help with the arrangements."

He risked telling her, "I'm still here... with him."

"Is it a godawful mess?"

"No, more like he's taking a nap."

"As if it makes a difference," she said and ended the call.

Evan straightened up and surveyed the lonely countryside. It was all Missouri flatland from here to the horizon. Where he stood was brittle, icy-hard, gnawed-down grass in Joshua Emmett's pasture. Beyond were a couple of acres of matted-down, dried cornstalks. Still farther off was a wooded area where some men took their teenage sons squirrel hunting with small-gauge shotguns. They'd go for rabbit or squirrel.

And why, oh why, did the preacher happen to be in this remote place at this ungodly hour of the morning? Nick Berner and Wiley Krause had invited him to their wild-turkey shoot. Evan was wearing a red Kansas City Chiefs ball cap so no one would mistake him for a deer. He said he wouldn't be bringing a rifle, didn't even have one to bring. Nick said not to worry, they wouldn't be loaning him one. No one manages to shoot anything on one of these outings, anyway, Nick admitted. Dumb as domestic turkeys are said to be (and that's *dumbass* dumb), the wild ones are clever as the dickens. It's just good sport to sit there in the weeds blowing on your turkey call and hoping sooner or later your amateur gobble will attract a hen or challenge a tom to raise its tail feathers in challenge. Then you might just get off a shot if you don't blink. Great sport, and by the time you've drained the whiskey in your flasks, you couldn't hit the broad side of a barn anyway.

Parking on the shoulder of the two-lane state road and traipsing through Emmett's field was the only way to get to where Nick and Wiley would be unless you had a helicopter.

It wasn't coincidental Evan thought about helicopters just then. A squadron of three choppers had flown over as he was locking up his car on the edge of the highway. He didn't think much of it at the time. There being three flying in close convoy, he assumed they were military. They were flying unusually low. He didn't know much about aircraft or their markings. Not usually being up at this time of the morning, he also didn't know whether those flights were routine, but he assumed they were. Locals knew that U.S. Army Fort Francis Blair was located just south of Lake of the Ozarks, east of Lebanon on the interstate, and military traffic, both in the air and on the roads, was a common sight.

Evan didn't have Wiley's number but considered phoning Nick. The preacher didn't know either of them very well. They were Bob's friends, but unlike Evan and Bob, they hadn't grown up here. Evan had only met them when he'd come back home, resettling in the countryside near Appleton City. Since the cops were on their way, he didn't want to go mucking up things by being the first to ask Nick the obvious questions:

Were you expecting Bob for the shoot? Did you hear the gunshot? And where's Brownie?

Bob's ever-faithful Lab-mix dog was nowhere in sight.

Perhaps run off at the sound of the shot. More likely, Bob made her stay at home with Edie.

The fact of the body's lying smack on the path to Emmett's woods suggested Bob knew about the meetup. He'd wanted his friends to find him. Maybe he'd expected it would be Evan.

I don't want to be in the middle of this. Best not to overstep. But something tells me I want to know what happened a lot more than some others might. The cops probably won't care why he did it. Will Edie?

Here came the St. Clair County sheriff's squad cars, two of them, lights flashing, no sirens. Followed by an ambulance.

First to approach was Sheriff Chester Otis himself. He was a large, broad-shouldered man with ebony skin and arms as thick as some men's thighs. He had the rolling gait of a wrestler and the sour look of a man who could smell mendacity. His immaculate gray Stetson looked too small for his round head. He seemed not at all happy to be doing any kind of business before he'd had his second helping of grits and sausage. His ample gut spilled over his hand-tooled black gun-belt and attested to his seldom having to skip a hot breakfast or any meal.

Behind the sheriff were three young male deputies, one red-haired, freckled, and white from the lead car and two lean, close-cropped, military-looking blacks from the other. The white guy, the sheriff's sidekick, carried a camera and a toolbox that must have held a forensics kit. Two paramedics, both female, an overweight white one and the other a trim Asian, were opening the back of the ambulance and setting up a gurney on which was stretched a heavy black-plastic body bag with a head-to-toe zipper.

"Reverend," the sheriff greeted him with a proffered hand.

Evan returned the manful grip as he confessed, "You understand, I'm not ordained."

The top cop gave a weak grin and said as he moved past Evan toward the body, "I won't tell if you don't."

As the sheriff stepped carefully around the scene, the red-haired deputy came up behind Evan.

"Friendly warning. Don't get invested in this," the fellow snapped.

"He was my friend…," Evan began, wishing his authority were above the law. He wasn't sure what to say next.

"I take it you didn't shoot him." It was a statement with an implied a question, craving but not expecting denial.

As the deputy slipped on a pair of rubber gloves, he introduced himself tersely as Deputy Malcolm Griggs, and he'd be in charge of the scene investigation.

The sheriff circumnavigated the corpse carefully, then bent down to have a closer look, his elbows resting on his thighs. He gestured to Griggs to come over, then pointed to the paper in the breast pocket of the suit. Griggs reached down and retrieved it with a gloved hand, then unfolded the paper, and they both read it. Otis gave a cursory nod, and Griggs slipped the note into a clear plastic evidence bag and tucked it into his toolkit.

Griggs walked back to Evan as Otis lingered near the body.

"What's in the note?" Evan asked the deputy.

"That would be confidential, for the time being," Griggs said, then demanded, "And who would you be?"

"Evan Wycliff, friend of the deceased," Evan repeated pointlessly and gesturing to the body added, "Bob Taggart. Back in the day, when we were boys, we used to play in these fields."

Griggs attempted to commiserate, offering, "Has to be tough seeing him like this." Then he resumed his strident tone as he asked Evan, "How do you come to be here? Were you with him when it happened?"

"No. I was heading into the woods over there to meet up with friends and found him like this."

Griggs shot him a look. "Odd time of day for a pow-wow."

"Kind of a sunrise prayer breakfast, you could say," Evan fibbed, not wanting to say he was on his way to make sure two drunken men didn't do anything crazy with their shotguns.

"We'll need their names," Griggs said.

You're not going to send somebody after them now? Those two officers over there aren't doing much. Okay, I won't ask.

Evan remembered to say, "Bob's dog Brownie. A big, mixed-breed and, well, brown. She was always with him. Could be on the loose, maybe panicked, somewhere around here."

"We'll keep an eye out," the deputy said dismissively.

The sheriff overheard as he approached. "Dogs run home. Smarter than us. No need to freeze our peckers off here, Reverend. Why don't you come by the office this afternoon and give us your statement? Griggs' work is going to take a while, and watching paint dry would be more stimulating." Otis didn't wait for an answer but muttered, "Helluva thing," as he shivered and stomped back toward his car. As he got in, he shouted back at Griggs, "Well, get a move on! Wilma and Darlene need to get him transported. And have Frank and Nolan here help you with whatever."

Wilma and Darlene had their gurney set up but wouldn't touch the body until Griggs had taken his photos. The two other officers were standing off at a distance by their car, waiting for instructions from Griggs as they shared a smoke and stamped their feet to keep warm.

The sheriff fired up the monster blown-V8 engine of his Crown Vic Police Interceptor. As the car lurched back onto the road, Griggs turned to Evan and said, "Like I said, don't get all invested."

"What do you mean?"

"Have you lost many friends before they got old?"

One who haunts me every day. And now this.

But Evan shook his head. He was in no mood to share with this guy.

Griggs offered with a swagger, "I did two tours, back to back. My friendly advice? The why? The how? I can tell, you're a smart guy, you've got a lot of questions. Don't go there. This is our job." Then he stepped closer to begin his survey of Bob's remains with his camera and added, "And we'll probably never know. Shit happens. Normal guys snap. Now go get warm someplace, and you be sure to drop by later for a chat with the boss. You're not a suspect, not unless I find something I don't expect."

2

WEDNESDAY 8 AM
EMMETT FARMHOUSE

J osh Emmett's hand quaked, his mouth went dry, and he felt stomach acid rising in his throat as he stared with disbelief at the official-looking letter in his hand:

Notice of Demolition

The U.S. Army Corps of Engineers? How could they do this?

The courier had just left, and Josh's first thought had been whether you're supposed to tip those guys. That was before he'd opened the envelope.

His wife Linda hadn't seen it yet. She now read over his shoulder and gasped, "This can't be happening!"

"It's saying by this time next week our home will be all smashed up. We're to be out of here, taking all our possessions, by midnight on Friday."

"I told you not to ignore that eviction notice!"

"Shhh! The kids will hear you!" In a voice he hoped was calm and reassuring, he explained, "I didn't ignore it. I went straight to Taggart. He told me he'd work something out."

"We're *two months behind.*"

"They don't tear your house down just because you can't pay. And in the middle of *winter?*"

"What can we do?"

"Edie must be behind this," he said, grabbing his coat.

3

WEDNESDAY 7 AM
TAGGART HOUSE

With rustic fieldstone-and-redwood exterior, the house was a handsome three-bedroom rambling ranch, having been custom-built to Bob's specification on the shore of a small lake less than a decade ago. Evan had visited a few times since he'd been back. Oddly out of keeping with the home's Western design, its carefully selected furnishings were colonial and expensive, although factory-milled. Drexel Heritage or Ethan Allen. Edie had moved in just three years ago, and Evan guessed she'd given all the first wife's stuff to charity and redone the place to her conservative tastes. Maybe then she could sit in the parlor and imagine she and her husband were in a grander New England gray-stone mansion in a swanky old-line neighborhood like Swope Park in KC. But Bob wouldn't have cared whether his chairs were covered in chenille or canvas.

Brownie did not greet Evan at the door, which was her habit. The preacher came in through the side entry to the kitchen, which was unlocked. The kitchen looked newly renovated, complete with high-end, stainless-steel appliances.

As Evan walked in on Edith Taggart, she was dressed in an oriental-print housecoat with fuzzy pink slippers. Her hair was in rollers, and she hadn't finished putting her face on yet. She didn't seem the least bit drowsy, and there were no streaks of residual mascara on her cheeks where they might have been wet from crying.

Why the rollers? Where's she planning on going? Or does she just do it out of habit?

She wasn't a stunner, more what the locals would call a *handsome* woman. Perhaps not yet forty, the second Mrs. Taggart had chestnut hair trimmed just long enough to hold a wave, a pale complexion with not a flaw, enigmatic hazel eyes that didn't blink when she wanted to make a point, and a lean figure. Evan judged she could analyze your loan terms or advise you on the rules of double-entry bookkeeping. So, to *handsome,* you could add *no-nonsense.*

"Where's Brownie?" Evan asked her, not knowing whether it was an insensitive question under the circumstances.

Edie sighed. "That mutt hasn't been around here for a couple of weeks. She was old and ailing, you know. Some dogs just sneak off to die."

Like her husband did.

"Bob didn't say anything about it?"

She glared at him and shot back, "What do *you* think? Apparently there were a lot of things he didn't tell me."

An awkward moment.

"I'm sorry," Evan said. "I'm so sorry. It's just... unbelievable."

Edie seemed to calm a bit as she took a breath and said, "You know, he thinks he botched Aunt Molly's will." She motioned for Evan to sit down at the kitchen counter and poured him coffee. He took a sip and was surprised to find it didn't need much doctoring. He'd need more sugar, but now was not the time to ask for special treatment.

"Is that what it says in the note?" Evan asked, not yet having seen the one the cops lifted from the body.

"Go figure," she said, handing him a single crumpled sheet of letter paper. "Your guess is as good as anybody's. It's not like he could express himself worth a damn."

Evan took the note. It was a neatly typed, double-spaced letter, a computer printout. The page had been neatly folded into quarters, and he guessed the crumpling was evidence of Edie's distress after she'd read it. He said to her, "Grief counseling isn't exactly my thing. But they do tell you, any emotion you're feeling is okay. Not just sorrow, but resentment. Even relief. You'll end up running the gamut. And it'll take at least a year, maybe longer, before you can draw a breath without wondering why you're here and he isn't. Don't blame yourself, no matter what."

Edie's kitchen phone has been ringing. She's letting it go to voicemail. I guess I would too at a time like this.

"Truth be told," she said, ignoring the phone again, "he's been dead to me for months now. I just didn't expect he'd do anything like this. Maybe he'd drink himself to death, overdose on that fruit salad of pills they gave him. But not this way." She gestured toward the paper. "Go ahead, read it. You tell me what you think he's trying to say."

My Dearest Ones,

By the time you read this, I've taken my own life. Don't come looking for me. Call the sheriff and tell them I'm at the northwest end of Emmett's east pasture. I'm truly sorry I've made a mess of things. I am also sorry for any hurt I caused. Now that I'm gone, it can all be settled, and no one can tell me it has to be different. They won't be able to come after me. I own my mistakes, especially my poor decisions. There is no plot for me, so let's keep it simple and cheap. Cremation, then bury my ashes at the cemetery between my parents. God willing, I will see my dearest ones again, and He will forgive.

Robert.

There was no handwritten signature. Just Bob's birth name in twelve-point Calibri font, same as the rest of it. Evan had trouble believing his friend was so fearful.

Evan remarked, "Odd this is printed. I'd expect something this personal to be in his handwriting."

"His handwriting was awful. I don't know what it was like years ago when you were cribbing off each other's exams in school. But as he got older, it got way worse, along with his eyesight."

The other obvious question was more troubling: "Someone was *after* him?"

Edie shrugged. "In his mind? What did he have that anybody wanted? But — my *dear ones?*" she demanded, raising her voice. "Who the hell else did he have but me?"

"Just you, as far as I know," Evan said. He knew of a prior marriage. The ex-wife was in the distant past, and they'd had no children. Like Evan, Bob was an only child, and they shared the sad fact that both of their parents had passed away by now. Most recently, they'd lost Bob's Great Aunt Molly, at ninety-four. Although not the officiant, Evan had said a few words at her funeral at First Baptist back in November.

"As far as you *know?"*

"He had some friends. Close ones," Evan said. "Joshua, Nick, Wiley. You know, his posse."

"You don't call drinking buddies and poker partners *dear ones.* Not in my language." When Evan didn't have an answer, she fumed, "He doesn't mention *me* anywhere in there! Do you notice the word *love?* Nowhere to be found!"

"Anger. That's totally okay." Evan tried to infuse his voice with a gentleness he wasn't feeling.

She stirred two more packets of Sweet 'N Low into a cup of coffee she hadn't yet touched.

"We'll burn him to a crisp, all right," she said as she stirred vigorously. "Twice baked, like a steakhouse potato. He'll get it in this world *and* in the next."

~

As Josh drove his Dodge Ram down State Route P at way over the speed limit, he tried Edie again on her cell phone. He'd already called the landline at the house twice. No surprise, she wasn't picking up. Maybe there was a way to permanently block his number? If she could've, she would've, he was sure.

Bob had been so easygoing. He seemed to like Josh, wanted him to stay on the property, mend the fenceposts, repair the dilapidated siding on the barn, and — the hard part — be smart about rotating and irrigating his crops, farming the land so it would make a decent living for the Emmetts and a reasonable return for the Taggarts.

Josh realized now, far too late, he should never have trusted Bob, should never have put an ounce of faith in the guy's lame assurances. Maybe Edie the prissy bean counter was the brains all along. Maybe they had always planned to sell the farm out from under him, and good ole boy Bob was simply shining him on, suckering him, stretching out the default long enough to justify throwing his family into the street. And then something in the guy's own life went upside-down, the sonofabitch put a bullet in himself, and his wife-hag says to hell with Joshua Emmett!

Josh's pump-action .20-gauge was loaded, clipped to the window behind his head, and he had six extra shells in his coat pocket. He'd make her give them an extension. He didn't know what more to ask or to demand. But if he had more time, surely he could get help. There had to be a way, now that he knew the Taggarts had made a fool of him. He needed to beg for help from somebody with more clout than them. Perhaps Mr. Shackleton at the bank would cut him a break.

He'd pick up Nick and Wiley on the way. Best to have his posse with him.

~

EVAN PAUSED A MOMENT, hoping for a shift in Edie's mood. He took a couple of sips from his own cup. The coffee was hot, fresh-brewed, and not your average canned, name-brand grind. More like dark-roast Kenyan. Something expensive. Like Evan, Bob had been more of an instant Folger's guy. It always took three heaping teaspoonfuls in Evan's mug to make it strong enough for him. He carried packets of instant in his pocket so he could add them to the dishwater house brew at the diner. Thankfully, there was real turbinado in her sugar bowl, and Evan helped himself generously.

Okay, sugar is my vice. And bourbon. And those nasty pills. Time enough to reform, but not now!

"You said on the phone I knew what he'd been going through," Evan said. "I'm not sure I know what you mean. Had he been depressed recently?"

I'm betting she doesn't know we argued, or what about.

"You should go have a talk with Doc Wilmer. Although the old cuss might not tell you anything. He's probably terrified I'll say he had some hand in this."

"Bob was seeing Wilmer?"

"For most of the past year. Depression? Sure. Also mania, nightmares, paranoia — you name it. A few months ago — it was right after Molly died — Bob comes home from Wilmer. He's got fistfuls of pills in trial packets. Like the sawbones says something like, 'Try these, one at a time. Find out what if anything works for you.' You know, country doctor. Throw the manure against the wall and see what sticks. So poor Bob chews them like candy, gulps them all down. If one is good, two must be better. And make sure you take a few of the yellow ones to go with the blue ones, along with gulps of Jack Daniels."

"Samples? He was taking drug samples?"

How did I miss this?

"With bourbon. He liked his Jack. Also Early Times, Evan Williams, Old Crow."

"We both did," Evan admitted.

With me, it's Vicodin for my back pain. I really shouldn't be mixing the two.

Edie explained, "For him, he drank whatever was on special in the half-gallon size at the Walmart. I poured the bottles down the drain whenever I found where he had them hidden. I suppose he was what they call a functioning alcoholic. Never acted drunk. He'd drink and drink, and then he'd be snoring in his chair. God help me. Booze and pills. You couldn't tell that man anything. A miracle he didn't off himself that way, by accident or whatever. That's what I've been expecting, frankly."

"Did you report any of this behavior to his doctor? Try to get him into treatment?"

"Like I said, Bob was stone deaf when it came to taking anything that sounded like adult advice. And calling that crank Wilmer a doctor would be like calling you the Pope. And I don't mean any disrespect."

Edie Taggart knew as well as anybody that Evan Jerome Wycliff was not an ordained minister, not a pastor of any congregation. However, the local ministry — from several different Protestant denominations, including the Baptists and the Methodists — did invite him to deliver guest sermons from time to time. So, Evan had something of a reputation, an honorable one, even if he wasn't exactly certified. That's how Edie, with a twinge of vengefulness, was now jerking his chain.

"I knew Bob was stressed, but I didn't think it was anything he couldn't work out," Evan said. "I'd have prayed with him."

I argued with him. Yes, we should have prayed instead.

"Evan, he respected you too much to tell you how disappointed he was with himself. When he spoke of you, it was with admiration. And he wasn't in the habit of talking about people. He was so ashamed."

"I don't understand. Ashamed — how? He was a good-hearted guy. Sincere. Everybody thought so."

She got up abruptly, went to the sink, tossed the rest of her coffee into it, and started to wash the mug compulsively.

"For most of our short marriage," she said with her back to him, "Bob was the guy you could trust. My mother liked him, and she hated everybody."

"What was it, then?"

She was staring into the sink as she said quietly, "Molly's estate. The guy had no head for business. I should have stepped in. The Emmetts are tenant farmers. It was Molly's land, now it's ours — I should say, *mine*. They're deadbeats."

Evan got up and stood by her side. He started to put a reassuring hand on her shoulder, then thought better of it. She hadn't come onto him, but something told him it wasn't out of the question. He'd been the one to say all of the emotions were okay, but he realized then that one of the possibilities was having to deal with the cliché of the horny widow. After all, she wasn't sobbing and she wasn't wailing. He had no idea how to read her.

"Blaming yourself," he said. "Don't."

She didn't look up. "Will you…?" She gasped, perhaps choking back grief or anger, then went on, "Help me with the arrangements? And the other, I don't know, *details?*"

"I'll handle it," he said. "His instructions were pretty clear. There will be an autopsy, of course. The drug screen might show something. Will you want a memorial service? Lots of people thought well of him. There will be less gossip if you give them all a sit-down and some chicken salad."

She finally turned around.

Her voice was as dry as her eyes. "We'll do the memorial service, then bury his ashes right after. But I want it private at the cemetery. I don't want any of those people at the gravesite. Wedging what's left of him between two coffins? What do *I* get? A can next to his? We'll do it his way, but the world doesn't have to know."

"I can find out what's possible, do what's necessary now." Evan offered. "But you don't have to decide about some things right away."

She dried her eyes pointlessly with her sleeve and asked him, "Can we do it in a week?"

"The memorial? Next *Saturday?*"

"Why not? There won't be anyone coming from out of town. If you make an announcement at the church on Sunday at First Baptist, you'll take care of most everybody. I'll ask Reverend Fortnum at United Methodist to inform his folks. And you can place the usual notices, whatever the papers do. Write something. You can text it to me, but I won't fuss over it. You want to contact Bob's cousins, or whoever they are, go right ahead. But don't lose any sleep. They won't."

She reached under the counter and pulled out a laptop and a smartphone, saying, "You might as well have a look at these. They were his."

"He didn't have his phone with him?"

She knew the plausible answer. "Maybe he was afraid he'd change his mind. And call me, call someone, for help at the last minute."

"Do you know the passwords?"

She shook her head. "That's why I'm giving them to you. Bob said you were clever with computers. Maybe you can find a way. My concern is, I don't want any surprises. If you find any evidence he changed his mind about things, you're not to tell anybody. You come straight to me."

"Did he leave a will?"

"His will and Molly's are in a safe deposit box at the bank. I know what's in them. Simple, it's all mine now. If you can't find anything to the contrary, I'll feel better. We'll know we're carrying out his wishes."

We will? Or will we know he didn't do anything to complicate yours?

"Where did he do his work at home?" Evan asked.

"We made the guest room into an office for him."

"Mind if I have a look around there?"

"Come back later today. I have to go out at two, but you can have the run of the place, for all I care."

The sound of tires skidding to a stop on the gravel of the driveway startled both of them. Evan parted the kitchen curtain slightly to see the black Dodge Ram, exhaust spewing from its tailpipe in the frigid air. The three occupants were keeping the motor running, perhaps while they decided what to do next.

"Looks to me like Josh Emmett's truck. And he's brought friends," Evan told her.

"This can't be happening," she snarled as she grabbed her private phone from the counter.

The truck's engine continued to run.

Maybe they don't expect to stay long? Could be good, or not so good.

The doors of the pickup opened. Josh Emmett got out of the driver's seat. Joining him, sliding out from the passenger side, were Nick Berner and Wiley Krause.

Josh had something in his right hand, which he held out of sight behind his hip.

Maybe a tire iron?

None of them looked happy. And the three of them had that purposeful stroll you see in the old movies when the showdown is coming.

Evan thought about calling Otis, but Edie announced, "I've sent the sheriff a text. Josh is in violation of the peace bond."

"These are friends," Evan said as if it made a difference.

She shook her head. "Don't go out there. *Don't.*"

At least, yesterday, these guys were my buddies. And some of the few Bob had. If I can't reason with them, I'd be a pretty poor excuse for a friend. Or a preacher.

Evan said a quick affirmation and stepped outside, without his coat. As Josh approached him, Evan could see that the tire iron he thought Josh was carrying was actually a shotgun. The preacher had never used prayer against a firearm before.

Evan forced a laugh and called out, "This is no way to treat a lady, Josh! And when you should be giving her your condolences."

"Did you kill Bob?" Josh wanted to know.

Evan figured Nick and Wiley had the news early, possibly because Otis had contacted them already. They'd have had plenty of time to share it with Josh on the way over.

Evan looked each of them in the eye in turn, then said, "That's the best guess you got? He did it to himself. The question is, did someone — one of us? — drive him to do it? I don't know enough yet to give you an answer. Maybe it was one of you guys."

"I need to keep my farm," Josh said. His voice was unsteady and his lower lip quivered.

"What has Bob said to you?" Evan asked him.

"Not much at all. That's the problem," Josh whined. "That man wouldn't say *shit*. And now I have till Friday to move my family off the place. Because they're tearing it down!"

Whoa. This mess just keeps getting thicker!

"There has to be a mistake —," Evan began.

Josh pointed at the kitchen window. "It's all *her* doing!"

"I'll talk to her, Josh. I will. But *you* can't. Not now. You have to understand, Edie's had the shock of her life."

"And I haven't? She gets to do this to me after all the work I've put in?"

Evan took a moment. The sun had disappeared behind a bank of cloud cover, and it was getting colder out there. He'd run out of placating words. He stepped closer to Emmett and in a cautionary voice said, "You really shouldn't be here. The sheriff is on his way. They've got a court order. You come near her, they lock you up. It's going to be kind of hard finding Linda and the kids someplace to live if you're in jail."

Josh's arm had been relaxed, the muzzle of his weapon pointing at the ground. Now he flexed his wrist, and the barrel started to rise.

"I need to see her," he growled.

Evan surprised even himself as he reached down slowly, calmly, and grasped the barrel of the shotgun.

Then he raised it the rest of the way and pressed the muzzle to his breastbone.

"Why don't you go ahead?" he said softly. "It worked for Bob."

The muscles in Josh's face went slack, and his jaw dropped. "You're crazy," he declared. He backed off a half-step, but Evan held tight to the gun. As luck or the stars or God's will would have it, the gun's safety was on. Otherwise, Josh's fierce grip on the stock and the trigger might have caused a good-sized hole to be blown in the preacher.

Josh frowned. "You got some kind of a death wish?"

Evan smiled. "You know, you're not the first person to tell me that."

Josh was at a loss. He shouted back, "Preacher, what's your part in all this? You found Bob like you knew where to look!"

Evan eased the barrel back down and let go, giving Josh a chance to retreat. Indicating the other two men, Evan said, "This morning, I was coming to meet you guys. Maybe Bob was too? Nick, Wiley — did you hear any shots?"

Nick looked like he was going to say something. His eyes were red and his face was flushed. But Josh warned him off with a wave of his arm.

Wiley, a frail guy who cowered to bullies but liked to crack wise, looked scared.

Someone should tell Wiley his experiment of a mustache just makes his upper lip look dirty. And sideburns? But his girlfriend Tamara is cuter than most women I've dated, so what do I know?

Taking a belligerent step again toward Evan, Josh demanded, "Now suddenly you're some kind of deputy sheriff? Poking your nose into my family's business?"

"Maybe you guys haven't noticed," Evan said, "but it's getting kind of cold out here? You want to have a chinwag, fine. I got nothing to give but time. But you can't go in there. Let's go to my place. It's as private as you could want." He tried another laugh. "I think I got enough coffee left to make us all a cup. With a splash of whiskey."

Nick and Wiley seemed like they were willing to go along — anything to duck this showdown. But Josh shot them another warning look and snarled at Evan, "I got nothing more to say to you." He stomped back to his truck, and the others sullenly followed. As they got in, Josh yelled, "Except *fuck off!*" The doors slammed, and they roared away, accelerating so hard the truck fishtailed in the slushy gravel of the driveway.

The affirmation prevailed against steel and gunpowder! This time.

Evan watched the truck go, then went back inside. Edie was visibly shaken, her head in her hands as she sat with her knees clasped tightly together on an elegant colonial armchair in the living room.

She's not giving me the whole story. And what's worse, she's dragging me down into whatever scheme she has going.

Evan was furious, angry with himself for taking such a huge risk with what he had to assume was a loaded weapon and angry with Edie for not being angry enough at losing Bob. He tried to rein it in. He knew screaming at her or making her wrong would just get him shut out.

"I saw what you did out there," she said. "Foolish."

"You should have stayed away from the window," he replied. "Not smart."

"I'm beginning to wonder about your judgment."

"Josh is not a bad person. Neither was Bob. But anything can happen when you push someone too far."

She glowered at him.

As he might appeal to child who was holding a burning firecracker, he asked, "Maybe now's a bad time, Edie, but what about Molly's farm? What was Bob going to do? Josh is under the impression you've given orders for his house to be torn down. On *Saturday?* We'd better reschedule the memorial. Give you both some time to settle down and deal with this."

She flashed him the stern look she must have given people who refused to accept the consequences of compound interest. "Never mind about those things. It's out of my hands. Get us through the memorial."

And she didn't say "please."

She must have decided Evan needed some kind of explanation. "The Emmetts haven't paid their rent for months, and Josh has been pestering us for an extension. The demolition is something else entirely. Bob was way too lenient with Josh, then he made no decisions about the other thing and kept putting them off. Now Josh phones me every time I turn around, and his latest voicemails are threatening. So I took out a peace bond. I've been afraid of something like this."

Evan said. "I hadn't realized."

Bob, did you think Josh was gunning for you? Or Edie and whoever else wants that farm?

Evan couldn't stay. He owed the sheriff his version of events, and he needed to clear his head before throwing more questions at Edie or anybody. In asking Evan to make the arrangements, Edie may not have expected to authorize him to look into whatever had driven Bob to death's door. But Evan wouldn't rest until he found out, even if he had to stare down a pack of demons. And keeping the Emmetts on their farm would have to be part of the bargain.

As he left, he grabbed the suicide note from the kitchen counter. Seeing him take it, Edie shrugged as if to say he could do with it whatever he wanted.

Shouldn't her interests be the same as Bob's? Deciding — and then getting approval — to destroy a building doesn't happen overnight. Was this Bob's decision and his plan? And he couldn't face the consequences?

A HALF-MILE down the rural route, Deputy Mal Griggs was sitting alone in the sheriff's Crown Vic, parked off-road and aiming his radar gun in the direction of Emmett's expected approach. Calculating what the target would do had seemed simple enough. After the courier's time-stamped drop-off, when Edie wouldn't answer the phone (which he'd expected she wouldn't), there was only one state road between the farm and the Taggart house. Griggs should have been able to time the intercept within a few minutes either way. Problem was, people don't always do the expected thing. Josh must have pulled off the road before the intercept to pick up his friends. Luckily, as Edie had reported in her second text to Griggs, this Wycliff guy had talked them down before they got inside. Three armed toughs against Edie, with or without the preacher, would not have turned out well.

For the second time today, Griggs figured he'd miscalculated. Emmett hadn't shown up yet. Of course, he must have stopped on his way back from the Taggart house to unload his buddies. No house party for them today. Just as well, though. Griggs would now have a one-on-one with Emmett. Much safer.

As Josh sped past him, Griggs clocked the speed of the Dodge truck at eighty-six, thirty-one miles per hour over the unmarked rural limit. He switched on his emergency lights and gave chase. For a while there, it looked as though Emmett was accelerating, perhaps in a rage on seeing the squad's flashing lights come up behind him. Griggs judged the fellow wasn't too drunk to ignore the warning, because the pickup eased over onto the shoulder and stopped. Drunk might have been better, a chance to rough the guy up *and* haul him in.

After the customary greeting and the preliminaries, Griggs wrote out a whopping speeding ticket. The fine would be a hundred-and-fifty dollars. As he handed over the ticket with the peace bond tucked beneath it, the officer asked the farmer, "Mr. Emmett, sir? Do you know what a peace bond is?"

Josh wasn't sure. "It's like for divorced people? If they fight, somebody goes to jail?"

"Not in this case, sir. Mrs. Robert Taggart has taken out a peace bond on you. If you ever go near her — and technically, that's defined as within five-hundred feet — you'll be arrested." Then Griggs actually grinned as he added, "And you can be sure of it." He rested his hand on the butt of his Sig Sauer sidearm and pronounced, "Because I'll be the one to do it. And when an arrest doesn't go smoothly, things can get out of control."

The two men parted ways. As events would unfold, Josh would not be heading home, and Griggs had a meetup this afternoon in El Dorado Springs.

4

WEDNESDAY 11 AM
EL DORADO SPRINGS

S tuart Shackleton was so nervous he willed his hands not to shake
— and so angry he could strangle a puppy. He felt a cold sweat
trickle down his right arm into his palm, and he worried the moisture
would compromise his tight grip on his weapon.

By God, no one is going to threaten me and get away with it. Ever!

It all happened in less than two heartbeats. He heard a noise, a single
footfall. He again scanned the dimly lit room, his head turning with a
mechanical slowness from right to left. And just as his focus rested
momentarily on the bay window to the south, he caught a blur at the
edge of his peripheral vision against the north wall, on his right. His
eyes flitted over there, ahead of his neck turn. As his right arm raised
his Sig Sauer to join the palm of his left, he took a half-step in that
direction to ensure his stance was wide and solid.

The blur was a head and then a torso. From a hiding place behind a
wine-colored, leather-covered divan, the dark intruder jumped to his
feet. His face was hidden in shadow, so it was impossible to tell
whether he was black or white or some shade in between.

The creep's right arm is in motion!

Shackleton held firm, willing his arms ramrod-stiff, his grip vise-tight, his shoulder muscles relaxed but ready to take the recoil. He lowered his head slightly, aimed, and fired a single shot.

Blam!

The intruder keeled over and fell backward, impelled by the impact of the nine-millimeter round as it tore through his chest at the midpoint of his collarbone, directly beneath his larynx.

Shackleton took a deep breath.

One down. How many more?

On his left, outside the bay window, another figure emerged running, coming at the house from some distance away, almost out of range. No doubt in a coordinated attack with the dead man, this malefactor was taking up the fight, sprinting with a weapon in his outstretched hand.

Shackleton chose not to wait, not to let him get close. It was a chancy shot at fifty yards. The first round would shatter the window, and his aim might lag the runner. But the second might hit home. Firing a third round might be a waste, especially if more criminals were lurking somewhere. The defender once again leveled his Sig Sauer and — *Blam! Blam!* — got off two shots. Coincident with the first shot, the window glass shattered in a crash, followed by a tinkle of falling shards, and the second shot found its mark. The runner hit the ground face-down and didn't get up.

Then the room went black!

After what would be a prayerful moment for a believing man, Shackleton took a deep, relaxed breath and let his right fist, still holding his pistol, drop to his side. With his left hand, he ripped off his ear protectors.

And the lights on the range came up.

A voice in the shadows behind him chided, "Top marks for marksmanship, reaction time, and technique!"

Griggs had removed his own earplugs. He stepped up to Shackleton, punched his shoulder (not too hard, he hoped), and declared, "But zero points for judgment under fire."

They stared at each other through their yellow-tinted protective eyewear.

"What are you talking about?" the shooter demanded, panting to catch his breath.

"The second guy was your neighbor, running up your driveway. The thing in his hand was his phone. He was probably about to call me to come save your sorry ass."

The RangeTime firing range in El Dorado Springs at Hayden and Park Streets is housed in a nondescript, long and narrow, single-story, brown-brick building. From the curb, the uninitiated might mistake the place for a two-lane, duck-pin bowling alley. But inside, the sound-proofed, double-walled shooting gallery is equipped with a floor-to-ceiling cinema screen, providing interactive, animated renderings of real-world locations, interior and exterior. Digital video simulations on the MILO Range LiveFire Shooting System are hyper-realistic, designed to challenge the most expert skill levels in all facets of critical incident training, situational awareness, judgment skills, and, of course, marksmanship with the client's choice of pistol-caliber weapons. You can even rent a gun, including some exotic pieces, for your session, provided you also buy your ammo from the establishment. And especially for law-enforcement clients, the system can also be used to train in de-escalation tactics, essential options for those all-too-prevalent and out-of-control domestic-violence calls.

Stuart Shackleton had just completed one of the home-invasion scenarios.

Griggs teased him, "By the way, who've you got to defend at home? Your kids are grown and away, your wife's in care, and you don't have a dog."

The older man didn't take it as a joke. He snapped at the deputy, "Let's just say, my stamp collection."

Clearly, from the set of his jaw and the throbbing veins in his neck and forehead, Shackleton was on edge, and getting his gun off, so to speak, had brought him no comfort.

Griggs seemed almost afraid to ask, "Are you upset about Taggart?"

"What do you think, you idiot? Suicide is a weakling's way out. You didn't know him, but many was the time I met him here. Nothing as sophisticated as this. Just plinking at paper targets. Let me tell you, he was not a guy to talk about himself. He was hard to read. But if I'd have thought he'd use that Sig on himself, I'd never have shot with him. And I'd never have sold him the fucking gun."

"Then again," Griggs said cautiously, "his demise won't be doing you any harm."

"I'm going to forget you said that, my friend. Banish those thoughts from your warfighter's mind. I didn't need him dead. Just out of the way."

Shackleton wanted to extend his session time and work through another scenario, but Griggs begged off.

"I've got to get back to the office," Griggs explained. "I've got a report to write."

"Don't you have to wait until you find out what the coroner has to say?"

The deputy shrugged. "I doubt there will be any surprises."

5

WEDNESDAY 11 AM
WITH EVAN ON THE ROAD

A s he drove his clunky but serviceable Taurus from the Taggart house to the sheriff's, Evan's heart rate slowed to almost normal, but his worry was strong as ever:

Why am I the only one who wants to know what happened?

Edie didn't seem anxious to learn why Bob had done it. In her deliberately straightforward view of things, her husband just wasn't up to the stresses of dealing with his troublesome responsibilities, which must have included some underhanded plan to kick the Emmetts off their farm. Evan hoped the authorities wouldn't be reluctant to share whatever facts they uncovered, now or later, Griggs' friendly advice notwithstanding.

Evan remembered what the existentialist philosopher Albert Camus said about dealing with evil:

Il faut jeter les mains dans la merde. You have to shove your hands in the shit.

For a country boy raised on what was little more than a dirt farm, Evan had studied a lot of philosophy. Although that morning he'd reminded Otis he was not ordained, few people in Evan's life knew that he was actually fully qualified to be a minister. He did not advertise, nor did he think more than a few people in the area knew, that he held a Master of Theological Studies degree from Harvard Divinity School. Raised on a farm outside Appleton City as a Southern Baptist, he'd intended to return from college and find a congregation that needed a pastor. But along the way pursuing his studies and earning his degree in religion, he found himself drifting toward Unitarianism (for which the nondenominational Harvard is noted), then toward Ralph Waldo Emerson's tradition of New Thought, then into a kind of epistemological horse latitude (where the breath of God isn't blowing strong enough to move so much as a dinghy), somewhere between Marianne Williamson's New Age and Richard Dawkins' atheism. Today, Evan was a profound I-don't-knowist, but a sincere one who could preach at length with conviction in just about any religious flavor.

As he drove, he fretted about his new conflict of interests, and he blamed himself for not defending his own peaceful state of mind. If he hadn't returned from Boston, if instead he'd fulfilled his mission and his promise to his mother as he'd set out to do, Evan wouldn't have been the one to find the body. And someone else would be delving into what was beginning to feel like a criminal investigation.

How is it that Evan Wycliff, one of the few pals Bob Taggart ever had, is led back to Southern Missouri just in time to see his friend perish but not knowing enough to prevent it?

It's all about choices. When the door you choose doesn't swing open, you wonder whether you're in the wrong place.

In his last year at Harvard Divinity, Evan had pitched his thesis topic to his tutor, Rev. Warren Ingalls, a fossil of a fellow who looked to be way past mandatory retirement age. They were both walking as briskly as the old man could down a classroom hallway. Ingalls wasn't good about keeping appointments (or remembering them), so it was a chance encounter when Evan caught up with him, at the top of the hour between classes, as students shoved past them to their next sessions. Evan had no idea where his tutor was going in such a hurry.

His goal could be a lecture to a hundred freshmen or a desperate dash to a urinal.

"I'm thinking about doing 'Astronomy in Dante's Divine Comedy,'" Evan told the professor excitedly.

"Hasn't it been done?" Ingalls asked.

"There's a classic by M. A. Orr, late nineteenth century and a more recent book by Alison Cornish. And some chapters in other recent works. But I want to explore the notion of harmony — the fusion of science and faith in the Church long before Copernicus and Galileo. And before Luther. You know, 'As above, so below.'"

"Is there all that much to say? Sounds like a one-page article."

"Oh, no. Dante's cosmography was highly sophisticated. For example, he describes the positions of the constellations in the night sky precisely — and accurately — on the date and time he entered the Dark Wood of Error."

Ingalls shrugged. "And why do you suppose he bothered?"

"I'm not sure. At least, not yet. That's what I want to explore. Maybe he thought it would give him intellectual standing among his patrons and the clerical readership. Or give credibility to his story. Or realism. Or maybe he just did it because it was another element of perfection for his poetry."

The tutor stopped, caught a breath, and told Evan, "I don't see the relevance. To our day, to our work. To your future. I take it you don't aspire to teach Italian literature?"

"No. I intend to find a congregation."

Ingalls was an ordained Unitarian.

The old joke is, the only time you hear the name of Jesus Christ in a Unitarian church is when the janitor falls down the stairs. Luck of the draw, I pulled this Joker from the deck.

"Then I suggest you find a subject more practical, more impactful," Ingalls said. "For example, the influence of the *Book of Revelation's* prophecies on the political activism of contemporary American evangelicals. I'd been hoping to suggest that one to you. You could make a name for yourself. Just remember about the sin of pride when CNN asks you for an interview."

"Has no one done it?"

"Many have, but perhaps without your insights," Ingalls said. "Might as well join the conversation!" And he left Evan standing in the middle of the busy hallway, wondering whether anyone in any church would ever let him talk about the nexus of metaphysics and astrophysics or any other kind of physics.

6

WEDNESDAY NOON

ST. CLAIR COUNTY SHERIFF'S OFFICE

B ob's suicide note was evidence — of what? It was intriguing for its oblique references and open questions.

Who did he think was after him? What could have been so complicated about executing the estate of an eccentric old lady who died with drawers full of now-useless books of S&H Green Stamps? Hadn't the plan for the demolition come later? And what was that paper in his pocket? Are there two different notes? Or two copies of the same note?

In his meeting with Sheriff Otis, Evan described what he'd experienced that morning, which included a more accurate description of his aborted meetup with Nick and Wiley. The sheriff said he'd follow up with those boys, but he didn't seem in any hurry to do it. Otis captured Evan's story on a digital voice recorder. Griggs wasn't present, and Evan assumed the deputy had plenty to do processing the evidence.

Evan informed the sheriff he'd already paid a visit to Edie. "Do you know anything about plans to evict the Emmetts and tear down their house?" he asked Otis.

The sheriff grew round-eyed and put a finger to his lips. He made the considerable and deliberate effort to hoist himself up and out of his chair. Then he went over and closed the door to his private office. Frank and Nolan were sitting just outside in the squad room, intent on the screens of their computers but probably straining to overhear whatever they could.

When he sat back down, Otis asked Evan, "Now how do you come to know anything about the Emmett farm? Other than once having harassed a few sheep there as a snot-nosed kid."

"Edie said Bob was distressed about dealing with his Great Aunt Molly's estate, which I take it somehow involves the Emmetts? But Josh wants to keep farming it. He's pissed Bob wouldn't tell him what's what, and now he thinks Edie wants to throw him out. About an hour ago, he showed up at Edie's with Nick and Wiley. I came out and discouraged them from going inside. She'd told me she has a peace bond, and that was news to Josh. He went away — angry, but he went away."

"Did they threaten you?"

"It didn't get that far. I was never close with any of them, but they're not thugs. I invited them over to my place for coffee and prayer. They didn't take me up on it, but they backed down quick enough."

"Any of them have a weapon?"

"No," Evan lied.

I thought I saw a tire iron. Josh was just checking the lugs on his tires.

"Can't file charges over a friendly chat," Otis mused.

"So what's this about tearing down their farmhouse on Saturday? That's the day Edie picked for the memorial service."

Now Otis was surprised. "I've known about the demolition for some weeks, but she's got stones doing Bob's sendoff on the same day. For sure, Josh will want to be on the farm until there's no hope left, and the rest of them will no doubt want to watch."

"Can you stop it?"

"I'm not the one planning the memorial…," he began.

"I mean the wrecking crew. Surely the knocking down can wait until all the parties understand what's at stake."

"Please put your phone on the table," the sheriff said. Evan complied.

Otis tapped the phone a few times with his thick fingers, then put it down. "Can't have you recording this," he said quietly. "Not quite ninety days ago, right after Molly's funeral, Bob was served notice by the U.S. government. They need to build some kind of access road, and it'll go right through that house."

"Access road? To where? There's nothing to access. And don't they need to hold public hearings? Eminent domain? Negotiate a buyout? Did all that happen?"

"Usually, yes. And in this case, no. All I can tell you is, I got an official visit. Two nice fellas from the Army Corps of Engineers. They presented me with a stack of near-unreadable fine-print paper and advised this office to keep a low profile on the whole thing."

"So Bob must have known about it."

Otis nodded and repeated slowly, "Yes, Bob *must* have known about it."

"Don't you think it's kind of coincidental he did away with himself just as this was going down?"

"I do, young man. I do."

"And you're just going to let it happen?"

"You can do what you want about the memorial service. I agree the timing is… awkward. As to the other, not only are my hands tied, but considering who's holding the rope, I really don't want to know anything more about it."

"But you just admitted the circumstances are suspicious!"

Otis looked as though Evan was trying his patience. "Let's wait and see the autopsy findings. If there's any indication of foul play, it'll be more than suspicious. But I'm gonna guess there won't be. That said, this office has no crimes to investigate until and unless someone brings us some evidence." Then he emphasized, "We're not in the speculation game. Nor do we get involved in real-estate disputes as long as the parties have their permits."

Evan had been hoping they could literally compare notes. He held up the one he'd gotten from Edie. "Bob left Edie a note. I believe there was another one in his pocket. Mind if I see it?"

When the crusty old cop demurred, the preacher asked, "What's the matter, Chet? Don't tell me I'm a person of interest."

The sheriff cackled as he swiveled aimlessly in the special-order, extra-wide chair behind his big oak desk. He wheezed, "Now that would be giving your sermons too much credit."

He's actually heard me deliver a sermon?

Evan shoved Edie's note across the desk. Otis read it and said, "Since you've seen this, I suppose there's no harm in telling you the other one is the same. Or almost. And also typewritten. I suppose when you're drunk it's hard to get your story straight. Edie gave this to you?"

Evan nodded. "She wants me to take care of the arrangements."

Otis again looked surprised. "You got her power of attorney?"

"Come on. Like she wrote it on some napkin?"

"I'll give her a call, ask what she has in mind. Then I'll have Nolan run over there with something she can sign. We won't worry about witnesses or notary. As long as her wishes are the same as Bob's and you're willing to go along, it's just a mess of paperwork. Griggs is off at the firing range. I think the poor kid needed to let off some steam. Provided I get her signature later today, you can come back tomorrow, get the details done, and we can both have a look at the autopsy report."

"So what happens today?"

Referring to his paramedic team, Otis said, "Wilma and Darlene are driving the body to Columbia for the autopsy. It usually takes weeks, but I got a guy at the lab, and I've put a rush on it." He explained the forensic experts are at University Hospital, which is more than a two-hour drive to the east when the roads are clear. Since Bob's last wishes specified cremation, it wouldn't make sense to transport the body back and forth. They could get it done there and ship the cremains back via UPS. Otis was proud to be saving the grieving widow a lot of dough. "You go through a mortuary, they job it out, and they'll mark it up on their invoice. And if there's to be a viewing, you'll also pay for embalming, storage, casket rental, and use of the chapel. Ridiculous waste of money. All so people can say goodbye to somebody who's already long gone?"

"I think it's about seeing is believing," Evan said. "So the family and friends see the person at peace."

Otis laughed. "At peace? Yeah, that's what they always say, 'Rest in Peace.' Do you know how long eternity is? Preacher, if there is *any* kind of an afterlife, the last thing I want to do is rest through century after century."

"Actually," Evan said softly, "the original meaning of the phrase is to rest in the assurance of salvation until the day of resurrection."

"If I'm dead, I'm dead. If somehow I'm still living, I want to be chasing pretty angels someplace. Which, if females are involved, guarantees no peace!" He chuckled and picked his teeth some more.

Evan nodded. He wasn't about to evangelize the sheriff, mainly because he wasn't sure he had any business trying to convince anyone. He also had his own thoughts about eternity, a state of timelessness, a state perhaps of knowing and feeling, perhaps of joy, but not of action.

Otis added as he showed the preacher out, "You can do what you want for the memorial service, but I'll tell you for free Bob was a Mason. Best pay a visit to Stu Shackleton before you firm anything up. He's head man in the Lodge."

"News to me. Bob never spoke to me about being a Mason." Evan asked the sheriff, "And are you a member?"

"Yes, as a matter of fact. Bob was Thirty-Third Degree. He'd earned all the merit badges, you could say. Me, I'm not that high up on the totem pole. But it's a way to give back, a good place to make friends in high places. Local business owners, public officials, bankers, lawyers — *judges.*"

Evan realized he'd forgotten to ask, "What do you make of that part in his note about they're coming to get him?"

The sheriff just said, "The guy was stressed. Maybe he fudged the mileage on his tax returns? Some things we'll never know. And, if I get a say, it won't be my job to find out."

"So, are you going to agree with Edie? I should keep my nose out of this?"

"I didn't say that, Preach. I don't know anything about the probate issues involving that farm. But it does seem all cocked up. Craves looking into. But not by this office." Otis parted the venetian blinds behind his desk to peek outside. "We had some sun there for a spell, but it's clouding up again. Mind how you go."

Otis walked Evan out to his car. As Evan got behind the wheel and the door was open, the sheriff bent down to say quietly, "Something about this has me bothered. From the evidence, I'd say nobody helped him do it. Now, assisted suicide is one thing, but driving someone to it is quite another. And legally, that's a tough one. Tough to prove unless there was some kind of specific threat. But what about an attempt to defraud? You and I know, it has to be all about that farm."

"So you do have your suspicions?" Evan asked.

"Yeah. But I haven't got a detective or a budget. Griggs hasn't been with me long enough. He was military police, then he took a couple of classes. I could deputize you, but that's too formal. And too public. We wouldn't be able to keep it just between us. You got that power of attorney. It could take you a long way. She might say it's limited to the memorial, but your interpretation might be different."

"Well, since I've got that, can't I do something right away to stop the bulldozers?"

"If Bob could have, he would have. Something is gumming up the works, but damned if I know what it is."

"I can't ask Edie, but I've got to find out what was in Molly's will. And in Bob's."

"You do that, see where it takes you. You get your ducks in a row, come back and we'll compare notes." And the sheriff walked quickly away.

Compare notes? Suicide notes?

7

WEDNESDAY 1:30 PM
WITH EVAN

E van had to skip lunch, a choice he rarely made. But he'd promised to return to Edie before she had to leave the house.

On the drive over, a few brief calls took care of some of the essential arrangements. Hill and Sons Mortuary. The office secretary at First Baptist. The two newspapers. He tried not to worry he was tempting fate by driving on icy roads as he juggled his phone.

For a guy who just wanted to let go, I'm up to my neck in responsibility.

Immediate pressing matters aside, Evan's thoughts returned to how he might have chosen a different path. He was beginning to suspect his returning here from Boston would prove to be a huge mistake, maybe even the onset of another blue period. Shrinks call it *depression.* Theologians call it the *long, dark night of the soul.* Crises of both faith and mortality had blown him back to his roots in the black dirt, but he'd assumed those storms were over. Now here was the jolt of another devastating loss, and he feared what was left of his faith couldn't withstand the hit.

How can I help anyone else when my own life is such a mess?

~

EVAN REMEMBERED Bob had once given him a lesson in generosity. They were twelve.

On most days during the school year, they couldn't play together because they had no free time. After school, they had chores at home. After chores, early dinner. After dinner, homework. After homework, early to bed. And farm kids wake before dawn because they have early morning chores before breakfast, then it's off to school.

Saturday mornings there would be special chores. Painting a fence or mowing a lawn. Those done, they might have some time to run off for a few hours of gloriously unsupervised and endlessly inventive searches for adventure. During the summer, every day was like a Saturday, with extra chores assigned at home to keep them busy and presumably out of trouble.

Evan's folks had a farm about a mile south of Appleton City and west of the Emmett place. Bob lived with his parents in town. Especially during the summer, Evan would often finish the chores at his house early, then ride his bike into town and over to Bob's to help him with his so they could start playing sooner.

At Bob's, the boys mostly did housework for Bob's Aunt Molly. The incident Evan remembered vividly occurred not long after Bob's mother Abigail had passed away from some chronic illness. Sweeping, scrubbing, painting — they'd do whatever needed doing, including polishing Molly's heirloom set of silverware. When they'd finish, she'd give them each a quarter, and the boys would head over to Taggart's pharmacy, where they could each buy a scoop of ice cream in a cone from the proprietor, Bob's father Lionel, who both as a matter of store policy and stalwart parenting insisted his son and his son's friends pay cash. However, he accepted their quarters as payment in full, even though to everyone else in town a single-scoop cone at Taggart's would cost a buck.

Bob had had a succession of female, brown, mixed-breed dogs, each of which he'd named Brownie. They were far from identical in appearance and breeding, except for the predominance of color in their coats. But Bob treated them as repeated incarnations of the same joyful, generous spirit. Who was to tell him otherwise? Although old gents with trophy wives might insist otherwise, Evan knew you can't replace people that way.

All of Bob's dogs were affectionate, but Brownie the First was profoundly adoring of Bob. She might have been what dog fanciers call a *Labsky*—a mix between a Labrador and a Husky. She had the build and bearing of a Lab, but with a short-haired, dark-brown coat and a streak of white on her muzzle. Like the other Taggart dogs, she was a foundling. She never had pups because Molly didn't want her hands full, and so they had the puppy spayed. Brownie's rapt attention to Bob's gestures, commands, and remarks to her ensured she could master whatever behavior Bob demonstrated. And, unlike the reputations some large breeds have for having short-term memories, Brownie retained what she learned.

During chores as at all other times, this first Brownie would follow the boys around continually, supervising their work and then escorting them to the store. Although pretty much useless as a worker, she was an enthusiastic cheerleader, and judging from the wagging of her tail and sometimes her whole body with it, she seemed to appreciate their shiny results as much as Molly did, probably because the sense of a task being done signaled that sweet rewards and recreational activities were sure to follow.

One bright day after a morning spent in diligent housework for Molly, Bob and Evan were sitting on the stoop outside the pharmacy and trying to lick their ice cream faster than it was melting in the summer heat. Bob startled Evan when he abruptly stopped and thrust his cone out toward Brownie, who was sitting at attention directly in front of them.

Brownie licked Bob's ice cream. Exactly twice, which must have been a strictly learned behavior.

Then Bob resumed his own happy consumption of vanilla, the only flavor Lionel stocked back then.

After a few more licks, Bob again let Brownie have a turn. And miraculously, it seemed to Evan, the dog didn't just gobble up what was left on the cone.

"Why'd you do that?" Evan finally asked his friend. "They say people food is bad for dogs."

Bob held up a finger to indicate he had to finish licking up the ice cream before he could talk. Evan recognized the wisdom of this, and they remained silent until all they held in their hands were the nearly empty cones.

Then Bob explained, "My mother always told me never to eat in front of other children. Not if they don't have any themselves."

"Well, Brownie's not a kid."

"When it's about food, it's just the same," Bob insisted. "I'm not going to eat in front of her when she doesn't have any. But I won't just give it away. If I got a candy bar or a cookie, I earned it. I'm not gonna break it up into little pieces and pass it out to every kid on the playground."

"Jesus did that with the loaves and fishes."

"Well, I'm not Jesus, and neither are you."

"I still don't see what this has to do with Brownie," Evan said.

"Brownie gets plenty of her own food. And she knows it's hers because it's in her bowl. But she never leaves me. She watches me when I sit at the table. And at times like now, when I've got something special." He smiled at Brownie and said, "So, we have this deal, don't we, Brownie?"

Brownie didn't bark an answer, but at the sound of her name, she wagged her tail.

Bob looked into Brownie's eyes intently as he explained to Evan, "Our deal is, whatever I'm having, she gets a bite."

Evan remembered Brownie died not long after that incident. The next time he saw Bob, he asked him what had happened.

"My dad says maybe airborne virus. But he doesn't know for sure. She didn't seem sick. And then one morning she was on the floor and didn't move."

Evan's friend seemed down, not so much grieving and miserable as in shock and mystified. The world did not make sense.

"Is that what happened to your mom?" Evan asked. At this age, whatever thoughts he had just came out of his mouth.

Bob didn't seem upset. He simply replied, "No, she had cancer."

Evan knew enough to say, "I'm sorry."

Bob went on, "My dad says death is a part of life. He says when I die, I'll see Mom and Brownie again. I miss them already. But I don't want to die. Not for a long, long time."

Evan's mother had told him it was selfish to pray for things. She reminded him, "Our Lord is not some Santa Claus in the sky. Don't ask for a bike. Yours isn't new, but it gets you where you're going. Pray for wisdom, pray for help, but mostly pray your friends and loved ones will accept God's grace."

The evening of Bob's Sermon on Ice Cream, before Evan tucked himself into bed, he made an exception and prayed for Bob's happiness. And for another dog for his friend.

Two weeks later, then-sheriff Burt Skinner pulled a female German shepherd stray off the street in Appleton City. Knowing about the losses in the Taggart family, Burt phoned Lionel to find out if they'd consider adopting the dog. And even though this mutt's fur was more black than brown, Bob anointed her Brownie the Second. Like the first Brownie, this second one was alert and intelligent. But, on balance, she was more lay-back, not as prone to knocking things over with the wild wagging of her tail. True to her predominant breed, she was a guard dog, never letting her watchful eye stray from Bob. But she never growled, never threatened, didn't jump up on strangers, didn't even nip. She was suspicious of children, but she never freaked out when she'd be sitting on the sidewalk and they'd come barreling at her with outstretched hands. Ever the careful medical professional, Lionel saw to it she was promptly spayed and got all her shots. Molly, God bless her, didn't object.

Even though Evan judged his prayer had been answered, he didn't regard it as a miracle so much as a necessity for life as he knew it to continue at all.

A MASTER's degree in divinity typically takes three to four years, mostly because there are spiritual development programs combined with the academics. All that work is in addition to four years of under-graduate study. Evan took even longer — almost nine years — to earn his masters. Even though he'd won scholarships and internships to subsidize his tuition, he'd had to take part-time jobs to cover housing and expenses. By the time he'd reached his thirtieth birthday, he had his degree, and he could have applied anywhere for an assistant minis-ter's position. Achieving that, it would typically take another three years before he could be ordained by invitation of the denomination.

Even though he could have applied for a church position anywhere in the world, he'd intended all along to return eventually to Southern Missouri. But upon graduation, he didn't apply, and he didn't return — at least, not until years later.

He titled his thesis "Creationism Versus the Theory of Evolution," with particular concentration on whether intelligent design, or divine engineering, might help reconcile those opposing views. He had hoped it might. His paper fell short of his goal, and, as with so many of his inquiries, he ended it having more questions than answers.

"Interesting treatment of the topic," Ingalls admitted. "But not likely to be decided in our lifetimes. Not in mine certainly, probably not in yours."

Upon his graduation from Harvard Divinity with honors, Evan was facing both a challenge to his faith and a crisis of confidence. By now he knew enough about the formal religions of the world to understand none of them had non-mythological answers to what he considered to be the fundamental questions of human existence. And therefore he doubted his ability to lead, counsel, and inspire parishioners in any of these traditions.

Astrophysics became another distraction, another force throwing him off-track. All during college, his curiosity about basic questions also attracted him to the scientific disciplines. He supplemented his divinity curriculum with science and math courses with the under-grads at Harvard College. Intrigued that he might get a peek at the mysteries of the universe from an empirical perspective, he aced calculus and impressed his professors in physics and astronomy, then in astrophysics.

After Harvard Divinity, having not quite shaken his self-doubts, Evan applied for and won a scholarship to the doctoral program in astro-physics at MIT. But he dropped out of that program and further schooling altogether during the second year, after his father called him with news of his mother's sudden and unexpected death from a neuroma.

He would always say Lena's death was the first major loss in his life. But it was Naomi's memory that still haunted him.

When he was at his most doubtful, he was never an atheist, not even fitting the definition of an agnostic. He didn't doubt God's existence. But, like Voltaire, too often he worried God had fashioned the universe like a clock and then retired to let it tick until it ran down.

In Evan's mind, his questions about his beliefs had stopped him. But in his heart there was a different obstacle — no, not an obstacle, more like a sheer cliff. He refused to discuss it with anyone, not with his best friends, not even with Lena, his mother, when she was alive. He tried not to think about it, although his upset kept him awake on many nights.

~

DURING HIS COLLEGE YEARS, throughout all of Evan's indecision, backsliding, and changes of direction, his parents held fast to the belief he was on a righteous, preordained path. Although they lacked the money to buoy his ambitions, the zeal of their prayers could have floated an ocean liner.

Evan's mother, Lena Pearl Zorn Wycliff, was a frail woman with a will of iron who never raised her voice, always refused to wear makeup, and only let her waist-length hair down from a tight bun at night to keep its sheen by giving it a hundred brushstrokes. Her one vanity was dissolving a packet of gelatin in her orange juice every morning, a nutritional supplement she insisted would prevent broken fingernails. She needed to get her work done, after all.

She was Evan's white light, his personal example of unconditional love.

One time when he was ten, she asked him gently to take out the garbage. He replied with a question, which in his little boy's voice sounded more like curiosity than defiance: "What if I don't want to?"

Lena smiled at him, rested her hand on the top of his head, and said softly, "Then you just say, 'Mamma, I don't want to. But I *will.*'"

When he was in high school, she'd plotted with Pastor Thurston to encourage her son's erratic progress as a student minister at First Baptist. The boy judged his own sermons to be awkward and murky, but Lena and the Reverend insisted those messages were brilliant in ways the congregation hadn't begun to understand.

All during his school years, Evan had long weekly phone conversations with her, every Sunday night. Sometimes, he'd have preferred email, but she refused to try it — even though she was an expert typist. Before she'd married Palmer Wycliff and moved into his family's farmhouse, she'd been a secretary for the Baltimore & Ohio Railroad in KC. She could also take shorthand and use a stenographer's machine.

"What are you finding to do?" she'd asked her dutiful son.

"Mother, I study and I stack books in the library."

"Is that a job or are you just helping out?"

"It's a job, the work part of my work-study grant."

"I'd prefer you not to work, and your father agrees. You need to concentrate on your studies. Don't go scrubbing pots until all hours of the night just to make ends meet. We'll find a way."

He knew they *couldn't* find a way, but all he said was, "Don't worry. I find time to get my rest."

"Any girlfriends? Nice? Christian?"

"Just some debate partners," he fibbed.

"Don't go being bossy. Sometimes you get this know-it-all attitude. You know you do. And that's no way to charm a lady. But you've got plenty of time."

As it turned out, he didn't. Not with his favorite debate partner.

Evan's father, Palmer Wycliff, was a gentle man of few words. He was short, stocky, and strong — a lumberjack with stubby legs. His childhood playmates called him Dutch because, in the local slang, a "dutchy" physique meant a long torso with short legs. Dutch was content to get news of his exceptional son from Lena. Even though his parents no doubt expected Evan to return to them one day, both of them encouraged his choices, even when his chosen subjects might throw him off his path into the ministry. No matter what Evan's course of study, Lena believed fervently, whatever he learned would do nothing but enrich his spiritual messages.

Likewise, Lena rarely disagreed with any of Evan's decisions. And Dutch backed her up. Evan remembered she'd disapproved of his request to wear crisply pressed chinos in high school. She didn't see why freshly washed blue jeans wouldn't be just as respectable, and she offered to iron them for him. But he bought two pairs of tan slacks from his chore money and ironed them himself.

When Lena eventually found out about Naomi, she disapproved.

"Do you plan to convert this Jewish girl?"

"I'm not sure that's possible, Mother."

"Is she expecting to convert *you?*"

"Not so far. I'm studying for the Christian ministry, after all."

"I don't see how this is going to work."

It was a serious problem between them, and one never to be resolved, except by parties absenting themselves from the planet and thus from the debate.

Lena's death had shaken Evan more than he thought was possible, for a person of faith. Its suddenness defied all expectation. She'd just turned sixty. She'd been healthy, vital, and downright talkative to the last. He'd spoken to her only three days before her fatal collapse. She was baking pies for a church social and repainting the sides of a chicken coop. Statistically, men were supposed to predecease their wives, and his father, who was fourteen years older than Lena and had emphysema from a lifetime of chain smoking, had been shrinking physically for years. Dutch had even written his will based on the assumption that his wife was his likely survivor.

The feeling of abandonment Evan felt called to mind early memories of him as a toddler accidentally letting go of his mother's hand in the supermarket. Here he was, just three, and in a moment shorter than his next breath, she was nowhere to be seen. Were he more mature, he'd have concluded logically that she'd simply ducked around a corner into the next aisle. But to little Evan, she'd disappeared with no promise of return. His anguished screams brought her running to him, but the boy wondered ever afterward, had he not complained loudly to the universe, would she have bothered to come back?

Evan returned from school for Lena's funeral and then lived with Dutch. They moved into a small apartment in Stockton after selling the family farm. Although Evan cared for his father dutifully, the old man didn't last long after losing Lena. Yes, his emphysema grew steadily worse until he was on an oxygen bottle all the time, but it would be just as true to say he died of a broken heart.

Today, Evan was neither pastor nor physicist. He got those guest-preacher gigs because pastors needed vacations, too, and people liked to hear him talk. Sometimes he'd do stem-winders for revival meetings, where he was expected to put the hard-sell on salvation. He'd usually receive a modest honorarium as a speaking fee, but not always.

As well, Evan was not a licensed investigator. But he was no stranger to investigative techniques, including police procedure, data search and analysis, forensics, and evidentiary matter. Evan Wycliff was an accomplished investigator because he worked on commission as a freelance skip tracer. Under contract from the local Ford dealer, he tracked down debtors who'd missed more than two payments on their cars or tractors.

After his father's death, Evan decided to stay in Appleton City. No place else on the planet was calling to him, and at least part of him, the boy in him, was at home here. It didn't take him long to occupy himself with the occasional pulpit assignments and the skip-tracer job.

His only close friend since he'd been back was Bob Taggart. They weren't constant companions, but one would call the other when something was bothering him. They'd share a meal at the C'mon Inn or drinks at the Cork 'n Cleaver. Bob was almost as close-mouthed as Dutch Wycliff had been, so Evan knew the type and didn't mind his friend's long silences.

He trusted me. Why didn't I make him spill his guts?

8

WEDNESDAY 2 PM
TAGGART HOUSE

E die was not behaving like a new widow. She was dressed for some meeting or social event. She had on a crisp print dress underneath her tailored herringbone overcoat with a velvet collar. She carried a designer handbag and had on matching pumps. She wore a hat that might be considered smart these days, but Evan wouldn't know. She'd taken some care with applying her lipstick, which was a deep, wet-look red.

Evan's first task this afternoon would be to look in Bob's office for an address book, the most likely place to find passwords. He'd brought two laptops and two phones, both his and Bob's. Not owning a brief-case, Evan had the laptops in an oilskin bag to keep them dry. The cold, crisp morning had turned into an afternoon drizzle.

Edie seemed pleased his return was punctual. She was forthright. "Did you take care of the arrangements?"

"I will authorize the cremation if we see no complications in the autopsy report, which we'll get tomorrow. And I made some calls. The cremains will be delivered to Hill and Sons. They'll provide a silver urn and a hand-carved walnut case with the appropriate Masonic emblem. His parents are buried in Rockville Cemetery, and I need to file that paperwork with Bates County. The car from Hill and Sons will take you and me to the cemetery after the memorial. I booked the church service and the reception at First Baptist for Saturday morning at ten. I reserved the obit notices in the papers. Do give me the family and guest list so I can make sure they're all notified. It's kind of late, but I'll do what I can to reach the ones out of town."

"Thank you," she said curtly. She was already moving toward the door. "I wouldn't know where to start. The door will lock behind you when you leave."

"I know you're in a hurry, so let's talk more about this later. Maybe I can help Josh calm down."

"Don't bother with him. What's done is done."

He hadn't planned to ask it now, but the question had been nagging him. "May I ask you, do you have anyone close who is on life support? Or terminal?"

"Whatever makes you ask?" She had her hand on the doorknob.

"Something Bob asked me. I never knew what it meant to him."

Edie sniffed. "No, no one close. There's Ann Shackleton, but Bob knew her hardly at all. She's in care, but she's not hooked up to some machine."

"Bob wanted to know how someone should make the choice between life and death in those situations. I thought he was talking about a sick relative. I never imagined he could be talking about himself."

When do you pull the plug? He didn't like my answer.

"Believe me," she said. "I'm sure you got more out of him than I did." And she left. From the kitchen window, Evan watched her get into her car, a white Cadillac CTS, and drive off, kicking up pea gravel from the driveway as the car made a hard right and spun out into the road.

∾

BOB MUST HAVE HAD his way with at least one of Edie's redecorating decisions. The guest bedroom was now a wood-paneled study and decidedly male. On the wall were engravings of mallards and a mounted Remington rifle of Civil War vintage. An engraved nameplate beneath it read:

To Jedediah Redwine
from Valencourt Griggs, 1865

There were built-in shelves full of leather-bound books. Evan resolved to study the titles, hoping they were not just stage decoration Edie had put there just to class up Bob's room.

For now, Evan had to remind himself his focus was on finding where Bob had written down those passwords. He had an executive-sized, roll-top desk that Edie must have found for him at auction. The top was open and the drawers weren't locked. Evan set the laptops and the phones on the hand-tooled leather surface as he covered every inch of the desk. There were no address books or notepads on the desktop. Evan's careful search of each and every drawer found nothing but the usual office supplies, and he was thorough enough to pull each drawer out to make sure there weren't stickers on the sides or underneath. Then he got down on the floor with his head near the modesty panel at the back and looked up. There was nothing taped to the underside of the desk.

Bob seemed like the kind of fellow who'd pick an obvious place.

Evan checked behind the pictures, looked in the closets, and concluded the room didn't have a wall safe. He was about to search the closets more carefully when he realized there was one striking item on the desk he hadn't inspected. It was a faded color Kodachrome photo of a light-brown, medium-sized, mixed-breed dog – Brownie the First, who would have been about two years old when this photo was taken. The dog held a dead duck proudly in its mouth. The photo was mounted in an expensive Sterling-silver keepsake frame, the kind with a plush easel stand people give as wedding gifts when they can't think of anything else.

Surprisingly to Evan, there were no pictures of Bob's other dogs, the later Brownies. Then he remembered, to Bob, they were all the same incarnated spirit.

The handwritten inscription in blue ballpoint under the photo read:

Brownie 1993

Evan sat down immediately in Bob's plush swivel chair and opened the laptop. *Brownie1993* was the password, and the four-digit code *1993* unlocked Bob's phone.

Evan was anxious to look at Bob's laptop, but, despite Edie's warning, he wanted to reach out to Josh. Evan didn't have the Emmetts' number on his own phone, but he found two numbers, labeled "Emmetts" and "Josh," on Bob's list of favorites. Evan called what he assumed was the landline at the farmhouse. Josh's wife Linda picked up. Like everyone else in town, she'd heard the news about Bob. Then Evan asked if he might speak with Josh.

Linda surprised him by asking, "I'm sorry, but why is that?"

"The short answer is I'm handling Edie Taggart's affairs for her. Bob didn't share much about anything he was doing with anyone, and I'm hoping Josh will have some answers."

"Who has answers? *We* don't! I'm packing suitcases and boxing up my china. I'm driving the kids to my mother's in Rich Hill. They're gonna *tear our house down on Saturday!* And where is Josh? Nowhere to be found! Answers? He's probably knocking down shots somewhere. He's not picking up when he sees it's me. If you find him, you tell him where we're at. And then tell him not to bother to come home because at this point I have *no idea* where that'll be!"

"Linda —"

But the line went dead. So Evan scrolled back through the phone's contact list, found "Josh," and dialed the number.

A tremulous voice answered, "Who the hell is this?"

The caller ID must have made the young farmer think he was getting a call from a ghost.

He'd be afraid not *to take it.*

"Please relax, Josh. This is Preacher Wycliff. I have Bob's phone."

"What do you want with me?"

"I'm making arrangements on Edie's behalf. And seeing if I can help with Bob's unfinished business. I need to ask — I know it might not seem important — but did Bob leave his dog with you? Maybe, for your kids?"

"His dog? Brownie? That fleabag? Naw. That guy," Josh choked. "Horrible he'd do that to himself. And just when he said he'd get it all fixed. Now it's all up to *her?*"

"Where are you, Josh? You've got Linda worried. Do you know she's packing up to go to her mother's?"

"I'm frustrated as hell, and I'm getting nowhere," he said, sounding like an exhausted and beaten athlete. "I'm coming home. I'll call her. She's right. We gotta clear out."

"Let me ask you, did Bob ever tell you what he intended to do with the farm?"

"He kept saying, like, hurry up and wait."

"Why?"

"It made no sense to me. He said he couldn't stop anything because he wasn't sure he even *owned* the farm."

"It was his Great Aunt Molly's!"

"Yes and no," Josh sighed. "Bob said the only guy who knows for sure is Angus Clapper. They were supposed to work it out, but I never heard back."

"Clapper?"

"Some lawyer guy from the old days. Lives in Knox now. I tried to call over there. They said I'm not family."

John Knox Village. A retirement home in Lee's Summit.

"Where are you now?"

"I drove to Osceola, asked at the Registrar of Deeds. They've got *no record* of who owns my farm!"

"Let's talk after you're rested," Evan suggested, trying to sound non-threatening. "Why don't you call me at this number when you're ready?"

"Maybe you can shake some sense into that bitch. We have no time!" Josh wailed, and he ended the call.

Josh never did call him back, and Evan didn't want to reopen the discussion until he had something more encouraging to tell him.

WHILE HE WAS STILL at Bob's desk and realizing Angus Clapper might have some key answers, Evan tried calling the name from Bob's phone. It rang and rang, and voicemail must have been turned off. He then called the John Knox Village main number. When he asked for Clapper, the receptionist said Evan's call was being transferred to the nurse's station.

"Critical Care," an officious female voice answered.

"May I speak with Angus Clapper?"

"Are you a member of his family?"

"No. No, I'm not."

"Then, I'm sorry —"

"This is Reverend Evan Wycliff."

Might as well use my all-access pass!

"Oh. Oh, I see." There was a long pause. "All I can tell you, Reverend, is that Mr. Clapper is unable to take calls or receive visitors now."

"Can you take my number?"

"No, it would be better if you'd call back tomorrow and ask for patient information. If all goes well, he may be moved back to his room by then. Perhaps you're trying to schedule a chaplain's visit?"

"Yes, certainly. If he's… responsive."

If he's a Catholic and needs last rites, I won't pretend to be your guy.

"Perhaps tomorrow, then," the nurse suggested. "I'm sorry I can't say more. I'm sure he'll want to see you. Thank you for calling."

SHACKLETON FUMED AT EDIE, "Why the hell did you give that Bible salesman your power of attorney?"

"First off," she said demurely, "the sheriff's office told me it was necessary if I didn't want to handle the details myself."

He cackled and stroked himself suggestively. "Seems to me like you've always been perfectly capable of handling whatever comes up."

He reached for her. She brushed his hand aside, but gently so he'd know her refusal was only temporary. "It's not that I couldn't deal with it," she said in her loan officer's voice. "But it doesn't hurt if they all think I'm so distraught I can't think straight. And you can say what you want about Wycliff, but they all think highly of him at First Baptist. And the crowd at United Methodist don't *dislike* him. Everybody needs to think I'm acting strictly in accordance with Bob's last wishes. I even pretended to Wycliff I don't care much about what's in the will." She seemed proud she'd exceeded Shackleton's expectations when she told him, "Wycliff wants to unravel it all, but he doesn't have time. We've made sure of that."

"I'm still not liking you telling him so much."

She rested her head back down on the pillow next to her old boss and added playfully, "If we keep everyone guessing, when the farmhouse comes down, the Emmetts won't know you're the big, fat prick who fucked them over."

"Oh, it's not me, precious," Shackleton protested. "Those rubes ignored a valid eviction notice two months ago. And no one can appeal the demolition notice because they don't have the standing as landowners to protest. As a matter of fact, neither do you. Bob got all bothered when he found out he didn't own the place."

"He never let me into his thoughts. It wasn't working. We'd have split up after the farm thing got settled." Then she thought to ask, "How does a demolition happen without anyone objecting?"

"Oh, technically, there's supposed to be a public process. But it's not eminent domain. That's what Bob refused to understand. And our partners aren't anxious at this point to go publicizing what's in that sinkhole. Way too early, before all the deals are in place. And besides, I got a tame judge who thinks he's going to be the next Worshipful Master, just in case."

"But… the *day* of the memorial? Why so soon? If someone objects…"

He got up on one elbow, and from his sweetened tone, he might have been telling a bedtime story. "Let's suppose, just for a moment, that knocking down the creaky old place is premature, maybe even illegal. But once the last of the low-life Emmett brood hightail it out of there and the place is nothing more than a pile of splinters, who's going to give a sour fart what we do with the property? Especially when we're ready to tell them about all the new jobs."

"I suppose you know what you're doing," she cooed. "One thing's sure, you won't get any argument from me." And she kissed him.

Edie neglected to share another reason why she didn't mind Evan's trying to find out what motivated Bob's final, desperate act: She didn't fully trust Stuart Shackleton. And if in his craftiness her beloved banker had overlooked something — or if he was planning to cut her out of his deals somehow — perhaps this dogged preacher might stumble on the evidence.

EVAN STAYED HUNCHED over the laptop at Bob's desk for a couple of hours. When daylight began to fade, he'd been at the task longer than he'd intended. Using his own phone, he called Edie to see when she'd be home, thinking he might as well wait for her so they could catch up. He especially wanted to know whatever she could tell him about the terms of the bequests, both Molly's and Bob's. (She probably wouldn't tell him, but he might as well ask.) The ambient noise on Edie's side of the conversation was loud with the hubbub of conversations and the clinking of plates and dinnerware. She said she wasn't coming home for a while and reminded him to make sure he locked up. She'd be visiting her sister in Higginsville. After the call, it occurred to Evan he hadn't seen her leave with an overnight bag. But maybe it had been already in her car.

There was nothing obvious on Bob's laptop. It wasn't that Bob hadn't used it. It was a recent model HP machine with updated Windows and antivirus software. But Bob — or someone — had deleted all his emails, along with the browsing history and its cache. And although the machine was set to back up regularly to the cloud, those files were gone, and the local trash had been emptied. The personal data that remained was the same address book he had on his phone, as well as a few files still remaining on the computer's desktop. The filenames were:

Catholics and Masons.pdf

Missouri Digital Heritage Collections Land Records.pdf

Note.docx

Nike Missile and Test Equipment.docx

Order 11 History.docx

Recorder of Deeds St Clair County Missouri.html

Redwine Family Tree.ged

XXX.docx

YYY.docx

Zillow Search Results.pdf

Evan quickly opened each file in turn. Most of the documents
appeared to be historical research about this part of Southern Missouri.

Bob was trying to figure out who owned the farm.

The Nike article seemed oddly out of place. It was about an abandoned
facility near San Francisco. The Note file was the suicide note, exactly
matching the printout Edie had given him. The XXX and YYY files
were locked, protected by passwords, and *Brownie1993* didn't open
them.

Enough for now.

Evan wanted to find some dinner, but he didn't think he should be
raiding Edie's icebox, even though she'd given him free access to the
house. As he got up from the desk, he took a closer look at the bookshelf. A handsome row of gilt, red-leatherette volumes was the *Standard American Encyclopedia.* Evan realized this set of books was very
familiar to him. When he and Bob were playmates in grade school,
Evan was enthralled with them whenever he visited. Bob's mother
Abigail was proud they owned all fifteen volumes of the encyclopedia,
which would someday be a valuable academic advantage for their son.
It was actually Abigail's mother who had bought them for her daughter, during Abigail's teen years, when they lived in Independence and
she was an indifferent student at William Chrisman High School. As it
happened, soon after this encyclopedia was first published in 1937, the
local supermarket featured it in a special promotion. Regular
customers could earn coupons by which they could buy one volume
per week. It seemed odd now to Evan that the set didn't allocate one
volume to each letter of the alphabet. Instead, the index was organized
so that each volume had about the same number of pages. Evan could
have recited the volume titles by heart, but here they were: *A — ART,*

ART — BOO, BOO — CHE, CHE — DIA, DIB — FOR, FOR — HER, HER — LAU, LAU — MOM, MON — PAT, PAT — REL, REM — SIG, SIG — TER, TER — UZH, VAA — WAT, and *WAT — ZYM.*

Evan knew this list as well as he could recite the sober recitation he memorized about the same time, "A Scout is trustworthy, loyal, help-ful, friendly, courteous, kind, obedient, cheerful, thrifty, brave, clean, and reverent."

It would be impressive for him to claim he'd read all the volumes from cover to cover. But, of course, he hadn't had time on those visits, and not all of the topics interested him. At various times, though, he had managed to thumb through the pages. The volume title pages claimed the set was "profusely illustrated." Indeed, the text was supplemented with thumbnail-sized black-and-white photos, line drawings, and engravings. He'd studied all of those. And he remembered reading about the city of Chicago, the tsars of Russia, early versions of the automobile (including electric-powered ones), and the process of photosynthesis in green plants.

He wondered whether Bob had ever cracked any of those books. The young Bob was an enthusiastic friend, but his curiosity was focused mainly on living things that crept and crawled.

On the row below the encyclopedia was an assortment of hardcover books with worn cloth bindings. All of them seemed related to Masonry, including *Morals and Dogma of the Ancient and Accepted Scottish Rite of Freemasonry.* The appearance of those books wasn't unfa-miliar to Evan either. He guessed they'd been on the shelf at the Taggart's, and they'd probably belonged to Bob's father.

Evan finally tore himself away from his nostalgia. He bagged the laptops, and as he stepped away from the desk, he decided to also take the framed photo of Brownie. He figured the safest place for the computers would be in the oilskin bag, stashed in the trunk of his car. The phones were always either in his pockets or plugged into the charger in the car.

He was about to leave through the kitchen door and lock up when he noticed something. Or the lack of something. There was no water bowl for Brownie where it should have been on the kitchen floor. Evan went back into Bob's office, where Brownie could be expected to hang out much of the time, and the obligatory second bowl was also missing.

All of the four incarnations of Brownie in Bob's life were rescues. They seemed to know they'd have been gassed had it not been for his abiding love.

Where is Brownie the Fourth? Maybe Edie guessed it. Maybe the dog did run off — one more heartache Bob was dealing with before he decided to stop his own.

But judging from the absence of those water bowls, Edie knows — or perhaps she simply hopes — the dog won't be coming back.

9

WEDNESDAY 8 PM
C'MON INN

I n the evening of the day of Bob's death, Evan found his appetite. He gratefully polished off a light meal of polenta and scrapple as he sat at the counter of the C'mon Inn. Cora had refilled his coffee cup faithfully with fresh-brewed Farmer Brothers from the glass carafe it seemed she never put down. To her credit, she didn't disapprove of his stirring in a couple of packets of Folger's crystals to thicken it up. Followed by his usual megadose of sugar.

The brain runs on glucose. That's sugar. There will either be time enough for me to mend my ways, or there won't.

The place was abuzz with the news about Bob, but no one suspected Evan had any special knowledge of it. Edie wasn't talking and neither was Chet Otis. Evan kept to himself, not just because of his ontological crisis but also because he intended to keep his inquiries confidential as long as possible.

It was a slow night at the diner. Only two booths were occupied, and Evan was alone at the counter. He was still dressed in the down jacket and jeans he'd had on since early morning, so he didn't look different from any of the other men in the place. They'd all parked their ball caps next to their coffee mugs. Cora was the type who was chatty and gossipy enough if you engaged her, but she knew to leave you alone if you were in a mood and wanted to keep your thoughts to yourself.

People say she's slow. She might not have made it out of grade school, but there's something glowing inside her.

Like most people in town, Cora had greeted him when he sat down as "Reverend," and he saw no point in correcting her. Sometimes he'd get "Rev." Most of them called him "Preacher" or "The Preach" because that's what he did on the occasional Sunday.

Cora usually didn't speak unless spoken to. Not because she was grumpy or cold. She wore an almost permanently serene expression on her face. No, perhaps because folks underestimated her intelligence, she was the town's confessor, and she was well suited to the role. But today she was looking wistful and forlorn.

She asked Evan confidentially, "What do we do when things happen? And don't tell me to pray. I've done plenty."

Evan replied, "I'd like to say what I usually say. That prayers are answered before you ask them. Your prayers need only ask for the wisdom to see what you already have, what God has provided especially for you from the beginning of time."

"But not now?"

"I've got no answers. Only a truckload of questions."

She took a moment like she was about to tell a friend she had a terminal diagnosis or some deep, secret wound. Then she said, even more softly, "I knew him."

Evan looked around. There was no one within earshot. He lowered his voice and asked her, "Can you tell me anything I don't know?"

"He was upset..."

"Yes," Evan began. "All those probate issues —"

"No," she said emphatically.

"No?"

"About his dog."

"Brownie the Fourth. You know, they were all named Brownie."

"Yeah," she said. "Talk about stuck in a rut. *I* could think of cuter names."

"The dog was sick?"

"Real bad. I don't know how it turned out."

"This was recent?"

"Last month."

"I visited Edie," Evan told her. "I didn't see the dog anywhere. *She* thinks Brownie ran off."

Cora stiffened as though her next thought was just too hideous. "Maybe she killed it."

And that's all Cora would say. She moved away with her Pyrex carafe.

Whoa. How can I get her to tell me more? Or is this as much as she knows?

Evan finished his fourth cup of coffee and his last gulp of pie at the C'mon. He left a twenty on the counter, more than enough for his food and a generous tip for Cora. (He still had some cash from his last commission check. He couldn't eat on what they gave him to preach.) He judged Cora was in no mood, and this was hardly the place to press her for more answers.

Evan's boss, Zip Zed of Zed Motors, liked to tease him about the possibility of his dating Cora. Evan wondered who else in town wanted to see him paired up with her.

But now I'm wondering how much of a thing she might have had with quiet, undemanding Bob.

As for mundane matters of his personal life, in coping with the day's events, he'd taken unauthorized time off. He'd fully intended to put in some work after the early-morning turkey shoot. Now, he promised himself he'd pay a visit to his boss in the morning. There would be no avoiding giving Zip a full and frank explanation.

10

WEDNESDAY NIGHT
EVAN'S TRAILER

Evan lived in a tiny, creaky, leaky old mobile home he'd rented for next to nothing from Zip Zed. Notable to anyone like Zip who fretted over real-estate investments, the mobile home would appear in any listings as "pre-1974." In that year, the building codes for trailer parks and prefab homes had been updated drastically. As a result, no bank would write a new mortgage on one of these older structures. The insurance companies didn't turn their backs, but they jacked their premiums. As a result, the only way for one of these vintage trailers to change hands was for the purchaser to plunk down the full amount in cash. Renovations, except for minimal repairs to keep the place habitable, wouldn't be a wise investment.

To make matters worse for the owner, the cost of moving or even demolishing one of these homes might be more than the land was worth. The best solution, which had already been followed for other lots in this neighborhood, was to summon the local fire department. They'd set a date to destroy the place for free in a controlled burn so their new recruits could have some real-world practice.

Despite its drawbacks, Zip still felt the place was rentable, albeit to low-income types whose alternative might be living in some shelter.

He didn't want to tear it down, and he didn't want to sell it. Zip was betting the land would appreciate as a long-term investment. So here was his skip-tracer Preacher Wycliff, who needed a roof over his head while he figured out what to do with the rest of his life. From Evan's point of view, he judged Zip should be paying him, since his occupancy and vigilance would prevent squatters taking over the place — or worse, turning it into a meth lab (not an uncommon usage of such premises in rural America these days).

So Evan lived in a space about half the size of a semi-trailer or boxcar. There was a good-sized propane tank outside, which provided a generous supply of LP gas for a wall-mounted space heater, an off-grid tankless water heater, and the bachelor-sized kitchen range. Zip had stepped up to repairing the aging swamp cooler on the roof — a repair bill of almost three-hundred dollars — and, with that luxurious amenity, living in this oversize closet was bearable even in the summer heat.

Evan got Zip to buy him a new microwave. The reconditioned half-sized fridge, although not frostless, worked just fine. The preacher didn't own a TV and didn't want to, but he sprang for the fastest fiber-optic Internet available, by which he got his news from YouTube and the digital editions of the *Springfield News-Leader, Kansas City Star, Washington Post, New York Times,* and *Wall Street Journal.*

Evan had a narrow, camp-sized bed with a new, ultra-firm mattress. He owed his tricky back that much. He'd bought his own sheets and towels — three sets (one in use, one clean, one in the laundry bag), and he'd found a double-thick woolen blanket at the Salvation Army that he'd taken promptly to a dry cleaner for sanitization. There was no place for a guest to sleep but on the floor. Entertaining girlfriends was not a priority. He'd found a plush beige carpet remnant for the floor, and he kept it reasonably clean with a manual brush-roller sweeper. Next to the bed was a low coffee table and a gooseneck floor lamp, also from the Salvation Army store. He had no kitchen table. An extension of the linoleum-clad, plywood kitchen countertop along one wall, under which he tucked two barstools, was his dining area.

He had one padded chair with a rigid back, and in front of the chair was his improvised desk — a rickety folding tray from which, as a child of yesteryear, he would have eaten his TV dinners. He refused to eat off this thing now, preferring the kitchen counter, but it was the right height for working on his cherished laptop — a recent-model Mac he'd bought refurbished on eBay.

The room was toasty. Despite the single-digit temperature outside tonight, Evan was comfortable in a Jayhawks sweatshirt, another Salvation Army find, and boxer shorts. Given that he was on the wrong side of the river to be rooting for Kansas, he wore the University of Kansas mascot mostly to bed where no one else would see it.

So, the little mobile home was downright comfy, provided you were a party of one with modest expectations. What you didn't want was rain, and most especially rain with a driving wind. Both window casements leaked, and there was still one elusive spot in the roof where, despite Evan's repeated efforts crawling around up there with caulking gun in hand, water inevitably found its way in. He had a bucket to catch the drips.

On settling in this evening, Evan plugged a pair of stereo headphones into his laptop and clicked his often-used bookmark for the YouTube clip of Roy Orbison singing "Only the Lonely" from *A Black and White Night*, a show at the Coconut Grove in 1987. If he were in a warmer, more nostalgic mood, his selection would have been "Pretty Woman." Those two numbers spanned the emotional extremes of his nonexistent love life. He was either missing Naomi or remembering her fondly. For variety, he might switch to Willie Nelson, but those themes of betrayal were usually far too bitter, unless his mood was downright sour.

His back was throbbing, so he popped a Vicodin. He told himself he'd wait before pouring himself any whiskey.

It might be easiest for everybody concerned if I could simply accept the obvious.

Maybe he was wasting his and everyone's time worrying Bob's suicide was a murder or even much of a mystery. Bob had murdered himself, the physical proof of which would no doubt be documented in tomorrow's autopsy report. As to why, the suicide note (or notes) strongly suggested an explanation: Bob thought of himself as a failure over some farmland deal, even if he was powerless to change things. However the deal was settled, some people would be disappointed, and Bob feared they wanted to do him harm.

Every so often, Evan would borrow a couple of minutes from his reverie to pour himself another two fingers of Wild Turkey, as long as it was at least an hour since he'd taken a Vicodin. Evan was ever-vigilant for shortness of breath, an early sign the alcohol and the painkiller were interacting, a potentially lethal combination if it got worse.

But enough of Orbison and Evan's thoughts of the uselessness of interior decoration. Time to dig back into Bob's phone and laptop and do some serious data drilling.

∿

As Evan sipped his bourbon, he scrolled through the call log on Bob's phone. This log and the contact list were the only remaining personal data. Bob either didn't use email on his phone or had deleted the entire app and its chronology.

The call log went back a couple of months, but not so far back as Molly's funeral. It was salted with familiar names:

Nick Berner

Buford's Fish and Game

Edie's Cell

Wiley Krause

Coralie Angelides

Angus Clapper

C'mon Inn

Emmetts

Josh Emmett

Stu Shackleton

Zip Zed

Zed Motors Service Department

There were a few numbers not associated with names in the address book. Evan searched on those in the browser of his laptop. Among the hits, he found:

St. Clair County Registrar of Deeds

Missouri State Historical Society

Fort Francis Blair, Public Affairs Office

Osage Nation Tribal Council

Evan then surveyed the files on the desktop of Bob's computer. He opened them one by one and skimmed the contents. The Zillow search was for the rural-route address of the Emmett farm. The property owner shown was Molly Redwine. The entry had a footnote:

Owner of record not verified.

Bob hadn't been the intellectually curious type, and yet from these phone calls and files, it seemed as though he was on a research mission about the history and ownership of Molly's land. The baffling part was, some of these documents went all the way back to the early nineteenth century, and Evan couldn't imagine why Bob should be having anything to do with the Army base or the Indian tribe.

Is Coralie Angelides our Cora at the C'mon? I never knew her full name. Buford's sells sporting goods. And ammo.

The password or passwords for the Word documents XXX and YYY could be difficult to find or to guess, even if they were something simple like Bob's birthdate. But if those files held what Evan suspected, the fates of many of the lives in this drama might well be different.

I'll sleep on it. Maybe my subconscious will have the answer?

~

EVAN DOZED off and had a vivid dream. It wasn't a nightmare, but it was unsettling. The Brownie of his boyhood brought a dead duck and dropped it proudly at Evan's feet. The dog ran off, and here came Brownie the Second, the shepherd-mix, with another duck, and dropped it. Brownie the Third, a tan Ridgeback Evan never knew, fetched the next round, and Brownie the Fourth, swimming like the Labrador she must have been, retrieved duck after duck from a pond and piled them in front of Evan. He didn't know what to make of it, didn't know what to do with all those dead ducks. He hadn't been the one to shoot them, hadn't asked for them, didn't want to eat them, was even ashamed about their wasted little lives, and didn't understand why the Brownies were so insistent he take them.

He awoke feeling bewildered, and as his consciousness merged with reality, he suspected that the ducks, like so many of the facts he'd garnered so far, were useless clues. He was indeed facing a pile of sense-lessly murdered ducks, and Evan had no choice but to get help sifting through those clues.

Silly as it seemed, he remembered:

Otis told me to get my ducks in a row.

The fattest duck in the pile had to be Angus Clapper, who was appar-ently in failing health. Evan said a prayer for Clapper, not sure whether he should be asking God to change the destiny of a man he didn't know, if indeed it was the fellow's time to depart this life.

So Bob got advice from Clapper. But did he follow through with it?

~

IT WAS three o'clock on Thursday morning. For a wake-up bracer, Evan poured himself another shot of Wild Turkey. Even though he drank it neat and tossed it back, he refused to drink from the bottle.

Bob and I weren't blood brothers, so much as bourbon *brothers.*

During his early college years, Evan hadn't been much of a drinker. But he didn't agree with the separatist Baptists back home who held that tipping up a bottle — any bottle, including soda pop — would lead to a life of drunken excess. During this time in the lonely valley of his spiritual and emotional journey, he became acquainted with Jack Daniels and Old Fitzgerald. When they were teenagers and learning to drink without getting sick, he and Bob had taken to bourbon.

When they were sixteen, Bob found a dust-covered but unopened pint of Old Crow his father had stashed in a closet, perhaps the teetotaler's insurance against a rainy day or for emergency application in case of a toothache. Safely installed in a grove of birches on the Emmett farm, they passed the bottle back and forth.

This incident was during the reign of German-shepherd Brownie the Second, who of course tagged along. Besides the flask of liquor in the hip pocket of his jeans, Bob carried a canteen case threaded through his belt so he'd always have fresh water for the dog.

"Now, Brownie," Bob announced as he took a swig from the flask, "we're not giving you any booze. You understand, it's not because I won't share. You know our rule. But it would be downright mean to give you something so nasty it would make you sick."

"What about me?" Evan complained. "Give me some of that nasty stuff!" And he snatched the flask from his friend.

Bob assured him, "You — and me — *we* need to learn how to drink, how to hold our liquor, so we don't pass out in some bar one day and have to be dragged home."

Bob had Evan cup his hands to catch water from the canteen, and Brownie lapped it up gratefully. For all the dog knew, the boys were just drinking dirty water that smelled too much like the vet's office.

"You know what they say?" Bob asked Evan after he'd had a few more pulls on the bottle.

"Wine on beer is queer?"

"No, this is adult advice. A Missouri gentleman can only drink bourbon. A rye drinker beats his wife, and a Scotch drinker probably lets his wife beat him."

They drank some more, taking gulps in turn, punctuated with coughs, thought about it, and finally agreed vodka and gin are for stuck-up foreigners, and rum is for beach bums.

And until his break with theology, Evan had considered his dietary habits sensible. For a while, his diet was vegetarian, then vegan.

"Someday, just the smell of meat or fish cooking will disgust you," Naomi had predicted.

After that phase, along with the bourbon, he reverted to the grease-and-potatoes habits of home. As they say in Missouri, he ate everything on the pig but the squeal. He put on forty pounds he had trouble losing long afterward. Surprisingly tall at six feet for the son of two short people, he had a broad chest and a muscular build. He carried the extra weight like a retired football player who had gone soft and forsaken the gym.

I'll do better. I will. Swear to God.

As, in the present, Evan dozed off again, he remembered: "Dumbass," Bob had called him.

11

THURSDAY BREAKFAST
C'MON INN

Despite having worked and worried through much of the night, Evan was up with the chickens and sitting in his usual chair at the counter of the C'mon Inn. Before Evan's return to his roots a year ago, the C'mon Inn had done business as The Blue Inn. Its one online review had a single begrudged star, awarded by a customer who complained he never got a refill on his coffee. Evan suspected Cora must not have been working that shift. (She gave you refills before you asked, "to keep it hot." Never mind he'd finally gotten the sweetness just right.) Also, this guy's Web avatar showed he was from California, and that alone could explain why the staff ignored him.

EVAN REMEMBERED one time he'd caught up with Bob at the C'mon, just as the preacher was beginning to feel at home again. They sat at their respective usual places at the counter, and Cora served them. Evan found his friend's dry wit to be as sharp as ever. Although other people often remarked on Bob's lack of expressiveness, when he was with Evan, he didn't hold back.

When Evan mentioned he'd come across the Californian's one-star review of the diner, Bob explained, "You don't wear your ball cap backward in AC. The bill of the cap is there to keep the sun off your forehead. If you want to prevent a burn on your neck, you turn up the collar of your shirt. You wear your tee shirt *underneath* your button-front shirt. Your jeans are flared for boots at the bottom of the pant legs. As for the boots, you prefer steel-toed, waterproofed lace-ups, unless it's Saturday night, when you might sport your Tony Lamas, if you have a pair, so to speak. You hold your jeans up with a wide leather belt, with a crafted silver buckle. And you buckle it no lower than two inches south of your bellybutton. Do it right, and you never show the crack of your ass, even when you squat to pet a dog. You *don't pet kittens* or ruffle the hair of little kids. You just *don't*. If you own any other kind of hat, it better be a Stetson, and then pretty much only for wearing on a Saturday night, unless you're heading to church or some kind of serious meeting."

Bob sold custom-built tractor-trailers — tankers for water or milk or chemicals, livestock and horse trailers, and refrigerated semis. Yes, he was a salesman, but he didn't need the gift of gab. His customers told him what they wanted to haul, and Bob knew which specs to put in the order. And because he didn't bend your ear unnecessarily, people tended to trust him.

Evan would talk about his own listlessness, his lack of direction. Bob silently agreed questions about Evan's bachelorhood were off the table. Maybe he assumed a minister was like a priest who'd walled off that part of his life. Evan didn't elaborate, and he never shared with Bob anything about Naomi.

As for Bob, he finally admitted to Evan he'd married Edie mostly for companionship. He'd hoped it would grow to be more, but it hadn't. Like Evan, Bob was in his mid-thirties, and Edie was a few years older. Bob never said how they met or what attracted him to her. Evan judged his friend wasn't a demanding husband.

And if I hadn't been so cocksure about giving him advice, maybe he'd still be here.

All through their meal at the C'mon, Brownie the Fourth, whose talent was radiating sweetness, had been sitting dutifully outside at the curb. She was a pretty dog with an elegant profile — Lab-mix, chocolate brown coat. Maybe there was some Collie in her? Even though she attracted admiring attention out there, she wouldn't stir. No leash necessary, she wasn't going anywhere. The spring weather this evening had been balmy. If it had been harsh and cold, she'd wait patiently in the cab of Bob's truck. And if it was sweltering summer heat, Bob might not have stopped in at all, since he judged neither the truck nor the sidewalk to be bearable for his furry friend in the hundred-degree heat.

When they emerged together from the diner, Bob was carrying a to-go bag Cora had just handed him. He pulled out the contents of a foil wrapper and gave Brownie two cooked hamburger patties, one at a time. The food was in her stomach in a matter of seconds.

"We share, don't we, girl?" he said affectionately as he ruffed the top of her head. Then he added, "But no bun and no fries. You know that stuff gives you gas."

THIS MORNING EVAN ordered rare steak and three over-easy eggs, crisp hash browns, a mound of grits, and buttered rye toast with strawberry jam. As she filled his coffee cup for the third time, Cora teased, "You just get out of prison?"

He forgot his mouth was full when he explained, "I was up late last night, trying to figure out a problem. I kind of lost track of time. Thinking is hungry work." He wiped his mouth and gulped. "Excuse me."

There was a brief news item in the morning *Springfield News-Leader*. (The *Appleton City Journal*, a weekly, hadn't yet gone to press.) The story recapped the facts of the suicide, so it seemed no one, including Edie, was trying to avoid mentioning the cause of death.

When there was an awkward pause, Cora decided now was as good a time as any.

"You wouldn't be up late with some girl?" she asked and risked a coquettish smile. "I know you got to write your sermons."

Is that eye shadow she's wearing? Mascara? I didn't realize her eyes were so big.

"Not really," Evan said, swallowing a mouthful of grits. "I've got three all-purpose that work pretty much anywhere. Kind of like jokes about those orange cones on the highway."

"You're pulling my leg," she said and giggled.

"Not at all. *Everybody* hates those orange cones, and they're *everywhere!*"

"I mean about those sermons. You just make stuff up?"

He counted on his fingers, "One: God is all that there is. Two: Every day is a gift. Be thankful and filled with joy. Three: Love yourself as much as God loves you, and you'll have a hard time hating anyone. I got this fourth one that we're all made of billion-year-old stardust, but that's kind of for special audiences. Like for the Unitarians."

"Wait a minute," Cora objected with a little laugh. "The Bible says the world got made in seven days."

He leaned forward and asked her, "So tell me. Before there was a sun in the sky or an Earth to whirl around it, how long was a day?"

"Let there be light! The sun had to come first."

"Who said the first light was from the sun?"

"Sure. From where else?"

"There was this thing called the Big Bang." He realized if he went on, things could get complicated — astrophysically, theologically, and personally. So he summarized, "Think of the Bible as poetry. A lot of it works better that way."

Starting to get up, he laid a ten on top of his bill, then added another five for her. As she picked it up, she confided, "You know, Preacher, that's more words than you've said to me all year."

He winked and said, "Must be the liquor talking," and he walked out.

As she watched him go, Cora muttered to herself, "I don't know what to make of that man."

Evan didn't know what to make of Cora either. She might have been Bob's only other close friend, but Evan didn't feel right pressing her for details on their relationship.

And I'm over-quota myself in the heartbreak department. It's not the love of God I lack. It's the love of Naomi.

His debates with Naomi were sporting. She was a fellow geek.

~

"WHAT DO you know about the *Book of Revelation*?" he once asked her.

"Never read it," she said flatly. "I think I caught some movie. Was it Netflix or Amazon?"

"*The Prophecy One and Two? The Rapture? Megiddo?*"

"I think it was a documentary." He could tell she was teasing. She knew the *Torah* in Hebrew, and she was a better student of history than he was.

"What bothers me," Evan said, trying not to let the discussion devolve into lighter-hearted teasing, "is how it all fits. I mean, we get the New Testament, and God has turned a cheek. We now have this compassionate, loving Father who can forgive the most heinous crimes if you will just believe and repent. Then here's this mysterious, possibly allegorical, apocalyptic text, and the vengeful God of the Old Testament is back in full fury. And most of its prophecies are extensions of old Hebrew war stories. And neat payoffs of prophecies. For centuries since it was written, Christian churches disagreed heatedly about whether it should be included in the Bible. But it made it into the King James Version and every major translation since."

"Hmm," she said. "You're forgetting about the heart of the story. *All* the books in the New Testament center on the sacrifice of Jesus. I mean, the *blood* sacrifice. Human civilizations through recorded time, and as late as the Romans, thought slaying animals would appease their gods. If you couldn't afford a goat, you'd say a prayer and snap the head off a mouse. Going back in the Jewish tradition, you have the ancient story of God asking Abraham to sacrifice his son Isaac, only tossing out a never-mind at the last minute. The passion of the Christ is a story designed to appeal to the most primitive human superstition, placating a blood-thirsty deity. These days, would anyone respect a president of the United States more if he cut his own son's throat on live TV?" She thought a moment. "Didn't Saddam Hussein assassinate his brother in public? But his was a power play, hardly a demonstration of love for his people. Or was it?"

"Maybe the crucifixion is a message about doing away with blood sacrifice… once and for all," Evan suggested.

"Think what you want, but I'd call yours a postmodern rationalization."

"I don't seem to be winning any arguments with you," Evan complained.

She smiled back at him. "Don't plan on it."

Evan told himself, sooner or later everyone must confront separation and heartbreak, some people more than a few times. He'd simply made his path more difficult by studying for the ministry while he was trying to learn what it means when one human soul is bonded in physical — and then all-consuming — romantic love with another.

12

THURSDAY 8:30 AM
ZED MOTORS

Evan found Zip "the Zipper" Zed IV in the service bay of Zed Motors, the family-owned Ford car and tractor dealership in Rockville. In the scheme of things in this part of Southern Missouri, Appleton City in St. Clair County is a one-silo town, nearby Butler (in Bates County, as is Rockville) is a two-silo town, and Springfield — more than a hundred miles to the south in Greene County — is the nearest big city. Rockville is a wide place in the road, with a population of about a hundred-and-sixty souls, which at any given moment might be growing or shrinking by a significant percentage, depending on what's happening in the beds of its lovers and invalids. Locating the dealership in this smallest of small towns instead of on the main drag of AC may have had something to do with the price of land or that the founder had expected the community to grow more than it ever did. As it was, Zed Motors was only a short side-trip from the teeming metropolis of AC, and Zip relished being the little town's undisputed business leader.

Zip was admiring a new delivery, a factory-new, late-model Ford TW-25 tractor. His service tech Max Alumbaugh was checking it over meticulously with the engine running, hooking up diagnostic connectors to a dashboard display to step through a sequence of metrics and detect any variances.

Zip glanced up from the maze of cables, j-boxes, piping, and valves surrounding the tractor's massive diesel power plant. The owner of Zed Motors was ten years younger than Evan, having inherited the business five years ago when his father's meticulously maintained Studebaker Golden Hawk hit a patch of black ice and collided with a telephone pole. Zip had won a degree with honors from the UM Rolla in mining and metallurgy with a minor in business administration.

Lack of confidence was not among Zip's shortcomings. Evan wondered whether, after a few more years, Zip would grow bored of running the dealership, although being a big fish in a little pond must have had its perks, including a loud voice in regional politics.

"Look at this sucker," Zip said. "Fully enclosed glass cab. Power steering and hydraulic activators. AM-FM and XM. Bose Surround Sound. Bluetooth smartphone interface. Wi-Fi with soft-screen controls, including GPS Nav accurate within about ten feet — if you're stupid enough to not know the lay of your own land. Programmable so it could be driverless, but let's not tell the family farmer. Time was," Zip sighed, "back in my granddad's day, you could fix one of these out in the field with a hairpin. One more reason to have a farm wife."

Knowing a punchline was coming, Evan asked him, "What about a girlfriend?"

Zip wheezed, "You shouldn't give a girlfriend time to put her hair up!"

"But what if she hasn't washed it or just wants to get it out of her way to do her chores?"

"Do you think there's girlfriends who *do chores?* Preach, that's why you live by yourself and still do your own laundry." The younger man's expression went slack as he asked, "Wuddya got for me, and how come I didn't hear from you yesterday?"

"You heard about Bob Taggart."

"Who hasn't? Damn shame. You gonna tell me you got something going with Edie?"

Evan drew Zip aside, away from Max, then confided, "I'm the one found him."

"Christ Godallmighty. Sorry you had to be the one. You knew him pretty well."

"Since we were in grade school in AC, yes."

"Must have been horrible to see."

"Shot himself in the chest. Just looked like he was taking a nap. They could do an open casket, but Edie doesn't want it. Him, he wanted cremation. So, it'll be private interment, but we'll do a memorial service beforehand."

Zip chuckled. "So you were, what? Counseling Edie all day?" Then he added, "Sorry, I should be more respectful. I didn't know Bob particularly, but people say she's hell-on-wheels."

"Will you give it a rest? She asked me to make the arrangements. I saw Sheriff Otis yesterday. They're doing an autopsy in Columbia. We should get the results today. Nobody expects any surprises."

"Edie trusts you with all that? And you're telling me you're *not* doing her?"

"Zip. Please." The youngest Zed had been married to the same strong-willed woman, born Delilah Carson, for eleven years. They had two smart-assed boys, playfully nicknamed Buzz and Whiz. Zip was reputed to be a good father and a doting husband. Amazing to Evan, Delilah gave Zip a long leash and didn't seem to mind how much he sniffed around, as long as he didn't slip out of the doghouse at night.

Still savoring the image of Edie, Zip informed Evan, "That woman has ice water for blood. You'd be better off hitting on Cora at the C'mon. That babe's got eyes for you, if you haven't noticed." Then he muttered, "Never mind. You haven't noticed."

"I'm not open to the possibility, just now."

"Well, what about that dog of Bob's? Edie won't want it. You could at least have some warm body in your bed."

"Brownie's disappeared. Edie thinks the dog was sick and went off to die."

"You preachers are supposed to spread the Good News," Zip cracked. "So far, you haven't brought me any."

Evan remained serious. "Did you know Bob was a Mason?"

"Come to think of it, yes. He was the one who approached me years back. I told him, from what I knew of it, too much mumbo jumbo and not enough picnics. That's why I joined the Rotary. Great-grandad was an Odd Fellow. Seems to me like those guys had something to do with the Masons. They hold weenie roasts and give out scholarships and such."

"Otis suggested I check in with Stu Shackleton on it."

"Now there's an odd fellow. His shit don't stink."

"You got issues with him?"

"There's a piece of land we both wanted. Don't get me started. And that fucker buys *German!* And the truck he pulls his boat with is a Chevy! I mean, Positraction was fine in its day, but let's move on. Shackleton's not only a Mason. He's Sons of the American Revolution *and* Founders and Patriots. So white, he shits vanilla ice cream. If you talk to him, I'd keep mum about that POA. You're just a friend asking for Edie about what those old boys expect to do for Bob's memorial. It's only logical. I assume you'll be giving the eulogy."

"How did you know the Masons do anything special?"

"Bob's father, Lionel Taggart. Also a Mason. His service was at Hill and Sons. As I recall, you were away at school. Like I say, mumbo jumbo. They came in their full regalia, leather aprons and all. Stood up there and spoke in tongues. Nobody understood what-the-fuck. They just did it for themselves, and then they left. Not one showed up at the reception. Maybe it's a religious thing?"

"Masons say they're nondenominational," Evan explained. "And that they're not a religion. But they're all about God, the Great Architect. That's where the masonry comes in. The Freemasons in Europe were formed in the eighteenth century as a secret society to stand against the pope and the king — all kings *and* all the aristocrats. So you couldn't be a Catholic or a royalist."

"Seems to me Stu Shackleton is Catholic. At least his wife was. Maybe he went along with it for her sake. I hear she's in a bad way."

"I heard that too," Evan said. "But that's all I heard."

"Surprises me a guy like Shackleton could be either Catholic *or* Mason. He thinks *he's* God."

"The Masons might accept a new member who says he's a Catholic. But I'm pretty sure the Vatican still forbids the faithful to be Masons."

Bob had the "Catholics and Masons" article on his laptop. Was he wondering whether Shackleton's leadership is legitimate?

Zip replied, "You ask me, they all collect money for charities, and they like their picnics and parades. The Shriners wear those Egyptian hats and tool around in their go-karts. These are old-timey men's clubs where they can get away from their wives, knock back their sour-mash-and-branch, and claim they're having sober discussions about helping the community."

"What about the Rotary?"

"We have our chatty dinners — you know, rubber chicken — and we sponsor community welfare projects worldwide. There might be a beer or two. It's not against the rules. We have quite a few women members, even some who are officers. There's an idea. We meet once a month at the Red Lobster. Join us next time and I'll hook you up."

"I thought you said I should go after Cora."

"Bring her, unless there's a chance you won't score because she'll think you're some kind of fucking straight arrow. Or you could take her to a strip bar. Find out if she likes to watch."

"I'm still working your list, by the way," Evan said, welcoming the chance to change the subject.

"I figured you were. That's why it's a commission deal. You don't get paid until I do. Who's next?"

"One Briana Caspar, over near the base. Ex-Army, single parent. In way over her head on a Mustang."

"I don't remember her," Zip said. "I must not have sold that one. But I do remember the *car.*" And he whistled. "When you gonna do her? If she's pretty, treat her real nice. We like repeat customers. After they've come to Jesus, that is."

"I should be able to run over there on Monday," Evan said. Then he added, "You know, you could do it a lot cheaper hiring some data driller to get you a current address. Then get the sheriff to serve papers. It doesn't have to be legwork these days."

Zip got uncharacteristically serious for a moment. "Since this establishment was formed in 1952 by a wounded war veteran, Zed Motors has never dealt with deadbeats. We sell to honest, hardworking members of this farm community who, except in rare instances of adversity, do not need to understand the fine print of their sales contracts. When we are faced with the unfortunate eventuality of nonpayment, there's always a reason. At those times, what I need is someone like yourself who can talk a scared cat out of a tree or politely scare the shit out of a goose. You find them, you have a sit-down, and you explain in words *they can understand* what's in the fine print. If I have to pay off the bank and carry the paper myself, I will. *I will,* as long as you tell me we've still got a customer who values our relationship and his or her future as a responsible citizen of this community."

"I didn't realize you'd carry paper. That's a helluva risk."

"I'm not saying my terms would be as favorable as the bank's. It's risk and reward, Econ one-oh-one. Besides, if I don't step in, the bank's gonna fuck 'em good. Probably find a way to grab their land or whatever else."

"Has that happened recently?"

"More times than it should've, yes," Zip said. "Then the bank flips the place to MFA or some other ginormous cooperative. They don't buy their fleets of tractors from me, but sooner or later, they all need repair."

"What about due process? Seems like the banks should be the ones offering the debtor a workout. Even after a judgment of default, there should be plenty of time to work out a settlement."

"Well, when you see Stu Shackleton, why don't you ask him?"

"Why him?"

"I'm giving the investigator news? You *have* been away. Around these parts, Shackleton *is* the bank. Bates Bank and Trust. Free trip to the cleaners with every loan."

EVAN GOT BACK in his car, and before he started the engine, he put in a call to Knox. This time he asked for the patient information desk, and he had to play the Reverend card to get them to tell him anything. Good news, Mr. Clapper was out of critical care but not yet able to receive visitors. Try back tomorrow, he may be back in his room by then. He'd be delighted to have a visitor.

Evan's next call was to Bates Bank and Trust in Rich Hill. He noted the irony of the bank's location. Growing rapidly in the 1880s and now about the same size as AC with its thousand-plus souls, Rich Hill was named not for its nutrient-rich soil or the gold in its citizens' pockets but for its coal deposits, to which Peabody Energy now seemed to hold the monopoly. As Evan expected, when he asked for Stuart Shackleton, he was told the bank's president was not available.

Perhaps the assistant manager could help? Evan declined the offer and explained his inquiry was a Masonic matter. He was politely given the phone number of the lodge in Osceola.

Having tried to breach Shackleton's firewall from the front, Evan would try the private entrance around the back. It was an approach he vowed to use sparingly, but he was beginning to appreciate the value of having Bob's phone.

"Who the hell *is* this?" was Shackleton's greeting.

"Evan Wycliff, Mr. Shackleton. I'm handling arrangements for Bob Taggart's memorial. On Edie's behalf, of course."

"I see," Shackleton grumbled. "You should change the ID on that phone. Might upset some people."

"We're planning a memorial service this Saturday morning at ten at First Baptist, and I'm told a Masonic ritual might be appropriate."

"The church has no objection?" Shackleton asked. "Some congregations aren't open to it."

"I'm sure Reverend Thurston will welcome you."

"We'll need about fifteen minutes following the eulogy, if you don't mind. We march in and we march out. I'll get back to you with details after I've conferred with the brotherhood."

"Thank you," Evan said. "I'm sure Bob would have wanted it."

Shackleton grumbled again. "God knows what that guy wanted. You were his friend?"

"Boyhood friends. We'd lost touch until I moved back into the area last year."

"I feel real bad about it, I don't mind telling you. He was a faithful member. I'd see him once a month at our meetings. But we weren't what you'd call buddies. He held his cards close to his chest." Then he added, "I sold him the gun, you know."

Gun? Chest? How does Shackleton have those details?

"Oh? When was that?" Evan asked instead.

"A few months back. After his aunt passed away. He got to thinking more about security for him and Edie. Home invasion, that kind of thing. You can't be too careful these days. I shot with him at the range. But, of course, I had no idea."

"Of course," Evan echoed, pretending to agree. "By the way, regarding the Taggarts' safe deposit box. Are you aware of the contents of those wills?"

Shackleton was caught up short. Evan had hoped throwing this grenade into the cordial conversation might cause the banker to blurt out something he'd rather hold back. "I don't believe that's any of your business, Reverend." Then he added tersely. "I have a meeting. We'll talk again before Saturday."

Evan managed to add, "We may have to reschedule. The Emmetts want to attend, but there's an urgent matter at their farm they need to take care of."

Before he ended the call, Shackleton muttered, "Mind how you go, fella. You're way off the reservation."

It was an apt metaphor. Evan was a lone warrior, and the Feds were closing in.

ALTHOUGH EVAN DIDN'T FEEL up to fighting city hall, much less the U.S. Army, he did want to try to understand how the demolition of the Emmett place could be done without public disclosure. Perhaps there would be a way to halt, or at least delay, the action. He phoned the public affairs office of the Army base and was transferred to the Corps of Engineers office in Stockton. After some throat-clearing and virtual paper shuffling, he was told, yes, the site was scheduled to be cleared, starting at dawn on Saturday morning. Water and power to the buildings would be disconnected, and the propane tank would be removed. Perimeter fencing would be erected and the farmhouse and outbuildings razed. Guards would be posted on the access roads, and the public would be barred from entry.

The reason given for clearing the land was to build an access road to an unspecified toxic cleanup site. No more details were available.

Evan had done some online research and had questions. He asked the officer, "Can you tell me, I know it's late in the game, but was the eminent domain process followed? Hearings? Negotiation with the landowner? Fair market value ascertained and accepted?"

"No," came the frank — and unexpected — reply.

Evan was speechless for a moment. "And why *not?*"

"Because that site is federal land."

13

THURSDAY 11 AM
SHERIFF'S OFFICE

Otis offered Evan a chair in the private office, closed the door, and handed him three documents — Edie's signed power of attorney, the medical examiner's report, and the sheriff's case report.

Evan scanned the POA's terms and conditions, which were concise but meticulously worded. Edie was giving him authority to "make decisions and execute agreements regarding all matters pertaining to my personal affairs, effective immediately and revocable forthwith on notice, whether oral or written."

"Wow," Evan said. "Isn't this unusually broad? And open-ended?"

"On the face of it," Otis surmised, "she's a distressed widow. Can't be bothered. Trusts you completely."

"And?" Evan asked cautiously. "What's her agenda, do you think?"

Otis leaned forward, lowered his voice, and said, "Could be she wants deniability. That is, if she decides to do something other folks might not approve of. Like maybe, try to stop the demolition?"

"I'd like nothing better, sheriff. But, turns out, it's not up to her. Not at all."

The sheriff looked genuinely surprised. "How's that?"

"The Corps of Engineers is telling me it's not her land. If she's not the landowner, she has no standing to appeal. Because there was no assertion of eminent domain in the first place."

"What?"

"The Army is saying it's U.S. government land. They don't have to ask permission from anybody. I'm guessing that's why Bob was so confused and upset about it."

"Well, knock me over with a feather," the sheriff said. "I'd just assumed Bob had given permission and accepted their offer, whatever it was."

"Somebody owes Josh an explanation, but the Emmetts have already decided to vacate. They're going to her mother's. Some guys from the church are helping them clear everything out."

"So there's nothing more to be done?"

"I doubt it," Evan said. "But I still want to know what's in Bob's will. And I want to have a long talk with some old attorney, Angus Clapper. He seems to be the only one who knows the history of the place. He's up at Knox, but he's been so ill they won't let me see him."

Otis grunted. "Not a name I know. Well, I'd say you're earning your nonexistent salary. You're welcome to take a desk out there and take your time with those reports. I just need your sign-off sooner rather than later on one item. We need your formal permission to proceed with the cremation."

"You sure you won't need more tests?"

"Let's not make this more than it is. I'm sure Edie wants to go forward, and for sure she won't want to pay storage costs for the body if you delay. But you're the POA, so I need you to sign off now."

"Before I've read the reports?"

"Routine, Preach," the sheriff said. "Nothing remarkable, I assure you." Then he lowered his voice and said, "If you don't do it today, you'll make that widow think there's more here than there is."

"Still," Evan said. "I just want to read through. I mean, are they really firing up the furnace today?"

"First thing in the morning, I expect. I was hoping I could send the form before I leave the office tonight and be done with it."

"Let me read your reports. And then I'll check with Edie, just to make sure."

The sheriff let out an exasperated sigh. "Do what you gotta do."

THE AUTOPSY REPORT was brief and mostly metrics. It had a line-art template drawing of the corpse with callouts and notations for distinguishing marks, such as scars and blemishes, the entry wound in the chest, and the exit wound in the back. The angle wasn't low-to-high, as Otis had predicted, but high-to-low. There were lab readings on blood alcohol, pharmaceutical residues, gastrointestinal contents, and wound location, along with affected bones and organs, and tissue damage, as well as dissection and visual inspection of organs.

The sheriff's accompanying report was lengthy and much more comprehensive than Evan had expected. Besides the investigation at the scene, it also summarized follow-up phone interviews with Edie and with Doc Wilmer.

The report had been written by Deputy Malcolm Griggs. To Evan, the most telling part of the report was an analysis of the autopsy results and evidence in light of eight standard criteria:

Ascertainment

In the following narrative, we assess the autopsy evidence in relation to established criteria for determination of a finding of death by suicide:

1. The method used is firearm, hanging, or another method common in completed suicide.

The fatal wound on the ventral side of the decedent's upper torso was caused by a single round fired from a SIG-Sauer P320 automatic pistol at point-blank range. The forensic investigator at the scene (and author of this report), Deputy Malcolm V. Griggs, was unable to find any spent rounds on the ground for a radius of 20yd, despite going over the area with a metal detector. The ballistics report (Exhibit A) shows a round had been fired from the weapon, and seven rounds were left in the magazine.

2. The decedent left a suicide note.

The decedent left two notes, one on the kitchen counter of his residence, presumably for his wife to find, the other folded and tucked into the right breast pocket of the suit coat on his body. We include the notes by reference in Exhibits B and C of this report. For reasons of privacy, the contents are held in a secured file in this office and not reproduced in the exhibits. Both notes explicitly state the decedent's imminent intent to take his own life, along with feelings of anxiety and guilt arising from unspecified causes.

3. Inspection of the decedent's body demonstrates self-injury.

As stated in response to the first criterion above, the wound in the decedent's chest appeared to be self-inflicted, subject to the exception stated in Note 1 below. (See also Note 2.)

4. There is a known pharmacological overdose.

Analysis of blood and tissue samples in the toxicology screen (summarized in Exhibit D) found no indication of pharmacological overdose, nor any evidence of substances commonly used in cases of deliberate overdose. Blood alcohol was 1.76%, indicating severe intoxication and physical impairment, consistent with ingestion of 4oz or more of liquor for a man of his body weight within a window of a few hours prior to death. Traces of Losartan Potassium (trade name Cozaar) blood-pressure medication were found, consistent with a routine daily prescription dose of 100mg taken sometime within the previous 8 hours.

5. Large quantities of pills are missing from pillboxes.

Decedent's spouse, Edith Taggart, reported to sheriff's investigator Griggs that in the preceding weeks her husband had taken doses of Xanax and Valium, perhaps in greater quantities than prescribed, but with no resulting visible signs of physical impairment or intoxication. As stated in our response above to Criterion 4, toxicology screens found no residual evidence of these substances. Inspection of the residence and the decedent's vehicle (parked on the shoulder of State Route P about 0.4mi south of the scene) found no remaining pills, pharmaceutical containers, liquor bottles, or sample packets.

6. The decedent has a history of suicide ideation or attempts.

According to the sheriff's investigator, the decedent's personal physician, Dr. Dudley Wilmer, reported that, over a period of the most recent 8 weeks, the decedent had expressed anxiety with paranoid ideation. No mention was made, however, of suicidal intent. Although concerned the decedent's depressive episodes might become chronic, the doctor saw no urgency or reason to break confidentiality and recommend a suicide watch. The decedent could not identify specific individuals who might be intent on doing him harm. In Deputy Griggs' interview with Mrs. Taggart, she described incidents of the decedent's confused thinking and anxiety, but no explicit mention of suicide or any intent to harm himself or others. She could identify no third parties who had threatened him or might wish to do him harm.

7. There are written materials or a computer website history of topics related to suicide.

Neither physical inspection of the decedent's residence and vehicle nor the investigator's interview with Mrs. Taggart discovered any such materials or relevant information. The decedent's smartphone was not found on the body, nor in the vehicle. The suicide notes appear to be computer printouts, but this office has not recovered or inspected a home computer or laptop. Further investigation per this criterion is not deemed necessary and could be a needless invasion of the privacy of the surviving spouse.

8. A relative suspects suicide based on their knowledge of the decedent.

As indicated in our response to Criterion 6 above, Mrs. Taggart's description of her husband's recent behavior noted anxiety and confused ideation, but no explicit mention of suicide or intent to harm himself or others. The decedent's apparent chronic depression in recent months would be consistent with potentially suicidal thoughts and behavior.

Findings

The conclusion of the Sheriff's Department of St. Clair County is that the decedent Robert Nathan Taggart died by suicide of a self-inflicted wound to his upper torso from a pistol registered in his name. The wound was causative and fatal, and the decedent therefore did not die of natural causes or at the hands of another.

Recommendations

We find no compelling reasons to preserve the decedent's remains for further evidentiary examination. The decedent's body is currently in the custody of University Hospital Forensics Unit by authority of the St. Clair County Medical Examiner. Since in his suicide notes the decedent explicitly expressed a desire for cremation, we recommend seeking permission from decedent's next of kin (Mrs. Taggart) to authorize cremation forthwith by the county's contractor.

Disposition

With the approval of Sheriff Chester Otis as indicated by his signature below, this investigation is closed and assigned file number 19-00034-6427.

Notes

1. Consistent with a conclusion that the decedent's fatal chest wound was self-inflicted, the M.E.'s report indicates cordite residue was found on the decedent's left hand.

2. Possibly irrelevant to conclusions of this report, the M.E.'s examination and tissue samples found Stage II (non-metastatic) cancer of the prostate gland. The decedent's physician (Dr. Wilmer) states that he and Mr. Taggart were aware of this condition. As is routine with male patients of decedent's age, during routine annual checkups, the physician provides

counsel about the prevalence of prostate cancer, along with other cautions, such as the need for regular physical self-examination for testicular cancer. During these counseling sessions, the physician typically asks whether the patient wishes a prostate-specific antigen (PSA) test to be performed. Because of the relatively slow progression of the disease and the potential emotional distress that might be caused by either a false-positive result or a condition that may not need near-term treatment, many patients opt to skip the test. Mr. Taggart authorized the test, and his PSA was out of normal range. Dr. Wilmer also stated that he was not aware that Mr. Taggart had sought medical care from any other providers during the last year. A Stage II diagnosis, which was suspected but never confirmed, is curable by a variety of aggressive methods such as surgery and/or radiation. In many cases, current medical practice typically advises only active surveillance without treatment. In short, the disease at this stage is far from fatal. Even though the decedent was aware of his condition, it would have been much less likely to be a motive for suicide than the other emotional and psychological factors cited in Criteria 6 and 8 above.

SHE ANSWERED on the first ring.

Evan came right out with "Edie, Otis is pressuring me to give permission for the cremation."

She didn't hesitate. "So do it."

"I've just finished going through the autopsy report and the sheriff's writeup of the case. I need to ask you — did you know Bob had prostate cancer?"

Again, no hesitation. "No. Is that why he did it?"

"I don't know. More importantly — was he worried about it?"

Now she took a breath, like she'd wanted to say something else. "That man wouldn't tell me if the house was on fire."

"I do have a lot of other questions —"

"Is there anything they need him — I mean, his body — for?"

Evan checked his impulse to make things more complicated than they needed to be. "No," he said, "I don't suppose so."

"Then let's get on with it, and you can come by whenever and ask any other questions you have till you're blue in the face."

AFTER HE'D STUDIED the autopsy report, Evan signed the cremation release and shoved it back across the desk to Otis. The sheriff beckoned across the room to Deputy Griggs, who promptly retrieved the document. As the young officer turned to go, Otis stopped him with a command: "And, Griggs. Fetch us some coffee, both black and with a fistful of sugars for the Reverend here. None of those wussy Styrofoam cups neither. Find us some *clean* crockery."

As Griggs turned his back to them and walked over to put the paper in his scanner, Otis gave Evan a secretive smirk and said, "So you got more questions? Fire away."

"How long had Bob been dead?" Evan asked. "I didn't see that anywhere in the writeup, but it's kind of a basic fact."

Otis shouted, *"Griggs!"*

As the deputy rejoined them, the sheriff beckoned for him to sit. "How long do you figure it had been since Mr. Taggart did himself in?"

"But how about the coffee?" Griggs wanted to know.

"Let's focus. You're the expert here, and the Reverend has a right to whatever we got."

"Not long," Griggs said. "He wasn't warm, but he wasn't frozen. No rigor mortis. Maybe he did it right before dawn? An hour before you found him?"

Evan asked the deputy, "In your report, you mentioned you searched his truck. Where did you find it?"

"Down the road, parked on the shoulder, about a half-mile to the south," Griggs said. "F-150, recent model. Metallic red. Sweet ride."

"His pride and joy," Evan said. "He'd be hosing it down, washing off the mud and the road salt, even in weather like this. Where is it now?"

"The keys were in his pants pocket. I drove the vehicle to his residence after we did our sweep," Griggs said. "And the sheriff brought me back. We had the widow sign a receipt."

"Your report said you didn't get a laptop or a phone. Weren't you surprised he didn't have the phone on him? Or that his laptop wasn't in the truck?"

"We judged we had enough to justify the seventh criterion," Griggs said. "Yeah, we could ask Mrs. Taggart for access to his computer, if she knows where it is and has the passwords and such. But why would we go invading her privacy any more? What would we hope to find?"

Evan asked Otis, "What about his personal effects?"

"After the autopsy, they burn the bloody clothes," Otis explained. "You can have the rest now. Wallet, belt, cufflinks, Masonic tie tack. Not much. Oh, and the gun. Sign the inventory sheet, and you can walk out of here with all of it."

"You're giving me the gun?" Evan asked.

Otis nodded. "With the understanding you will return it to its new owner and advise her she must reregister it if she intends to keep it. We'll keep the ammo from the clip, since I doubt you have a license to carry."

"And what about the note?" Evan asked. "The second one he had in his pocket."

"We'll be keeping it in the case file," Otis said. "You've seen the other one. Same, same."

"Could I have a look at it?"

Otis declined for a second time. "I've sent it to the lab for tests. Like I told you, there's nothing more to see. But I have to go through the motions. In case, I don't know, somebody else's spit is on it. That kind of thing."

Weird answer. But what can I do?

Otis stared at the deputy for a long moment. The sheriff cleared his throat and ordered him, "Okay, so clear out that crap from the locker, and we'll have our coffee *now,*" and Griggs jumped up.

Then Otis said to Evan confidentially, "I've got some questions of my own."

"All right. I hoped you would."

"How come you came to be in that place at that hour?"

"I told you yesterday. Nick Berner and Wiley Krause invited me to their turkey shoot."

"Where was your shotgun?"

"I don't own one. No other firearms, for that matter. It was kind of a lark. Those boys know I don't go in for hunting, and they didn't even say they'd loan me a rifle. Wiley said it would be a blue moon if they got anything. Why didn't I come along, help them drink their whiskey-spiked coffee, and pray for the turkeys?" Then Evan remembered to say, "Oh, and I was running late."

"Amusing," Otis muttered. "That's right, legal turkey hours begin a half-hour before dawn. Problem is, regular firearm turkey season was in October. There's a short archery season, but that's over as well. Squirrel and rabbit season ended two weeks ago."

"Maybe those boys are not all that careful about their permits."

"Enforcement used to be lax, that's true. But not anymore. You fire off shots, somebody's going to report it. And the penalties are stiff."

"Did anyone report hearing the shot that killed Bob?"

"Berner told me they did," Otis said. "I didn't bother to ask Krause to corroborate."

"They probably thought it was some other hunter," Evan said. "But they made it sound like it was a lot of sitting around, drinking, and pretending to be toms by blowing on their bird calls. I think they'd get a kick if they even saw a turkey."

"Was Bob invited too?" the sheriff asked.

"I never heard anybody say he was."

"How long since you'd seen him?"

"I gave the eulogy at Molly's funeral."

"November, as I recall. The week after Thanksgiving."

"That's right," Evan said. "Then he stopped by my place three weeks ago."

"Did he tell you he was going through a bad patch?"

"He was glum at the funeral, no surprise there. Molly had been a mother to him. But, this last time, he was agitated, and he wouldn't tell me why."

"He must have said something."

"He wanted to know about pulling the plug. How you decide. Said he was asking for a friend. I'm sure it wasn't about Molly. She'd expired on her own. I didn't know who he was talking about, and he wouldn't tell me."

"So, do you think now he might have been talking about himself?"

"I suppose he was. But I didn't pick up on it. And I'm not sure anything I said helped."

Griggs returned with two steaming mugs. One bore the official seal of U.S. Army Fort Francis Blair, and the other was inscribed with "This Is

What a Feminist Looks Like." Otis muttered his thanks. He fished in his pocket for a five-dollar bill and handed it to Griggs. "We'll need some crullers to go with," he said with a mocking grin. Griggs took the money, grabbed his coat from the rack, and headed out the door into a day that was sunny and bright, even downright warm, if you're talking sub-freezing temperatures.

Otis took his coffee black in the Army mug and handed Evan the other mug along with the packets of sugar and a wooden stir stick. Then, as he took a long, noisy sip, the sheriff continued the interview by asking, "Were you all bundled up on the morning you found him? Were you dressed for the shoot? I mean, what did you have on besides the jacket and pants?"

Evan was surprised by the question. "Thermal underwear, jeans, down jacket. Work boots. Red ball cap. I had a wool scarf and lined gloves in the pockets of my jacket. Even with that, I wasn't sure I was going to be able to stand it. I was counting on the whiskey and coffee to see me through."

"I believe the temp was nine degrees when we arrived on the scene. And, as you saw, Bob was dressed for a prayer meeting. Like we'd just load him into a casket and be done with it. He wasn't wearing long-johns neither."

"Okay, he suited up. I imagine that's typical."

"Yes, as a matter of fact, it is. Your war veterans put on their uniforms and their decorations. I guess it's their last formal occasion." To his coffee cup, the sheriff said, "I tell them to double up on the measure, and it's still weak as shit."

"So where are you going with this?" Evan asked, regarding the wardrobe question.

"I want to know," the sheriff went on, "why he picked that spot. His note told his wife not to go looking for him. So, he could have done it under his favorite tree on his own property. But he drives out to the Emmett farm, and — what's more puzzling — he doesn't park where you did, but a half-mile down the road. So seems like he'd have to hike

all that distance to the spot — before sun-up when it's teeth-chatter-
ing, bone-rattling cold — and he's not dressed at all for it. I mean, I
assume some woolen underwear and a ski jacket would not be
improper when you go to meet your maker. Why be uncomfortable?"

"I see. I guess he was tanked up on booze. But, you're right, even with
that, he wouldn't be able to stand the cold for very long."

"Then we've got your story about heading to the turkey shoot. The
path you took, which leads from your parking spot into Emmett's
woods, is the only cleared way in there from that road. And there's his
body, smack dab in the middle of your route."

"What do you make of it?"

"I'm guessing he knew you were going to that shoot. Maybe he'd been
invited too. And he did it there because he wanted you to be the one
to find him."

"And why would that be?"

"I was hoping you could tell me."

"I've known him for a long time," Evan said. "I thought he was one of
the good guys, and I think he trusted me. But we'd fallen out of touch.
I'd have been the first one to help him, if he'd asked."

"And then there's the question of how do Berner and Krause figure
into this, if at all? You said you got there late, but you didn't see their
cars parked on the shoulder, and neither did we. And if where Bob had
left his truck was some kind of meeting spot, there weren't any other
cars there either. At least, not by the time we checked. A logical question is, were those guys really in the woods waiting for you? Maybe
they were never there at all. Maybe the hunting party was just a story
to get you and Bob into those woods."

"Wow," Evan said. "That theory is totally paranoid. Why would they
do that?"

"I'm expecting you to find out," the sheriff said.

"Me?"

"Look, Preacher. Officially, I'm closing this case. I can't go spending more time and resources on this. I have not the slightest doubt Bob Taggart pulled the trigger on himself for reasons none of us mortals may ever understand. And I don't think he had help — at least, not from the standpoint of assisted suicide. But if someone drove him to do it, it might help the future peace and tranquility of this community if we knew who it was and what they hoped to achieve."

"I hadn't planned to let it go, no matter what Edie decides."

The sheriff shrugged. "For now, you got that POA. And you've got my permission to talk to anyone you like. What else have you got on your plate?"

"Like I say, there's Angus Clapper. I should also have a word with Wilmer about that cancer diagnosis. I really wonder how much it might have worried him. Bob was a Mason, you know, and I guess they want to be involved in the memorial."

"Stu Shackleton. Which brings me to another question — the weapon."

"Not exactly a rabbit gun."

"The Sig Sauer is a mighty fancy piece for one of these humble farmers to have. You don't own that gun so you can plink beer cans in the backyard. It's a preferred police sidearm, and it's also standard Army issue. It's the kind of one-shot, thug-killing cannon a pro keeps under the pillow. Now, it *was* registered to Taggart. So as the means of this self-inflicted suicide, it's open and shut. But he'd only bought the piece in December. Second-hand. From Shackleton."

"Shackleton told me," Evan said, "without being asked, when we had a brief, very brief, conversation about the memorial."

"It's Griggs' favorite weapon too. Me, I carry a revolver."

~

EVAN WONDERED about Nick and Wiley. If they were hunting on Josh Emmett's farm, they would have gotten permission from Josh, who, by all rights, should have informed Bob. Maybe they didn't give a rat's ass for the rules of the Missouri Department of Conservation, but no idiot goes traipsing around farmland with loaded guns without making sure the farmer is okay with it and knows exactly where you'll be and when.

Maybe it wasn't supposed to be a turkey shoot. It was an early-morning meetup, including Josh, far away from eavesdroppers, for a full and frank exchange of views. After Molly's passing, Josh would have been anxious to reaffirm his lease. And for reasons perhaps only Clapper understood, Bob was hesitating to give his answer. Which probably made Josh think Bob was stalling, planning to sell the farm out from under him.

14

THURSDAY AFTERNOON
EVAN'S TRAILER

van hadn't told Otis about the files he found on Bob's laptop. That Bob had been researching the ownership of the farm was not so surprising. But the fact of the two encrypted files with anonymous labels nagged at Evan. *Brownie1993* for the computer had been a lucky find. He'd have to try to guess the password or passwords for those two files.

Brownie, 1993. The year the dog died. Also Bob's mother. Now we have that in common.

≈

As BOYS, when Evan and Bob weren't poking around AC, they'd meet up at the Emmetts. Bob had permission from his parents as well as from the Emmetts to roam those pastures. Only later did Evan realize it was because Bob's Great Aunt Molly owned it all (or thought she did). It was a short hike from the Evans' farm to the Emmett's, so the boys regarded it as their personal recreation area. Although unsupervised, they knew they weren't allowed (and didn't have access to) firearms. But they plinked at everything they saw with BB and pellet

guns, and slingshots. Brownie (the First) was there to scout elusive
prey. But when she spotted a squirrel or a rabbit or even a mouse, she'd
bark excitedly, nonstop. As a result, she'd startle the animal, which
would scamper away before the boys had a chance to get off a shot. It
was enormous fun, and the boys never faulted themselves for not being
expert hunters or crack shots.

Brownie, 1993. The photo of the dog with a duck in its mouth.

Evan didn't remember ever having gone duck hunting with Bob.
Although Brownie was an enthusiastic but unskilled stalker, from the
evidence of the photo at least, she was a good retriever.

Evan recalled the sudden and tragic passing of Brownie the First, when
he and Bob were twelve, in 1993. He hadn't known Bob's other dogs
as well. He'd met this last one, Brownie the Fourth, a few times at the
Taggart home and also when she'd accompanied Bob to the C'mon.
When the boys were in high school and Brownie the Second was Bob's
companion, he and Evan played less at the farm, and both of them
became preoccupied with dating. (A notable exception was their exper-
imental drinking in the forest with their watchful Good Shepherd,
after which only the dog felt no sickening consequences.) In their
teens, the boys were obsessed with *thinking* about dating and which of
their self-nominated, prospective girlfriends would be lucky enough to
entrap them. So, not surprisingly, Evan and Bob grew apart. Then
Evan won his scholarship and was off to college. Bob, Evan had heard,
enrolled in an animal husbandry program at a trade school in Sedalia,
where his devoted roommate was the unacquainted Ridgeback,
Brownie the Third. Bob didn't finish school because Lionel died
prematurely in 2004 from a tetanus infection, which, as some doctors
are prone to do when it's their personal health, he'd waited too long to
treat. Bob moved back to town to live again with Molly and manage
the business side of the pharmacy.

∼

EVAN NOW HAD Bob's wallet and therefore could try variations of
birthdate, home address, and full name as passwords. None worked on

those locked files. Then he tried variations on Edie's name and his own. Again, no luck. He tried just plain Brownie and brownie. Nope. Variations of duck? Duck hunting? Mallard? Negative.

THINKING about secret words and phrases that might be passwords brought up more memories for Evan.

He and Bob were ten. Brownie the First had just grown out of puppyhood, and Bob's mother Abigail was still alive, although already bedridden at the house, where Molly was pretty much in charge.

Bob called Josh's father "Uncle Dick" even though he was no relation. But he was an important authority figure because he was the tenant, and therefore gatekeeper, of their private theme park and playground, the Emmett farm. Uncle Dick didn't always leave the boys to fend for themselves, especially when he found it amusing to take them hunting. He owned several .22-caliber rifles and .410-gauge shotguns, which he kept cleaned and oiled. On some of those Saturdays when the boys were playing on his property, he'd watch after them in what seemed a fit of sincere fatherliness.

Dickie's son Josh wasn't yet old enough to tag along. He was left to play in the yard with a dozen or so stray cats, and the highlight of his day might be getting to pet a sheep. Also in the yard were crazed chickens running around unaware they were destined for dinner, as well as some itinerant ducks, in transit from here to God-knows where. The farmhouse was surrounded by sidewalks which went nowhere but the gravel drive, which emerged on a dirt road to town. Dickie was continually scolding Josh for stepping in the "duck shoe-polish" that adorned the sidewalks.

Dickie started Bob and Evan out learning marksmanship, aiming their .22s at his used beer cans set on a railing out in a field. They'd go after rabbits and squirrels with the shotguns. Uncle Dick was the one who taught them the unwritten rules. You never fired into a squirrel nest, and you never shot at a sitting rabbit. It had to be on the run. If your shot hit but didn't kill the animal, you approached at close range and blew its head off. But it didn't go that way with rabbits. Even when hit, the thing would take off like *it* was shot from a gun. That's why you didn't so much as aim at one if it was at rest. Even if you got it with a fatal wound, it could run for a mile before it dropped. But hit it on the run, you'd see where it dropped. Humane, they called it. If you saw English sparrows, fire away. Too many of those damned imported pests.

As when they went fishing, Bob liked to assume the role of junior mentor to Evan. Except when he was around Evan, Bob was not at all assertive with the other boys in school. It was a special bond of their friendship that Evan put up with Bob's coaching cheerfully, even when Bob teased him without mercy.

Then or now, Evan never thought of himself as a sportsman. But besides the episode of a fish that got away, Bob would have no doubt remembered two notable episodes in which Evan showed unexpected talent.

The first instance was the one and only time they tried skeet shooting. Once, for target practice, rather than lining up cans on a rail, Uncle Dick had brought the shotguns, along with a spring-loaded contraption called a *trap* with a handle like a hammer and a box of Danish-pastry-sized clay disks. He explained this was how hunters practiced shooting birds, such as pheasant, on the fly. He never told them whether those birds lived on his property, and he never took the boys on a hunting trip to shoot birds of any kind. But he was entertained by the idea of throwing these clay targets in the air for the boys to learn to track with their shotguns, and, with some coaching and a great deal of luck, succeed in blasting out of the sky.

Before Dickie let them load their shells, he coached them carefully about the importance of having a firing line and respecting it. The shooter stood on the line, and the thrower and any observers stood well behind it. The thrower pointed out the range where he'd toss the target, in this case in a clearing bounded by two tall trees. No matter where the clay might fly, the shooter was never to fire anywhere but into the gap between those trees. Observers and inactive shooters should keep their guns unloaded and broken open when not on the firing line. The shooter should step up to the line, load, remove the safety, and tell the thrower to "Pull!" Using the trap, the thrower would fling the target into the air, and the shooter would track it, swinging his gun along the path of the clay's flight, always aiming just slightly ahead of it, then pulling the trigger before the clay started to traverse the second tree.

Another important responsibility was for the boy who wasn't on the firing line to hold Brownie on a leash. She was still young and inexperienced enough at hunting to be spooked by the gunshots.

Evan had not done this before. He went first and blasted five out of five clays to smithereens.

Bob muttered, "Beginner's luck." He stepped up and totally missed all five.

Uncle Dick was preparing for another round when Bob announced that it was lunchtime, he was hungry, and he'd had no breakfast.

After lunch, Uncle Dick brightened and suggested they go after some live game. Brownie, after all, promised to be a hunting dog at heart and would bark whenever she spotted a squirrel in a tree.

Bob marked his second humiliation of the day when Evan bagged two squirrels, his uncle got three, and he got one, but in a way that brought him unforgettable shame.

Evan's and Dickie's shots had been clean kills. Bob's first shot only wounded the squirrel, and the poor animal dangled in agony from a tree branch and cried out.

"You know what to do!" Uncle Dick shouted urgently to Bob.

Bob loaded another cartridge, dutifully marched under the tree, pointed his weapon skyward, and fired a point-blank shot that blew the squirrel's head clean off.

That's when Uncle Dick decided they'd had enough excitement for one day. They bagged their kills, broke the barrels of their shotguns open, made sure they'd gathered up all their spent shells, and walked back to the farmhouse.

Uncle Dick carried the game bag, and, unlike other times when she'd be clinging to Bob, Brownie followed close behind the leader with her attention riveted on the bloody prizes.

Evan was at a loss. He knew Bob felt awful, but he couldn't think of anything to say to make him feel better. Evan hadn't made any effort to best Bob in competition. He hadn't thought of their time together as competition at all, and yet here was this string of incidents that tallied to an inadvertent winning score. He felt like apologizing, but acting ashamed of winning might only make Bob feel worse.

"It took guts to do what you did back there," Evan finally told him.

Bob studied the ground as he walked without comment. Then, as they neared the farmhouse, he turned to Evan and said, "My uncle says he figures you could do anything you set your mind to."

Evan was speechless for the rest of the day.

The boys watched Uncle Dick as he pulled out a Bowie knife and dressed the squirrels over a wash basin at the back of the house. Brownie sat just inches away at rigid attention. Dickie sliced an animal from gullet to tail, then along the axis of each leg. He pried the skin away from the body, and with a single strong tug, pulled the furry coat up over the head. He then sliced through the neck, severing the head from the body. Now there was a limp sack of skin with a golf-ball-sized skull inside. He tossed it to Brownie, who caught it in the air and swallowed it whole, in single gulp.

The boys were aghast. Uncle Dick thought this was great fun and would surely lighten Bob's mood. "Don't worry, boys. The dog ain't gonna choke. They got stomach acid like you wouldn't believe. Dissolves fur and bones and all."

Bob petted Brownie's head lovingly. She looked up at him gratefully, then turned her full attention back on the man with the knife.

Uncle Dick slit open the stomach and removed the guts, which he flung at the dog, who made quick work of them and licked her lips.

After he'd cleaned all six squirrels, he announced, "It's not a lot for dinner, but we'll make do. Bread 'em and fry 'em up like chicken. You get a leg, it's about as much as a chicken wing. We got some catfish in the freezer, so nobody's going hungry. But you got to learn to eat what you shoot, am I right?"

"I guess so," Bob said, as if unsure he wanted squirrel in his diet. But he brightened when he bent down to Brownie and said, "We share, don't we, girl?"

Uncle Dick rolled another smoke. He took a deep drag. He was determined to make Bob feel better. A man learns to face up to things, after all. He pointed to Brownie and said, "Look at that there dog. Happiest moment of her life. That's why she sticks with us, hunts with us, barks at those critters up a tree. Don't tell me dog food from some can makes her happy as that."

"Brownie likes ice cream," Bob insisted, confessing a secret he'd shared with no one but Evan.

Dick sneered. "Never spoil a dog, son. They're working animals." This from a guy for whom work was to be avoided as if it were a dread, infectious disease.

"I guess that's right," Bob said sullenly, possibly wondering whether he was destined to be a failure as a hunter-provider and Brownie's future meals in the family kitchen would now be devastating disappointments.

❧

WHEN THEY WERE BOYS, Evan hadn't worried much about competing with Bob or the effect his winning at contests of skill would have on his friend. Now he remembered that it was after the squirrel-hunting and skeet-shooting episodes that Bob had begun to tease Evan with the nickname *Dumbass.*

The password dumbass, all lowercase, unlocked both files.

What Evan read was not a solution, but it was not a dead end.

All the more reason to pray for Angus Clapper's speedy recovery!

15

FRIDAY MORNING

ON THE ROAD TO PECULIAR

E van had a scant breakfast of toast and coffee in his trailer and phoned Knox promptly at 8 a.m. to inquire about Clapper. The preacher was elated when the old fellow came on the line and, in spite of some phlegmy coughs, seemed downright chipper and chatty.

"The Redwine farm or the Taggart farm or the Emmett farm — whatever you want to call it — was the nastiest ball of snakes it was ever my misfortune to deal with. But I've been retired for thirty years, which is what I told Taggart all along. And these days I don't like to waste my time. I did enough of that even though I was often paid handsomely for it. So on your way over, be thinking about whether you prefer checkers, backgammon, or chess. I'm equally bad and a sore loser at all three!"

Thirty years in retirement?

Evan did the math. Clapper had to be in his mid-nineties by now.

Evan agreed to the lawyer's adamant terms and conditions. The preacher would have to be patient and play along during some recreational game to gain the fellow's cooperation. They agreed to meet two hours from now, and the old lawyer said he'd give Evan as much time answering questions as he needed. But, with a sadistic chuckle, Clapper warned Evan he might leave with more questions than he'd brought.

KNOX IS a little more than an hour's drive from AC. The route is straight up I-49 until you get to Harrisonville. There you can veer off onto state and local roads for a straight shot north to Lee's Summit.

This morning was partly cloudy, and it was spitting snow. The temp was considerably warmer than the morning when Evan had stumbled on Bob's body. Today, it was just subfreezing. Evan worried they were in for a gloppy, wet storm. In such weather, he preferred keeping to the interstate superhighways. That meant staying on I-49 at Harrisonville, which took you farther west than you wanted, then bearing east on I-470 to double back to Lee's Summit. This long way around added perhaps a half-hour to the trip but was more likely to provide a cleared roadway, especially if the temperature dropped suddenly, causing the back roads to ice up.

Besides, staying on I-49 past Harrisonville took you through the town of Peculiar. Who would want to miss that opportunity? If there were anything peculiar about Peculiar, Evan didn't know what it was. In fact, in his years living in the area, both as a boy and now as a wannabe holy man, all he'd experienced of the place was its road signs, which seemed both mysterious and precautionary. When Evan had been checking his route to Knox on MapQuest, he'd seen the route through Peculiar. He also found an attractive way station in Merle's American Tavern, where the menu on the Web touted their specialty, chicken-fried chicken. So in addition to his preference for taking interstates in bad weather, here was another reason to navigate through there. Checking Wikipedia, he also found the origins of the town's name, of which there were two versions of the story. The most colorful was that in 1868, the town's postmaster Edgar Thompson petitioned the U.S. postal service to register the name *Excelsior*. His request was rejected because there was already another town in Missouri by that name (and

Missouri has a wealth of peculiar town names). The persistent Post-master Thompson's repeated alternative suggestions were also rejected because they were not unique. In frustration, he wrote back that he didn't care what the name was, as long as it was "peculiar."

Careful what you ask for!

Had the postmaster's vocabulary been more precise, this wide place in the road might instead have been named Distinctive, Missouri. The other version of the story has an early settler gazing out over the land-scape and pronouncing (apropos of what, history does not record), "Now, that's peculiar!"

The town's motto is "Where the 'odds' are with you." Why is there no casino?

So Evan decided to go a little out of his way to pass through, but he didn't plan to tarry. He wasn't a casual tourist but a man on a mission. He was eager to see Clapper. Still, a superstitious part of his otherwise rational brain wondered whether he'd feel at all peculiar as he rolled through Peculiar.

After all, I still feel like an odd duck here.

After he sped past the Flying J Travel Center on the interstate, he got off at the 211th Street interchange. Which, in itself, is peculiar.

What small town has 211 parallel streets? Manhattan doesn't have that many, counting from the Bowery to the Bronx. And numbered starting from where?

It didn't take Evan long to find 1st Street, Peculiar's main drag. It hardly seemed two-hundred blocks away from the off ramp. The strip was just a few blocks long. Evan passed storefront signs advertising classes in karate, ballet, and theater. A prominent attraction was The Frog Pond Bar and Grill, which must vie for clientele with Merle's, where Evan intended to stop for a hearty lunch on his way back from seeing Clapper.

Evan circled back from the town's business core, mindful of the need to get to his destination but wondering why he'd been drawn here. As he turned onto Highrise Trail, he spotted the ruins of an old granary. It was a crumbling two-story brick structure with a watchtower perched atop a pair of squat silos. The hoard must have been precious to require such diligent guarding. Evan guessed the building was a relic of the Civil War era. He stopped the car and got out to read:

> Historical Spotmarker
> In 1861-1864
> While bloody battles raged
> throughout the southern states
> nothing happened here.

Perhaps the latter-day historian didn't know much about the strife in this region back then. Or, perhaps the town is in denial?

Corn and soybeans were the staple crops of this area, grown in rotation. The wheat fields are west of here, in Kansas. During the war, transporting grain across territories had probably been hazardous and therefore intermittent. And then they guarded it once they had it.

Evan got back in his Taurus and drove on. In the short time he'd spent in Peculiar, the sky had gone from fluffy white to gunmetal gray. He hoped the hard freeze would come before the storm, after which the roads would be snowy but not treacherously icy.

He passed the Peculiar United Methodist Church, where he'd yet to speak. He resolved to add them to his list of attentive congregations.

Maybe I can try out one of my oddball sermons on them.

Many of the homes Evan saw were recent, developer-built, situated on full-acre plots, and large. Some were probably five thousand square feet, enough for three or maybe four bedrooms, a family recreation room, and a home theater. Some had swimming pools. Near these upscale residences was the Peculiar Golf & Learning Center.

What course of study do you get with your golf? Zen Buddhism?

Who lives here?

16

FRIDAY 11 AM
JOHN KNOX VILLAGE, LEE'S SUMMIT

As Evan arrived at Knox, a copious snowfall had begun. He wanted to take as much time as necessary with Clapper, but he worried weather conditions could worsen and complicate his drive back.

When Evan reported to the reception desk in the vestibule, he had to first sign the register, which he did as Preacher Evans. So he was within his rights simply writing *Preacher* in felt marker on his stick-on visitor's badge. The security guard at the desk summoned a pimply faced male orderly, named Darnell, who accompanied Evan to the solarium on the second floor of one of the residence buildings. Perversely thinking about his newly adopted sister village, Evan wondered about the impression he'd give if he'd written *Peculiar Preacher* on his badge.

Maybe no one would get the joke?

Angus Clapper was seated in a wheelchair with a plaid blanket covering his lap. Clashing with the blanket was his heavy wool hunter's shirt, also plaid but of a different stripe. A translucent plastic tube hung from an elastic band hooked around his ears, connecting his bulbous nose to a small oxygen tank mounted on the back of his chair.

Evan shook the frail, dry hand Clapper offered him and sat down opposite the fellow at a small rollaway table. The chessboard was already set up.

If Evan had looked in the *Standard American Encyclopedia,* he'd have seen that Clapper bore a remarkable resemblance to the U.S. president Martin Van Buren. His freckled, shiny pate was entirely bald. As though in compensation for the barrenness of his dome, unruly frizzed white hair stuck out horizontally from both sides of his skull. He had mutton-chops sideburns, and his ears were nearly covered with downy white hair.

"I thought you said we'd choose the game," Evan said as he sat.

"I told you to *think* about which you'd prefer," Clapper snapped. "Now depending on how this introductory game turns out, your opinion might change — for the next time." Then he coughed up a wad of phlegm, spat into a handkerchief he kept wadded up in one fist, and added, "If I'm fortunate enough to live that long."

How sick has he been? He seems sharp mentally.

To lighten the mood, Evan looked around and exclaimed, "It's looking like a blizzard out there. I'm glad to be with you in here, where it's so cozy. And I'm pleased you've taken the time to see me."

"You're a preacher?" Clapper looked skeptical.

"Yes," Evan emphasized. "Freelance, more or less."

"I wasn't so bad at oral argument in my day," Clapper said. His eyes were red and watery, probably from some allergy — unless he was sneaking forbidden smokes. His bleary, mournful look was all the more touching because of his sarcastic comment about his mortality.

Evan started to say, "Of course, the reason I'm here —"

"Will be addressed in due course. I have whatever time I have, and I expect you're in no hurry. You're welcome to stay to lunch if you don't mind cafeteria fare. But, please, no conversation during our game."

Evan noticed the board was set up correctly — white square in the lower right, Queen on her color. Clapper had the white pieces on his side of the board. To choose sides, it was customary for one player to hide a pawn of each color in either clenched hand for the other to choose.

"Aren't we drawing for color?" Evan asked.

"I'm defending the whites," Clapper wheezed. "Welcome to Missouri politics. Story of my life. Which means *I* go first." And he laughed at his own joke.

Clapper advanced King's Pawn to King Four, the standard opening move.

Evan responded with the same move on his side. The two little pawns faced off against each other in the middle of the board, a black soldier defying the white man's advance.

From here, there was no telling how the game would go. That pair of moves — which is typical and gives neither side an advantage — indicates one thing: Both players have played this game before. The next move, which would be Clapper's, might tell whether he was as bad at this game of strategy as he claimed. Evan's move after that could well decide how masterfully the rest of the game would go.

Evan had played chess hardly at all by the time he got to college. In Cambridge, he had a roommate, Karl Meister, who was obsessed with it. Especially on long winter weekends when neither of them had dates, chess became their main distraction from hitting the books, which in their first undergraduate year involved a lot of late-night, headache-inducing philosophical proofs. You'd think more mental exercise would hardly afford any relief. But fretting over — and arguing about — chess got their brains spinning in other directions until one of them successfully threatened the other's king or they were both drowsy enough to call it quits.

Karl was impatient for Evan to get to his skill level. So, especially in their early contests, he doled out the advice liberally. Karl told Evan all competent chess players have memorized at least a dozen time-honored opening sequences of moves, including the Ruy Lopez, the Sicilian Defense, and the Queen's Gambit. Those strategies have variations and counter-strategies, which also have names. An expected strategy against the Queen's Gambit is the Albin Counter-Gambit. As a result of executing these strategies by rote, a game between advanced players can seem unimaginative until one of them breaks a familiar pattern. Then things can get *really* interesting.

When you are playing someone whom you've never played before, suspense in the opening phase of the game is acute. If the other player follows a pattern — any of the traditional patterns you know — you can be sure you're dealing with someone who is no stumbling beginner. However, if instead those moves appear to be illogical, erratic, or even foolish, you don't know what to think. You could be dealing with a stumbler who is making it up as he goes along. Or, you could be facing a genius who knows tricks that will bewilder, astound, and ultimately devastate you.

Clapper's second move, another pawn advance, left an opening in his flank for attacks on his queen, which could indicate either carelessness or cluelessness. And, more importantly for Evan's assessment of his opponent, the move didn't fit any of the patterns Karl had taught him.

Maybe the old lawyer is as bad at chess as he says he is.

But newbies don't insist on silence, as Clapper had, during a game. Screwups don't cast you furtive glances, looking for a tell that you're wise to their devious plots.

Evan decided to play along. After all, he was the guest. Silent minutes and several moves passed. Evan took Clapper's bishop with a knight as he tried to hold an expressionless gaze.

"Well, I didn't see *that* coming," Clapper muttered as he moved his threatened queen out of danger.

Clapper proved to be a wiz at chess and a shameless liar. He had Evan checkmated in four more moves.

"I see you've played this before," Clapper cackled.

"Not nearly enough, I guess," Evan said with an embarrassed shrug.

Alluding to the sample chess games in the newspaper, Clapper quipped, "I bet you play a decent game of *New York Times*. But you're not so good at what I'd call Country Boy."

"Story of *my* life, I guess," Evan said, and they both smiled.

"Thank you for that," Clapper said. "Lets me think I've still got it, at least in one department." He wheezed and glanced up at an approaching nurse. She was thirty-something, mocha-skinned, and a sight for his watery eyes.

She stood next to Clapper and took his wrist. She was close enough for Evan to read her badge — *Monica*.

Without any introduction, she gave Evan a commiserating look and cracked, "Oh, he's a handful, all right."

Clapper looked up at her admiringly and shot back, "You got a couple of gorgeous handfuls there, but I'm going to remember I'm a Southern gentleman."

Monica decided not to stay. She called back to Clapper, "Holler if you need anything. Lunch is at eleven-thirty. Let us know if it'll be in your room or in the cafeteria with your friend." As she walked away, the rhythm of her hips betrayed a serious lack of offense.

When he'd made the appointment on the phone, Evan had briefed Clapper on his role as Edie's representative.

"So what's the problem with Molly's estate?" he asked the crusty chess champion. "The federal government is saying she didn't own the land the Emmett farm is on. And the Army has served notice they intend to demolish the house and barn, a week from tomorrow."

"The Army!" Clapper exclaimed. "Those rascals. You'd think they'd never get around to it. But this is news to me. Though hardly surprising."

"Is it true? Is the Emmett farm on government property?"

Clapper chuckled until he managed to wheeze, "No one's had a proper answer to that one for two-hundred years!"

"What's the problem?"

"Problem!" Clapper laughed. "A whole snake pit!"

Clapper paused as he seemed to lose his train of thought.

I'd better let this guy tell it his way. If he loses the thread, he might not find it again.

After a minute, Evan prodded, "So you were Molly's attorney? Were you also Bob's?"

"Neither," Clapper insisted. "Call me an advisor. I helped them sort through some things, then they could have some snot-nosed kid with a license do the paperwork. As for Bob, I gave him the name of a bright, young fellow. But I don't know what he did about it."

"So you weren't Molly's attorney?"

"I drafted her will and she signed it. I advised her to have someone who was still practicing to give it a look-see, but she wouldn't hear of it. So, even though I hadn't bothered to renew my license, her will was legal and binding. What was anybody going to do? Sue me for malpractice?"

"So there must be an original document somewhere."

"Oh, yes. Bob had it. We discussed it — *at length.*"

"Do you mind telling me its terms?"

"Simple enough," Clapper puffed. "She left it all to Lionel, Bob's father, with the boy as contingent beneficiary. She didn't have any children of her own, and she'd raised Bob. Excluded her brother-in-law Arthur. She said he had enough of his own already, which he still does. Of course, Lionel passed some years back. Stepped on a rusty nail, or some such, and it went from bad to worse. So that left Bob holding the bag of family assets — and responsibilities."

"All what?"

"Her will says 'all my assets.' I told her she should list the farm, the walnut groves, the bank accounts, and whatever else. She said all that detail wasn't necessary. She might forget and leave something out. I explained we'd just say, 'including but not limited to,' but she wouldn't have it. She said she wanted to keep it simple. With Lionel gone, Bob was the sole beneficiary and the executor. My secretary and Arthur Redwine were the witnesses, and it was duly notarized."

"So, where is the document?"

"Last I had anything to do with it, Bob had the original in a safe deposit box at Bates Bank."

"So how did you advise him?"

"I told Bob I'd give him all the background, whatever files, but he was eventually going to have to retain counsel, preferably someone who not only handles probate but understands the quirky aspects of land sales in these parts."

"Did he do that?"

"I doubt he got that far. He got his tail in a twist about the complications. I don't know whether he was trying to save money on fees or whether he just didn't yet know whom to trust. But he didn't get any paperwork started with me."

I'm going to try to make it clear. With these old guys, they're sharp when they're giving you history, but details in the present moment escape them. And I hope he can hear me well enough to understand.

Evan leaned forward and dropped his voice, careful to speak slowly and distinctly so Clapper could follow. "On Bob's laptop, I found a scan of Molly's will. It's an encrypted file, but, go figure, I could guess the password. It has handwritten edits, changes so as to make it *Bob's* will. Maybe, like you say, he thought he was saving on legal expenses. All the terms were the same except Edie gets it all, and she's to be the executor."

Clapper chuckled, "So whatever mistakes I made, he duplicated!"

Evan said, "The document is obviously a draft. If there's a signed copy, I'm guessing it's the one in the safe deposit box at the bank."

"Poor Taggart," Clapper mused. "All this may not mean much, in the end."

Let's hope you're wrong about that!

Evan went on, "Then there's a second file, a later version, also hand-written, *gifting* the farm — to the extent Bob owned or controlled it — to Josh Emmett. Edie gets the house and the joint bank account. But then his other assets, including some walnut grove, go into an escrow account to help the Emmetts with any legal expenses enforcing the terms of the will. Once ownership of the farm is settled, the rest would go to First Baptist. And I'm to be the executor through all this."

"Any idea whether that document was ever executed?"

"No," Evan replied. "Sadly, not."

Clapper cleared his throat, wetly, then said, "If you can't find the executed will, you've hit a wall. Handwritten wills — also called *holographic* wills — aren't valid in Missouri. It has to be typed, signed, witnessed, and notarized."

"But let's say I could find the document. What then? Could we prevent the Army from tearing down the Emmett farmhouse?"

"Maybe yes, maybe no."

This guy's fees must have been astronomical!

"Can you explain?"

"The government says they own the land, but the *presumptive* owner — or the legitimate heirs of such owner — should have the standing to sue to claim otherwise. That is, provided you have some *proof* of title."

Evan politely suggested, "Well, seems like you'd be the one to know."

Clapper went silent. He stared into space.

Is he expecting the arrival of some angel — or perhaps the smell of lunch?

Uh-oh. He's lost it.

Indeed, Clapper abruptly changed the subject. He dropped his voice, leaned forward, and asked, "You were close to him? You *found* him?"

Stay with him in the present! Follow that agile mind wherever it goes!

"Yes, I found him," Evan replied. "We were pals growing up. I went away to school, only recently came back. We'd lost touch in recent years."

"An awful thing," Clapper sighed. "I keep thinking if he'd had someone to give him perspective, someone to talk him down, maybe he'd still be with us. And, of course, he should have hired a good lawyer the minute I told him he needed one."

"Edie thinks dealing with Molly's estate somehow sent him over the edge. I take it you'd agree?"

"I'm not so sure. Yes, it's complicated, as I'll explain. And there's no clear way out. But it's nothing to go ending your life for."

"He left a suicide note. No specifics, but he did imply someone was out to get him — as if he *deserved* whatever was coming. The question is, had he become delusional? Or is paranoia just a heightened state of awareness?"

"I never heard it put that way," Clapper chuckled. "Just right. I don't know of anyone who had it in for Bob, but there will certainly be plenty of upset stakeholders in any deal."

"I guess I need the whole story," Evan said.

Maybe if he begins at the beginning, he can get to the end.

Clapper wet his lips and wriggled to get comfortable. "Okay, Molly came to me, said she'd put off writing a will long enough. That was in 1993."

Brownie, 1993.

"How old was she then?"

"She was born in 'Twenty-two. That would make her seventy-one. I was a bright-eyed and bushy-tailed sixty-nine. But already retired, as I said."

"Had she made a will before that? Why did she up and decide to do it then?"

"Why do any of us ever get around to doing it? Maybe she had a glass of sherry and it gave her heart palpitations. She was at an age when a flutter might keep her up at night."

"So there was nothing specific. She didn't give a reason?"

"She wasn't sick, if that's what you mean. One day I went around to pay my respects on her birthday. I found her on the roof. She was replacing a tile." Then he muttered, "A remarkable woman. Jake had this eccentric younger brother Arthur. Always trying to give Molly half-baked advice. Maybe he was onto her about doing a will. I don't think he ever liked me. I always thought he was a lunatic. Molly was fond of him, but she didn't trust his judgment about money. I guess he had plenty of his own. She told me he kept giving buckets of it to some church. I suppose that's why she didn't leave him a dime."

"I believe I met Bob's Aunt Molly a few times when I was a boy. In church. And, then, sometimes we played at his house, and she was ruling the roost. Bob's mom, that would be Abigail, she was laid up in bed most of the time. Then, I believe it was in 'Ninety-three, she died, and his aunt continued to live there, cooking and cleaning for Bob's father, who was at work every day minding the store. Molly was always well turned out, clean and crisp, but no makeup."

"She didn't need it! She was a widow, you know. Her husband Jacob Redwine died in 'Forty-four, I think it was. Battle of Guadalcanal. Jake had a farm, a bit less than five-hundred acres, and some other land holdings over near Stockton. Walnut groves, I believe. Not long after she got word about Jake, Molly moved to a house in town in AC.

Lionel Taggart's. And she rented the farm to Josh Emmett's father, Richard, who promised to keep it up and farm it. Richard — we all called him Dickie — supposedly told her if he could turn a profit on the farm, she'd get not only her land rent but also a portion of the yield."

"Oh, I remember Dickie," Evan told Clapper. "Uncle Dick, Bob called him. Bob and I used to play on the Emmett farm, and from time to time, but not all that often, Uncle Dick would take us hunting or fishing on the property." Then Evan asked, "So, all this time, it wasn't really the Emmetts' farm? Did they have a lease?"

"As near as I can figure, Molly had agreed to rent to Dickie sometime around 1950. Neither of them had a lawyer. It was a handshake deal. So there's no land sale, no lease for the farm, nothing in the public record. Except Molly had her bank deposits of the Emmetts' rent payments, plus some extra in the good years. So I guess Dickie knew what was expected of him."

"So Molly was the owner and the Emmetts' landlord?"

"*Presumptive* owner. But hold on. We haven't caught up yet." Clapper fidgeted in his wheelchair. "I can't abide the electric ones," he said, referring to the chair. "You can't believe the incompetent drivers in this place! And the traffic jams! Those things actually have warning horns and bells, like on bicycles? Sometimes in the hallway it's a chorus of *Beep-beep! Chirp! Rrrrrring!*" Then he confided, "Besides, if I could get around by myself I wouldn't have Monica to push me!" And he cackled. "They got coffee, tea, and lemonade. I do wish I could offer us something stronger."

"Yes," Evan said. "Black coffee. Heavy on the sugar."

Clapper caught the eye of Darnell, the orderly who'd shown Evan into the solarium. The boy dutifully came over. The old man whispered their order to him and then fished in his pocket for two quarters, which he handed over with a devilish grin.

As Darnell retreated, Clapper winked and quipped proudly, "Got to take care of them that take care of you."

"Indeed," Evan said, wondering whether Darnell thought his fifty-cent tip was meant to be a joke.

"Now, where were we?"

"Molly's farm. Handshake deal," Evan prompted. "Presumptive owner."

"Oh, yes." Clapper paused to collect his thoughts as he shoved the tray with the chessboard to one side. Signaling their newfound intimacy, he wheeled his chair forward to close the space between them. "Time was, handshake deals were not uncommon in these parts, but more like a nineteenth-century way of doing things. As things stood, I'm guessing Molly and Dickie thought they had no choice. At least, they probably hoped, possession being nine points of the law (which it isn't, by the way), maybe nobody would ever bother to ask for the bona fides."

"What was wrong with the deal?"

"Simply put, the land might not have been Molly's to begin with." Clapper looked wistful, as though he blamed himself for not doing better by her.

Yes, that's the question.

"And why is that?" Evan asked.

Darnell brought their drinks. He cleared away the chessboard and set two steaming mugs on the tray. "Gentlemen," he said solemnly, and retreated.

Clapper stretched the breathing tube away from his nose and tucked it under his chin so he could take a long, noisy sip. "This one must be mine. No sugar. Black like the delicious Monica." He stayed unplugged from his oxygen as he smacked his lips and continued the story.

Evan ignored the opportunity for locker-room banter and drank his coffee. "Bingo. A good dose of highly refined carbohydrates with my caffeine."

"As to Molly's ownership of the land, there were at least two problem issues. I learned about them when I drafted her will. That's when, as a matter of due diligence, I tried to dig into the title work. But there wasn't any. As I said, no documentation whatsoever."

"How could that be?"

"Because of the two issues. And, mind you, all this is guesswork on my part." He grinned proudly. "I'm something of a historian, you see. If you don't need the details, I don't want to bore you. But it makes a helluva story."

What choice do I have? If he draws a mental blank, if he has a senior moment, he may never remember!

"No, please, go on." Evan urged.

"First issue, a little skirmish called the Civil War. Missouri was a border state. Meaning we had sympathizers on both sides living next to each other. Most, if not all, of those farmers were either home-steaders or squatters. The homesteaders were supposed to have a land grant from the federal government saying they'd get ownership after some years of active farming. The squatters, of course, had no such proof they had any right to be there. Some claimed to be sharecrop-pers, and those folks were neither fish nor fowl. Now here they all were — blues and grays — happily tilling the soil cheek-by-jowl in what is today Bates County, right on the Kansas line, and in St. Clair, to the east.

"Understand, at the outbreak of the war, Kansas had just been admitted into the Union as a free state. And it starts annoying the hell out of those pro-Yankee Kansans that Rebel gangs are hiding out nearby in Bates County — in many cases being sheltered in the homes of sympathizers. The Rebs cross over in raids to harass the Kansans, then run back to safe harbor provided by the Confederate under-ground. The Kansans form a militia they called the Jayhawkers. The Rebs called themselves the Bushwhackers. And very rapidly, it esca-lated into one bloody skirmish after another. Not a place you'd want to call home, if you had a choice."

Clapper raised his nosepiece to take a hit of oxygen, then he lowered it again and drank some more coffee. "It's weak. Sorry. They think our shriveled kidneys can't handle anything stronger." He went on, "Yankee leadership figures this all could get out of hand. So in 1863, the Feds issue General Order Number Eleven."

A file on Bob's computer.

Clapper went on to explain, "Union soldiers go from house to house in the area, lay this paper on them, giving the farmers notice they all have to clear out. They totally evacuate the area, which becomes a military-enforced no-man's land for the duration of the war."

"Uh-oh. I think I see what's coming," Evan said.

"Yep. End of the war, people go back to what they think is their home and they might find squatters there. Squatters who claim they were always true Yankees. Maybe the rightful claimants don't have their federal paperwork saying *they* were loyal all along. The Yankee government says it's federal land until and unless you prove otherwise. Most people couldn't. Didn't have the paperwork. Who keeps paper during a war when you're running from place to place? The Yanks don't throw the people out of the houses again, but maybe they don't ever formally bless their right to stay. So, that's issue number one."

Evan recalled the antique rifle hanging on the wall in Bob's office. "Do the names Jedediah Redwine and Valencourt Griggs mean anything to you?"

Clapper snorted. "Family feud! Valencourt Griggs was a federal circuit court rider. Went from town to town presiding over hearings on disputes — including all those home ownership messes. Just a few weeks after the war ended, Griggs was on his horse following a dry creek bed, and he was ambushed. Shot out of the saddle in cold blood by Bushwhackers. Reb stragglers who didn't want it all to be over. Some said the Redwines were Rebs. I doubt it, but could be a reason they never had title to their land."

"Sounds like complication enough to queer a sale," Evan said.

I'm wondering whether Deputy Griggs knows Bob Taggart's Great Aunt Molly married a Redwine.

"Oh, but it gets better," Clapper wheezed. "A reason the Feds might not have been so eager to issue paperwork was probably they weren't sure which of their land-grabs from the Indians applied to any particular parcel around here. There were two main indigenous tribes in the area in the early nineteenth century — the Otoe-Missouria and the Osage Nation. If you look at a map of tribal territories, the arbitrary border the Army drew between the two tribes runs right through this general area. They couldn't be precise about it because Indians didn't exactly build fences or have written treaties or even stay in the same place for very long. The Feds forced the tribes out in two proclamations, both entitled The Great and Little Osage Accessions — one in 1808 and the other in 1825. Then somebody noticed there were still some stray Kickapoos around, and — ha! — they *kicked them* out in 1832! So, there's issue number two, and I think you see the complication."

"Another reason for no proof of title."

"Now," Clapper sighed. "Fast forward to where we were with Molly's will. You understand, in 'Ninety-three that dear woman had been a widow almost fifty years. Never got close to the altar again, although she had plenty of suitors — including me. Oh, I chased her around the table a few times." The emotion of the memory must have been intense because Clapper was suddenly wracked with a succession of barking coughs. He shoved his inhalation tube back up to his nose and snorted several restorative gulps of air. Evan saw Nurse Monica step from the shadows in the hallway and peer over toward them with a look of concern.

The old man's coughs subsided, and when he was calm again, he cracked a devilish smile as he continued, "She wouldn't have me, though. I'd have made her an honest woman at any point, but it was like she slept with Jake's ghost every night. I admit, what I had in my heart was lust, but I can't imagine a love like that. Can you, Preacher?"

Clapper's question was disarming.

How should I answer?

Consuming romantic love was not a topic Evan wished to discuss, much less think about. "I've read about it," he replied with a forced chuckle. "Pyramus and Thisbe. Romeo and Juliet. Burton and Taylor — for a time, anyway. But up close and personal? I don't know much about it."

True enough. Not that I haven't had the experience. But am I wiser? Ha!

Evan was lying, but besides his aversion for the subject, he feared sharing more with Clapper would pull them seriously off track. Not to mention, keep Evan awake tonight.

Please, Angus! Stick with it!

Clapper took a gurgling breath and resumed, "In drawing up the will, I figured, best do what we can to tie up loose ends. I told her, it wouldn't be out of the question to get a title insurance company to step up. The premiums might be higher than usual, but that's why they're in business. You'd think they'd be eager to assume the risk since we're talking long-ago history — with all the likely claimants long since dead? I recommended applying for the title insurance, then drafting a formal, back-dated lease agreement with the Emmetts."

"How do you back-date something like that?"

"You start the document 'Dated As of.' Then in the language both parties stipulate there has been a valid and ongoing oral agreement since that time to the present. And the purpose of this document is to affirm and memorialize that deal and its terms."

"Sounds like you found a good way to settle it."

"Yes and no. *She wouldn't let me do it!*"

"Why ever not?"

"Because that's when the *third* issue came up. And it was not like anything I'd ever seen before — or am ever likely to see again."

"Let me see if I got this right. All this fretting about the title work and the farm lease was something separate. Things you wanted to get nailed down *before* you started writing her will?"

"Yes, establish the preconditions as undisputed facts. *Recorded* facts."

"What else could there be to prevent Molly from acknowledging the lease?"

Clapper's face grew red, and he spat out, "Dickie Emmett was always a skinny, mean sonofabitch. Pardon me, Preacher. But he was a bottom feeder and a no-good."

Evan took a guess, "Did he also have a thing for Molly?"

Clapper just smirked, meaning yes, and went on, "He was younger than me, but not much younger. Not so much frail, but wiry. Shoe-leather face with a permanent squint. Rolled his own smokes and spat no matter where. Disgusting human being. In his later years, around the time I was struggling with that will, people said they'd never seen him on a tractor, never seen him at Grange or Rotary meetings, never heard him talk about what he had planted or how he was rotating his crops. Yet here were Molly's bank records. On paper, he was making his nut and then some. I asked Molly about it, and she came back right away with, 'Oh, Dickie's got it all in the soil bank.'"

"Soil bank? I heard the term years ago," Evan said. "But I never quite knew what it meant. When I was a kid, farmers used it to talk disparagingly about somebody who was cutting corners, not pulling his rightful weight."

"That's right. The Feds used to pay you not to work." Clapper said. "Farm subsidies were common because, only a few decades after World War II, farm production was so abundant it was driving down prices. You might have been able to raise a family on soil-bank money as late as the 1960s. Over the years since, those subsidies got cut back and back. Now, there are precious few allowances left. Those don't pay enough to buy groceries. Like I said, the Emmett place is just shy of five-hundred acres, a small farm according to the Department of Agriculture. It would be hard to get rich if you farmed every square inch of it. Setting any of it aside just wouldn't be smart."

"So how was Dickie Emmett getting by?"

"He may have worked that farm in the early days. But he didn't go off to war, God knows why. Maybe he had asthma or flat feet or something. But during the postwar era, I doubt if he worked much, if at all."

Despite Clapper's enthusiasm for his subject and his delight to have such an attentive listener, his physical energy was fading. His coughing fit had left him looking shrunken, as though he'd collapsed into his chair. Now he was starting to wheeze. He pulled the oxygen tube back up to his nose and took a long drag. As he did, Nurse Monica materialized behind his chair.

"Reverend," she said to Evan. "Mr. Clapper's a wonderful storyteller, and he can bend your ear for hours. But I think we should call it a day."

Clapper looked up and asked her, "Shall we run off together?" Then he squealed delightedly, "She's abducting me!" even as his eyelids started to droop.

Evan pleaded with her, "Just a few minutes more?"

Monica shot him a stern, silent rebuke and informed him, "You can help yourself in the cafeteria. Just tell the wait staff you're Mr. Clapper's guest."

Evan declined with a polite wave of the hand. He wouldn't mind if the fare was only acceptable, but if Clapper couldn't talk more today, Evan wanted to get back on the road. Outside, the snow was flying thick and fast.

"It's been a pleasure, counselor!" Evan called out as he stood and the nurse wheeled the old fellow away. "Let's do this again soon?"

Maybe he can give me five more minutes on the phone after he's had his supper.

Clapper yelled back, "I've got a theory, but it's only a theory."

By THE TIME Evan was on the interstate driving back from Knox, the snow accumulation on the highway was only cleared by the hot tire tracks. Visibility was a car-length, at most. He put his headlights on and kept his speed at about fifty, ever watchful for slower vehicles and those with no taillights. He said a quick prayer for each fearless driver who passed him as if he were standing still on a dry road:

Right here and right now, the power and the presence of God is.

He'd mutter the same affirmation whenever he'd pass a dead animal or emergency vehicles on the road.

Don't ask for solutions to problems. Don't ask for a miracle cure or a new car. Ask to see the truth. Ask to appreciate and use the power you have always had within you.

It wasn't that Evan didn't believe God answered prayer. As he'd told Cora, he believed all prayers have already been answered, from the dawn of time to the end. Not being able to hold to that faith (and it was impossible for even the most devout person at some time or other) might well be the source of all human suffering.

At least, that's what Evan tried to believe, as much of the time as he could manage it.

He phoned Edie. When she answered, he could hear her clattering around in her kitchen. He wanted to tell her all he'd learned about the farm from Clapper, especially if she knew anything about this "third complication."

But I don't know enough yet to guess which side she's on. If she really doesn't own the farm, she's as powerless as the Emmetts are.

All he said was, "Edie, I have a lot of questions."

He was afraid she'd rebuke him for exceeding the scope of his assignment. But instead she brightened, as though they'd been discussing plans for a party and not a burial. "Why don't you come on over? You deserve a hot meal."

Her shift in mood startled him. Even though he had questions for her, he wasn't sure how to take the invitation. "Okay," he relented. He thought about the travel time. "But don't wait your own lunch on me."

"Never mind me," she said. "Don't go buying yourself one of those readymade gas-station sandwiches."

Actually, he'd been thinking about doing just that. Maybe with a chocolate-milk chaser. Sometimes his food choices were all about speed and convenience.

Then he asked the question he'd wanted to start with. "Did you know Molly probably didn't have clear title to her farm?"

Edie avoided the question by saying, "Look, we can talk this to death when you have your lunch. Keep your eyes on the road and both hands on that wheel, do you hear?"

And that was the end of the conversation.

So Molly asked Angus to help her make a will in the same year Abigail died. How much does Edie know about the wills? Does she know — or does she suspect — Bob changed his mind?

Clapper was right. Evan had left with more questions than answers.

What could be the third complication? How could it be so unusual that an experienced lawyer like Clapper hadn't seen anything like it before? And how could its effect be so threatening or devastating that it discouraged Molly from formalizing her lease deal with Dickie Emmett? She must have gone ahead with her will, since, there at the last, Bob was fretting about his responsibilities as executor.

Evan was tempted to phone Knox and ask Clapper the crucial question. But the preacher feared the fellow might not yet be rested, and the old lawyer's explanation, even if he could summon it, might not be brief.

17

FRIDAY AFTERNOON
TAGGART HOUSE

I t was two o'clock by the time Evan got to Edie's. The snowfall had abated, but a blustery wind had kicked up, and the dense cloud cover imparted a general gloom. As the locals say, "If you don't like the weather in Missouri, wait five minutes and it'll change." But Evan remembered they'd said the same thing in Massachusetts.

When Edie didn't respond to the doorbell, Evan let himself in. These ranch homes don't have a mudroom, as the farmhouses do, but there was space in the entryway for him to remove his slush-caked work boots and hang up his soaked ball cap and down jacket. He tucked the bag with both computers behind a box of fire logs. He wasn't yet sure how much he wanted to tell Edie about his data drilling. After all, she'd authorized him to make arrangements. And so far he hadn't followed through with the details of the memorial service. But he figured it was his responsibility to at least understand the disposition of Molly's estate. And he was hoping — or fearing — those discoveries would shed some light on why his friend felt he had to die.

Having removed his wet gear and his cap, Evan was more or less neatly dressed in a flannel shirt and khakis. But he'd be plodding around her neat house in his damp wool socks. Somehow exposing his bare, hairy feet didn't seem appropriate. He called out to Edie, and her voice from another room shot back, "Sit yourself down and eat!"

The place at the head of the dining room table was set for one, with a steaming hot meal and a pot of fresh coffee.

He didn't have to be asked twice. Meatloaf stuffed with mushrooms and oregano. Julienned carrots with brown-sugar glaze. French-cut green beans sautéed in ham fat. Mashed sweet potatoes smothered in melted butter.

Hey, baby, it's cold outside. A body needs fuel.

As he sat, he said a quick, silent thanks. Then he nailed his most urgent desire by pouring himself a cup of Edie's inky Kenyan coffee and ladling in a couple of heaping teaspoons of sugar. Fortunately for someone who consumed both sugar and alcohol in what some health practitioners would consider excessive amounts, Evan was hypoglycemic. He therefore thought he had low risk of developing diabetes. That's not to say his food choices would support his future wellbeing.

I just choose for now not to worry about the consequences of my petty vices.

As he lifted a fork and inhaled the food aromas deeply, a different kind of pang shot through his craven stomach. He felt a twinge of panic. All during his newfound relationship with Edie, he'd been fearing the new widow might set a man-trap for him.

Here it is. Situation ethics. Søren Kierkegaard.

It had been a hot topic in his studies of theology. The Danish philosopher held that what might be immoral in one set of circumstances could be acceptable — or even *necessary* — in a different situation. Legally and practically, he and Edie were both available. They were about the same age, both attractive and healthy. And, Evan assumed, they both shared a gaping wound. And they both needed to be comforted. But her husband, his friend, had been cooked to an ash only hours ago. No matter how long it had been since Evan's last intimate encounter, the ethics of the situation certainly didn't feel righteous.

And, yet, here he was thinking about it, debating the morality of it like a schoolboy writing an essay.

He ate hungrily, if not sloppily. His place setting included an immaculately folded linen napkin. As he tried not to gulp the food, he thought about how he'd counseled her. He'd said she'd go through all the emotions, and he'd advised her to understand that any and all of them were okay.

He still believed his own advice. He'd found it true for himself several times when his dearest ones had left him. Whether the person expired or packed up and left, the feeling of abandonment was the same. Even if you were holding their hand as they passed or felt the coldness of a goodbye kiss, there was the initial reflexive onset of denial. Surely, they'd be coming back. This couldn't be the end.

There is a life after this one. There must *be.*

He was surprised to see teardrops falling into his plate. His eyes had suddenly flooded, and wetness was coursing down his cheeks. He was finally mourning for Bob.

But it didn't affect his appetite. Or appetites.

Edie entered quietly on barefoot. She sat down next to him at the table. Her hair was wet, and she was wearing a lavender silk kimono with a scrolled monogram on the left breast pocket. She smelled of lemongrass soap. She had her robe tightly cinched at the waist, which prevented its falling open but also emphasized her proud and rounded bustline.

So, here was the man-trap. He'd walked in with his eyes wide shut. If he hadn't been so hungry, maybe he'd have turned down the lunch invitation and the meeting. They had a lot to say to each other, but he worried it wouldn't be about the arrangements.

What am I doing? Bob's wife? I have no business putting myself in the middle of this. And Bob had no right to expect that I would!

Edie saw Evan's tears, and perhaps she understood the depth of his feeling. But instead she asked, "Don't tell me you're allergic? I didn't think to ask."

"No, no," he sniffled as he wiped his face with his napkin. "It just all caught up to me. I attend a lot of funerals, and in my sermons I can't help talking about how you deal with death. But this was in my face, personal in a way I can't describe. I was seeing myself lying there. I guess until this moment I've been numb, not letting myself dwell on that moment. He was my friend. Or, he had been years ago. We hadn't had much to do with each other lately. Not since I decided to quit school and come back here. I don't know yet, but maybe *I* let him down somehow?"

"Why should it be your fault? That's just out of nowhere. Maybe somehow I made him do it. We weren't happy campers, you know."

That much, I guessed.

If Edie had planned to seduce Evan, his tears were his best defense. In a sense, Bob's ghost was now in the room. There was no denying why Evan and Bob's wife had been thrown together and what their obligations were to this person who'd been important to both of them, although at different times.

Evan had to admit he was tempted. She'd created a situation, she'd opened a door. But she wasn't rash enough to push him through it. He'd look obtuse if he didn't at least take the hint.

Ethics aside, I just don't trust her.

He ended up staring at his plate too long. She got the message.

"I'm sorry. I should have dressed," she said quietly, with a touch of shame. "I worked up a sweat in the kitchen, so I did a half-hour on my exercise bike and took a shower. The workout is one way I cope."

"The meal is delicious," he said. "You went to a lot of trouble." It was not what she wanted to hear at that moment.

"What else do I have to do?" she asked simply, although with enough of an edge to suggest he could think of other ways to amuse her.

Do? To seduce me? Or to convince me you're on the side of the angels?

Evan had stopped eating. He was about half finished when she'd joined him. She gestured to his plate and said, "You go ahead, and I'll put on a sweater and a pair of slacks. This house gets drafty. Then I think we should have a sit in the parlor and have our talk."

THEY SAT in the living room. Edie had made herself a cup of chamomile tea, and Evan was on his fifth cup of coffee. She'd offered him whiskey. But much as Evan was fond of the gentleman's substitute for Missouri River water, somehow draining the last of his friend's bottle of Old Fitzgerald seemed irreverent under the circumstances — unethical in this situation.

Behind her danced cheery flames in the fireplace. It was a natural-gas fire set with ceramic logs.

The box of wood in the entryway must be for show. So much of what she does seems to be for how it will look to others.

Okay, I'm not going to pretend I'm not looking into Bob's worries. She either knows more or she doesn't care to know. Either way, I have to find out.

So, he asked her, "How is it, for so many years, Molly — and everybody else — thought she owned the Emmett farm? It's kind of late for the government to be saying it's theirs."

"I told you not to fret about any of this."

"But the Emmetts are being evicted, and the house — which by all rights should be yours — will be torn down on Saturday!"

"All right." She took a breath. "I will tell you what I know and this will be the end of it, as far as you're concerned."

She looked to him for agreement, and he nodded his head slightly.

I heard you. Doesn't mean I agree.

"A week after Molly died, Bob received a notice from the government. This was the first anyone knew his family didn't own the land. Bob looked into it, tried to fight it, but then he seemed to give up. If we had any proof we owned the place, we could go to court. But we don't. Not a scrap of evidence."

"Do you know Angus Clapper?"

The question obviously made her uncomfortable. "I believe he's the gentleman who helped Molly with her will, and I believe he also counseled Bob."

"Well, I met with him."

An angry flush came to her face. "Evan, that was way beyond —"

"He seems to be the only one who knows much of anything about this. Hear me out."

She didn't reply, just straightened herself in her chair.

Evan went on, "I take it at some point you read Molly's will?"

"Yes."

"And Bob's will?"

"Yes. As I told you, both documents are in the safe deposit box."

"So you know that, against Clapper's advice, Molly didn't list her assets. She just gave everything to Lionel, which then went to Bob. And Bob did the same, giving everything to you."

"That's right."

"So it will be up to the probate court to determine what, in fact, Molly owned, what she gave to Bob, and what he's given to you."

"That's right." She must have decided rounding out the picture for Evan wouldn't do any harm, and maybe it would finally shut him up.

She added, "Because it's government property, and because they don't seem to want to talk about whatever toxic waste is there, they wouldn't give us any information besides the demolition notice. They won't even be specific about the boundaries of their claim. It was stressing Bob so much, I finally asked for Stu Shackleton's advice. Bob wasn't aware. Stu said, while the government might own some of the farm, it might not own all of it. So, once they're done with their demolition and their access road and their cleanup, perhaps we can compel them — go to court if necessary — to give us a survey and have the court make a determination. Understand, at today's prices, the farm isn't worth much. And with the Army camped out in the middle of it pushing dirt around, no buyer will want to go near it. We can't do anything for the Emmetts, especially since they don't pay their rent anyway. We'll have to let matters run their course. Once we know what we own, we can decide what to do with it. And it might not be worth the legal expenses — and time — to contest any judgment."

"You seem to have a good grasp of it," Evan said. "But who is *we?* You said, 'we can't do anything' and when 'we know what we own.'"

She wriggled in her chair again. "Why, Bob and myself, of course. I should have said, 'When *I* know,' of course."

"So you didn't share Shackleton's advice with Bob?"

"Bob was too agitated. And he wouldn't listen. I tried to tell him there isn't a way to stop the Army project, and we might as well wait. That was the essence of Stu's advice, after all. But no, I didn't give Bob all the details."

"Including the interesting fact he might yet own a big chunk of that land?"

"Like I said, he was too upset to take it in."

I'm not going to tell her what I found on his computer.

Evan paused and smiled, hoping to indicate her explanation was more than sufficient and reasonable. Then he asked, "Edie, you say Bob had recently given up. Do you think he may have had some new information, perhaps a change of heart? He kept telling Josh Emmett he was going to work things out."

She shook her head and sighed. "He might have had good intentions. But he had no way to back them up."

"Well, I don't think Josh will be bothering you anymore. The Emmetts are packing up their things, and I believe they'll be going to live with Linda's mother in Rich Hill until they can figure out what's next for them."

"So they will allow the demolition to go forward?"

"I believe so, yes."

She was visibly relieved, saying, "Look, Evan, I know you want to get to the bottom of things. Frankly, I don't have the patience to delve into it now. From what Stu says, the case could take years — if I decide to pursue it. Let's get Bob buried, give him a warm send-off, and get on with life. Here's the list you wanted of folks who will want to know about the memorial service." She reached into a monogrammed, leather-bound appointment book on the coffee table and handed him the list. It was neatly hand-lettered on light-blue stationery, and, like her kimono and her little leather book, monogrammed *ECO*. The letter *C* was bigger and in the middle. So Evan guessed the initials were *EOC*. That's right, Zip had said Clark was her maiden name. She must have a supply of fancy personalized stuff and had never bothered to have things done up for her new status as queen of the Taggarts.

The list had a dozen-or-so names. They were almost the same as the favorites on Bob's phone. Except Angus Clapper wasn't on her list, and there were two additional names.

Maybe she doesn't want Angus there? They probably wouldn't let him out, but that's no reason not to notify him.

"How about Ezra Bailey and Arthur Redwine?" Evan asked.

"We have the Baileys on a Christmas list. I don't know them. Arthur is Jake Redwine's younger brother," Edie said with a smirk. "An eccentric old crank. Doesn't answer his phone. He must get mail, but I wouldn't be surprised if he doesn't bother to open it. He has a place south of Rockville. You couldn't call it a farm. All gone to seed. Five fishponds. Smallmouth bass and catfish. Bob said he fished there as a boy."

I remember fishing with Bob. Yeah, there was a crusty dude named Arthur, but he never paid much attention to us.

Edie had given mailing addresses for most of them. Opposite Arthur's name was a rural route box.

"If Redwine can't be reached by phone and he's family, I guess I'll head out there and have a talk with him," Evan said. "How do I find the place?"

"It's off Route P on the way to Rockville about five miles south of the town. Maybe go by daylight and ask for directions at the gas station in Rockville? I never visited him, so that's as much as I know."

I'm guessing you think he's clueless about the farm. I'm hoping he's not.

Evan was down to the dregs of his coffee, and he set his mug down on the table.

Edie looked annoyed again, and her lips tightened as if she were composing a speech. She got up quickly holding her bone-china teacup. Then she snatched Evan's empty mug from the table and walked briskly to the kitchen sink. As she ran the water, she spoke over her shoulder, "Listen, Evan. I want your help, but you seem to have the priorities all backward."

Evan didn't get up. He figured she'd be coming back to sit. He turned toward her in his chair and asked, "Don't you want to know how Bob intended to work it out?"

She turned around to face him and said sharply. "No. No, I *don't*. And neither should you."

Evan got up and started to go to her. She made a gesture to push him away — but he was still halfway across the room. It stopped him. He didn't think his moving toward her could have been interpreted as an intimate approach.

"But what about his note?" Evan asked her. "He seemed afraid. Don't you want to —?"

"*No!* That's what I'm trying to tell you. We'll probably never know exactly why Bob did what he did. As I said, even on good days, he couldn't express himself. And here he has his last chance — when you'd think he has all the permission he needs to say exactly whatever was driving him nuts — and he can't find the words! *Dearest ones?* Are you any closer to being able to tell me who *that* might be?"

"No," Evan said softly. "I'm sorry. I do want to help, and I thought you were as mystified as I was why he would do this to himself."

"Whatever the issue is with the ownership of the farm, there's a solution. It'll all be about lawyers and money. I'm telling you, I don't care." She gestured to take in the room. "This is a nice house. I've put a lot into it. It's paid for. And I don't believe in ghosts."

Evan moved toward the door. "I should be going. You went to a lot of trouble, and I'm grateful. And now I'm fortified."

She came over. Now her body language said he couldn't leave soon enough. "I was going to say, I should have been more specific about my instructions. When the sheriff gave me that power of attorney to sign, it was their form, and I didn't give it much thought. But I didn't mean for it to be a blank check. I want you to handle the memorial and the burial. I'd like you to attend both, and I'd appreciate your saying some kind words about him on those occasions. But the will, the farm, the other assets, all those things — I'll decide how to deal with them in time."

"Do you have anything to say to Josh and Linda? Do you want me to reach out?"

"No, don't put yourself in the middle. If Joshua Emmett has a question or a complaint, he can raise it with me after Saturday. I'm not like Bob. I was in the business world for years. I'll know what to say."

Having donned his coat and his Chiefs cap, Evan reached down behind the firewood box to pick up the oilskin bag.

"Were you bringing me a present?" she asked coyly, her tone changing back to almost flirtatious.

"Oh," Evan said. "My computer. Didn't want to leave it out in the cold. My favorite toy, you know."

"Every boy needs one," she said as she managed to both dial her emotions back and imply he could've done better.

Evan tucked the bag in the trunk of his car, got in, and started the engine. Before he pulled out of Edie's driveway, He couldn't wait any longer to satisfy his curiosity. It was dusk, the weather had calmed, and he hoped Angus Clapper had enjoyed a restorative nap. He hoped the fellow wasn't having his dinner yet.

Edie was watching Evan from her kitchen window. She no doubt wondered why he was lingering, whom he was calling on the phone. The receptionist at Knox put him through to the second-floor nursing station.

He recognized Nurse Monica's voice. "Reverend Wycliff?"

"Yes," Evan said jovially. "I wanted to give Angus a quick tip about his chess game."

Her voice dropped. "I'm sorry to inform you that Mr. Clapper passed away peacefully this afternoon."

Evan felt the wind knocked out of him.

Now time has stopped for Angus Clapper too.

"I'm sorry. I'm really sorry" was all he could find to say. "So vital, such a character." He was going to say he'd only met Angus today, but he held back. Better she think they'd been friends going back a while. The "Reverend" thing got him through a lot of doors.

Am I supposed to say, 'May he rest in peace'? Like Otis says, if there's a life after this, who wants to rest? Certainly, not Clapper!

"He enjoyed your visit," Monica said.

"And he admired you," Evan told her.

"Yes," she said, understanding that Evan meant it with good humor. "Yes, he did." She became officious: "We have a next of kin as Henrietta Bailey in St. Louis, but we're not getting an answer. We can't text to the number, and there's no email. Do you happen to have any family contact information?"

Bailey? *Ezra* Bailey? Evan fished Edie's guest list out of his shirt pocket. Sure enough, in the dim light he could read the Baileys' address — in St. Louis.

Situation ethics.

"Yes," Evan said. "I believe I did know a member of the family." True enough, he'd known Angus Clapper, however briefly. He gave her the mailing address from Edie's list. Then he asked, "Do you have their phone? After a time, I'd like to offer my condolences."

She read him the number. He wasn't sure whether he was supposed to have it, but he didn't hesitate to punch it into his phone's address book.

The third complication. I can only hope Clapper's theory didn't die with him.

18

FRIDAY NIGHT

WITH EVAN

N*ow Clapper's dead. What is life but heat? Time flows in one direction — from low to high entropy, from hot to cold. Angus with the flushed cheeks is now cold. Warm-hearted Bob is now ash.*

After that ample meal at Edie's, Evan didn't feel much like having dinner. On the way home, he stopped in at a convenience store and bought a can of aerosol cheese and a box of Ritz crackers. There not being any Wild Turkey or Jack Daniels on the shelf, he opted for a fifth of Old Crow.

Edie hadn't yet asked him to return Bob's phone or computer. And he certainly wasn't ready to tell her what he'd found. Maybe she figured he'd never found the passwords. When he got back to his trailer and settled in, his first task was to back it all up into the cloud.

THE ALCOHOL MADE Evan's dreams vivid, his sleep fitful. Edie's coming onto him had stirred old emotions. Images of her flitted by. She was arranging things in neat rows, punching buttons on a calculator, chairing meetings, sucking up to her boss. Only sometimes he'd look at her and she'd be Naomi. Dream identities morphed and flowed. He wasn't sure of anything, which actors were in which roles. Much less, how he fit in.

Through the night, Evan had fits of wakefulness. His eyes would pop open as he roused from some vivid dream and it could be hours, if ever, before he could get back to sleep. As much as he tried to keep thoughts of Naomi from distressing him, these were the times she'd demand his attention. On these nights, his experience was a mashup of memories and dreams.

HE'D MET Naomi during his experimental-agnostic years, between his divinity studies and his decision to undertake astrophysics. It was an unfocused time for him when he held a wet finger in the air hoping for a puff of wind from any direction. Female companionship might have helped, but he didn't know where to look. He didn't want to spend more time with students for the ministry, and even though science intrigued him, he expected socializing with empiricists might be disappointingly dull. He needed a complementary, contrasting personality. Someone from a walk of life he'd not yet explored.

So he enrolled in an evening acting class at Boston University's extension school. Perhaps he could learn to pretend to be interesting to someone who wasn't a wonk.

The instructor, L. Greg Foster, was a disaffected middle-aged man in a worn cardigan and jeans, with a paunch and chronic indigestion. He'd grown tired of playing supporting Shakespearean roles in regional theater. His gray hair had thinned to a wisp on top, compensated for by a bushy goatee. His puffy face wore a perpetually wistful look, which disappeared when he smiled, usually in sarcasm. In the substrata of Foster's quirky personality, there existed a layer of wry humor. But most people, and particularly his intimidated students, never dared to dig deeply enough to find it. He claimed to own an approach and a technique, which he said he'd developed from the teachings of the Actor's Studio, where he'd never been. At his worst when leading a class, he enjoyed teasing students with assignments and exercises he hoped would evoke frustration, fear, or anger. In this, he was more eager audience member than mentor, but his close attention served his instructional purpose.

"The focus of my class will be scene study," Foster informed his dozen students in the first class session. There were eight women and four men. "We'll rehearse scenes from dramatic literature. Then we'll change some assumptions and run through again as you learn to explore and improvise." He might as well have said he was the experimenter and these wannabe actors were his lab rats.

He went on, "The most captivating scenes, you'll find, begin with a disagreement about action and end with an argument about values." He scanned the room, no doubt looking for callow faces. "Who can give me an example? A disagreement about action."

No one wanted to answer. Foster pointed to Evan. "You!"

Evan offered in a low voice, "Uh, where should we go to dinner?"

"Speak up! My God, this is an *acting* class!" Foster stressed with feigned annoyance.

Evan repeated, with more lung power, "Where do you want to go to dinner?"

"Excellent!" Foster pronounced. "And an argument about values?"

Naomi, who happened to be seated next to Evan in the semicircle, answered vehemently, "You never loved me!"

Foster smiled to himself and cooed, "I'm going to enjoy this class."

Without hesitation, Foster handed scene scripts (which the students learned to call *sides*) to Naomi and to Evan. The play was the romantic comedy *Two for the Seesaw*. Evan's sides were labeled *Jerry* and Naomi's were marked *Gittel*. Jerry Ryan is taciturn, sincere, and inexperienced. Gittel Mosca is brash, opinionated, and worldly. It was spot-on type-casting for both. Evan suspected Foster's calling on him initially had not been coincidental.

Foster didn't give them long to study their lines before he had them on their feet. As they took their places in front of the class, he quipped, "As I said, a disagreement about an action, followed by an argument about values. So, what's the action? How does that action play into the difference in values? What strong feelings come up from those differences?" He paused, then added, "This two-person play is ideal material for this. I would have assigned *Who's Afraid of Virginia Woolf?*, but I'm sure none of you have endured partnership long enough to understand why *Woolf* is best played as a comedy."

Indeed, most of the students were in their twenties, except for Evan and one retired postal worker, a confessed movie buff. That fellow later admitted he'd joined the class out of curiosity about how actors manage to fool themselves into being people they're not.

Predictably, Evan and Naomi stumbled through their scene. Jerry thinks it's about time they were intimate, and Gittel "wouldn't sleep with Columbus on the first date." They ran through several times, interrupted by Foster's coaching, which was taunting and sarcastic. Evan's Jerry was suitably understated, mainly because of his lack of confidence. Her Gittel was heated and overacted, for the opposite reason.

"Looks like you two have some chemistry," Foster observed.

"Chemistry, fine," Naomi replied to Foster. Paraphrasing Gittel, she shot back with a glance to Evan, "But no biology on the first date."

Her crack drew a chuckle from the others — except for Foster, who smirked. He never liked being upstaged.

Afterward, Evan was bold enough to ask her, "Go for coffee?"

"I'd prefer something stronger," she deadpanned, "if you're not in some program."

~

NAOMI WEISS WAS twenty-nine and Jewish. Her physical resemblance to the young Shirley MacLaine in the movie version of *Seesaw* was striking — dark-haired, fair-complected, trim, and perpetually animated. Naomi's face was longer and thinner, and her nose more Romanesque, which made her look a touch austere, more thoughtful.

They spent a couple of hours in a wine bar. Theirs was just get-to-know-you conversation. She liked that he'd studied theology and liked even more that he was thinking of turning his focus to science. Despite Evan's diligent efforts to venture into the liberal arts for new friends, he learned Naomi held a day job as some kind of analyst for one of the big aerospace firms on Route 128. He'd hooked up with another wonk, but this one had the personality of a standup comedian who could do calculus. He would discover she was a better chess player than Karl Meister, but Evan wasn't yet skilled enough to know the difference.

Their after-school date ended with his walking her to the St. Paul Street station of the Green Line. She had a studio apartment in Brookline. As Naomi had predicted, there were no biological exchanges involved, but both of them obsessed about the chemistry on their separate ways home.

As ANY DUTIFUL SON MIGHT, Evan viewed each new prospect for a girlfriend as to whether she was a suitable candidate for marriage. Until he'd met Naomi, the question was mostly hypothetical. Here was his first real test case, and she was from a devout Jewish family! But it didn't take him long to learn in their get-to-know-you conversations that, like him, her background in the sciences had turned her cynical about traditional faiths. These days, she was a seeker, intrigued by some aspects of the New Age. She loved the notion that "thoughts are things," that strong beliefs can shape new manifestations of reality — that simply believing might make it so.

As Evan became more fascinated with her as a partner, he began to rationalize away their differences. After all, Harvard Divinity graduated a lot of Unitarians, and he could decide to be one of them. Maybe she could meet him in the middle?

Also like Evan, Naomi had studied theology. She'd grown up at a time in the Jewish Reform movement when girls were being admitted to Talmudic studies that had traditionally been restricted to males. She found she had a talent — and enthusiasm — for rabbinic *pilpul,* the process of debating all sides of a scriptural question with equal conviction and vehemence.

"That's why Jewish boys make such good lawyers," she told Evan.

"And what about the girls? You just told me they can hold their own now."

She laughed. "No, the girls grow up to be Jewish wives and mothers, and they win *every* argument. The opposing point of view dare not even speak!"

By virtue of his divinity studies, Evan was no stranger to logical analysis and debate. But Naomi gave him a whole new taste for the game. Even though they came to think of themselves as like-minded people, they rarely agreed. That's because whatever statement Evan offered, Naomi would claim its opposite — convincingly — whether or not it was her personal opinion. Pilpul was how they communicated, as well as how they entertained each other.

Now Naomi was no longer with him. Half of his brain was missing. At those times, especially when he was worried or fretful, he'd invoke her spirit as an interlocutor, her Watson to his Holmes.

She'd say those roles should be reversed, but, these days, I get to decide.

It had been a long and tiresome day. Evan was still awake at three in the morning. While he was data drilling in Bob's phone and laptop, Evan had devoured the box of crackers, continuing to chomp on them even after the can of cheese spread was empty. And he'd drunk more than half the bottle of Old Crow.

He sat cross-legged on his bed, his bad back propped against it on the three pillows he owned. Even then, his posture made his back hurt.

He'd had so much booze, he resisted the strong temptation to pop a painkiller. As he cataloged the new ducks piling up in his stack of mental frustrations, he imagined Naomi sitting in the chair beside him, her hot breath just inches away.

"So," she challenged, "what's got your stomach all tied up in knots?"

"Edie didn't ask whether I had Bob's laptop in the bag," Evan told her. "I was afraid she'd ask for it back, along with his phone."

Naomi shrugged and said, "She either thinks there's nothing useful on them or she thinks you couldn't crack the code. Either way, you know she'll ask for them back, and soon. Did you get all you could get, or did you just sit here smelling your farts and getting drunk?"

"I copied the contacts — phone and email — into the cloud. And those documents on the desktop. But, from what Clapper told me, I can guess what Bob was looking for, some proof of ownership. And I have Bob's notes for his revised will — there's a bombshell — but if I can't find a formal document, it was just good intentions."

"All right, smart guy. Who's next? You haven't exactly exhausted all the sources of information."

He thought for a moment. "Arthur Redwine has to go near the top of the list. He might be a daffy old duck, but he probably knows a lot more about whatever happened in 1993. And maybe a *lot* more."

"What about Nick? And Shackleton?"

"I'm thinking I'd better find out as much as I can from as many people as I can before confronting Stu Shackleton."

"Cautious, if not cowardly," she observed. "How about seeing him sooner rather than later? You could make it all about the Masons until you know where he's coming from."

Her mentioning the Masonic ritual made Evan think about the memorial, and he checked off in his mind what more he had to do. "Sure," he said, "Edie is relying on me to handle the details of the cremation, memorial, and interment. But she also has to understand, I can't just close my eyes to the rest of it."

"Doesn't she know you still have Bob's personal effects — including the *gun?*"

"Like you said, maybe she thinks none of it is important. She's expecting me to go along with the cops. Open and shut."

Naomi said, "What I'm wondering is, will Edie be proactive about changing the terms of the power of attorney? Yesterday she lit out of the house and gave you the run of the place. Today she's telling you there are compartments you're not supposed to open. What happened?"

"She was prepared to come onto me today," Evan admitted. "But she stopped short. Or, my hesitation stopped her. Maybe she thought I should have been more enthusiastic about the opportunity. If it had gone the other way — if I was in bed with her right now — what would she think she was getting out of it?"

"You flatter yourself, Preacher," Naomi teased. "I doubt if she changed her mind because you turned her down. I'd say it's more like she decided she couldn't make you an ally, and now she doesn't want you running around poking your nose everywhere. But if she makes a big deal about trying to stop you, she'll be tipping her hand. That is, if she's really a player in all of this."

"She's awfully uncaring about that house coming down."

"What's with all the monograms?" Naomi prompted. "And in her maiden name? When was she in business, and why isn't she doing it anymore?"

"I don't think she was ever all that invested in being Mrs. Taggart. But she's getting used to the idea of being the widow who controls all the Redwine assets."

"She used to be some kind of accountant?"

Evan's eyes were starting to glaze over. "Bates Bank. The bank that writes most of Zip's car loans. The bank Stu Shackleton manages."

Naomi reminded him, "And the bank where Bob locked his secrets in a safe-deposit box."

"He wouldn't have put the new will there. Not if he'd changed his mind. He'd know they'd destroy it or hide it, and no one would be the wiser. And it would actually be smart to leave the old one there, to throw them off the track."

"I think it's time you got some sleep," Naomi said. "You're almost up to the task when you're awake and sailing on caffeine. Sweet dreams."

19

SATURDAY BREAKFAST
C'MON INN

Evan wanted to press on with the priorities Edie had warned him off of. He hadn't agreed to stop asking questions. But if he got the arrangements for the memorial service set, maybe she'd stop worrying what else he might be doing. He didn't have to go running proudly to her every time he was gifted with another dead duck. Especially when he didn't yet know how to interpret those clues.

He disliked the image of a dead animal as a portent. Those ducks were nothing more than fantasy images. But now real dead people were piling up. Angus Clapper. Evan had been actually looking forward to winning a chess game off the old coot. And then there was the lawyer's theory about the third complication, whatever that was. But theories aren't proof of anything.

If Evan had been a minister in the truest sense of the word, he wouldn't have left Clapper without asking after his spiritual welfare, without talking about the endearing fellow's preparedness for what would come next, sooner than both of them expected.

Evan knew, as an agent of the divine order, he was supposed to be inspiring the workers in the field with hope and zeal for their earthly tasks. Comforting the sick. Reassuring the dying. Instead, he was asking after dead people, who, of all the humans needing his care, undoubtedly needed it the least, if at all. (Praying them out of Purgatory was not in his belief system.)

We have so many close-knit families in this part of the world. Arthur Redwine is younger brother of Jake, Molly's deceased husband. Molly and her sister Adelaide were Baileys. Adelaide's daughter, Abigail, was Bob's deceased mother. Angus Clapper was Molly's suitor as well as her advisor. Was he also somehow related to the Baileys — Ezra and Henrietta of St. Louis? What kin are they to Abigail's side? Are they husband and wife or brother and sister? Henrietta was listed as Angus's next of kin. Maybe she was born Henrietta Clapper?

The first step after breakfast would be to sit down with Reverend Thurston, pastor of First Baptist and Evan's spiritual mentor since he was a boy.

Breakfast was two heaping stacks of buckwheat pancakes at the C'mon. Drowning in butter and pure maple syrup. Sugar and alcohol were Evan's vices, at least the two he recognized. He spooned just one teaspoonful of sugar into his coffee and told himself the scales were balanced, at least for today.

Evan asked Cora if she knew Angus Clapper. "I knew *of* him," she said. "Bob Taggart complained about him."

"Bob discussed Clapper with you?"

"Bob would sit here and go on and on. I'd think he was talking to me, you know, letting off steam. But he didn't do any explaining, like you'd do if you wanted a friend to understand. It was more like he was talking to himself — but he knew I was listening if he needed something."

"What did he complain about?"

"Mr. Clapper was supposed to get to the bottom of something and he didn't. Bob said time was running out."

"Do you know what that meant?"

She smiled. "Not a clue."

Evan was about to get up. "We may never know," he sighed. "Mr. Clapper passed away last night. He was a colorful fellow. In his nineties. He must've been a sharp country lawyer in his day."

Cora shot Evan an odd look, then said, "Did he help Bob with his will?"

This stopped Evan. "Yeah. What do you know about it?"

In a hush, she leaned over and told him, "I was never supposed to tell anybody. Bob made me promise."

"I'm handling things for him. And for Edie, now. Please tell me."

As before when Cora had confided to him, there was no one at the counter to eavesdrop. She said quietly, "The week before he, you know, left us. He had a paper, very official. Came in here with it, and he had a lady with him. Somebody who signs things with a stamp?"

"A notary public."

She pointed. "Him and her and me sat in that booth over there. The lady said we needed one more to sign, so I got Evelyn to come over. She was on the lunch shift with me that day, brought us all coffee because it took a while. We signed two copies, and the lady stamped them. We had to make fingerprints in her book and sign it too. Then Bob gave me and Evelyn fives for tips, paid the lady, and he was outta here."

"Did you happen to read any of the documents?"

"No. We didn't get a look at the other pages. I heard the lady ask him if he made any wills before this. So I guessed that's what it was."

"And he didn't say anything about what was in it?"

"Not a word."

"Did he happen to say who he would be giving those papers to?"

"Not to me."

This is incredible news!

Evan thought to ask, "Do you happen to remember the lady's name? The notary?"

"Nope. Sweet gal. Some Mexican last name. Maybe about your age. And she was chubby." Cora thought about it. "No! She was pregnant and showing."

"Thanks, Cora," Evan said as he gave her another oversized tip. "This could be important. But, as with Bob, this stays our secret. Okay?"

"Sure, Preacher."

Not only did Bob change his mind. He made a new will. And somewhere on the face of this Earth, there's a legally enforceable, certified document.

Evan thought Clapper's passing had created a dead end. But if the terms of this will Cora signed were the same as the handwritten changes in the file on Bob's laptop, the Emmett's house might still come down, but the future of this part of Southern Missouri might well be different.

Where did you hide it, Bob?

20

SATURDAY MORNING
FIRST BAPTIST PARSONAGE

E van expected to find Reverend Thurston in his study at the church preparing his message for tomorrow. But when he phoned over there, the secretary told him the pastor had stayed home this morning. Evan worried his old friend was sick. He didn't want his mentor to be the next to expire.

And, note to selfish self, I'm in no mood to take Thurston's place in the pulpit in the morning — or maybe ever.

Seventy-two-year-old Thurston was hardly ill. Dressed in a pair of bib overalls and a tattered chambray shirt, he was down on his knees using a hand shovel to turn over the soil in the flower garden in back of the parsonage.

Since dawn, the temperature had warmed up into the forties, but the ground must have still been hard from yesterday's freeze.

As he entered the yard, Evan called out, "I've got news for you, Pastor. Spring isn't for a couple of months yet."

"Evan!" Thurston cried happily. He stood up, wiped his mud-caked hand on his pant leg, and extended it to Evan. The hand was big and meaty, and its grip could crush a rock. Thurston wasn't the only

African-American in St. Clair County, but his social status as a religious leader made him the most distinguished. First Baptist had a few black members. United Methodist had none.

Why is it always First Baptist? Is there a Second Baptist somewhere? Maybe that's where people of color used to go if they felt uncomfortable in the other place.

"I thought you'd be writing your sermon," Evan teased.

"Roses don't die during the winter, you know. Helps to open up the ground and let the roots breathe, let the meltwater trickle down."

"Sounds like something I've heard you speak on. Tending the garden."

"Oh, yes, a theme and its variations," Thurston chuckled. "And relating the seasons to recycling is a thing these days. You got any better ideas?"

"I'm not asking to sub for you," Evan assured him. "But how about one I like to kick around, 'God Is All That There Is?'"

"Okay," Thurston scratched his head. "God expresses in the flowers. But are you telling me the Holy Spirit is also in the rocks?"

"Why not?" Evan insisted. "If in the beginning there was nothing, how could the creation be separate from the Creator?"

Setting his trowel down, Thurston suggested, "Conversations with you are never short. Let's go inside."

THE PARSONAGE, an old clapboard place down the block from the sanctuary, was small, tidy, and well maintained. But the linens and the draperies might have been a hundred years old. Thurston was a widower and did most of his own cooking and cleaning. He insisted it wasn't necessary, but the board of deacons had hired a housekeeper to come in once a week. She didn't find much to do, and what she did he quibbled with. The older man suspected the real reason she was there was to confirm to the deacons he was still breathing.

Like Evan, Thurston was a faithful user of instant coffee. His brand was also Folger's. Evan asked for his usual, making it stronger with heaping spoonfuls. The wrinkle was that the pastor tolerated no sugar in his house. He preferred the substitute stuff in the blue packets. Evan doubled up on that too.

As they huddled and drank in Thurston's sitting room, they made quick work of the memorial service arrangements. The coming Saturday morning date didn't give them much time, but, as of old, feeding the multitude had to be a primary concern. Thurston said he'd reach out to the Loving Embrace committee, a woman's group that supported bereavement, mostly by setting up the reception and providing the food. There wouldn't be an abundance of flowers at this time of year, but Evan had arranged for Hill and Sons to ship some in. Edie had said not to overdo it.

Evan asked Thurston, "Did you counsel Bob recently?"

"No, I didn't," the pastor sighed. "Bob wasn't one to ask for help, as you know. Wasn't one to attend services much either. I'd see him around town now and then. I could tell something was bothering him."

"His Aunt Molly's will. And the eviction of the Emmetts from their farm."

"I've heard about that. They're not members here, but we're providing assistance. We can't pay their rent, but we'll help make it easier for them to make the move. Our community-service committee is helping them pack up, move their stuff someplace temporary. Mr. Zed donated storage space for however long until they get resettled."

"Josh and Linda are resigned to it, and it doesn't seem as though there's a way for any of us to stop it."

"Possessions and property? Not much in the scheme of things. Certainly no reason for Bob to play God like he did and leave a suffering wife."

Suffering? I think not. Or maybe she's in denial?

"Did you get to know Edie?" Evan asked him.

Thurston stopped him with an upraised hand. "Evan, I got no trouble telling you what I know about anything and everything. And that's not my way with everybody. In our ministry, we don't have a formal ritual of confession, but a pastor who can't keep secrets is not a good shepherd."

"I respect that, Marcus," Evan said, using the pastor's given name for the first time today. "But you have to admit these are exceptional circumstances."

"I knew Bob since he was a squirt, but you were closer to him. And seems to me like you're the only one who really cares why he did what he did. I respect that."

"So do we have an understanding?"

Thurston shook his head solemnly. "No, Evan. No, we don't. This confidential sharing has to work both ways."

"I don't see why I can't tell you what I know."

"I'm not talking about Bob. I'm talking about *you.*"

"Me? I don't have much to tell."

"Oh, I beg to differ, young man." Thurston glared at him. "A year ago you returned to this community. You came back because your mother had just made her transition and your father needed your help and support. Now he's gone, and why have you stayed?"

"You can't imagine I'd like it here?"

"No, I can't. After Harvard, maybe you didn't want a ministry of your own, but I'd expect you to at least be a professor somewhere. Theology, philosophy — how about *ethics?* There's a word we don't hear in business or in politics anymore. It's an opportunity for you to make a difference in this world."

"Frankly," Evan admitted, "I had a crisis of faith. Science and technology are changing our world so fast, and all the religions are stuck in the distant past. I wanted to find out if any of the new theories offered better explanations for questions like how humans came to be here and what we're supposed to do about it."

"Those answers are in scripture. Eternal truths don't change."

"You and I will disagree about this, but we've never had anything like eternal truths. We've got some ancient writers' versions of what they think God revealed to them. Writers who don't agree at all with each other, by the way. And over the centuries, those human interpretations of revealed truth *do* change. Do you mean to tell me that the vengeful deity of the Old Testament — 'an eye for an eye' — is the same as the loving God of 'turn the other cheek' and 'do unto others' in the New?"

"As humans, as mortals, as *sinners* who can't help themselves, we can only see through a glass darkly. Then *and* now."

"Do you think a doctrine forbidding contraception is correct? When overpopulation threatens our very life on the planet?"

"I counsel our couples to be responsible parents. What other churches say about it is not my concern."

"But what about condemning homosexuality? In an overpopulated world, from the viewpoint of the biology of a limited ecosystem, homosexuality, as long as it's not practiced by the entire population, might be a healthy adaptation for survival."

"But it's not Biblical."

"You and I both know the story of Onan has been bent way out of shape to justify an intolerant point of view. And in terms of both contraception and homosexuality, those doctrines were pushed by churches that cared only about maximizing the population of their own believers so that they would never again be dominated politically by pagan kings."

"So those two questions got you sidetracked? Made you give up your plans for the ministry?"

"Not at all! I just started with a couple of easy ones. What about stem cells? Fertility clinics? Artificial intelligence? Genetic engineering? Virtual reality?"

"We must hold to our faith as we're tossed on a sea of storms. Mental confusion is like the weather. It'll pass."

"What got me really perplexed is *time*. The more I got into astrophysics, the less sense I could make of anything you'd call reality."

"What do you mean by *time?* That our time in this life is so short?"

"What bothers me is that time shouldn't exist at all. If you study the math of relativity — Einstein's equations — you begin to realize, as his friend and colleague Kurt Gödel did, that time is nonessential to every physical process in the universe. Out in space, when a cloud of gas and dust gets big enough, it will reach critical mass, it will ignite, and — presto! — a star is born. It doesn't make a difference whether it takes a hundred-million years or a billion for that to happen. It's all about mass, gravity, and temperature. Time has nothing to do with it. Nothing in the universe depends on a clock, and all clocks will disagree anyway."

"Why is that upsetting? Does the notion of eternity bother you?"

"At the level of stars and galaxies, time doesn't exist. And eternity? There may be no such thing. The universe will expand forever or fall in upon itself. Either way, it and any kind of life or intelligence will cease to exist — someday."

"Perhaps Satan is misleading you. Covering your spiritual eyes with deceptive illusions."

"Oh, I've heard that argument. The fossil record is a hoax to make us doubt the Creation story. The evidence we have from telescopes of the vastness of the universe is a curtain of fakery to convince us we're not the center of God's creation and the only intelligent beings that ever existed anywhere." Then Evan added, "And, by the way, I don't believe in Satan. Evil is ignorance of the presence of God. Darkness has no power of its own. It's just the absence of light."

Thurston smiled and said, *"That's* a longer conversation! But let's stay on track. What is it about time that upsets you?"

"If time doesn't exist out there, why is it so important down here? In our little lives, there's no denying time governs everything. I don't see why, if time is nonessential, that we have to die."

"We don't die. Our souls live for eternity."

"I don't think the fossil record is a lie. But I suspect the concept of eternity might be."

"My son," Thurston sighed. "I can't pretend to comprehend all the implications of your advanced learning. And I can assure you, there is a dark night of the soul, and it is an agonizing test, a necessary part of your spiritual rebirth process." Then he added, "But what you have been describing is a crisis of logic, a confusion of reasoning. I grant you these issues are serious and perplexing. Perhaps beyond the ken of ordinary folk. But I don't believe for a minute any of this is why you chose to stay here with us in Southern Missouri."

Thurston can't be fooled. He knows, as a father would know, as a close friend might know, that the critical mass of any crucial human decision is reached, not when the weary brain gives up, but when the heart breaks.

Thurston asked softly, "All this aside, were you perhaps disappointed in love?"

Evan stared into his cup, then drained it and confided, "If I admit it, which I've told no one, could we promise to talk about it another time?"

Thurston laughed. "Time, is it? If time doesn't exist, I'll give you all I've got for free!"

Evan took a deep breath and smiled gratefully. He had dodged a bullet, for now.

I might have known Thurston would be the one to draw me out.

"So what about Bob and Edie?" Evan asked, grateful this wise man gave him permission to change the subject.

"I married them. Neither of them had much in the way of family left. She has an unmarried sister, Claudia Clark. Maid of honor. You could have been best man, but you were away at school. Nick Berner stood with Bob, and Nick's wife Louise came with him. Also Wiley Krause and his girlfriend Tamara. And the Emmetts with their two kids. That was it. Edie's church had been United Methodist back in the day, but they'd just hired a new assistant minister — Agatha Philpot — and for some reason she and Edie don't get along. Reverend Fortnum should have retired years ago."

"I don't quite know how to say this," Evan said, "but Edie and Bob didn't exactly carry on like newlyweds. But dealing with her now, she doesn't seem to be the kind of person Bob would be drawn to. What I'm trying to say is, I can't figure why they got together."

A sly smile appeared on Thurston's face. "A pastor isn't supposed to know these kinds of things unless they are shared with him in confidence. But, you know, it's a small town. I keep my ears open and my mouth shut."

"Except now," Evan insisted. "When Bob's friend needs to understand what isn't making sense."

"Bob's first wife Karen up and left him for nobody knows whom or what. Her leaving tore him up. I'd guess he blamed himself somehow." Thurston got up to get them some more boiling water for their coffee. "You're what, in your thirties now?"

"Thirty-six," Evan said.

"You quit school, when? That's a long time to be earning a degree."

"I was six years at Harvard Divinity. Then I did teach for a few years before I decided to apply for the physics track at MIT. That was five years ago."

Thurston sat back down and they busied themselves with getting the mixtures in their mugs just right. Thurston took a tentative sip, smiled with satisfaction, then went on: "With an empty nest, Bob was a lonely fellow. He got to playing hold 'em poker. He and Edie met in a casino in Branson. He played the sports book and she played the ponies. Besides those hobbies, the other thing they had in common was they liked to drink."

"Doesn't sound like much of a romance."

"It might have been all about companionship. She'd never been married. Maybe she'd given up on the idea. But I believe I know why she'd stayed single for so long."

"She told me she'd had a business career."

"Yes, she was an assistant manager at Bates Bank and Trust. Has a good head for the numbers, I believe."

"She'd have worked for Stu Shackleton."

Cue the sound of limp duck carcasses falling on the soggy ground.

"Yes. She did for years."

"If you're dropping a hint, it could explain a lot."

"Shackleton's married. His wife is an invalid. Alzheimer's. In assisted living, I believe."

"How do you know all this? From people unburdening themselves in counseling sessions? Secrets of the confessional?"

Thurston chuckled. "Now I have a confession to make. And I expect you to keep it in the same sacred trust to which I accord your private thoughts."

"Wow," Evan said. "You finally got a girlfriend?"

The pastor almost spit out his coffee. "Don't wish that on me! No, one of my vices is hold 'em poker. Strictly penny-ante, you understand. Twenty bucks is my limit. I was never at the table with Bob, but some of the fellow addicts I play with did. You get a few drinks in them, and those fellows gossip like blue-haired ladies."

"Marcus, you've been more than generous. Thank you. You've given me a lot to think about."

Thurston helped Evan on with his coat, as though he were a doting father sending his boy off to school. He gave his protégé a gentle pat on the back and teased, "You *would* have given *me* a lot to think about. That is, *if* you'd fessed up about your love life and *if* I understood a word you said about relativity."

As Evan stepped out on the porch, the pastor asked him, "See you in church tomorrow? It's been a while."

"I guess I owe you that," Evan said as he pulled on his ball cap.

"No," Thurston intoned in his best commanding bass. "You owe *yourself.*"

21

SATURDAY AFTERNOON
ARTHUR REDWINE FARMHOUSE

There would be a reckoning with Shackleton, Evan was sure of it. But he didn't want to confront the banker until he had as much information as he could get elsewhere, particularly about the will and the land-title complications. The person who might know the most, if he could express it coherently, would be Arthur Redwine.

As Edie had suggested, Evan pulled into a gas station off Route P to ask directions to Redwine's place. Evan didn't recall which brand the station had sold before, but a new sign read ZipGas. He suspected his boss had made another potentially profitable investment as a reseller of surplus fuel from the big operators. But the prices here were no bargain.

The kid who worked the station was seated behind a double pane of Plexiglas with a pass-through dip for exchanging payments and receipts. He was underage, much too young not to be in school. But it was the weekend, so he was probably filling in for somebody. He looked forlorn and freezing, dressed only in a sweatshirt hoodie with a long woolen scarf wrapped several times around his neck and a stocking cap pulled down over his ears. He said he didn't know of the Redwine place, but he punched the rural route address Evan gave him into his phone, and then he scrolled through the satellite view of Google Maps to zero in on the five ponds on the property. Evan could have done that himself, but he hadn't guessed that entering a postal route number would result in a hit on the geographic location. The kid held his phone up to the glass so Evan could see, but it was hard to read in the glare. Evan took out his own phone and traced the same search, with the same successful result. He grinned and tipped the kid five bucks, not something he'd normally do, but in recognition of a colleague. He wondered whether the boy was a relative of the Zeds, or even one of Zip's kids.

Learning the biz from the ground up.

The sun was out and the temperature had fallen. Turning off Route P onto a succession of back roads, Evan's Taurus mounted hills still coated with the dazzling white of yesterday's snowfall. In this part of the landscape, all the trees were old-growth deciduous — white and pin oak, sweetgum, silver maple, ash, and American elm. There was no ever-greenery. All the leaves from last season were under the snow. The dry, brown branches on the tree line reached up to the sky like supplicants:

We're not dead. Our roots grow deep. We will live again soon.

Redwine's old, whitewashed house sat atop the crest of those hills. The view of the surrounding countryside included the five finger-lake fish-ponds but no other houses. The ponds were small enough they'd ice up quickly during a freeze — ideal for skating parties. But Evan wondered if anyone besides the old man was allowed on the property these days. He guessed Redwine owned the land, maybe since the days of Jake's father. Another handshake deal? Evan remembered Edie had said something about the family's owning walnut groves over near Stockton.

Evan parked his car behind, of all things, a Model-T roadster that appeared to still have serviceable, inflated tires and a current Historic Vehicle license plate.

A stooped man in overalls with a bushy white beard, granny glasses, and a felt slouch hat was already out on the porch wondering who had the nerve to visit.

"You lost?" the fellow called out in a hoarse, high-pitched croak.

"Mr. Redwine!" Evan responded jovially. "I'm Preacher Evan Wycliff." And he climbed the four creaky wooden steps to the porch. The porch was strewn with rolls of fence wire, paint cans, and implements — all so rusted they hadn't been used in years. A broken glider swing was canted over. Perhaps, years ago, some visitor had sat on one end and broken it, the repair having been deferred indefinitely.

Evan wondered how Redwine got along, since Edie said the fellow typically refused to answer a phone.

"Is it true you don't have a phone?"

"'Course I do," Redwine huffed. "Just no sense turning it on most days."

He must have been in his nineties. He was frail, with parchment skin, and with his stoop, no doubt from advanced osteoporosis, he was fully a foot shorter than Evan.

Redwine squinted up at Evan and snapped, "I told you people I won't be writing any more checks until next quarter. Leave well enough alone."

"I'm sorry, sir. I don't know what you're talking about." Evan spoke slowly and politely.

"You're not from the Daughters of Calvary?"

"Nossir. I don't even know who they are."

"Well, I only give to them. So you're barking up the wrong tree in any case."

"I'm not here soliciting donations," Evan assured him. "May I call you Arthur?"

"Evan," the fellow pronounced, and touched the side of his own head, indicating his memory was still sharp. "*The Wycliffe Bible Commentary.* I own a copy."

"I didn't write it, but Wycliff really is my family name. We spell it without the *e* on the end. The book dates back to fourteenth-century England."

Perhaps not wanting to expose his limited grasp of history, Redwine snapped, "I never said you wrote it."

Evan smiled and suggested, "Perhaps you'd like to invite me in. I'm handling the arrangements for Bob Taggart's memorial service. You were aware he —?"

"Cursed thing." Redwine shook his head. "A fine boy, he was. Makes no sense." He studied Evan, then asked, "If you'll permit me?"

Evan had no idea what the man planned to do, but he said, "Okay."

"Lean down closer to me. And take off your cap."

Evan complied. The old man placed his palm on the top of Evan's head and then ran the flat of his thumb across the preacher's forehead.

Redwine nodded with approval, and Evan straightened up.

"Prominent frontal lobe," Redwine said sagaciously. "My son, you have a propensity for remembering names, dates, and events."

And that's when Evan remembered meeting Arthur Redwine twenty-six years ago. Evan and Bob were both ten, old enough to know better but too young to have had much experience making choices.

ONE SATURDAY MORNING when the boys were being particularly rambunctious at Bob's house, Aunt Molly suggested Bob's father run them over to her brother-in-law's place to go fishing. Lionel, who had come home just long enough for an early lunch, gulped down what was left of his sandwich and begged off. So Molly called Dickie

Emmett and asked him to do it. Dickie readily agreed, possibly because he wanted to stay on Molly's good side or because for whatever reason he wanted to suck up to Arthur or simply because he was bored. Molly said they could take Brownie, but her permission was unnecessary because the dog wasn't about to leave Bob's side.

Bob had two long bamboo poles with lines, hooks, and bobbers. They'd ask Uncle Dick to stop at the bait and tackle in town so they could buy a can of worms for a nickel. As they climbed in to sit beside Dickie in his old pickup, Molly handed them each a sack lunch and instructed them all to be back by sundown. Uncle Dick wanted Brownie to ride in the pickup bed, but Bob wouldn't have it and neither would the dog, who sat head-up and alert the whole way in the front seat, wedged on top of the boys. As Uncle Dick put the truck in gear, Molly warned them they should be respectful and not go wandering off, away from the pond. Arthur didn't have much patience with children, she said, but he stocked his ponds faithfully, and with patience they were sure to have good luck. She mentioned the mysterious fact that her brother-in-law was a phrenologist, a believer in the correlation of skull shapes with traits of intelligence. She also told them he didn't like dogs.

Redwine was a widower, an eccentric, and a recluse even then. At that time, his full beard was bushy and black. Wearing overalls, a soiled tee shirt, and no shoes, he stepped out on his porch just long enough to let them know in which of his five ponds the fish might be biting. He informed Dickie, "There will be no drinking or cussing or smoking in front of these boys." He looked down at Brownie, who looked as though she expected to be invited in. "And keep the dog with you." Uncle Dick almost always had a hand-rolled smoke in his mouth, but he didn't right then. His grin showed missing and tobacco-stained teeth as he said, "You bet."

And, sure enough, Arthur bent down to run his thumb across Evan's sweaty forehead, then pronounced the young man's "propensity for remembering names, dates, and events."

Bob giggled, "Naw, Uncle Arthur. This guy's a dumbass!"

Arthur snapped back, "Young man, if you can't say anything nice, don't say anything at all." He pointed them to the footpath that led to the pond stocked with catfish and smallmouth bass and retreated into the house.

As they stepped off the porch, Bob confided, "He says the same thing to everybody, you know. Don't let it go to your head, dumbass!"

Uncle Dick leaned against his truck long enough to roll another smoke. Then he wished them luck and promised to return to fetch them before sundown. Brownie stayed loyally with the boys.

Evan was squeamish about loading a wriggling earthworm onto his hook. Bob showed him how, explaining that these two- and three-inch-long ones were just the right length. You didn't want some big night crawler but a bite-sized little thing, so much better if it still squirmed when it was in the water. Both the taste of the worm and its motion could attract a fish. The little pond didn't have a rowboat or a dock, so the boys stood a few feet apart on the muddy bank and cast their lines in different directions. Bob chose to sink his near a rotted stump that protruded from the water. He informed Evan that such locations, including sunken barrels and tires, were notorious hangouts for fish, which were inclined to congregate there as they investigated all kinds of nooks and crannies looking for tasty morsels (of what, Bob didn't know).

Having imparted the extent of his wisdom on freshwater angling with live bait, Bob didn't say much more. Brownie plunked down at his side, basked in the sun, and took a snooze.

After a time, Evan broke the silence by asking, "Do you think a fish thinks about anything? Do you think it *can* think about anything?"

Bob shrugged. Other questions occurred to Evan, but he decided to keep quiet. Maybe silence was a necessary strategy for catching fish.

When they got tired of standing, they sat, muddying their jeans, then, keeping their lines in the water with their poles pointed at the bobbers, they reclined a bit higher on the bank in the soggy grass. There wasn't any shade from the hot sun. Neither had thought to bring a hat, and sunglasses were an unknown vanity at this point in their lives. Evan grew tired of squinting, but his anticipation at hooking his first fish unaided by an adult had him ignoring all discomforts.

Every now and then, Evan's line would twitch. "That's a nibble," Bob said. "Pull it out." Sensing the excitement, Brownie woke up and began barking excitedly. When Evan pulled his line out of the water, the hook was bare.

"Clever critters," Bob said. "But that's a good sign. You get a nibble, you'll get a bite. They're not touching mine." And he baited Evan's hook for him so they could get on with it without a fuss.

Moments after Evan recast his freshly baited line, there came a sharp downward tug on it as the bobber disappeared below the surface. Bob exclaimed, "That's a strike! Pull back — *hard!*" Evan leaned back, jerking his pole quickly upward, and the line stayed taut. The tug had set the hook in the fish's mouth.

Bob helped Evan pull his line in, hand over hand (their simple bamboo poles didn't have reels). And three feet down from where the bobber was set was a glistening, five-pound smallmouth bass. It was about two feet long and fat. Maybe a female full of eggs.

They hadn't thought to bring a net or a bag to hold their catch.

"Wow!" was all Bob could say, with profound respect. Brownie barked in a fit of ecstasy. Her master had performed a miracle, summoning life from the sea!

"What do we do with it?" Evan wondered as they watched the creature flopping and gasping in the mud.

"Well, Mister Dumbass," Bob grinned. "Don't you know how to clean a fish?"

"No," Evan announced remorsefully. "I don't. I never did. Did you?"

"I did," Bob said proudly, but then he frowned. "But I didn't remember to bring a knife. Did you?"

"Of course not," Evan said. "I wouldn't know how to use it, and, besides, who knew we'd catch anything?"

"*We* didn't catch it," Bob fumed. "*You* did. Beginner's luck!"

"Maybe I should run back to the house and get a knife."

Bob shook his head. "That guy is scary. My aunt says he has a temper. Let's don't go asking him to go looking for any knife."

"What do we do, then?"

"Why, I guess we throw it back," Bob said. He bent down and with a twisting, wrenching motion managed to pry the hook out of the fish's throat. "Times like this, you need a pair of wire cutters for the hook. That's so you can get it out without doing much damage to the fish. They heal, though. I've heard these old boys talk about they catch a big one, one that's been around a while, and there's some old hook grown into its mouth. From another time when it snapped the line and got away."

And he tossed the fish back in. The big *ker-plop* as it hit the water attested to the impressive heft of the catch. Brownie was startled and hardly understood why this miracle had to be undone.

Bob explained to Brownie, "We're going to let her swim back to her family."

As he watched the ripples subside, Evan said, "I guess we should have at least brought a camera."

Bob chuckled. "Nobody's gonna believe you now. That's for sure! Dumbass!"

"GETTING ON TOWARD TEATIME," Redwine said to Evan. "You hungry?"

"Sure," Evan said.

With so much time on his hands, perhaps the recluse has learned to cook?

They went inside. Redwine bade Evan sit at the kitchen table, which was covered with a red-checkered oilcloth. Its design was worn in places, but the tabletop appeared to be clean. There was a wood fire going in a potbelly stove. The floral wallpaper in the kitchen had the look of old parchment and must have been peeling for years. The room was toasty warm, even overheated. In the center of the table was a circular object about the size of an automobile tire, draped with a white cloth. Redwine put on water for tea, then set out two Melmac plates, which looked scratched but clean. He whisked the cloth away, revealing a cheese wheel. It was covered with greenish-white mold. Redwine cut out two pie-wedge-sized slices, set them on the plates, and then Evan watched with amazement as the old man trimmed the mold from both pieces of cheese and threw the trimmings in a garbage pail.

From a tin on the pantry counter, Redwine produced a loaf of store-bought rye bread. He placed one slice on each plate. With the addition of two crisp, green apples and steaming cups of Lipton tea (no sugar), their sumptuous repast was complete.

The cheese was Emmenthaler Swiss. Buttery sweet, perhaps the best Evan had ever tasted. The bread was only slightly stale. The tea was welcome because it was hot.

"So, Preacher," Redwine began. "Are you spreading the Gospel? Telling the good news?"

"I give guest sermons from time to time," Evan said. "I guess you'd say I talk about introspection and insight."

"Now you listen to me, young man," Redwine growled. "With that brain structure of yours, you could be too smart for your own good. A righteous preacher is not a philosopher. If he's worth spit, he's a *salesman*. The only message that counts is the one that brings lost souls to our Redeemer."

Evan finished his generous slice of cheese.

My next worry may be constipation.

Evan wanted to get on with it. "I hope you don't mind if I ask you some questions about your sister-in-law's property. You see, Bob was trying to sort through her probate issues when he, well, when he met his untimely end."

"Jake's farm? There you got one royal mess."

"Whatever it was must have worried Bob. I understand the date of the will was sometime in 1993. Why do you think Molly decided at that time she needed a will?"

"Our niece, Bob's mother Abigail, got cancer, lingered, and then died way too young. Molly pretty much raised Bob, his father being locked up in that drugstore at all hours."

"Makes sense," Evan said. "Molly was reminded of her own mortality, and she wanted to make sure Bob was taken care of."

"And then later in 'Ninety-three, of course, Brownie died."

"And then Bob had other dogs, each named Brownie."

"Yep," Redwine said. "All mutts, all brown." He sighed. "Molly left me out of her will, you know. Ancient history. She knew I had no use for that farm."

"One problem is, there seems to be no record of a deed, no evidence of title. Did Molly really own the place?"

"You need some history," Redwine said as he wiped his runny nose with his sleeve. "After I'm gone won't be anybody around here to remember. Best I tell you."

"I got some of the history from Angus Clapper. You might not know, I'm sorry to say, he's passed on."

"That horny little shit! Chasing after Molly? Wasn't even a lawyer anymore and dishing out advice like it was ice cream!" Then Redwine mumbled, "Sorry to hear."

"Clapper explained conflicting claims to the land. Civil War homesteaders and squatters, and before that, Indian tribes. The government should have straightened it all out, but they didn't."

"If the government don't care, and unless somebody wants to sell the property, what business is it of anybody else's? Molly intended to keep it in the family."

"How did you come to settle there in the first place?"

"The year was 1847. Believe it or not, I was not born yet. Truth can now be told, the Redwines were Rhinesbergers. Swiss-German. Folks around here didn't like newcomers much, particularly if they didn't speak English or spoke with some weird accent. For our part, we were Freethinkers — not Catholic — doubting Protestants, you might say. In the Swiss cantons, the Catholics were fighting the Protestants. In Austria and Prussia, other wars were starting like brushfires. Here we were pacifists and minding our own business, and now we're afraid our boys are going to get drafted into somebody's army. So we came here. Steerage on a steamer to Baltimore, then railroad to Kansas City. With as much furniture as we could pack into the crates. You could homestead in Missouri. Climate more or less like home. Some other Germans around, you didn't feel alone. Changed the name to Redwine. End of story."

"Angus Clapper told me that, when Molly was writing her will, he'd advised her to buy some title insurance and formalize the rental agreement with the Emmetts. For some reason I don't understand and he didn't explain, she wouldn't let him go through with it. Clapper called it the 'third complication,' but he never told me what the problem was."

"Molly kept saying there was a big sinkhole on the back forty. That thing would be sure to bring down the value of the property because maybe that land couldn't be made usable."

"Are sinkholes all that common around here?"

"Sure," Redwine said. "Depends where. You see a pond, it might have been a sinkhole. Where it's hilly. Not so much on the plains. You farm the flatland. You don't have to drill down very far into this black Missouri dirt to hit limestone. That's ancient ocean. Flat. Yeah, to the south you've got all those lakes, but those aren't sinkholes. The lake beds were gouged from the rock by glaciers at the end of the last Ice Age."

The old man went on, "When Molly told me about it — and you're right, that was 1993, the year she was getting all that crappy advice from Clapper about her will — I got curious. So I go hiking into the Emmett place from the south so as not to go near the farmhouse. I'm making my way toward the patch of land she says is unusable. And what do I see? Barbed-wire fencing for a long stretch. It had to be acres. I didn't pace it all around because I was caught up short. Signs every fifty feet along the fence-line read, 'U.S. Government Property — No Trespassing.' And then here come the barking German shepherds and the guys in uniform carrying automatic rifles. I say something lame like, 'Sorry, guys. I thought this was a shortcut to my friend's property.' They say, 'Sir, you can't be here.' I ask, 'What is this place?' They say, 'What the sign says, sir.' And I hurry out of there."

"Wow," Emmett breathed. "That's a complication all right. What do you think was in there? You don't put armed guards around a sinkhole. And what business is it of the government?"

As he was about to clear the plates, Redwine grew solemn. "Ever hear of Area Fifty-one? Could be like that. Those boys must be flying saucers in and out of there."

Evan tried mightily to keep a thoughtful, receptive expression on his face. "Have you been over there since then? Is this sinkhole, or whatever it is, still there?"

Redwine cackled. "Was I fool enough to go back? But you go right ahead, if you're itching to. Send me a postcard from Mars!"

BEFORE EVAN LEFT the Redwine place, he remembered one more thing about his boyhood visits there. Bob and he had disobeyed instructions, strayed from the pond, and explored the barn. There, to their amazement, was a Model A Ford touring car. It had no wheels, perched up on blocks. And whatever color it might once have been (undoubtedly black), it was now totally covered in a fine patina of red-brown rust.

When they returned to Bob's house that evening, the boys asked Molly about the car. "You see," she said, drawing a breath for a story she wasn't willing to tell at length, "when Mr. Ford came out with those cars during the first war, Arthur thought they were dandy enough, but he worried this horseless-buggy fad wouldn't last. So he bought a fine Model A touring car, and he looked forward to driving it into town on Saturdays with him dressed up for a rich night out and his wife Sedalia in some frilly dress. He bought the Model T, a cheaper model with the same engine, for spare parts. Then Sedalia died of consumption before she was forty, and he decided he'd drive the Model T on errands. He put the Model A in storage, and he's never drove it since. And, year after year, he keeps donating money to churches in Sedalia's name."

22

SATURDAY NIGHT
EVAN'S TRAILER

A s Evan settled into his trailer for the night, he wondered whether, despite the pastor's assurances, Thurston would invite him to speak tomorrow.

If I were a stronger person, or if I knew more, I'd talk about depression and suicide and the power of prayer.

Sheriff Otis seemed satisfied the case of Bob's suicide was a closed book. And as far as Griggs was concerned, Bob was just another wacko who owned a gun. Fortunately for the rest of the community, Evan's friend hadn't decided to take out his anger or disappointment or frustration or lunatic fantasies on any other living being but himself.

Evan knew personally some of the people who'd been gunned down last year as they worshipped in their little church less than a hundred miles away, just over the state border in the hills of Arkansas. The murderer was a war veteran who'd been diagnosed and treated for post-traumatic stress. But not all bad actors in the plethora of such cases around the country were distraught servicemen. Some were students who judged what their peers might think of as temporary setbacks to be irremediable life reversals. Others felt betrayed by a love that hadn't been sufficiently reciprocated. Some were acting to rid the world of a

particular race or religion. And, yes, not a few of the murderers —
who more often than not ended up dead before they could be appre-
hended — wanted the fame that publicity about their sensational
crime would bring them, even if posthumously. You'd think, no matter
what their fate in any afterlife, their souls would be beyond caring.

One of the recurring themes of Evan's sermons was the age-old question, reformulated years ago by Rev. Robert Schuller, "Why do bad
things happen to good people?" Evan found only one sensible conclusion he could draw from such senseless acts of violence:

All mass murders are hate crimes.

Not in the sense that racial or religious bigotry drives them. Rather, it's
because, in all cases, the perpetrator hates *himself* most of all. When
the last glimmer of God's light goes out in any human soul, the feelings of isolation, the profound emptiness, the abject darkness — those
states of nonbeing must be terrifying. In what was left of Evan's
notions of religion, that sense of abandonment was what Jesus had
described as Hell, using specific imagery of agonizing fire and brim-
stone that his audience could understand. But if you don't have a body,
you can't feel fire.

*It's not punishment. It's judgment. And it's self-imposed. Bob's low opinion
of himself was premature.*

Simple as it might sound, Evan preached that the first commandment
is to learn to love yourself. In loving yourself, you find God, who
dwells in everyone "closer than your neck vein," as some translations of
the scriptures say.

But Evan was fairly sure, even if his friend was stressed beyond
endurance, that Bob Taggart did not hate himself.

For the first time in Preacher Wycliff's life, when he'd forced himself to
recall what he felt looking down at what was left of his friend lying on
the frozen ground, the horror was no longer abstract. It wasn't in a
headline or an email or a social-media post. It was here and now, as he
relived feeling the flush in his own ruddy, breathing face as he gazed
into his friend's pale, slack face, getting colder by the minute. What

Evan was confronting was not just the absence of good but the palpable presence of evil, the sucking void of godless existence.

So what held Evan back from pursuing his investigations was not fear of physical harm from anyone outside himself. No, he was strongly tempted to accede to the sheriff's lack of curiosity because he feared the undoing of what little faith he had left. Evan's was a crisis of belief. Getting to the heart of Bob's motivations could lead his own soul into that dark corner where there was no light and no hope.

Evan didn't want to go anywhere near there. Not again.

Even so, Evan wanted to help himself understand.

I need to not only get on with my own life but also to shake the feeling I'm a fraud.

What did the preacher really believe — and not just preach? What did Bob's nonsensical act mean in the scheme of things?

If I can't find a reason, I'll have to decline the next invitation to preach, and many more after that.

23

SUNDAY MORNING
FIRST BAPTIST CHURCH

The First Baptist Church of Appleton City is a narrow, block-long structure, distinctive for its austere plainness and lack of ornamentation. There's no steeple — just a large, white cross set into the modern façade, the design embedded in the floor-to-ceiling glass panes around the entry. On this Sunday morning, the crisp and clear weather from the previous day had carried over. Perhaps because the roads were clear, or perhaps because the Loving Embrace ladies were serving warming coffee, cucumber and egg-salad sandwiches, and home-baked cookies afterward, the attendance was better than usual. Evan had decided to put in an appearance, not so much to soothe his dark night of the soul but as a way of placating Thurston. Evan did not expect to be asked to speak. Besides, he hadn't polished any of his stock messages, and he was in no mood to wing it.

The congregation stood to sing the opening hymn "What a Friend We Have in Jesus," followed by the choir's rendition of "Amazing Grace." Then a deaconess took the pulpit to read the week's announcements. Among these, she gave the details of the memorial service for Robert N. Taggart, a cherished member of the church, to take place at ten this Saturday morning in the sanctuary, followed by a reception in the fellowship hall. She did not add personal comments to the written announcement, nor did she make sure to state whether the service would be for friends and family or anyone who wished to honor Bob's memory. The notice included no mention of the cause of death, other than the adjective *untimely*.

There was no apparent reaction among the congregation. By this time, everyone knew what had happened to Bob. The Catholics say suicide is a mortal sin. The Baptists just refuse to talk about it.

Edie Taggart was not seated in the congregation, which probably came as a surprise to nobody. Zip Zed was there, but without his family, sitting by himself at the end of a pew in the back, ready to get up early and dash out the door. By force of habit, Evan had taken a seat on the aisle in the front row.

Reverend Thurston stepped up to the pulpit to give his welcoming remarks. Then came the moment Evan had been promised would not happen.

"We have with us this morning one of our longtime members, Preacher Evan Wycliff, who has returned to the fold after extensive studies at Harvard Divinity School and laboring mightily in the field. I'd hoped Evan would do us the honor of delivering the message this morning. But I do understand he has had his capable hands full with arrangements on behalf of our dear Bob Taggart's widow Edith. Be sure to remember her in your prayers this week, and I encourage you all to attend the memorial service for Bob on Saturday. I know Evan will have some insightful and inspiring words for us then."

An inspirational reading from scripture, setting a theme for today's sermon, would usually come next. As Thurston adjusted his reading glasses, he raised a bushy eyebrow and pursed his lips. He'd had a new thought. Or maybe he'd planned it all along, and he was just a good actor. Glancing up, he said jovially, "You know, at my advanced age, I'm aiming to slow down. Work in my garden. As you all know, we don't have an assistant minister just now — someone ready to step into my shoes?" He looked squarely at where Evan was seated in the pews. "My personal preference would be for the brilliant Preacher Wycliff to pull on his work boots and step up!" He shot Evan his dazzling smile, and a ripple of polite laughter went through the congregation. "With that tantalizing prospect in mind, I'd like to invite Preacher now to at least share a few words as a foretaste of glory divine!"

As Evan reluctantly stood and came forward, Thurston raised a beckoning hand and added, "I do believe he has some penetrating thoughts on the nature of *time.*"

Thurston yielded the pulpit to Evan and took his chair on the dais behind it. Evan smiled weakly and surveyed the congregation. Some were in their work clothes, but most had taken care to don their Sunday best. Evan didn't own a suit, which he realized now might be a hindrance to any career goals as a minister. Although he no longer had any such goals. He wore his only sports coat, a Harris tweed that was showing wear at the cuffs and elbows. He'd selected the more conservative of his two ties, a sincere-blue one, and at least he had a freshly laundered white shirt he'd taken this morning from its dry-cleaners box. (He had the same scheme for dress shirts as he used for underwear — three of each: One to wear, one to be laundered, and the other freshly done on the shelf.)

"Reverend Thurston, the honor is mine to be able to share some thoughts with you all this morning. You now know, and we've made the announcement about his memorial, that my friend Bob has passed on. As you may have heard, he took his own life. Why he chose to do this, I doubt if any of us will ever know."

They might as well know how he died. Let's be honest, at least here.

Evan continued, "Some of you may have also known a dear fellow, a recent acquaintance of mine, the retired lawyer Angus Clapper. I visited him yesterday at John Knox Village up in Lee's Summit. I'm sad to say Angus made his transition last evening, dying peacefully of natural causes. He'd lived a full and rich ninety-seven years."

Evan paused, expecting a stirring among them. There was none. Maybe nobody was old enough to remember when Clapper was active in this community.

"I'm a man of faith, and I believe in God's grace and the promise of a joyful hereafter. But I'm also human, and any death — particularly when it's someone I hold dear — disturbs me. Unsettles me. Makes me question what it's now like for those souls. None of us can know for sure, because it's not for us to know while we're here. The Bible talks about streets of gold, but I really doubt that God's heavenly children have any use for gold. Or streets. Those are images, used to describe something so grand and glorious, something far beyond the understanding of a limited human mind."

No way I'm going to make them understand why Einstein's math ignores time. They have smartphones and watches. They catch the evening news on TV right at six. They set their alarms and see the sun rise and set. They watch as people die, and they count the years.

"I chatted with Reverend Thurston recently about the nature of time. What I can say for sure, is, for Bob and for Angus, their earthly time is at an end. For them, time has stopped. The choir blessed us with the hymn "Amazing Grace," and today I heard something new in its familiar lyrics:

> *When we've been there ten thousand years,*
> *bright shining as the sun,*
> *we've no less days to sing God's praise*
> *than when we'd first begun.*

"Here's an image used to describe eternity. An image to help our child-like minds grasp the incomprehensible. *Eternity.* But one thing I'm almost sure of, eternity is *not* just a long, long time. Time has a stopping point, as it did for my departed friends. Eternity is *timelessness* — *no* time.

"You see, in a state of timelessness, where Bob and Angus must be now, there is no action. If you perform an action, if you drive down the street or walk across a room, you can measure the time it takes with a stopwatch. But if there's no time, nothing moves. Now, there is *joy.* I'm sure of that. But no soul in heaven, no angel, no spiritual entity can take *any* action. An angel can't so much as pick up a teacup.

They'd have to incarnate, take human form, to be in time, to take action, to move anything on this earthly plane.

"Why is this idea of timelessness important? And why is it important to us, who still have time left on this planet? Because we are the *only ones* who can take action here. If God needs a teacup moved or a field planted, some human has to be inspired to do it. We are God's hands. We do God's work. And if we don't do it — before time stops for us — it won't get done."

As before, no visible reaction, no astonished gasp, passed through the congregation. But there was a hush. Kids stopped fidgeting as their parents sat still, not necessarily because they understood Evan's words, but because, like worshipful dogs attuned to the moods of their guardians, they sensed their folks had grown serious.

Evan was frozen in place. His remarks were much briefer than a full-length sermon, but he'd said all he had to say, all he could say.

Thurston rose to place a fatherly hand on Evan's shoulder. "Thank you, Preacher Wycliff. You've given us a lot to think about."

Thurston gave a sermon on patience. A couple of people dozed off.

ZIP CORNERED Evan at the reception and drew him aside.

"I know you've got a lot on your plate, but you've still got a job."

"You know, Zip, if slacking off in my work will bring you to church, I should make it a habit."

"You spoke to Clapper?"

"Yes, a few hours before he breathed his last."

What does Zip care about Clapper? Did he even know him?

It seemed odd to Evan that Zip should make this furtive appearance for the simple reason of getting him back on task encouraging nice people to make good on their car loans. Evan prodded him, "I thought you were worried about your past-due customers."

"Briana Caspar. That's a tricked-out Mustang. Mag wheels, candy-orange metallic paint, the whole disaster. Not a car I wanted back, no matter how well she'd maintained it. I mean, who around here buys those? Do you know where she is?"

"Yeah," Evan said. "Lives over near the Army base. She's a veteran. Undergoing some kind of counseling at the VA center. That's how I found her."

"PTSD or some shit? Maybe I don't want to hear. Don't make me feel bad for chasing her."

"I didn't find her through health records. These days that's next to impossible unless you're some Russian hacker. No, she rolled through a stop sign near the VA center, and she got a ticket. Some police records aren't so hard to get."

"So you'll have a talk with her tonight?"

"It's Sunday, Zip. Maybe she's going to prayer meeting. It won't seem so tacky if I drop by in the morning. Maybe I'll offer to buy her breakfast — on *my* dime."

Here came Zip's sly grin. "I have no clue what she looks like. Like I said, I wasn't the one sold her the car."

"I didn't mean it that way. I'm not looking for a date. Just a decent breakfast somewhere besides the C'mon for a change. Maybe we'll go to Denny's and tell them it's her birthday."

"Call me the minute you're done," Zip said seriously.

"Zip, what's this really about?"

"Helluva thing, Clapper expiring like that. Keep this up, you'll get a reputation. Angel of Death."

"Not the least bit funny, but I know you'll keep trying."

"You also had a talk with Arthur Redwine. Congrats on putting up with that loon."

"He doesn't do phone. How'd you know I was there?"

"You asked my kid for directions."

"ZipGas." Evan congratulated himself on his powers of deduction. "What's the story there?"

"Now *you're* changing the subject." Zip protested.

"I've been trying to figure out what there was in Molly's will to get Bob so upset. According to Clapper, she didn't have clear title to the Emmett farm. And according to Redwine, there's a huge sinkhole in back of the place that'll drag down the appraisal value. Then the Army is claiming it's been federal land all along."

"A sinkhole, huh?" Zip wasn't much of liar.

He must know it's not a sinkhole.

Evan told him, "I don't know what's going on out there these days, but back when Molly was fretting through the legal details with Clapper, Arthur went over to have a look. Claimed it was fenced off as government property with armed guards."

Zip looked nervous and thoughtful all at once. "You know, you know? I'm thinking about that Mustang now. Now it's *three* payments? That's looking like she won't be the type to step up, even if we make her a good deal."

"So what do you want me to do?"

"Forget about her. You got that address? I'll get the repo paperwork started."

"I don't have an exact address yet. I have a six-block area. I figured I'd drive around, spot the car, stake it out." Then he added, "You sure about this? Even if you start the repo, I could still go over there and have a chat. Especially if you don't want that car. If I can find a way for her to keep it, everybody wins."

Zip shrugged. "Next month my gas-pump jockey turns sixteen. He'll need a car." He popped a chocolate-chip cookie in his mouth and said as he chewed, "Don't approach her. Text me that address when you get it."

And the kid will need a trust fund to underwrite his speeding tickets.

A FEW MINUTES later at the reception, Evan was about to score some cookies for himself, when a fellow he didn't know approached him.

"Preacher, might we have a word?"

Evan now recognized the fellow as the church sexton. Evan didn't know the fellow's name. A quiet man, he always sat in the last row in a seat close to the door, just where Zip would be if he decided to duck out quickly. This man was old, frail, and African-American. He was darker-skinned than Otis. He was dressed in a well-worn suit of uncertain but bygone vintage, with a collarless shirt buttoned to the top. The guy had the wizened look of a freed slave who'd survived the Civil War, but here he was living and breathing in the twenty-first century.

Evan suggested they step into Reverend Thurston's office. Evan closed the door behind them, and they sat in guest chairs around the coffee table.

"My name is Fred Birchard. But they call me Birch, like the tree."

"Birch, glad to know you. How can I help?" Evan asked.

"Well, sir. I work as a janitor at the Myerson Clinic. My sexton work here at the church is only part-time."

"You're a maintenance engineer."

"Call me what you want, but I sweep floors and clean toilets."

"What kind of place is it?"

"Like a hospital, but private. Drug rehab. Alcohol. People come in, maybe their families bring them. Some in the ambulance. All strung out."

"Does it bother you being there?"

"I don't mind the work. Not at all. I've been doing it a long time."

"But you must see a lot of pain. People suffering."

"Withdrawal. People screaming. Seeing things. Demons, I guess. Sounds something awful."

"You can't help but feel for them."

"It's like you said in your message. We must all do whatever we're put here to do, or it doesn't get done. I feel I'm supposed to be there, do what I do, but I'm no doctor. How do I know I'm using the time I have left the way God wants? What more can I do?"

"I'm going to guess you're already praying for those people."

He nodded. "Every one of them. Every day. I don't do it out loud. It's not that kind of place. Some people might take it wrong. And I don't speak to the screamers, but maybe I should."

Evan told him, "I haven't lived as long as you have, Birch, but over the years, I've noticed something. I notice it particularly when I spend some time in a place, more than a few days. It could be a hospital or a school or a business or a church — someplace a group of people live or work together, day in, day out. In the group, usually not right away, but eventually, I notice a person. One person. Someone who is quiet. Often, unusually quiet. In the background, hardly noticed."

Birch chuckled. "That's me."

"I often think that person must be an angel. Someone who is there to anchor the consciousness of the group. To cherish them, support them, sustain them. Not in action, but in thought." Evan looked Birch in the eye and thought he saw a twinkle. "Maybe you're that person."

Birch looked embarrassed. "I suppose I could be. I never thought of it that way."

"If that's so," Evan told him. "It may not be important what you do. You may be sweeping floors or painting walls. Or just sitting in a corner, if that wouldn't get you fired. It's important what you *know*, what you hold in your heart to be true. That the eternal, loving presence of God abides there and can never leave, even when other people refuse to see it or feel it."

Birch smiled and nodded his appreciation, as though Evan had poured holy oil on his head.

Evan said a brief prayer with him, and Birch left in silence.

Oh, for a planet full of humans like Birch!

EVAN DIDN'T WAIT for the reception to finish. Thurston was still exchanging greetings and giving blessings at the door.

"Thanks for the use of the hall, Reverend," he quipped as he shook his mentor's hand on the way out.

The older man smiled broadly. "I know less is more, but when we do this again soon, stretch out the *timing,* and don't give me a chance to talk."

24

SUNDAY AFTERNOON

ON THE ROAD TO THE ARMY BASE

Evan climbed into his Taurus and checked the route to Fort Francis Blair on his phone.

He glanced in his rearview mirror and was not too surprised to see Naomi sitting in the backseat.

"Sorry, she said. "I couldn't help noticing you need some more coaching."

I should have known she'd be back. A woman having the last word. I admit, I need her now.

Evan posed this to her: "Zip told me at one time he and Shackleton had wanted the same piece of land."

She smirked, "Let me guess. Was it by any chance the Emmett farm?"

"I'm thinking Zip's visit here was no coincidence, and he has no interest in that Mustang. He knows Briana Caspar is ex-military and near the top of my to-do list for him."

"And his boy told him you'd gone out to see Redwine."

"Which confirms to him I'm digging deeper into the issues surrounding Molly's will and her rights to the Emmett farm."

"Hmm," she said. "Sometimes it takes you so long to connect the dots. Do you suppose Zip's warning you off talking to Briana has something to do with what you guys are calling the *third complication?*"

"I'm betting it's at the root of Clapper's theory. Fort Francis Blair is a big military presence in the area, and due to her proximity to the base, there's a good chance Briana was stationed there at some time or other."

"This third thing, whatever it is. Why do you think it's such a problem?"

"It's something about that sinkhole," Evan said. "It has to be the basis for the government's claim to ownership. And it must be the issue Bob felt he couldn't cope with."

"You need to do better than that," she said. "When you didn't have your nose in some textbook, weren't you always reading some trashy mystery novel?"

"Travis McGee," he admitted.

"A sexist pig!" she fumed. "More macho than James Bond. But it was the Hugh Hefner era. Not to be forgiven, but to be understood. Go on."

"All those titles with a color in them — *The Dreadful Lemon Sky, The Long Lavender Look, Cinnamon Skin, The Deep-Blue Goodbye* —"

She stopped him so he wouldn't rattle on with the entire list, which, of course, he could easily recite. "Who were the bad guys in these disgusting stories?"

"Greedy rich men. Florida real-estate developers. Land grabbers."

She emphasized, "Land grabbers," and paused. "What do we have at stake here?"

"Farmland."

"What's it worth?"

"It's a smallish farm. Not a lot in the scheme of things — not these days and not with these corporate-owned commodities markets. Maybe even less profitable to own than to sell."

"So this third complication. If it's a toxic site, wouldn't that make the land worth even less? A lot less?"

"I suppose."

"But assuming your suspicions are correct — Edie, Shackleton, and Zip, and who knows who else, might be falling all over each other to grab it."

"So whatever is in that sinkhole must have value. And no matter who gets the place, Josh Emmett is in the way."

"Mineral rights?"

"I doubt it. In this state as in most places, when you buy land, you don't own whatever is underneath it. The big exploiters hold options on anywhere there might be anything underground."

"Maybe the government doesn't want it anymore, but they don't want anyone else to have it."

"I don't see how that could make the place a lot more valuable. You grant the government an easement or a lease or whatever, and you get on with life. It's not like you can negotiate with them, especially if they're already there and have a prior claim."

"So who might know about this?"

"Briana Caspar?"

"You'd better find her as soon as possible," Naomi warned, "before Zip starts pestering you for her address."

"You know," Evan said. "Zip might be greedy, he might be a sharp businessman and a land speculator, but he's not a bad guy."

But that was all she had to say on the subject.

25

SUNDAY AFTERNOON

WITH LT. BRIANA CASPAR

E van's not stopping to grab a sandwich before he hit the highway was powerful testimony to his sense of urgency.

The outside temperature was still in the forties with partly cloudy skies and not much of a wind. Spotting the metallic-orange Mustang with the fancy wheels was all too easy. Even though Evan hoped Briana had better things to do, he found her in her carport, bundled up against the cold, hosing the salt off the sides of her muscle car.

He stopped his Taurus in front of the Mustang. Because the carport had a rear wall, Evan's maneuver effectively blocked Briana from making a hasty exit.

As he got out, he called to her, "Would you be Briana?"

She recognized him right away. "Why, you're the preacher!"

"Yes," he admitted, surprised, as he touched the bill of his ball cap. "But my day job is I work for Zed Motors."

She didn't panic. She shut off the hose and actually laughed. "How do you come to be doing Satan's work on a Sunday?"

"Mr. Zed is hardly Satan, Ms. Caspar. Just a businessman who wants to keep his customers, and keep them happy."

"That's Lieutenant Caspar, to him," she said. "And Briana to you."

"So, do you want to keep this car?"

"Frankly, I'd rather sell it. Not my type of ride at all."

"Then why'd you buy it?"

"Pretty as it is, I didn't. My boyfriend Ellroy bought it. He gets me to co-sign, then he declares bankruptcy and up and split with some mulatto chick from KC. I had his car keys hid, but he split anyway. She had some trashmobile and whisked him outta here. *And* extensions? No way her hair could be that blond and that straight. I bet those boobs are fake too. Like softballs, you know? How'd you find me? The apartment lease is in Ellroy's name."

"Your driver's license is still in the system and linked to the car plates. You got a ticket over by the hospital, which put you in the vicinity. If you want to go hiding from people, you really should turn off the GPS on your phone and don't go doing meetup searches on your Facebook friends."

"Well, I guess welcome to the twenty-first century," she sighed.

"Look," Evan said in his best aw-shucks manner. "I really want to find a way to let you keep this car. You must've heard me preach somewhere?"

"Bethany Baptist in Stockton," she nodded. "God is all that there is. I remember. We'll make an exception for Ellroy and his phony blonde." And she laughed.

No slacker boyfriend is going to unnerve this soldier.

"Then you know I'm a straight shooter," Evan assured her.

"O-kay," she agreed cautiously.

"I haven't had lunch yet, and I was thinking of finding a Denny's so we could have a sit-down and a chat." Then he took his chance. "And I'll buy, if you're willing to answer a few questions about your military service. Just curious for a friend. Nothing to do with your loan."

"Is this, like, a date?" She grinned, revealing a pair of deep-set dimples.

"It's a business transaction. I expect, a *friendly* business transaction."

"You got a deal," she said meekly. "Or I guess the start of what *could* be a deal. Just one condition?"

"Name it."

"Let's make it Applebee's."

"Done. We'll take your car, and if you don't mind, I'll drive."

She gave him the keys. He pulled his Taurus forward, then got in the Mustang and drove it out of the carport. He got back in his Taurus and parked it in her spot. He drove her car for the practical reason to find out how well it had been maintained. Doing so would also prevent its mysterious disappearance when they returned to the carport.

"What did you do in the service?" Evan asked her after they'd ordered.

"Air traffic controller. They have to retire you at thirty-five, or else your frazzled nerves will make you go screaming into the night."

"You served at Francis Blair?"

"First at a logistics base in Kabul. Then here, yes. Like it was supposed to be easier."

"And you were injured? PTSD?" She didn't have any apparent wounds.

"What makes you think that?"

"Your traffic violation was over near the VA center. After I got that location, I saw you went there twice a week. Sick friend?"

"No, psychiatric counseling. During my tour, I was raped. Twice."

"How awful for you. By the enemy?"

She laughed. "Well, he was after he did it. And got away with it."

"I'm sorry," Evan said. "I really didn't need to know, and I shouldn't have asked."

"Well, with those super-snooper skills of yours, I figured you knew already."

She was plus-sized and round-faced. She was having the fruit plate with yogurt and granola. Evan was chowing down on biscuits and gravy with a side of pork sausage. She had tea with lemon. He sipped his usual syrupy coffee with four packets of sugar.

Having taken the edge off his appetite, he swallowed so as not to speak with his mouth full, and asked her, "So. Are there any Army toxic cleanup sites around here?"

"Wow," she said. "This is what you want to know about? You working for Greenpeace or some shit?"

"A friend is having some problems with selling his farm."

"If they ever close Francis Blair and want to repurpose the place, of course there'd be cleanup issues. You know, fueling stations and such."

"No, I'm not talking about *on* the base. There used to be some kind of installation on my friend's farm over in western St. Clair County. Maybe as much as forty acres? Right in the middle of private land, but the Army has it fenced off and is telling everyone it's a sinkhole."

"I don't know this for sure. But back in the day, and considering where you say it was, maybe an abandoned missile site? Nike Ajax, then the Nike Hercules. Antiaircraft, antimissile missile. The first technology to hit a bullet with a bullet. And from what I hear, it was damn good. There was a ring of those sites around Kansas City and also around St.

Louis. But they decommissioned the program and closed them all in the seventies."

"Do you know whether there were Nike sites around here at one time?"

"Nope. But I can take a scientific wild-assed guess. Francis Blair is a training base. Maybe the site you're talking about was just one pad, and maybe not for the big show. For training."

"My friend's old uncle said there was still a military presence on the place in 1993. But from what you say, the site would have been long since abandoned even then."

"The active programs were decommissioned, yes, which means the sites aren't operational and there's no more funding. But the place would be a hazmat problem until somebody paid millions of bucks to clean it up. Here you'd be talking about residues of rocket fuel and lubricants. And radioactive contamination? I dunno. Maybe no nukes if it was for training."

"That's what they had Superfund sites for," Evan said. "I read that the old Lockheed Skunk Works out there in L.A. is now a shopping mall."

"Yeah, and the list of Congressional Superfund sites was public. But if this site didn't get on the list — especially if they officially denied its existence — maybe its cleanup was never funded. Those political hacks in DC these days don't seem to want to go doling out taxpayer dollars for environmental cleanup. For any reason."

"In all this time — fifty years since the program was closed — you'd think somehow they'd get it taken care of. I've looked at the online satellite maps of the area," Evan said. "There's nothing at that location. Just grass."

Briana smiled, sipped her tea, and smacked her lips. "I bet if you zoom in on those pixels, you'll see a pattern that is *very* regular."

"You mean, like the photo was patched?"

"Like they want you to think it's polo grounds or a bowling green? Some places, like where you know there's something, they might just put a black patch over it. But if they did that here, they'd be telling you some of what you want to know — that something's down there they don't want you to see."

Briana thanked Evan for lunch, and he assured her she'd given him valuable information. They chatted for a while longer. Briana told him she had a four-year-old son in preschool. She had a part-time job on the customer-support desk at Best Buy, and she was looking around for something more permanent. But if she wanted to keep up her therapy sessions, she might have to take a night shift. She'd like something in aerospace, but in that case, she'd probably have to move to St. Louis or KC. Her mother was local, in poor health, so she'd like to stay around. And, yes, sad to say, she'd been having trouble making ends meet.

"Do you want dessert?" Evan asked her.

"Preacher Wycliff!" she scolded.

"Evan."

"Okay, Evan. I just had the fruit plate with yogurt. What do *you* think?"

"All right," he said with mock seriousness. "Next question, we might as well do some business. Do you want to keep your car?"

"I need wheels, sure enough," she said. "But I'm not in love with that car. And, besides, it reminds me of Stinko."

"You'd like something more practical? With lower payments?"

"It would be an answer to prayer." She had the puzzled look of a contestant on a quiz show. What was behind the door she'd just won?

"Let's go back to get my car," Evan said. "I'll have a think on the way. I might have a solution."

Evan drove Briana back to her carport. They sat in her Mustang and agreed to his workout plan. He had a draft used-car sales contract on his laptop. He filled in the blanks with what he thought were reasonable numbers, emailed it to her phone, and she replied with an electronic signature. She got her title for the sports car out of its glove compartment and signed it over to Zed Motors. Evan gave her the keys to his Taurus and transferred his evidentiary cargo, including Bob's empty gun, into the trunk of the Mustang. Evan had offered her a test drive in the sedan to make sure she knew what she was getting. She'd said no, she was running late, and for sure he'd hear from her if there was a problem. He verified her contact information, which he double-checked against the contract header, bid her a sweet goodbye, and drove off in the Mustang.

The Taurus was carried on Zed's books as a loaner. Evan credited Briana with the market value of her Mustang, minus a deep discount including the loan balance and her missed payments. He ignored the jacked interest penalties. Then he credited the net amount to her purchase of the Taurus. She actually came out ahead. Zip Zed would have to mail her a check for $1,249.50.

So, let his kid have the Mustang. Worst case, if Zip is pissed, he'll loan me some clunker.

Evan was elated over the win-win deal he'd engineered with Briana. If only his job always worked out that way.

On the cushy drive home in the performance car, his elation built to excitement.

Zip said he and Shackleton once wanted the same piece of land.

The ducks at his feet were resurrected! They flopped about, got on their feet, started quacking madly, and then began to line up like good soldiers.

I'm getting my ducks in a row!

As he'd promised, he phoned Zip, ostensibly to give him Briana's current contact information. But then he was quick to add the details of his swap.

"Are you fucking *nuts?*" Zip screamed.

"Take a breath, Zip," Evan said soothingly. "Do the math."

After a long pause, Zip admitted, "Actually, financially, it works. How'd you convince her to take that piece of shit in trade?"

"She's a practical type. The muscle car was her ex-boyfriend's, and all she wants is reliable transportation."

Then Zip said in a low voice, "You know I told you not to see her. I said I'd handle it."

Evan stayed cheery. "I felt like taking a drive after church, and I had a hunch I could do a deal. You just agreed it's a win-win."

Zip feigned a lighter mood and asked, "Did you guys talk about anything else?"

"What do you mean? Like, does she need a boyfriend?"

"Evan," Zip said with a sudden edge. "I think you know what I mean."

"Not sure I do, boss. You know these military types. They're trained to tell you only what you need to know."

Evan had drawn a line in the sand, and Zip chose not to cross it.

"By the way," Evan asked, "have you got something else I can drive?"

"Meet me at the dealership in an hour, and we'll figure something out."

26

SUNDAY DUSK

DRIVING BACK FROM FORT FRANCIS BLAIR

O n the drive back to AC, Evan summoned Naomi.

Naomi asked him, "So what are you going to do? Do you run right back to Zip and tell him everything you learned?"

"I'm not sure meeting up with Zip would be a good idea," he replied. "I mean, maybe he's not a bad guy, but he might be in business with people who did not wish Bob well. Or who want the Emmetts off their farm."

"Okay," she said casually, "you've got Bob's gun in the back. You could drop by the bait and tackle and buy some nine-millimeter rounds for it. You don't have to be a defenseless dweeb."

"You know me better than that. And how do you happen to know the caliber of that weapon?"

"You must have read it someplace. Look, these are exceptional circumstances," she insisted. "Okay, you're a man of God. But you're also a human being who would not last long with a bullet in his chest."

"Do you think Zip is capable?" Evan asked.

"No idea. And neither do you, and that's a problem."

"I don't have to keep that date with him. I'm thinking it might be a very good idea to have a chat with the sheriff first."

"And you'd rather trust *Otis?*" she asked. "I don't think he's been entirely straight with you either."

"At this point," Evan admitted, "I have to trust somebody."

And on this early Sunday evening, Evan drove, not to meet with Zip, but straight to the sheriff's office.

27

SUNDAY NIGHT
SHERIFF'S OFFICE

E van found Griggs sitting at his boss's desk with his feet up. He was watching the evening weather report on a small, wall-mounted TV.

The deputy looked up and said, "We're in for a big blow tonight. Guess I'd better oil up the jaws of life. Who says this job is boring?"

"Not me," Evan said. "It's just that sometimes being in the center of the cyclone can *seem* calm and quiet."

"So you were bored and dropped by looking for excitement?"

"Looking for the sheriff, actually," Evan said.

"He's on his way in. Seriously, he's worried about the storm. Might not be the greatest idea for you to be hanging out here instead of tucked away in your own kip."

Griggs switched off the set and took a sip from his steaming mug. It was the one with the Army insignia on it.

Evan sat down in the guest chair and asked him, "You were at Francis Blair for a while, right?"

"Military police. Now *there's* a boring job. Unless you get a bomb scare. *That's* no fun." Griggs took his feet off the desk, suddenly embarrassed by his rudeness. "Coffee? We got no sugar, no sweetener even. There's creamer, if you want."

"Sure," Evan replied. "As long as it's hot. I'll take it as it comes, right out of the pot."

Griggs got up and returned with the "This Is What a Feminist Looks Like" mug. Evan took it and asked, "So you have just the two mugs?"

The young man pulled up a second guest chair and sat down, cradling his half-full cup in his lap. "We also got 'Who Shot the Sheriff?' I got him that one. He doesn't always think it's funny." He'd positioned himself in preparation for the arrival of the man who owned the desk. Then, in his renewed guise of rectitude, he asked, "Is there something I can help you with?"

"I have a friend who used to be stationed at the Army base. I understand it's a training facility?"

"Yep. Logistics, supply chain, munitions, network operations. Amazing what all it takes behind the lines to keep soldiers deployed."

"What about missiles?"

Griggs shrugged. "Small-scale stuff. Perimeter defense. These days, the Air Force and the Navy own the boomer programs."

"What about the Nike?"

The fellow looked surprised. "Army, yes. But ancient history. Way before my time."

"Any of those around here?"

"Where'd you get that idea?" he asked.

"My friend is kind of a history buff. She thought the base had something to do with the old program."

"Couldn't prove it by me," Griggs said. "Don't tell me that's what brought you here."

"No, just curious." Then Evan asked, posing a new thought, "How about that Sig Sauer of Bob's? Had you ever seen it before?"

"I had one at the base, have another one now. A fine piece. Never used it in anger. I saw what it did to your friend, though. Sorry you had to see that."

"But that particular weapon? Was it new to you?"

"Why shouldn't it be?"

"You said the Army gave you one like it, and you police officers carry them. Chet said Stu Shackleton must have sold the gun to Bob. I was just wondering where he might have gotten it."

"Gun show? Internet? The guy collects weapons, you know. Old and new."

"And how do you know that?"

"This office uses the commercial firing range for our mandatory practice and recertification. I've seen Stu there, but we don't talk much. Enough to know he knows his weaponry."

"So you don't know much about him?"

"I guess Chet and him go back a ways." Just then, Otis walked in, brushed the new-fallen snow from his leather jacket, and hung it on the coat rack.

Indicating the sheriff, Griggs said to Evan, "You might as well ask *him.*"

"Ask him what?" Otis demanded. "And where's *my* coffee?"

Griggs jumped up as his boss slumped into the executive chair behind his desk. "Coming right up, Chief."

"You said Stu Shackleton sold that Sig Sauer to Bob," Evan explained. "Since it's a standard service weapon, I wondered whether either of you had seen that piece before. I mean, where would Shackleton have gotten it from?"

"Free country, Second Amendment," Otis sighed. "You might as well ask, 'Where did you buy your Ford?'" He shot Evan a look and added, "I really doubt whether the provenance of that weapon has anything to do with anything. Taggart had a permit, we checked. Knowing Shackleton, he has his paperwork too. What brings you here on this Witch's Sabbath of a night?"

"I've been lining up ducks," Evan said. "Thought I'd catch you up. And maybe you could fill in some gaps."

"Griggs…," Otis began.

Knowing he was about to be dispatched, Griggs stood and replied, "Yessir."

The sheriff pulled a twenty out of his wallet and handed it to the deputy. "I know you like pizza, but, frankly, it clogs me up. I'm thinking KFC — two buckets because it may be a long night — and don't skimp on the trimmings. But you can have the corn. I don't digest it so good."

Griggs grabbed his leather jacket and was gone.

Otis got up and helped himself to coffee. As he sat back down, he did a take to his mug. "I gotta tell him, next time he's at the Walmart, get us some plain cups. No writing, no jokes."

"Christmas has come and gone," Evan said. "But when's your birthday?"

Otis ignored the joke and asked, "He tell you anything?"

"Griggs? About what?"

"About anything."

"I'm not sure he knows anything."

"He has a lot to learn about some things," Otis said cryptically. "So what have you got?"

Here goes. If Otis is a bad actor in all this, I'll be making a mistake. But at this point, I'd rather have him inside my tent pissing out.

"The problem with Molly Redwine's will was that she was never sure whether she actually owned that farm. She didn't have clear title, so legally she'd have trouble selling it or even gifting it."

"Clapper told you that?"

"Yes. And when it came Bob's turn to deal with it, Clapper had what sounded like a reasonable solution. Pay the title company for some kind of special insurance and a waiver, and get on with life. But there was another problem, what Clapper called the *third complication.*"

"Which was what?"

"There's a sinkhole on the land, and for some reason the Army thinks it's theirs. Is that something you know about?"

Otis smiled like a poker player who is about to show his hand. "You think there's anything goes on in my little old jurisdiction I don't know about?"

"Was it a Nike base? Part of Francis Blair?"

The sheriff gulped his coffee gratefully and chuckled. "Yes and no. From what I understand, and this was even before my time, it was never an operational site. When you and Bob were boys running around on that farm, did you ever see Army trucks?"

"Come to think of it, yes. Tankers, troop carriers, and some long flatbeds. Everybody knew about the base, so military vehicles weren't exactly a remarkable sight on the highway."

"Well, those flatbeds sometimes had missiles on them, draped in canvas. The standing instruction they gave this office was, if anyone asks, their cargo was telephone poles and radio towers."

"But the Nike program was decommissioned in the seventies. Why should anybody care about it now?"

"And who do you think that might be? What deep-pockets outfit would give a crap about that little farm these days?"

"I'm pretty sure Zip Zed and Stu Shackleton were bidding against each other for it. Edie Taggart thinks whatever part of it the government doesn't own will be hers. At that point, I believe she wants to sell. At first, Edie was all for me tying up loose ends. The arrangements and, I assumed, the estate matters. But she got all dressed up one day, drove off to some meetup or date, and then she had a sudden change of heart. Take care of the burial and the service, she told me, but don't bother sorting out any problems with the wills. Plenty of time for that, and she'll handle it. I'm guessing she's more than friends with Shackleton — and has been before and all during her marriage to Bob. If I want to be really paranoid, I'd say she took up with Bob expressly so she could get control of that land. Even if Bob hadn't gone and taken himself out of the picture, she had to figure hers was the head for business in the family and he'd be more than happy for her to tell him what to do."

"Five-hundred acres, even planted to the fences with corn and soybeans, doesn't amount to all that much."

"That's what has me stumped. Why would the Army care about it, and why would anybody else but Josh? The area they're calling the sinkhole has to be both the problem — and somehow the *asset.*"

"The problem is pretty easy to guess," Otis said. "For years after they rolled up the missile program, the place would have to be protected as a toxic cleanup site. And even if they ripped all the gear out of it, there could still be a security risk. You don't just walk away from something like that until it's completely and totally sanitized. Like those silos out West they converted to condos? So, assuming government budgetary insufficiency and the persistent procrastination of the military, it's not difficult to imagine nothing much being done out there."

"And the asset value?"

Otis savored his coffee. "I've found one way-out possibility, and I've been thinking about it for a very long time."

"You have my full attention."

"You know about those folks who reenact battles of the Civil War?"

"Sure."

"And then you got your antique gun collectors. Love their flintlocks, their Colts, and their Winchesters."

"Lots of them in these parts. Bob had an antique rifle on the wall of his study. Griggs told me Shackleton collects guns."

"Well, at least one old Nike base near San Francisco is still there. There's a group that wants to turn it into a monument, a kind of Cold War museum."

"Loads of fun for the whole family."

"What sane person who's ever been in a firefight would want to relive Gettysburg or Shiloh? The Nike system never had to be used. Some folks think that system, just as much or maybe more than the big ICBMs, kept the peace for a very long time."

"Okay," Evan said. "Tell me how this works. If the government wants to turn one of its installations into a historic site, how does anyone else benefit?"

"Because these days," Otis explained, "the government isn't in the business of building visitors' centers, hotels, or concessions. They might own the land, but they give contractors licenses to develop the site and operate it. In a few years, a new tourist attraction so close to Branson would turn the adjacent dirt farms into hospitality-industry goldmines, particularly whatever part of the Emmett farm Edie can claim she owns."

"So, for purposes of development, maybe nobody cares about the sinkhole itself. They just want to build on every inch around it."

"Bingo," the sheriff said.

"But what about Dickie Emmett? Surely he knew what was behind those fences on his place. He'd know if vehicles were coming and going, even if by a back road and in the middle of the night. He told Molly he didn't have to farm because he had the land in the soil bank."

"I bet Molly and Dickie were both in on it. Whether the government asserted its rights to the land, it would have been simple paperwork to pay them both for an easement — to Molly because presumably it was her farm, and to Dickie because otherwise they'd be infringing on his rights as a tenant, rights of privacy and also of land use. And all those agreements would have to be secret."

"Why?"

"They wouldn't exactly want to hold public hearings. Do you think they'd want to tell these farm families they'd be living with nukes in their backyard for decades?"

"What about Bob? How much of this did he understand?"

"Now there's something neither of us knows. What did he think of Josh Emmett?"

"When we were boys, Josh wasn't old enough to play with us. He's in his twenties now, just getting started. But farming is in his blood. It must've skipped a generation with Dickie. Josh is sincere, honest, and hardworking. He wants that land to be a productive farm. Bob admired him for that."

"Then, let's suppose, if Bob hadn't died, he might not have listened to Edie. Maybe he wouldn't have gone along with the plan. Maybe he'd have wanted to keep Josh on as tenant."

"But the Emmetts aren't mentioned in either of the wills. Molly left it all to Lionel and so to Bob, and Bob left it all to Edie."

Otis shrugged, "Then I take it there's nothing to be done."

Do I tell him? He didn't have to tell me what he knows.

Evan steeled himself and took a chance. "Now, here's where I've uncovered some things you may not know."

"I figured if anyone could, you would."

"First, I found a marked-up draft of Bob's will on his computer. A *new* will. He gifted whatever he owned of the farm to Josh. And he has some clever provisions in there. His scheme might not prevent the house from coming down, and it might not settle things right away. But when the dust clears, Josh and his family will be well taken care of."

"No doubt this development is what some people have been afraid of. But if it's a draft, it won't hold up in court. Might show intent, but Edie's lawyers could claim he changed his mind again and didn't go through with it."

"Secondly, I've learned he had a clean printout signed, witnessed, and certified."

For the first time this evening, Otis looked startled. "So, who has it? Do you?"

"Nope," Evan replied. "That's just the thing. There might be more than one copy, but no one knows where they are."

Otis pulled a ring of keys from his pocket, reached over, and unlocked the file drawer on his desk. He pulled out a green folder and handed it to Evan. "It's time you saw this."

Evan opened the folder. It contained the second suicide note, laid out flat in the clear evidence bag, the note that stuck out of the breast pocket of Bob's corpse.

Otis has been holding out on me!

As the sheriff had told him on that first day, the note was identical to the one Edie had found on her kitchen counter. Except for a handwritten line scrawled at the bottom:

Now dumbass Evan will have to clean the cellar by himself! Ha!

His handwriting is terrible, but maybe he was writing this in the cold, trying to keep his hand from shaking.

"Something told me to bogart this until you were ready to see it," Otis said.

"And why have you held back? Especially if you thought it might be important."

"If I'd shown it to you before, neither one of us would know what we know now. And I wasn't sure who's side you were on. Or, for that matter, who all the players are, and how they line up."

"You do now?"

"Nope, I'm still not sure. But I *am* sure you are who you say you are, and if you have an agenda, it's something to do with finding the truth."

Evan read the note again, shook his head, and felt his eyes welling up with tears. "Sorry to disappoint, sheriff. It's a lame joke."

"It's not some kind of clue?"

"Afraid not. You see, when we were boys playing together, and we misbehaved, we'd be ordered to clean the cellar. It was a chore Bob hated, all the more because I think he felt guilty he dragged me into it."

"Dumbass?"

"His term of endearment for me. His way of getting me to do most of the work. He'd say I drew the short straw, when we never drew. Which made me the dumbass. He never got tired of the joke. I never did either."

Otis must have grown up in the area. The boys hadn't known him then. The schools were segregated in those years, and there were many fewer blacks than whites. But the sheriff knew the history. "I believe after Bob's mother took sick, his Aunt Molly moved into their house in town."

"That's right. We preferred having the run of the Emmett farm, but on rainy days, we'd play at Bob's house."

"Wasn't that place torn down? I mean, there couldn't be a cellar there now, could there?"

"You're right, that old house is gone," Evan said. "Molly lived there by herself for a while after Lionel died, but then when she fell ill, Bob moved her into a rest home and sold the place. It's a parking lot for the furniture store now. There's no cellar for me to clean. Bob's just saying I'll be stuck with sweeping up after him. Again."

"So," the sheriff sighed. "If this isn't a clue about where he stashed his will, I suppose there are no more loose ends. You'll continue to handle the memorial, and Edie will decide when she wants to start probate."

"I still need to have a talk with Shackleton," Evan said. "But only about the Masonic ritual for the memorial service." He studied Otis's face for a hint about what to say next. Finding none, he added, "I suppose there's no need to quiz him about the gun or his intentions for the land deal. Whatever is going to happen, it looks like Edie's in control. Except, it sounds like she wouldn't be able to stop the demolition, even if she wanted to." Then Evan lied as he got up, shook the sheriff's hand, and assured him, "Yes, no more loose ends."

Evan's was a sin of omission.

Cleaning the cellar was our punishment. But it was the cellar of Lionel Taggart's pharmacy.

28

SUNDAY 10 PM
TAGGART'S PHARMACY

I n the short time Evan had been with the sheriff, snow had
accumulated on the Mustang. Evan scolded himself for leaving his
ice scraper in the trunk of the Taurus. He didn't want to wait around
for the car's defrosters to melt the snow, so he got in and started the
engine for the warmup, then got out and brushed the snow off the
windshield with the sleeve of his coat.

He jumped in the car and drove through the thick downfall to
Taggart's Pharmacy, which was only four blocks away on U.S. 52. Bob
still owned the building and the business. He had recently hired
another in an inconsistent series of druggists, young Phil Vanderhorn.
That store and the C'mon Inn were the only businesses open late on a
Sunday night in AC. Other than the rare medical emergency, on the
weekends Vanderhorn sold painkillers for hangovers and condoms for
wishful party animals.

Naomi was in the passenger seat. She framed it as a question, but she
knew the answer: "It's not a joke, is it?"

"Oh, it's a joke," Evan told her. "But it's also an instruction. Bob is still
giving me orders."

"Do you think Otis bought your story?"

"I don't know. He was sure hoping there was someplace else to look. Maybe he knew all along there is something else to find."

"Is he after justice, or something else?" She knew the answer to that one too.

"Otis has known about what's in the sinkhole longer than anybody. He could have been the one to tip off Shackleton there was money to be made. Then again, I wouldn't be chasing down all these clues if he hadn't egged me on. Like he wanted to get to the bottom of it as much as I did, but he didn't have enough evidence to justify an official investigation."

"There's another possibility," she suggested. "If you want to be paranoid."

"For the sake of argument, consider me paranoid."

"Maybe Otis got you all spun up about digging for clues because, if Bob made an amended will, you're the best bet to find it. Edie has no idea. You were buddies with the guy, knew where he hunted. If you can't find it, maybe no one can, and they, whoever *they* are, can all relax. Or if you do find the amended will, maybe like a good dog you'll fetch it and bring it back to him."

"And Otis would, what, tear it up? Give it to Edie?"

"They'd have to destroy all the copies. And probably also find the lawyer who helped Bob, and pay that guy off."

"We can be sure the lawyer wasn't Clapper. Edie might worry there's a new will, but you can bet Bob didn't tell her about it or tell her who helped him."

"You've got Cora's description of the notary," Naomi suggested.

"Wow," Evan said. "That's brilliant. But we're running out of time."

Then she asked, "What about Zip?"

"He's in the game somehow," Evan guessed. "But I doubt he can make a deal with Edie that cuts Shackleton out of it. So he must be trying to leverage a partnership. He might pull that off, if he has something they want."

"What could he have?"

"I'm guessing, but he's been into the land deals ever since he got control of his family's money. So he could own adjacent property, or at least an option. He could have water and drainage rights. He could be cozy with some Indian who could get them a gaming license. He could have loaned Molly money for back taxes and therefore holds a lien on whatever property she *did* own. But he couldn't be in it this late in the game if he didn't have an angle."

"So Zip wants what they all want?"

"Like I say, Zip plays to win, but he's not unscrupulous. That said, if he was in it with somebody else, he might not be able to control them."

"You're late for your meeting with him."

"He sent me a text. I put him off until tomorrow and blamed the weather. He still wants to meet, but I didn't reply."

AT THIS HOUR of night and in this weather, the city's main drag was deserted. As Evan's car approached the drugstore, a pair of headlights appeared behind him. The lights were large and rectangular, set high on the vehicle. The powerful halogen beams flooded the passenger compartment of the Mustang like brilliant daylight.

Must be a truck.

Like a pair of menacing, predatory eyes, the lights drew closer, too close. Visibility was poor in the driving snowstorm, and Evan worried about stopping distance. Now the truck was practically riding his bumper!

This guy's crazy! If I have to stop or swerve, he'll either flatten me or drive me into a storefront!

The truck was so close Evan could hear the throbbing of its big diesel engine.

The engine revved as if preparing to ram the Mustang.

Okay, Josh, settle down! This gets you nothing!

Then the truck's emergency lights above the cab switched on, it pulled alongside to pass, and it roared away, its huge tires biting into the icy asphalt. Down the road, Evan saw it slow to make a left turn onto a side street, and it disappeared behind a row of buildings.

Okay, I drive like an old lady.

YOUNG DR. PHIL VANDERHORN was alone in the pharmacy. Evan knew him hardly at all, their contact having been limited to his occasional purchases of prescription Vicodin for his back. Evan flashed the POA on his phone. He explained he remembered there was a boyhood keepsake in the cellar, and Edie wanted it for the exhibit table at the memorial.

White lie. Situation ethics. Besides, there could *be some memento down there, besides whatever it is Bob is sending me searching for.*

"Sure," the pharmacist said. He didn't look up as he ran totals from the day's receipts on his sales terminal. Then he looked up and added, "Helluva night to be on an errand. You hearing that ruckus out back?"

Besides the howling of the wind came the throbbing sounds of a truck engine and the clattering of heavy chains.

"I believe it's a tow truck," Evan said. "It was behind me on the road coming in."

There was an alley in back of the store, just wide enough for a car or a small delivery van. Evan remembered the tow truck had turned off in that direction as he was parking on the street.

"Some poor soul's stuck back there, I bet," Phil shrugged. "Like I say, helluva night. You're nuts to be here."

Evan offered a weak smile of apology. "Well, I figure, if it's something the lady wants, it's the least I can do."

"Sure," Phil said again. "Sure, why not? I suppose those mementos could mean a lot." As the fellow's expression grew serious, Evan realized Phil had been waiting all along to ask, as his voice dropped, "You wouldn't know what she plans to do with the store?"

"She hasn't mentioned it," Evan told him. "All she said was, she's going to take time to sort things out. So you might as well figure it's business as usual, at least for a while. By the time she decides, I doubt if I'll even be involved."

"I believe she has a head for business. I had to practically force the monthly reports on Bob."

"If Bob trusted you, and I'm guessing he did, he'd pretty much leave you to decide how to do your job."

"I'm sorry," Phil said softly. "Losing a friend like that."

The blizzard's winds were coming in gusts, rattling the windows of the old building and howling its way through cracks and around corners. Despite the lateness of the hour and oddity of Evan's taking care of this errand when a storm was raging outside, Phil saw no trouble letting him downstairs through the interior access door. It wasn't even locked.

Phil apologized, "Good luck finding anything down there. The light circuit's fried, and it hasn't exactly been a priority." There were no windows, so putting off the search until daylight wouldn't help. "I had a flashlight and batteries, but I sold it this afternoon, and I'm waiting for fresh stock."

"I'll use the light on this phone," Evan said. "It shouldn't take long."

"I'm fixing to leave," Phil said. "If it's all the same to you, I'm not eager to go down there. You sure you can manage?"

"I'll be fine," Evan said. "Like I say, I shouldn't be long."

Phil said apologetically, "Our kid is teething. I catch hell for working late. When you go, you just pull the door shut and set the code."

"I can do that," Evan said.

Might be better if he leaves and I can take my time to poke around.

Phil asked, "Did you park out back?"

"No," Evan replied. "I'm on the street."

At this hour and in this weather, the orange Mustang might be the only car on the street. I doubt if anybody cares, but I wish it weren't so noticeable. Somebody could be looking for me.

"The reason I ask," Phil said, "is I'm parked back there and that truck better not be blocking me. If I don't holler down to you in a few minutes, you'll know I'm gone."

Evan remembered there was also a storm-cellar door on the back side of the building, which he figured had been permanently closed off. "What about the old storm door?" he asked. "I suppose you've sealed it up."

"You got a good memory. Maybe you'll find whatever you're looking for after all. But as for the access door from the alley, it's always had a rusty padlock on it, and I don't have the key. Okay, I guess it's lousy security for a place full of drugs. But we've got a safe up here for the hard stuff, and we've never had a break-in attempt — from the back or from the front, for that matter."

"You might as well get going. So, what's the code?"

"It's one-two-three-four."

"Are you kidding?"

Phil said, "You know, I can remember Latin names and complex formularies, but passwords just don't stick." He smiled, turned, and left.

AC must be really low-crime. But where are all those addicts who are looking to score opioids?

As Evan switched on the phone light, he noted the battery-life indicator was at just fourteen percent. He hoped it would last long enough. As he opened the cellar door, he felt a blast of cold air and smells of mold and dust. Before he went down, he tried to remember the layout down there, rehearsing mentally how he'd find his way to the wall and its hidey-hole.

WE WERE THIRTEEN. *An awkward and a perverted age. Brownie the Shepherd followed along with us as we undertook our chores at Taggart's Pharmacy.*

"Come on down!" Bob yelled. "And bring the broom and that dustpan! And a handful of those old rags."

Evan started down the rickety stairs with the cleaning supplies. "Why do *I* have to do this?"

"Because you drew the short straw, dumbass."

"When did we draw?"

"Last Saturday."

"I don't remember."

"So you're a dumbass *and* you're lazy? Better get to work!"

Having arrived at the bottom, dutiful Evan awaited his orders. Brownie had descended with Bob and lay curled up on the floor in the middle of the tiny cellar.

"Tell you what," Bob said, taking the rags. "You sweep the floor and I'll dust the shelves. We can't have some stumblebum dropping these rare samples."

"What about the dog?" Evan asked.

"You nudge her nicely with the broom, and she'll move. But *nicely.*"

The cellar was lit by a single bulb on pair of twisted wires dangling from a two-by-six floor joist above. The wiring was ancient, maybe dating from the days of Edison himself. The wires were covered with knitted cloth, and where they separated at the joist, they were held in place by porcelain insulators the size of sewing-thread spools.

It was the middle of summer, and the cool dampness of the cellar was a welcome relief from the heat and humidity. The funky smells weren't bad if you didn't think about dead rodents or rat mess. Evidently there were no critters to chase, because Brownie was unperturbed.

On one bare-brick wall were four rows of wooden shelves. Bob was referring to blue-tinted glass jars that held mysterious colored masses bathed in liquid.

Evan crept closer, enthralled by the orderly arrangement of carefully preserved organic matter. "What's in those things?"

"I don't know for sure," Bob said, adopting a dramatic, secretive tone. "And you don't want to find out. I bet it's brains and testicles and such. You know, diseased tissues? My father's a doctor, you know."

"Wow, that's gross," Evan said.

"Here," Bob offered, shoving a jar at him. "I think this one is cancer from some monkeys. Maybe you want a taste?"

Brownie sat up.

Evan recoiled. "Awwwwww! No way!"

He watched in horror as Bob twisted off the top of the Ball mason jar, shoved two fingers into the brine, retrieved a glop of yellow-colored flesh, and gave it to the dog, who gulped it down!

"My God, Bob. What have you done? She could die!"

Bob looked into the bottle quizzically, fished out another morsel, and popped it into his own mouth! He savored the residual taste and smacked his lips. "Definitely not monkey brains. Maybe goat's pancreas."

"Ewwwwww!"

Then Bob asked Brownie, "Wuddya think, girl? Should we tell him what he's missing?"

Brownie whimpered. It might have been a giggle.

Bob's poker face broke as he was overcome with a fit of hysterical, wheezing laughter. "You... *dumbass!*" As his laughter subsided and he gained control of himself, he rotated the jar so Evan could read the handwritten label:

Pear Preserves

"You jerk!" Evan exclaimed, wanting but not finding a stronger word. "What are those doing down here?"

Bob caught his breath. "There was a cellar in my aunt's house when she lived there with my Uncle Jake. But now she's with us in town, we don't have a cellar. So when she does her canning at the end of the summer, she stores the jars down here." Then he added, "I'm going to have to tell her pears are your favorite, and you did such a good job sweeping up, that's why I let you open one of her precious jars. We're supposed to save them until winter."

The other jars were labeled:

Spiced Apples

Green Tomatoes

Prunes

Blackberry Jam

Rhubarb Pie Filling

I would have preferred the jam.

THE STAIRS CREAKED JUST as they had years ago as Evan made his way carefully down. He clung to a handrail on the right, not remembering and not finding one on the other side.

Accidentally stepping off in that direction would be a bad idea.

At the foot of the stairs, he expected he should turn to the right. He remembered the array of mason jars used to be on the wall to his left. He was tempted to survey whether any were still there, but he didn't have the luxury of time, especially if he expected the phone battery to survive. The wall parallel to the stairs would be the place to look for his objective.

But his way was blocked.

Navigating the cellar as it was today would be no easy task. The place was filled, as most attics and crawlspaces these days are, with the empty boxes of purchased appliances and electronic gear. People took seriously the warranty terms requiring a defective product to be returned to the manufacturer in its original packaging. Problem was, the stored and forgotten packaging almost always outlived the product. Here were boxes for a telephone answering machine, a portable computer the size of a briefcase, the now-obsolete sales terminal that replaced a cash register, a credit-card imprinter, two space heaters rendered unnecessary by the upgrade to baseboard heating, empty refillable bottles for a water cooler that no longer served, and assorted suitcases larger than carry-on regulations that no one would ever want to use again. All of it was covered in a thick layer of dust, as if these artifacts were being held in the historical archive of some museum as testimony to the legacy of a contemporary small-town drugstore.

The wind continued to rage outside. Evan could hear the slatted sides of the storm door rattling as the drafts whistled through.

He soiled his hands as he set boxes aside to clear his path to the wall. If the hidey-hole had remained undiscovered, it would be behind some loose bricks about knee-high up on the east wall.

Evan's light threw bright illumination on a spot only about two feet wide directly where the phone was pointed. And that spot had grown noticeably dimmer just in the brief time he'd been down here. The ambient light from the phone was faint, and the space in back of him was pitch black.

He was startled as some boxes tumbled over.

Is someone here? I must have stacked them carelessly.

Even with the light, the location of the loose bricks wouldn't be obvious. Evan had to get down on his knees and feel his way with his fingers, working upwards from the damp floor, searching for telltale gaps in the mortar.

Behind him, another box fell down.

Was that a puff of wind? A poltergeist? I'm freaking out here.

Just where he remembered, he found the loose bricks. There were six of them, arranged two high and three wide. Removed from the wall, the space in the gap was deep enough to cache a tin toolbox.

Then, another sound. Not a box falling. Not the wind moaning.

The scuff of a shoe on the gritty floor!

The power and the presence of God —

Evan's hand shook, and the phone dropped to the floor, extinguishing his light. The cellar went pitch black, then became blindingly bright as the intruder switched on a halogen lantern and turned it on him.

What's that smell? Fried chicken?

Then came a skull-splitting blow, and Evan's world faded to black again.

29

MONDAY 1 AM

IN AN AMBULANCE

T he first thing Evan heard as he regained consciousness was Otis's raspy voice: "Relax, Preacher. You're still among the living."

Evan opened his eyes to find himself riding flat on his back in an ambulance, the plastic cone of a respirator covering his nose and mouth, and an IV plugged into his arm. His neck, which throbbed mightily, was immobilized in a collar lashed down to the stretcher. The heavy blanket covering him was a decided comfort. Paramedic Darlene Cho sat on his left, monitoring his vitals. Sheriff Otis was on his right.

"You're no angel," Evan said to him woozily.

"Question is, are you a thief?" the sheriff asked, not whimsically.

"Why is that even a question?"

"You could say I'm dealing with conflicting versions of events," Otis said cautiously. "Do you feel like talking? Do you know what happened to you?"

"Somebody hit me from behind. Hard."

"BP one-fifty over ninety," Darlene reported into her headset. "I've got tachycardia."

Yeah, I guess you'd say I'm starting to get upset!

"Why were you in the basement of that store?" Otis asked. "And why tonight, when any sane person would be tucked in at home? We had so many wrecks out there, the paramedics might have skipped right over you."

"The note you showed me. The cellar of the pharmacy."

"Okay, for now, I'm going to ignore you lied to me. It couldn't wait till morning?"

"I was looking for the document. And I was afraid someone else might be after the same thing. Including maybe you."

"Me?"

"You held back that copy of the suicide note. You guessed the scribbled message was important. You waited until I might know what it meant. Who else knew about it?"

"Griggs," the sheriff said. "He had to inventory and review the evidence for his writeup."

"Who hit me?"

"Griggs." The sheriff wasn't guessing.

"So he's the bad guy in all this?"

"The deputy tells it this way. He responds to a call about a stalled vehicle in back of Taggart's. He dispatches a tow truck and meets it there. Owner nowhere to be found, and that gets him worried. He has a look around the alley. As the tech is rigging the tow, Griggs notices the storm door of the pharmacy has come loose. The wind is tossing it up and down. He goes over and sees the padlock was sheared off. He remembers seeing a car he didn't recognize out front on the street — an orange Mustang. He's thinking illegal entry, grabs his lantern, goes down, and finds this guy rummaging in a hole in the wall. He says you had a brick in your hand and raised it up to threaten him. That's when he hit you with the butt of his service weapon. In a way, you're lucky, because, if he really thought he was in danger, procedure would be shoot to kill."

"I didn't threaten him! I didn't even have a chance to see who it was. How about he just identify himself and ask me what I'm doing?"

"Back entrance to a drugstore? And he's thinking you are, what, some kind of opioid addict?"

"You've gotta be kidding. Ask Vanderhorn why I was there. He let me in."

"He wasn't there. The front door was unlocked."

"That's right. He was in a hurry to leave to take care of his kid. Told me to lock up." Then Evan asked, "Does Griggs have the box?"

"Your secret stash, you mean?" Otis chuckled. "No, he brought it to me. You see, if his version of events is true, he had nothing to gain by keeping it. So I've got two plausible stories here. Your word against Griggs'. I'll have a talk with Vanderhorn, but I've given orders for the deputy not to leave the station at the end of his shift, and you can be sure I'll confront him on this."

"If I'm not the guilty party here, don't you think he'll run?"

"The guy is not stupid. His cover story will probably hold, even if it's not entirely accurate. It's all about what he *thought* was going down, you see. He could get a reprimand or a suspension. But if he defies my order and takes off, well, he'll be in deep shit. If you're right about this, maybe he was on an errand for someone else. Somebody who really wanted that box. Or didn't want *you* to have whatever was inside."

"So, what did you find in it?"

"Why don't you tell me what you *expected* to find?"

"It's a rusty tin fishing-tackle box. Back in the day, it had aggie marbles, an electric yo-yo, a couple of genuine Indian arrowheads, a lock of Samantha Smith's hair, and a Civil War penny."

"And?"

"A certified copy of Bob Taggart's last will and testament. It's the only thing that would explain what Bob wrote."

"Well," Otis replied, "this helps your story, your reason for being there. And you're exactly right. Except, there were no documents."

"Did Griggs have a chance to open the box before he gave it to you?"

"If it ever had a lock, it doesn't have one now. And he didn't say he did, didn't say he didn't."

"If there was a document, he could have already destroyed it."

"Tearing it up would be a serious crime. If I was him, I'd return it to its rightful owner and say I thought I was doing the right thing." He let this sink in, then said, "They'll keep you under observation until they know your neck's not broke and your brain still works." Then he added, "It might be a good idea to find another minister for the memorial service."

"YOU WERE SUPPOSED to bring me that box!" Shackleton shouted. He stood in the parking lot with his shoulders hunched against the brisk, cold wind.

"There was nothing in it," Griggs insisted. He was looking down, avoiding the gaze of his angry taskmaster, as he stamped his feet and rubbed his gloved hands together.

"Nothing? The guy's dying thought, and he sends his friend to find an empty box? I don't buy it."

"Kid's stuff. Toys and trinkets. No document, not even a scrap of paper."

"But your instructions were to *bring it* to me. Maybe there's some clue you missed."

"Think about it. If it doesn't have what you want, why risk implicating yourself? I gave it to the sheriff, and he'll give it to Edie. It's her property. Maybe she can make sense of it. But, this way, the case is finally closed. And I mean, really closed."

"I've still got a bad feeling about this," Shackleton grumbled as he turned and walked away toward his idling Mercedes-AMG S65 and its passenger, a handsome woman huddled in her politically incorrect fox fur who must have been wondering whether these unscrupulous men might be getting her into more trouble than any deal was worth.

SHACKLETON DIDN'T like Edie giving him lectures. She was worried Griggs had grabbed the will and would be selling it to the highest bidder. Or using it to blackmail her somehow.

Shackleton told her, "Just let me handle it. You don't need to know details." And he stayed seated behind the wheel with the engine running as she opened the car door on her side, ducked her ears into the softness of her fur coat, and marched up to open the door of the house where she now lived alone.

As she turned her key in the lock, she looked back at him. It was difficult for him to read her expression in the snowstorm, but he judged it was not fondness but suspicion.

Before he drove off, he called Wilmer.

"Yeah, I know it's the middle of the night and the roads are treacherous and you'd rather sit home with your brandy. But get yourself over to the clinic right away. They're bringing a dear friend of mine in an ambulance. The poor bastard's hooked on opioids. The cops caught him breaking into the drugstore, if you can imagine. So we're doing an intervention. I'll foot the bill, whatever it costs. You're to admit him for as long as it takes to set him straight." Then Shackleton stressed, "And for sure he won't be happy about it, so, until he comes to his senses, you'll probably have to sedate him."

30

MONDAY MID-MORNING
MYERSON CLINIC

W hen Evan awoke next, he was comfortably installed in a private hospital room. The breathing tube and neck brace were gone, but there was still a spike in his arm. The regular pattern on a heart monitor told him he was still alive in humanoid form with a heartbeat and not in some alternate dimension.

I guess my neck's not broken. Who is paying for this? Hey, I didn't think they let you go to sleep if you have a concussion. Well, I'm still here.

There was a nasty knot of pain at the base of his skull, and he expected a multicolored bruise would blossom there. Even though he'd been kneeling when he was struck, the fall to the packed-earth floor of the cellar had wrenched his back. The pain ran all the way from his neck to his tailbone. His prior torments were but a preview of coming attractions. He could now understand and forgive the people who had no other God than Oxycodone.

The room is nice. Too nice.

It was clean and upscale. Geometric pastel designs on the cream-colored damask wallpaper. Light-oak guest chairs upholstered in dusty rose. Ceramic-clad medical gear in a matching color. Worktable in faux-granite. Glistening stainless-steel sink. Accent lighting recessed in the light-oak wainscoting that surrounded the room.

To die in comfort?

Springfield or Columbia? If they'd taken him to Springfield, they'd chosen the closest large, urban hospital. Fine. But if he was in Columbia, they'd had some reason to take him to the UM teaching hospital, somewhere they'd have the most expensive machines.

And doctors with exotic, cutting-edge specialties. Excuse the pun. Not so fine.

He was groping for the call button while praying for some relief when he looked up and saw her grinning at him.

Uh-oh. Maybe I'm in the other place, after all.

Naomi sat in the guest chair. She was wearing a Radcliffe sweatshirt, black stretch yoga pants, and a new pair of designer running shoes. In sharp contrast to Evan's present state of sorry health, she looked relaxed and vital. In fact, she was never lovelier, which was how he wanted to remember her. When she saw his eyes were open, she smiled more broadly and said, "I guess they're going to keep you around a while longer."

Perfect teeth, gleaming raven hair, and flawless, ivory skin. A goddess descended from the Pantheon of genius. Only the hint of a few freckles across her cheekbones and the whimsical sparkle in her eyes bring her down to Earth. What is the point except to torment me now with this vision? What's the sharper wound — love or loss?

"I was wondering when you'd show up," he said, delighted to see her in any circumstance.

"Maybe you should have bought those bullets when I suggested it."

"I don't see how the gun would have helped."

"There might be a next time."

"Oh, you can see the future now?"

"No more than you can. But I can assess probabilities, just as you can when you're thinking clearly." It was her way of reminding him — teasing him, really — that she was only a manifestation of his vivid imagination. And his longing.

"So, you're thinking sometime soon I'm going to need the gun?"

"No," she said, talking to a child. *"You're* thinking that."

I'm a sitting duck here. A lethal injection, some accidental overdose? And with the sheriff looking the other way?

He willed himself to stay awake, at least until the painkiller arrived, but he drifted off to sleep again.

THE ONLY CONFIRMED, hard information Evan ever got was "fatality from friendly fire." He was not her next of kin, although she had only one living family member at the time, an uncommunicative brother. She wasn't military personnel, so no one owed him an answer according to protocol, and there was no formal public procedure to be followed. If she hadn't ignored her clearance and shared some details of her posting before she left, he probably never would have found out what happened.

The company had sent her to Lebanon on temporary assignment. It was supposed to last a month or two. On separate occasions, when he'd teased her about her secretiveness, she'd given him hints about the nature of her job. When he taunted her she was working for a weapons manufacturer (which he'd done in a fit of frustration and later regretted), she replied curtly that some weapons save lives. One other time, she admitted she worked in "perimeter control" but did not elaborate.

While she was away, he followed all news reports from the Middle East closely. He got no news from her, or of her. She didn't call and she didn't email. He supposed it was a security thing.

The incident made headline news for a day. A United Nations observation post on the Lebanese side of the Golan Heights had been destroyed by an Israeli missile. The missile was a countermeasure launched in immediate response to a Hezbollah attack that had been fired from a portable, shoulder-mounted device moments before from a location near the post, perhaps even from somewhere inside the compound.

Evan phoned the company hoping to confirm that Naomi was safe and nowhere near the site. He was routed to the HR department, and when he admitted he was not a family member, they refused to tell him anything. He left his contact information with them.

A week later he received a call from the same office informing him that civilian contractor Naomi Weiss was among the fatalities in a friendly fire incident. No further details could be provided. The reason he was getting the call was she'd given him as the emergency contact in her employment records. Did he know how they could contact her family? No, he had never met them, and as he understood it, none were living now except a brother, last known location somewhere in Canada. He didn't know how to reach the fellow.

Future skip-tracer Wycliff used his online skills to search for Leon Weiss. There were lots of matching names. But brother Leon, like his recalcitrant sister, must not have been an avid user of social media. After Evan got negative responses to his queries from a few of the likely subjects, he gave up the search. What was the point?

But he was diligent in his research about the scenario of the incident. He learned that perimeter control involves gates, barriers, and guards, along with sensing and monitoring devices to prevent unauthorized intrusion. Recent innovations, and possibly tools Naomi had helped develop and deploy, were radio- and audio-frequency motion detectors, night-vision sensors, and license-plate recognition systems that could retrieve vehicle-registration data in real time.

As to the countermeasures that took Naomi's life, the story was ironic but not unique. For a time during the Palestinian-Israeli conflicts, Hezbollah was said to have used a tactic of firing shoulder-mounted missiles and mortar rounds from the precincts of vulnerable civilian locations, especially from the campuses and even from the rooftops of schools and hospitals. Israeli defense systems included antimissile missiles, as well as retaliatory counterstrike ballistics. If those automated response systems could be fired in time, they stood a good chance of intercepting and destroying an incoming projectile. At the same time, they might also fire antipersonnel weaponry targeted on the attackers. Of course, when the retaliatory blow might hit noncombatants, a command decision should be made. Ordinarily, you'd think an officer would need to authorize the target. But, in practice, the time required to do so would almost certainly give the attackers time to flee the area. Eventually, in response to the mounting prevalence of these attacks, no time was allowed for human decisions. Use of automatic countermeasures was perhaps deemed justified by the rationale that anyone with security so lax (or sympathies so suspect) as to allow a terrorist on their property risked being targeted the same as combatants. Otherwise, it was feared that mobile rocket units would continue to exploit such sensitive locations. The benefit to the attackers was double: They'd also get the propaganda bonus of portraying the Israeli defense measures as callous and inhumane because of the collateral damage to civilians. In this case, not only did the UN and public opinion chastise the Israelis, but also the attackers gained an advantage in discouraging the presence of observers they hadn't wanted there in the first place.

Whether the company ever repatriated Naomi's body, Evan never knew. Even if he had been able to take any action, he wouldn't have obsessed over the disposition of her remains. He didn't believe in the sanctity of a corpse any more than he cared about the discarded cells of his own body he flushed down the toilet. And, as for having a place to visit and pay respects, he didn't believe spirits hovered over their graves waiting for tearful homage to be paid them.

31

TUESDAY – WEDNESDAY
MYERSON CLINIC

E van slept on and off for what seemed a long time. He hadn't realized how tired he was. Staying awake to fend off some pharmaceutical attack was pointless. He craved the injections because they were painkillers. The opaque curtains in his room were drawn and the interior lights dimmed. So he had no sense of whether it was day or night, or days or nights. Sometimes he'd look up and see Naomi sitting there patiently. But she didn't say anything. Nurses and attendants would come and go. They didn't say anything either. Or if they did, he didn't remember.

THE DRUGS they gave him did more than sap his energy. They made him extraordinarily sensitive to light, to noise, and to the maelstrom of images racing through his tormented, post-traumatic brain.

Outside, the raging storm which had begun when Evan was down in the cellar continued unabated. The driving blizzard winds whirled and whined. Evan's hospital room was insulated from outside temperatures but not from those woeful sounds. In his dimmed mental state, as he drifted in and out of consciousness, the fury outside inspired and magnified his inner visions.

It wasn't a dream because it made too much sense. Perhaps it was a semiconscious vision induced by his delirium, because Evan remembered it afterward in vivid, color-saturated detail. It began with a pleasant, realistic memory and ended with an overwhelming, surreal horror.

THE TINY GREEK island of Patmos. To its sun-drenched summer tourists, the port of Skala is a quaint fishing community with those characteristic stucco houses, all painted a sun-dazzling white, with flat or red-tile roofs. The village is orderly as the streets of heaven might be orderly, its immaculate appearance unreal, the tiny houses neatly arranged side-by-side, in tiers, ascending the steep, twisting and turning roads leading up the island's central peak.

Having disembarked just an hour before from the cruise ship *Oceanos*, Evan and Naomi were hiking happily upwards, making the half-mile trek on the road that led to the mandatory tourist attraction — the Cave of the Apocalypse, also known as the Cave of St. John. Island lore says it was here — in the mountain heights above the village — where one of the early Christian writers set down the *Book of Revelation*.

The cruise around the Greek islands was supposed to be their honeymoon trip. Their commitment to marriage, made in the spring, had been tentative. But as time grew closer to the date in June, Naomi informed Evan she was simply not ready. Evan was upset but not irate, partly because they'd told no one else, especially his family back in Missouri, and he hoped she'd change her mind again eventually, which, considering the spritely personality he had come to know and love, was not unlikely. She had no one to tell except her recluse brother and a former roommate. The couple, which they still were, decided to take the tour of the islands anyway because Naomi had researched the packages and booked nonrefundable tickets months in advance. She'd nailed a good rate at a high-season time of year, when that part of the

Aegean Sea is typically overrun by British schoolteachers on summer vacation, interspersed with professor-tourists-turned-residents on their yearlong sabbatical leaves of absence. The age-old popularity of the Greek islands with these Britons (dating back at least to Lord Byron) may account for the prevalence of English spoken by Greeks as a second language (well before there was such a thing as the European Union to mandate it), as well as the reason, when you ask any Greek waiter in English for the breakfast menu, the reply will inevitably be "English breakfast," in which case you'll get the international standard fare consisting of fried eggs, chips, baked beans, bacon *and* sausage, buttered toast or crumpets, and grilled tomato, along with a pot of inky black tea blandified with steamed milk.

As a result, they were acting like shameless tourists and thoroughly enjoying it. The food on the block-long buffet table onboard the cruise ship was stunningly ample and various, although concocted more for the eye than the palette. A minor annoyance was their dinner-table assignment. When they had come on board, the ship's steward had asked them which nationality of people they might prefer for company. Naomi insisted they wanted French companions. Evan knew she wanted to practice the language, in which he knew only a few phrases. The steward, who was Greek like the captain and most of the crew, looked at her incredulously, shook his head, wrote a table number on a slip, and handed their assignment to her with a courteous nod and an insincere smile. That night during their first meal on the ship, they discovered they'd been seated next to a soft-spoken dentist from Indiana and his talkative wife. The others at the table were Dutch and German, who did their best to ignore the Americans. Those Europeans were themselves outcasts from the numerous French and Italians, who were gregarious and chatty among themselves in their separate groups.

On their hike up the hill, Naomi reminded Evan, "I've never read it," referring to the most sensational, some say the most unbelievable, book of the Bible. He couldn't resist giving her a lecture, because here was one of those arcane scholarly controversies he'd endured at Harvard Divinity. He explained, "This John may have been John the

Divine, John the Revelator, or John the Theologian, or perhaps John the Apostle or John the Evangelist or John the Presbyter. These latter three might have been contemporaries of Christ, and at least one of them was the disciple John referred to in gospels, but *not* John the Baptist. Scholarly opinion varies on whether these Johns were multiple personages or which, if any of them, was the John whom the Roman emperor Domitian exiled to Patmos."

"So that's how he ended up here," Naomi said dully, indicating she was following along courteously but not at all interested.

"Yes. Legend has it that, toward the end of the first century, Romans put John in boiling oil in hopes of killing him in excruciating pain. But he survived. The miracle pumped up his rock-star reputation with the rebellious and defiant Christians, so the emperor sent him here."

"Ouch and ick," she said.

Evan ignored her sarcasm and continued, "Presumably, John the Revelator was so named to attribute authorship of the apocalyptic book to him, so the name is not so much a differentiator of a historical character as a tautology, as if to say, 'whichever John wrote this book.' There's a monastery named for one of these Johns at the top of the peak, but it was founded long after the exiled fellow was dead. There's also some doubt as to whether this cave we are going to see was the authentic site or someplace nominated by the locals in their oral history and exploited as a tourist venue."

"What do *you* think?"

"I don't know. Maybe I'll have an opinion after we see it."

The cave is a grotto about the size of a small hotel suite, now decorated as a chapel with a hardwood-paneled narthex and golden chandeliers suspended from a naturally formed archway in the rock. Just inside the entry is a mosaic showing John standing over his seated scribe Prochoros as he dictates the hellacious prophecy. Venturing deeper inside, the headroom becomes uncomfortably confining in a small chapel. There have been installed an altar and a few rows of single-plank wooden pews. The curators of the shrine have fenced off John's closet-sized sleeping area, featuring a hammered-silver plate where the saint is supposed to have rested his tormented head.

Evan's first thought was that the barrenness and the marginal livability of the ancient cave were obscured by its repurposing as a place of worship. The shrine looked cozy, but the habitation in ancient times must have been stark and forbidding.

"Not much to call home," Naomi said.

Evan imagined the place stripped of its ornamentation, its bare rock glistening wet with the constant seepage and dripping of condensation from onshore winds.

That's when his reverie changed to horrific fantasy. The fury of the brutal winds swirling outside his hospital room merged with his memories of the cave. As he'd stood there with Naomi and a few other gawking tourists, he'd imagined what it would be like to actually survive in that place, from year to year, from season to season. He imagined John huddling in a corner here in December or January, the coldest months, when it could be chilly and rainy, sometimes freezing and blustery during violent sea storms whipping around the tiny island. Most days, the air in the cave would be dense with smoke from the wood fires inside. But if the weather had suddenly turned harsh and no wood had been gathered, riding out a storm in this remote cave would have been a fearsome, bone-chilling experience.

As John shivered in the cold and damp and recoiled from the storm's wrath outside, what visions came? Greek wine was thick and even syrupy, often laced with drugs, both good reasons to dilute it with water. In fact, it was so strong some said drinking it undiluted would kill you. A few sips to warm the blood, consciousness fading as sleep eventually overtook John in the early morning hours, and here would come the hallucinations, the Four Horsemen stampeding into his fearful brain with a vengeance.

As Evan lay curled up in his hospital bed and the storm raged, his docile brace of ducks transformed into a murder of giant, screaming crows. Huge now, and blacker than the night, they spread their giant wings, blocking all light and looming over him as he cowered and squirmed on the wet ground. Their eyes glowed fiery red, and their raucous cries became a unison chorus rising in crescendo as a piercing cry:

Caw! Caw! Screeeeeeeeeeech! Who. Killed. Your. Friend?

EVAN HADN'T SEEN a doctor yet, although he might have snoozed through morning rounds. He'd never had a concussion before, so he didn't know whether feeling dizzy and woozy was to be expected. Even so, he felt drugged and overmedicated. He didn't see why he needed to be kept that way. And, he thought, these days when you show no dire symptoms, they are usually in a big hurry to boot you out of your expensive bed.

The pain in Evan's neck and back had subsided to the point of a dull throb. Perhaps some medication they'd given him had done its job. He was both drowsy and hungry, not sure whether he should want to sleep or eat.

The room lights flared up full as a nurse waltzed in followed by a handsome middle-aged man in expensive casual clothes. He had close-cropped, greying hair and cosmetically tanned skin. He was wearing slacks, golf shirt, and a cardigan cashmere sweater. He must have checked his winter wear with someone downstairs. He was dressed for Palm Beach or Palm Springs, whichever coast.

"You have a visitor!" the nurse announced, and left.

The guy invaded the space by the left side of the bed, towering over Evan and shining down his best thousand-watt smile. "Stu Shackleton, Reverend. We hope you're feeling better."

Without waiting for a response, he pulled the guest chair close, sat down, and crossed his long legs.

"I'm not ordained," Evan said groggily.

"I understand you sustained a concussion," Shackleton said. "It's normal to be a bit confused. You know, disoriented. Some amnesia, even. Do you remember what happened to you?"

Evan reached down for the button on the railing of his bed and raised himself to sitting position. He looked directly into the man's ice-blue eyes and said, "I'm not the least bit disoriented. I know who you are, Mr. Shackleton, and I believe I know what you want."

The guy was amused. "What I want is for this ice and snow to go away so I can get my boat out of dry dock and go back to tooling around the lake with a cold Tanqueray-and-tonic in my hand. Other than that, I can't imagine what it is I might lack."

"You want the Emmett farm. You and Zip."

Shackleton actually laughed. "Now what would you know about that deal?"

"Most people don't know there's an old Nike base on the property, and you and some developers think it would be a dandy roadside attraction."

"It's a pile of collapsed concrete with a pit full of oil sludge and God knows what other contaminants. Hardly a magnet for tourists."

"I think Bob changed his mind about his will, perhaps just days before he died. I was looking for proof when I was rudely deprived of consciousness."

"That's why I'm here, as a friend of Edie. And Bob. And *you,* if you'll allow me," the smooth talker said. "I fear you've been the victim of an extremely unfortunate misunderstanding. You've suffered undue stress. You needn't concern yourself with the Taggart family probate matters."

"You're right," Evan conceded. "If Bob never amended his will — or if there's no evidence that he did — there's no reason for me to be involved."

"Exactly right," Shackleton said with a condescending smile.

I might as well tell him.

"Except…," Evan began.

A look of mild surprise. "What else could possibly matter?"

Much as Evan wanted to berate this guy so loudly the entire angelic host could hear, he tried to keep his voice calm and steady as he informed him, "On Bob's laptop, I found a scan of Molly's will. It was an encrypted file, but, go figure, I could guess the password. It had handwritten edits, changes so as to make it *Bob's* will. Maybe he thought he was saving on legal expenses. All the terms were the same except Edie got it all, and she was the executor."

Shackleton nodded. "I do believe that's the document we have in the family's safe deposit box at the bank."

Evan went on, "Then there was a later version, also handwritten, *gifting* the farm — to the extent Bob owned or controlled it — to Josh Emmett. All else except the house and the joint bank account — Edie would keep those assets — would go to First Baptist, and making me the executor."

For the briefest moment, Shackleton's face muscles went taut, as though he'd been slapped. He recovered immediately and relaxed as his iron will took over.

"Sorry to say a handwritten will's not worth a crap, my friend." He shook his head, feigning fondness for their dear, departed friend, and commented, "Nice gesture, soft-hearted Bob. Sad to say the congregation will lose out. Perhaps, knowing Bob's last wishes, Edie will be generous. A sizable donation, I'm sure."

"I was hoping those were drafts. And the certified originals are — or were — in the tin box."

"You're right," Shackleton said thoughtfully. "If there were a valid codicil — all typed out and duly certified — it could be a different story. A *very* different story."

"So, let me guess. Griggs brought the box to you — unopened?"

"Let's just say I am reliably informed there was nothing in that box but childish playthings. If Edie wants them displayed at the memorial service, I can't see why not."

No wonder he's not worried. Either there was no document in the box or he's already destroyed it. Sorry, Bob. It's probably game-over for me.

Evan finally thought to ask, "Where is *here*? Which hospital?"

"This isn't a hospital. It's a private rehabilitation clinic."

"For a bump on the head?"

"I'm told you may be addicted to opioids," Shackleton pronounced solemnly. Then he flashed his approximation of a gracious smile. "Don't worry about the expense. It's all taken care of." As he got up to leave, he added, "Do get some rest. Don't be in any hurry to get out of here."

So Shackleton's version of events would be the same as Griggs'. And it gives whoever is running this place a justifiable reason to keep me here.

There was, of course, the outstanding matter of the memorial service, the details of which Evan had failed to discuss with the Worshipful Master of the Alabaster Lodge of the Ancient, Accepted and Free Masons of Southern Missouri.

As he stood in the doorway, Shackleton turned back to him and added, "Oh, and Mr. Wycliff. You needn't concern yourself with the details of the memorial service or at the cemetery. We'll get Reverend Fortnum to handle it. And, you forgot to ask, but I'll offer, the Masons will provide a tribute during which I'll say a few words. I'm sure you'll approve. Like I say, it's one worry less for you." And he left.

I'd get up and walk out, but whatever they've given me has sapped all my energy. If they've got people thinking I'm an addict, what else are they saying about me?

So much for all my responsibilities. Fortnum is the withered wimp from United Methodist. Sorry again, my dear friend.

Oh, and I needn't bother trying to muck up the demolition.

Evan was still hungry, but he couldn't keep his eyes open.

FURTHER CONFUSION as to whether Evan's visitors were real or phantasmagorical came when Doc Wilmer showed up, standing at the foot of his bed and wearing a white lab coat. Evan recognized him from United Methodist, where the old fellow taught a young-adult class in Sunday School. Both addle-brained fossils, the old doctor and Fortnum might have been brothers.

"I'm sorry, doctor, I've been meaning to call you," Evan said as he sat up.

"Oh? Why's that?" The questioner hadn't expected to be questioned.

"I wanted to ask you about Bob Taggart's diagnosis and treatment."

"That's all very well," Wilmer started slowly. "Mind if I sit?"

"Not unless if you mind if I don't."

He doesn't get the joke.

Wilmer sat carefully, using the armrests as he lowered his brittle bones into the guest chair. "I expected you'd be asking me about *your* diagnosis."

"Uh, are you *my* doctor now?"

Yikes. Just when I was starting to be thankful I'm not dead, I get this quack. Quack!

"I'm the attending physician here at the clinic," the doctor said importantly. "Addiction therapy isn't my specialty, of course. But I'm responsible for our clients' general health." He laughed and said, "You could say, if your heart stopped, I'd be the one to sign your death certificate."

I'm hoping that's his idea of a joke.

"They're trying to keep me here against my wishes, you know," Evan said.

"They all say that," Wilmer replied dismissively. "You're actually free to go after initial observation."

Funny, I was thinking this was some kind of conspiracy. You showing up isn't reassuring me any.

"I'd leave, but my body feels like it's covered with lead weights," Evan said. "And I feel dizzy, like now, whenever I try to sit up."

"I can explain. There's the question of the extent of your head injury and whether brain function is impaired. They'll be running tests, you know. We have a neuro man for that. As well, when anyone is brought to this type of facility, we don't know whether you intend to harm yourself or others. We don't yet have an evaluation of your state of mind. We have a couple of shrinks, both lovely ladies, for that. Now, it's against the law to restrain you physically. So in an abundance of caution, we give you a mild sedative so you don't go jumping up and doing anything crazy, if you'll excuse the expression. Also by law, we have seventy-two hours to make an assessment."

"What happens then?"

"If we judge you're not at risk, you're free to go. That is, if you don't choose to stay, which would probably be to your benefit if you need to follow our program. Which, in all probability, you do. By that time, we'll all know what's what."

"I understand you treated Bob Taggart."

"That I did. Tragic. I confess I didn't see it coming. Did anyone?"

"I have his wife's power of attorney," Evan said, although he wasn't sure it was still true. "I read the autopsy report. It showed he had prostate cancer. Did that have him worried?"

If Wilmer was concerned about the propriety of disclosure, he didn't show it. He said simply, "We knew his PSA numbers were on the high side. It didn't bother him all that much, and he didn't want to pursue treatment. But he was stressed, certainly, about whatever else. It was affecting his blood pressure, and I got him started on Losartan — a low, maintenance dose. He seemed anxious, so I gave him a sample of Xanax. He never let me know whether it relaxed him at all. And once he had the pills, he missed his follow-up visits."

"What was stressing him?"

Wilmer gave a doubtful smirk. "He wouldn't say. Just that all of a sudden he had to make decisions, and he wasn't sure he was up to it."

"Decisions? Plural?"

"That's what he said. Sorry I can't tell you more. Condolences to his missus." And he got up, resigned there was no more he could do.

His missus? *As a member of United Methodist, Wilmer should know Edie well. Maybe she doesn't go. Or his relationship with her isn't exactly cordial?*

"Perhaps you could order me some food?" Evan asked.

He smiled. "I do believe it's on its way. Around here, you can set your watch. Provided, that is, you're old enough to prefer to wear a watch. The young ones seem to use their phones these days. Did they let you keep your phone? They don't always."

Evan glanced at his nightstand. There was a wall-mounted beige handset, a pitcher of water, a plastic cup, and nothing else. "I guess not."

They took my watch too.

"Just as well," Wilmer assured him. "Enjoy your meal, be glad you can ignore your friends on Facebook for a while, and get some rest." He walked out with some difficulty. His shoulders were hunched forward, and he had the stiff, halting gait of a man with arthritis in his knees.

BEFORE HE LEFT THE CLINIC, Shackleton confronted Wilmer in his office.

"What are you proposing to do about our friend?"

"He belongs in a hospital for his physical injuries. Head trauma should be monitored. He's not insane by any definition. Legally, we can't keep him here much longer if he doesn't agree to stay for treatment."

It was not the answer Shackleton wanted.

"Find a way to keep him here. At least until Sunday. After that, I don't care what happens to him."

32

WEDNESDAY DINNER
MYERSON CLINIC

D inner was on a rolling tray brought by an underage female intern in faded jeans and a blousy smock the same rosy pastel color as in the wall designs and the upholstery. The food was also red-themed but did not quite match the decor: There was cream of tomato soup, a grilled-cheese-and-tomato sandwich, and a small dish of red Jell-O with an embedded ring of pineapple. The coffee was decaf instant in a dainty foil packet that would require strong fingernails or a sharp instrument to open. Evan ate it all but drew the line at tolerating the coffee. He hit the call button and asked the intern with attitude for a teabag (*Red Rose would be appropriate,* he mused), which never came.

When the intern did come back, she bore no gifts but announced, "You have a call."

Evan did a take to the phone, which had been silent.

"How do you know?" he asked her.

Then the phone purred briefly, once.

"Because it's ringing," she said and pranced out.

"St. Clair County Jail," Evan answered.

"Evan?" came Edie's irritated voice. "You're not picking up your phone."

"That's because I don't know where it is," Evan said.

"How *are* you? What's going *on?*"

"I'm not really sure about that either," he said honestly.

"Oh, my dear," she said. "I've loaded way too much on you."

"Too much or not enough," Evan sighed. "The jury's still out. Never mind. There won't be a jury."

"Are you feeling okay? You're sounding weird."

"Somebody hit me from behind and stole something Bob had wanted me to have. I'm in some kind of clinic, as you know because you called here. Stu Shackleton is my new best friend, and he's insisting I stay as long as he likes." Evan took a breath. "You and I really are overdue for another chat."

"I told you not to worry about the will," she said curtly.

"Short answer," Evan said, "is I didn't think those things concerned me, but now I have some new information that leads me to suspect it all concerns me very much."

"Evan, what are you trying to say?"

"I'm saying Bob must have had a change of heart right before he died."

Now it was Edie's turn to take a long breath. Then she said, "You said you talked to Stu?"

"I did. A most congenial meeting. Love the guy."

"Then, trust Stu," she insisted. "He'll set you straight."

She thinks she'll turn it all over to him. No need to give me explanations now.

In the next long pause, Evan didn't agree or disagree, and the call was over.

I've lost track of time. What will be the order of events? Expiration of the seventy-two hours? The memorial service? Or the flattening of Josh Emmett's house?

Ah, well. On Sunday it will all be over.

33

THURSDAY MORNING
MYERSON CLINIC

Perhaps the seventy-two hours had come and gone, because Evan's head felt clearer, and his lethargy had lifted. The IV spike had been removed from his arm, and he was no longer hooked up to the heart monitor. Maybe there were risks to keeping him sedated, or for some reason he couldn't guess, they'd changed their plan to hold him here.

By the way, who are they? *Does Shackleton own this place? What do they hope to achieve? Keep me out of the way until the house is gone? If they knew the terms of the will, they'd realize that's not enough.*

As he sensed his vitality and strength returning, he wondered how he'd manage outside dressed in his flimsy pajamas and paper slippers. If they were intending to keep him, picking up the bedside phone wouldn't be any use. It rang the receptionist, who placed any outside calls. When he had tried, he'd been politely informed that making calls and taking walks on the grounds were privileges to be earned in the program. For any urgent need, he should press the nurse-call button.

What would Travis McGee do? Maybe he'd recruit an accomplice who would sling him over his shoulder and carry him through the snow drifts to safety. James Bond would have a miniature device hidden in his mouth to summon a remote-controlled car. Philip Marlowe would guess there was someone in the clinic who could be tempted by the promise of a bribe, possibly Doc Wilmer.

If Evan were to remain true to character, he'd *pray* his way out of this mess.

But what to pray for?

Maybe there was a reason he was supposed to be here. He wasn't being tortured. No one had threatened to harm him — at least, not after the nasty crack on the head. Presumably, his caregivers were competent enough to help him recover from the head injury. The only threat had been to cure him of an addiction he didn't have.

I could pray to see that the means of my salvation is already here.

Maybe he wasn't supposed to see the future. There's a reason we don't know the hour of our passing — or even what's lurking around the next corner. But he wished he'd known he would have so little time with Naomi.

I could pray that all is well, that I will be delivered. That's there's a plan, and I'm doing my part in it.

But, Evan realized, he should believe that all day, every day.

I could pray for calmness and presence of mind.

Their drugs had already done as much. Perhaps he should pray for a panic attack to motivate his escape. As it was, he had no interest in doing much of anything.

WHEN EVAN next opened his eyes, an angel was standing by his bed.

The angel was dressed in clean coveralls with a patch on the breast pocket that read *Birch*.

"You had a rough night last night, Preacher. You were screaming."

"Birch. I'm glad to have a friend here."

"You gave me a gift. And I sincerely appreciate it. I wake up every day, and I know what I'm about."

"I didn't give you anything you didn't already have. I helped you see the truth."

"That you did!"

Evan said quietly, "You know how I said you didn't need to take action?"

"That you did!"

"Never mind. I need you to do something for me. Call my friend Zip."

In the next few minutes, they hatched a plan, and, with a sly smile, Birch hurried off to carry it out.

Miss Attitude entered in high dudgeon and threw his clothes on the bed. "You're to get dressed. Quick. Your ride's already here."

And she left.

He did as he was told.

Situation ethics. The end justifies the means. Something like that.

In the lobby, Evan was met by an impatient Zip Zed.

Seeing Evan, he exclaimed, "It's about fucking time! I told them we have to get going!"

Ornette, the stiff-backed receptionist, called out from behind her desk, "I told you, Mr. Zed. I don't have a written order for this."

Zip closed in on her. "And I told you, this is last-minute. There's no time. The CT scanner in Springfield is booked two weeks in advance.

They had a cancellation, and we got an appointment in less than half an hour. If you care anything about this client's welfare, I suggest you let us get on with it!" Then Zip demanded, "Did you give him his wallet back?"

"Why, no," Ornette said.

"Duh? Won't he need his ID and health insurance card?"

"I suppose so," she said, unlocking her desk drawer to hand Zip the wallet.

"And his keys, for chrissake! I'm his landlord, and he's stiffed me two months' rent."

She cowered and handed him Evan's keys.

"*And* his phone. I'll take it as security."

She turned it over.

Then Zip grabbed the mute, startled Evan by the arm and led him out of the building, complaining for all to hear, "They don't have the equipment here! My God, how did they even know your neck's not broken?"

The second surprise was parked outside in the circular drive with its engine running. A squat Fiat Cinquecento. In robin's-egg blue. Zip hustled Evan into the passenger seat and then got in behind the wheel and drove off.

The weather had finally cleared. Mounds of new snowdrifts had transformed familiar landscapes. The sun was out, the temperature was above freezing, and the roads were wet but passable.

"About the Mustang," Evan began, "I left it parked in front of Taggart's."

"Yeah," Zip fumed. "I know."

"So you got it back? I mean, I was sort of overcome by events."

"Just shut up!" he barked. He was so excited he needed a moment to catch his breath. Then he went on, "The sheriff told me to go pick it up. I sent a guy, my lead tech Max. His wife dropped him on her way to work. He got in, found the key in the ignition, got out on the highway, and the fucking engine exploded."

"Wow," Evan said. "Max got out?"

"Yeah, wow. Max is fine, if you don't count getting scared pissless and shitless. Those high-performance turbo cars, if you don't steam-clean the engine and it gets covered with grease and gunk, you're asking for trouble. You run it at high rev, the manifold heats up, the oil covering it hits the flash point, and you're ablaze. That is, *if* this was an accident. Maybe it was, maybe it wasn't. With the weather, by the time the fire crew got there, the whole thing was a cinder. Did you have anything in the vehicle?"

Evan drew a breath. "Just Bob's personal effects, along with his laptop and the pistol he used on himself."

And my *laptop.*

"In other words, all the physical evidence."

"Now that he's been burned to an ash, yes. Pretty much all the evidence."

"What do you mean 'pretty much?'"

"Tell me where we're going and why, and maybe I'll decide to confide in you."

Zip glanced over at him. His face was ashen.

"I don't want any part of this shit," Zip fumed. "You know me, somebody tries to stiff me on a loan, what do I do? I send you to kill them with kindness. Rigging a car to blow up? What lowlife would do something like that?"

"I have many of the nice folks we know short-listed for that award."

"Ah, but it gets better."

"By all means, don't hold back," Evan told him.

"While you were in rehab there, somebody broke into the little love-shack I rent you and did an early spring cleaning. Tossed your shit everywhere. Do you know what they were looking for?"

"Documentary evidence Bob changed his mind about leaving property to Edie."

"And would they have found it?"

"Nope. There's none to find because I don't have it," Evan said.

"So — there's no such evidence?" Zip asked. Evan noted his rescuer's curiosity on this point.

He knows what they were looking for. Maybe he was the one who broke in? I hate that everybody's a suspect.

"I didn't say that," Evan said.

Maybe if I spill it, I'll find out how much he knows, how much he's involved.

Evan explained, "There may be a certified copy of an amended will somewhere. I was looking for that too. What I did have were Bob's notes about how he wanted his will changed. Those files were on his laptop."

"But now those files would be history," Zip concluded, tentatively.

"Not so, Mr. Zed. I already sent them to data heaven."

"What do you mean?"

Evan couldn't control where his mind wandered, which paradoxically often happened when he was under stress. At this moment, he was probably in more mortal danger than at any point in his life. But embracing his fate brought him emotional release. He was no longer worried whether Zip was friend or foe, protector or plotter. He mused out loud, "There's a theory in metaphysics that immortal souls who incarnate on this plane of existence have reinvented in the physical world many of the capabilities they have in heaven. To regain telepathy, they invented the telephone. For clairvoyance, television. To create life from dust, genetic manipulation. To support planetary consciousness, the World Wide Web. And the Internet cloud is a manifestation of an ancient concept called the *Akashic record.* That's a kind of spiritual storehouse where every thought and action from the beginning of time is stored indestructibly for eternity. So, I copied Bob's files to the cloud, on multiple platforms. An NSA operative might be able to find them all, but not your local scum-suckers, even with expert help."

Zip didn't look reassured. He appeared more nervous than ever.

This guy is my answer to prayer? I don't have to panic. Zip is freaked enough for both of us.

"Answer me this," Evan said. "If you don't spin me some yarn, if you're totally straight with me, it'll make all the difference."

"I'm on your side, Preach," Zip assured him.

"Okay. You said you and Shackleton wanted the same piece of property. Was it the Emmett farm?"

"Are you kidding? That bean patch? What would I want with it?"

"Do you know there's a sinkhole on the property?"

"Get outta town! What do I make of that, an Olympic-sized pool?"

"You really don't know?"

"The property Shackleton and I were bidding for was Molly Redwine's walnut groves. She had almost a hundred acres of mature, bearing trees."

"There's big money in nuts?"

"No, knucklehead. The nutmeat is not nothing, but it's the nut *shells.* Pulverized walnut shells are the best abrasive for cleaning jet engines. There's an engineering firm in St. Louis. They supply GE, Pratt and Whitney, Rolls Royce, and the military. Those are the big customers, including companies with service contracts for airline maintenance and air bases. Supplying that stuff would be like a license to print money."

"So, you're not in business with Stu Shackleton?"

"Over the years, he's offered to cut me in on what he calls big deals. But, you know, being married is challenging enough for me. I don't do partner well."

"Do you know he's after the Emmett farm?"

"No, but he shouldn't have any trouble getting it. He's got Edie, and now with Bob gone…"

He's got Edie? Does the whole town know?

"Do you think he's behind what happened to the Mustang?"

"I know he put you in that clinic. He called me to say you'd be out of work for a while, he and some of your friends had done an intervention. You're hooked on painkillers, he said. It just smelled wrong to me, and then the car fire got me all anxious somebody has it in for you. Then Birch called, and I'm happy to help."

"Most of the facts of the autopsy make it look like Bob killed himself. But I've been trying to figure out whether anybody helped him, or maybe drove him to do it." Then Evan asked him, "How'd you find out about the burglary at my place?"

"Otis called me, said there'd been a break-in, told me to go over there and check it out. He said his officers were keeping an eye on the place while you were in the hospital."

Watching for burglars? Or accomplices? Or fugitives from drug-treatment programs?

"I need to have another chat with the usual suspects," Evan said. "So, where are you driving me? I assume you're not taking me home."

From his coat pocket, Zip handed Evan his wallet, keys, and phone. "You're dropping me at the dealership, and then you're driving yourself in this dandy little coupe to anyplace you might want to go. I'm done.

Don't drag me into this. You want to come back to work, fine. It's not exactly a muscle car. It's another one I took in trade. No one around here wants it."

"It's an Easter egg with wheels!"

"It's a sweet ride," Zip beamed. "And oh-so-easy on the gas!"

34

THURSDAY MORNING

ON THE ROAD WITH EVAN

After leaving Zip at Zed Motors, Evan pulled back onto the interstate. The midday sun was shining brightly and the sky was a dazzling blue, not quite matching the paint job of his too-cute Fiat. The driving experience was decidedly different from the Mustang's. He feared a strong gust of wind might blow him off the road. But the car's low center of gravity, combined with its aerodynamic shape, made it surprisingly stable on the highway. Evan figured he could get used to it, even enjoy its nimbleness, but then he realized its distinctive appearance would needlessly advertise his whereabouts.

He congratulated himself on being remarkably calm for someone who might easily have met his untimely demise in a car fire. Briana Caspar impressed him as someone who would maintain her vehicle meticulously, even if its bling didn't fit with her personality. And if the engine needed steam cleaning, she'd have it done, no matter what time of year. No, he had to assume the unfortunate accident was not an accident. However, he assumed the intent was to destroy the evidence in the trunk of the car — including the signed will, had he somehow managed to find it — not to banish his soul from the land of the living. After all, he wouldn't have been the one to move the car. They'd already put him in a hospital bed.

Nevertheless, he decided not to head home, at least not right away. His first impulse was to drive to the sheriff's office, there to confront Otis and get a sense of where he stood in this present iteration of the multiverse. A lot of it was not making sense.

Naomi ran her delicate fingers over the dash panel. Her nail polish was turquoise, exactly matching the car color.

An oh-so-subtle touch of passive-aggressive mockery?

She was wearing a spring dress, a crisp cotton A-line with a bright-yellow floral pattern. He'd seen her in it before, on dance night aboard the *Oceanos.* The sight of her in it made him take a breath.

She teased, "First the gray Taurus, then the fiery Mustang, now this little Continental puddle-hopper. Maybe your problem isn't opioids but multiple-personality disorder."

"You have a way with words, my dear," he said admiringly. "I'll have you write my next sermon."

"Good idea. You should work up some good, old-fashioned, vengeful-God-of-the-Hebrews righteous anger. Get a trumpet, blow down a few walls." Then she asked, "For now, I'd give a pass to Zip. But is Otis in with the plotters? The guy is hard to figure."

Evan thought for a moment, then said, "You've got me there. I was pretty sure he was on the side of the angels but keeping cool. Wanting me to follow through with the investigation even though he couldn't officially. But, now? He didn't have them take me to the hospital emergency room but to that private clinic. That's suspicious. Then again, with the storm, maybe the ER was jammed. Surely he doesn't buy the opioid addiction story, much less the lie I was trying to break into the drugstore. *Someone* sent Griggs to follow me to the store and get the box. The deputy told a cocked-up story. Otis didn't say he believed it, but then he said Griggs' version could stand up."

"If the sheriff knows the truth — and yet acts as if he believes otherwise — that's the definition of a bad actor," she said, knowing Evan would prefer to believe otherwise. "Otis is either in bed with the bad guys, or he's looking the other way while he knows full well what they're up to. It's pretty simple. You have to ask yourself, who benefits?"

Evan answered, "Shackleton wins if no new will is found and any evidence of foul play is destroyed. So either Otis sent Griggs on a nasty errand to get the box or Shackleton did, with the sheriff's knowledge. And it's pretty much the same if you ask who set up the car fire."

"Don't forget," Naomi said, "it was Otis who told Zip to have the car moved. If the car was rigged, it wasn't intended for you."

"So maybe Zip was the target, along with the evidence?"

"Maybe not. I doubt if it was a bomb," she said. "If a fire starts in the engine compartment, there should be time for the driver to get out of there before the whole vehicle goes up — *if* it does. Car fires don't always end in explosions. Max was unhurt." Then she asked, "What about Zip? Do you think he's been straight with you? Seems like he was in with them, now he wants out. He's not acting like a ringleader."

"He is a car salesman, after all," Evan said. "His panic seems genuine enough. His story about the walnut grove is plausible. And his description of the car fire, also plausible."

"I don't think he was worried so much about your safety in the clinic as he's freaked his pals would use violence. And he'd be implicated. But why would anyone make that connection? Again, we're back to Otis, who gets to decide which crimes to write off as accidents."

"Zip did have a lot more information than he should've," Evan said. "All I said in my message through Birch was 'Come get me.' He had that excuse about my needing a CT scan, about the possibility my neck had been broken. He said Shackleton called him about putting me in the clinic. But how would Shackleton have those details?"

"I'm sure they meant to keep you at that clinic," Naomi insisted. "Zip spoiled their plan. But what *was* the plan? To keep you drugged into immobility indefinitely? Or long enough for the Taggart probate case to clear? Would they take the chance you'd just get up and walk out one day?"

"Sounds like a drug overdose would be a convenient solution. And Doc Wilmer would be the perfect idiot to make the mistake."

"Another nasty crime Zip couldn't stomach," Naomi said. "After all, he gave you the car, your wallet, your keys, and your phone. And he's trusting you to make up your mind about what to do next."

"Zip is washing his hands," Evan said.

"Before you're crucified?" She wasn't laughing.

"Homing in on Otis right now might not be the smartest thing."

"That's what they'd expect you to do," she said. "They know you need to know what the sheriff knows."

"So where to now?" Evan asked her.

"You're still a target, and so is Zip. No use going back home just now. Maybe you make some inquiries by phone. From a safe place. Didn't you see a motel in Peculiar?"

"The Ak-Sar-Ben Motor Inn."

"That's *Nebraska* spelled backward," she giggled.

The quickness of her response was impressive. He hadn't wondered about the origins of the bizarre name. "Yes, I guess it is."

"Odd to name a motel in Missouri after some other state."

"They've got Nevada and Lebanon. And Warsaw and Vienna. And they don't need reasons in Peculiar," he said. Her smile warmed him.

If she'd been incarnate and this had been a vacation road trip, she'd take a nap about now. Instead, she just disappeared, and he drove north in lonely silence, to a town with a magical name where he hoped he was not yet famous.

35

THURSDAY NOON
AK-SAR-BEN MOTOR LODGE

The Ak-Sar-Ben is a cluster of separate fifties-style bungalows, a haven for one-night-stand truckers and even shorter-term trysters. The cabins are small and overheated. The microwave and the mini-fridge were new when Nixon was president. The Sony Trinitron TV screen is a CRT with knobs for controls. The ersatz wood paneling on the walls is lithographed vinyl laminate on plywood, a proud feature of the "recreation rooms" of a bygone era. Two small framed Audubon art prints show those ubiquitous, insolent mallard ducks.

Ducks!

The bathroom tile is linoleum, the counters Formica, and the carpet in the bedroom is worn down along the traffic pattern almost to the sisal backing. To Evan, the place smelled faintly of mothballs and disinfectant. But the bed linens were clean and the towels fresh. The horsehair blanket was old-school heavy and would keep a body toasty against the winter chill.

And the modest price was right because Evan's sole credit card couldn't take much more.

The area around his head wound was tender, and his back ached something awful. He didn't have so much as an aspirin. He'd run out of his personal supply of Vicodin days ago, and he'd taken no meds from the clinic. After inspecting his bruises in the mirror above the bathroom sink, Evan relaxed in a nearly scalding shower, a sweetly painful experience he was delighted to prolong. He was tempted to stretch out in the bed, but in his recent involuntary experience, bed equaled confinement. So he dressed again in his one set of clothes, which at least the clinic had seen fit to launder. He thought about having someone go by his place to fetch more clothes and some personal items. That is, if the place was still standing. But then he realized, if his house was staked out, his friend would be followed back here. Not a good plan until he knew more without exposing his location.

The room had one guest chair, a Naugahyde-covered recliner. Evan sat down, tilted it back, and pulled the phone from his pants pocket.

Bob's phone!

Evan had used it when he descended the stairs at the pharmacy. He'd taken Bob's and not his because this one had a flashlight feature. Now he remembered he'd left his on the counter by the pharmacist's sales terminal. This phone had almost no juice then. He assumed now it was dead, but nevertheless he tried to turn it on. The screen lit up. Someone must have powered the phone down, perhaps to avoid its being tracked by GPS when he was at the clinic? There was still five percent battery remaining. He phoned Taggart's. Phil picked up.

The caller ID has to be a shocker. Remind me to stop pretending to be Bob's ghost.

"Edie?" Phil asked.

"No, Phil. It's Preacher Wycliff."

"Well, I guess you're calling about *your* phone. Don't worry. I've got it here."

"Listen, Phil," Evan began cautiously. "The cops have some weird story about my trying to break into your store. Did you set them straight?"

"Officer Griggs called me at home that night. Said they were taking you to the hospital, wanted to know how to lock up and set the alarm."

"What else did he say? Did he ask you why I was down there?"

"He said he'd had to subdue someone he thought was a prowler in the basement. He didn't know it was you until you were out cold. And, yeah, he wanted to know how you happened to be there, so I told him. Then he asked me whether I believed your story. He suggested you might have been planning to come back up into the shop after I'd gone. You know, to steal drugs. He said they'd recovered a metal box. Maybe you had drug paraphernalia in it from the old days?"

"Is that what you think? I thought the stuff I was looking for was in that box."

"I told him I don't know you well, but I really don't believe you're some kind of addict. I've dealt with more than a few strung-out people. Maybe they're not all in withdrawal with the shakes and such. But they're all desperate."

"And did you also talk with Sheriff Otis?"

"He called later that night, and we went through the same drill again. I told him, just to be on the safe side, I'd gone back after his deputy locked up. I made sure nothing was stolen. Then he apologized, didn't say exactly why. Something about it may all have been an unfortunate misunderstanding. He said he'd have someone come to pick up your car. I didn't realize the Mustang was yours. I didn't tell him I have your phone."

An "unfortunate misunderstanding?" It's the same phrase Shackleton used. Is this more reason to think he and the sheriff are working together?

"Thanks, Phil. You know I have to take something for my back now and then. But if I have a habit, it's whiskey."

"Are you still on the Vicodin?"

"Yeah," Evan admitted. "But I'm cutting back and trying not to do both at the same time."

You'll tell them I'm not hooked. You'll say their story is ridiculous!

"Are you still in the hospital?" Phil asked. "I guess you need your phone."

"No, I'm holed up in a motel," Evan answered. Then he fibbed when he added, "The heat in my place is on the fritz."

"So where are you?"

This time he stuck to the truth. "I'm hiding out in Peculiar." And he laughed. "No jokes, please."

"Tell you what," Phil said. "I deserve a long lunch today. I did more than my quota of childcare last night. I finally got the store assistant trained. She's licensed, so she can cover for me. I'll run the phone up to you and I'll buy you a burger or whatever. Maybe it wasn't exactly my fault, but I did bail out of there sooner than I should've, and maybe if I'd stuck around, things would have been different. I don't know, I just feel so bad you got hurt in my store."

Evan was starving. Breakfast at the clinic had been cornflakes and half a banana. "There's this place Merle's American Tavern I've been wanting to try. Right off the I-49."

"See you there at two?"

"You gotta deal, doc."

36

THURSDAY AFTERNOON
IN AND OUT OF PECULIAR

On the way to Merle's, Evan stopped at a convenience store and bought a toothbrush and travel-sized toothpaste, deodorant, and two phone chargers. To which he added a pint of Old Crow and a bonus-sized bag of pork rinds. He knew he'd be flirting with the limit on the credit card, especially if he didn't know how long he'd have to hang out in the retro rented room in Peculiar.

He didn't hesitate to buy the whiskey, but he wondered for a moment whether he should restrain his impulse-grab for the pork rinds. Throughout their friendship, Naomi had been on his case to turn vegan. She didn't lecture, but whenever he'd order a meal or load up his plate, she'd gently remind him there was another way — which was not only *moral* but also *sustainable.* He'd tried it, then soon cheated with eggs and fish and cheese whenever they weren't dining together. Cutting out animal products might be more sustainable for the planet, but as an individual he found it nearly impossible to practice routinely. Even now, he'd resolved to at least aspire to a healthier diet again, someday. Maybe he could survive on salad all the time if he lived in Miami or Tahiti. But during the ice-bound months in the Midwest, he was convinced his body must have meat. At least, that was his excuse, for now. Never mind the sugar, the salt, the fats, and the alcohol.

Those were vices without excuse. He'd minded his mother, and he would have happily obeyed Naomi. Maybe he would find another good woman who could make him behave, but he doubted it. After all, if the Holy Spirit couldn't knock sense into him, who could?

But if practicing veganism faithfully would bring my lost love back, I'd take it up again without complaint. I'd eat raw sprouts and live on ice floes. Because I'd have her to keep me warm.

At Merle's, he arrived before Phil and took a table for two. He watched NFL football classic replays on one screen and an Australian tennis final on the other. Worried Phil might be delayed, Evan went ahead and ordered. He forsook the signature chicken-fried chicken and went for a double order of the daily special, a hearty beef stew, starting with New England clam chowder. And, of course, double-thick coffee, which he achieved by adding requested extra packets of instant to the house drip grind as he poured in sugar liberally from a shaker.

Phil didn't show up, and Evan was comforted in the wisdom of his selfishness. He celebrated his good fortune with thick-crusted, home-made apple pie topped with two scoops of cinnamon-vanilla ice cream.

I'll take an afternoon nap, charge up the phones, and then make some calls. I'll make sure Edie rescinds the POA to take me off the hook. I'll inform the sheriff there's no evidence Bob had a change of heart. I'll insist I'm off the case, officially and unofficially, and what's done is done. Maybe I'll even tell him I'm going back to Boston.

Will that be enough for them to leave me alone? Maybe moving away wouldn't be such a bad idea.

Such was his tentative plan, and it was making more sense by the minute. The problem was that time-worn joke about how to make God laugh.

∼

IN HIS LIMITED LARGESSE, Zip had put less than a quarter-tank of gas in the Fiat. With the indicator reading below Empty, Evan pulled off the interstate and into the Flying J on his way back from Merle's. Before he got out to unhook the pump, he looked down at the console where he had been charging Bob's phone. He switched it on, and the screen lit up with two text messages from Phil, minutes apart, about an hour ago:

Sorry. Childcare issues!

We must meet. Not just your phone!

Evan tapped Phil's name on the message to place a voice call.

"Where are you?" Phil asked when he saw Bob's ID.

"On the interstate, just south of Peculiar. Where are you?"

"Home. Emergency run. Pampers for the kid and Tylenol with codeine for Clara."

"What have you got?"

In a hushed voice, Phil said, "I'm beginning to understand how you might be in trouble."

Evan did know Phil well enough to guess how sharp he was to pick up on clues. "O-kay."

"I think I know what you were looking for. In that box. I mean, what you were *really* looking for. A couple of weeks ago, Bob gave me an envelope to put in the safe. Told me you'd come looking for it."

Uh, about those plans to get out of Dodge…

Evan didn't believe the pharmacist had been holding out on him. But he was appalled that the guy had failed to mention something so obviously important. "You're just remembering this *now?*"

"I told you," Phil said, almost in a whine. "Postpartum stress. And I tend to be absent-minded about some things."

"Did you open it?"

"Of course not," Phil promised.

Other people would've. They'd give the excuse they needed to make sure it wasn't something urgent. Which, of course, it is. Bonus points for being honest, though.

"Listen," Phil went on, "I don't know what's in it, but I'm smart enough to guess someone else wanted it bad enough to jump you."

On target, Ace.

Evan asked him, "Do you know the Arthur Redwine place?"

"Actually, yeah. We make deliveries out there. Redwine turns on his phone about once a month, long enough to order Lotrimin for his jock itch and low-dose Bayer for his angina."

"How long will it take you to get there?"

They agreed to meet in half an hour. Phil said he would be setting out from home, so he wasn't worried about being followed. Evan told him to be careful anyway.

Just when I was sure I was out of it. If I did leave, I'd feel bad for a while, maybe for the rest of my life. But, even with those regrets, I might live a lot longer.

37

THURSDAY 4 PM
REDWINE FARMHOUSE

They sat around Arthur Redwine's kitchen table. Evan stared at the unopened business-size envelope. It bore an attorney's preprinted return address and *Evan* hand-lettered for the addressee. He and Phil had declined offers of cheese. In front of each of them was a smudged glass of cloudy well water. Evan was glad to have his phone back, but its battery was depleted.

Evan apologized to Arthur, "I had your number on this phone, but it's dead. Thanks for your hospitality. Under the circumstances."

"I'm not antisocial," Arthur Redwine explained. "Just reclusive."

With a knowing glance to Phil, Evan said, "I guess we're all alike that way."

Redwine smiled. He was among co-conspirators, wise men who could stomach only so much of the mundane world at a time.

Phil asked, "Evan, do you want to open it in private?"

"No," Evan insisted. "I need you two as witnesses. In case anyone tries to say I forged it."

He tore open the envelope, which contained five legal-sized sheets, along with a note-sized slip. He read in silence for a couple of minutes.

"It's what we need," he announced quietly. "What I expected. It's not an amended will. It's a revocation of the old one, and this one is totally new. He gifts the farm to Josh. Edie keeps the house and the joint bank account, which are already hers anyway. All the rest goes to First Baptist, and I'm executor."

"Lucky you," Redwine said with a sarcastic wink.

"Some people are not going to be happy," Phil said. "And you'd better watch your back. I take it those other assets are substantial?"

"Yes," Evan said. He studied the document some more, then added, "He's been pretty clever about this. Recognizing the will is likely to be contested, he directs the assets going to First Baptist to be held in escrow as a reserve against any expenses we might have defending and enforcing his wishes. And he stipulates the Emmetts are to maintain their tenancy until probate is fully adjudicated, land disputes resolved, and the farm's title is recorded."

"Airtight?" Redwine wondered.

"He was trying to make it that way," Evan said. "Whoever drafted these terms must have listened carefully to Bob's story and took a lot of care working through the details."

Phil looked bewildered. "I guess this means the church owns the store. Or will, unless it has to be sold to pay Josh's legal bills."

"I think that's exactly what it means," Evan agreed. "And there's a little matter of a walnut grove some interested parties will covet and perhaps want to buy."

The suicide note said he was afraid they'd be coming after him. Yeah, some angry folks who'd want to talk him out of what he'd done.

The slip enclosed with the will was not an explanatory note from Bob, as Evan had hoped. It was a receipt for fifteen-hundred dollars for legal services from a law office in Butler.

"The lawyer is Jeremy Bailey," Evan told them. "You have Baileys in your family, don't you, Arthur?"

"No, not on the Redwine side. Molly was a Bailey, married my brother Jake. And her niece Abigail, Bob's mother, married Lionel Taggart. The Baileys were St. Louis," Redwine mused, rolling his eyes back, looking into the gray matter in his own prominent forehead as he searched his encyclopedic memory of names, dates, and events. "Never heard of any of them being in Butler, but it's not like we're all pen pals. Henrietta Bailey, wife of Ezra, was a Clapper, sister to Angus. No love lost between the Clappers and the Baileys, nor between the Baileys and the Redwines. The Bailey girls came to St. Clair County to teach school. Their older brother Ezra stayed in that sinful big city, ran a dry-goods store. The Clapper folks were in Rich Hill. They didn't approve of their gal running off with Ezra all the way to the other side of the state. This lawyer fella could be one of those Baileys. To be a relative to Molly and to Bob, he would have to be the grandson of Henrietta and Ezra. He'd be Bob Taggart's nephew, a first cousin once removed, and Angus would be his great-uncle. Maybe no coincidence he took up the law." Redwine blew out a puff of air, winded from his mental exertion. He helped himself to a gulp of well water, then qualified his opinion with, "But I suppose it's a common name."

Inspecting the signatures at the bottom of the last page, Evan reported, "This will is the real deal. Dated February twenty-fourth. That was the Friday before Bob died. All duly notarized. The witnesses were Evelyn Rose and Coralie Angelides. The notary was Betty Ann Vasquez. Also from Butler."

"Do you know those witnesses?" Phil asked.

"They were Cora and Evelyn from the C'mon," Evan told them. "Cora said they'd signed something for Bob, but he wouldn't tell them anything about what was in the document."

PHIL VANDERHORN TURNED out to be an eager ally. Perhaps anything to occupy him besides cuddling a screaming baby and changing diapers. As they stood on Redwine's porch, Phil indicated the Easter-colored Fiat and said to Evan, "Kind of a noticeable vehicle."

"Yeah, it's a loaner from Zed Motors. Must've been all they had in the used lot."

"You know you can't be driving around in that," Phil said. "There's a rental agency over at the body shop in Rich Hill. There's probably one closer, but you don't want to be tooling around your usual stomping grounds. Why don't I take you there and we'll get you something more plain vanilla? Just until, you know, you get things settled."

"My card's nearly maxed out," Evan said.

"Your credit's good with me. I won't use the store's account because you-know-who will get the bill. I'll have to explain it to Clara, but seems like I do a lot of explaining these days."

If Evan had obeyed his honest impulse, he'd have left the Fiat parked at the nearby ZipGas station with a note on the windshield. It would be an ironic choice because Zip's kid might end up as its new owner anyway. But Phil cautioned him not to do that. He said there'd be no use Evan's letting anyone know he was no longer using the car. Evan agreed Phil's instincts were right, even though the pharmacist was unaware Zip was still a possible conspirator in Evan's list of bad actors.

Then Evan remembered Arthur Redwine had the old Model A perched up on blocks in his barn. There would be plenty of room for the puddle-jumper. When they asked him, the old fellow didn't object and marveled any red-blooded American would want to drive an Italian car that looked like it was made for the clowns in a circus.

Redwine wished them well and said they could keep the "useless Catholic thing" in his barn as long as they wanted. But if any of the Pope's minions came for it, he vowed they could take it back with his blessing.

38

THURSDAY EVENING
RICH HILL

P hil rented Evan an anonymous-black, all-wheel-drive Subaru Forester, which came with a dandy new set of snow tires. The preacher was pleased because here was a car with more heft and traction, much less likely to put him in a ditch.

Unless someone chases me there, that is.

He thanked Phil profusely and sent him home, an exile the fellow did not appreciate. "Let me know if there's anything else I can do," he said hopefully, then added, "and be careful out there."

The car had a full tank of gas, so Evan wouldn't need to stop anytime soon to refuel. He figured the motel was still the safest place to hang out. When he got into the Subaru and fired it up, the first thing he did was plug in his phone.

Then he turned GPS tracking off on the phone, as he'd already done on Bob's. And he punched through the soft menu on the Subaru. Sure enough, it also had a built-in location finder, so he turned it off.

He'd have to pass through Butler on his route back north on I-49 to Peculiar, but by now it would be after-hours at the law office. Not wanting to alert the lawyer about who was calling by using Bob's phone, Evan used his own to leave voicemail, requesting an appointment first thing tomorrow at Bailey's office. He said he wanted to discuss probate matters. He didn't identify himself as the executor of Bob's will, just gave his name as a prospective new client.

Who knows what this guy knows? Or doesn't?

He'd ignored the inevitable string of missed-call and voicemail notifications on both phones. Now he studied them. He'd expected the half-dozen attempts by Edie, who'd reached him eventually on his room phone at the clinic. But there were also calls to him from Josh Emmett, Nick Berner, Zip, and Sheriff Otis. There were text messages on Bob's phone from what looked to be a bill collector.

Never mind that, for now.

Evan didn't want to call Edie, Zip, or especially Otis until he'd met with Bailey. Once Evan could be assured the will was duly submitted into the probate process, he could let the others know of its existence — and its consequences. If he was careful until the information was in the public record, perhaps none of them would have a reason to harm him.

Because the contingent executor isn't Edie, but Cora. Oh, Bob. What tangled webs we weave!

Unless any of them had a hand in Bob's death. Then they'd be right to fear me.

Evan thought he didn't have anything to fear from Josh. But he didn't want to spring the good news on him until Bailey explained exactly how the terms of the will could benefit the Emmetts. Despite Bob's cleverness, it appeared as though the farmhouse would still have to come down.

Bob put his trust in this fellow. But if he's a protégé or even a relative of Clapper's, why didn't the old coot tell me about him?

The weather remained clear and bright. After sunset, the night sky was almost cloudless, with a scattering of stars, and there was a full moon. The soft moonglow rimmed the snow drifts in the broad fields with silver. Evan took a deep breath, not quite a sigh of relief, as he pulled onto the I-49 and headed north.

~

As Evan tucked himself in for the night at the Ak-Sar-Ben, he decided he'd call Nick, who was about the last one he'd suspect of collusion with the usual suspects.

"I know it's late, Nick. I'm calling you back." Evan apologized, saying, "They had me in the hospital. Some knuckleheads thought I'd overdosed on painkillers."

Nick's voice came back low-key, almost sullen. He must have been drinking all through the evening. "Yeah, bro. You gotta take care of yourself. The whiskey works for me, most of the time."

"Like I said, you called?"

"I meant to say for some time and sorry I didn't — Josh shouldn't have gone off on you like that. I mean, you're not the bad guy. You don't want to throw him off his farm."

"No, I'm not," Evan assured him. "And I don't. Do you know who does?"

"Josh asked Bob over and over for more time to pay his rent. And to stop the eviction and the tear-down. Bob just told him to calm down, no worries. That's about all he said, from what I get. Josh got all bent out of shape because he thought Bob should've been able to give him some kind of guarantee. But he stopped short. Like he wouldn't make any promises. Or *couldn't*. That got Josh really riled."

Evan switched on his pastoral voice. "I'm sorry, Nick. Sorry you're worried about Josh. Sorry I haven't been able to give him any comfort. But things will change. And soon. Josh and Linda are going to be fine."

"But how do *you* know?" Nick asked skeptically. "I mean, I'm sure they're grateful to have your prayers and all, but righteous words don't pay the rent. No disrespect."

"Let me put it this way. I can't make promises either, just now. But I know what was in Bob's heart. Maybe better than anybody. And I can assure you, and I'll tell this to Josh, we might not be able to save the farmhouse, but his family is going to be well taken care of."

Nick sighed. "That Edie. Hell on wheels. Do you know what's in *her* heart?"

"Edie won't be a problem," Evan insisted. "But let me be the one to tell Josh. You don't need to go carrying messages for me. Just stick by him, as I know you have." He paused, then asked, "So, is this why you called me? You're worried about Josh?"

"No, actually," Nick said reluctantly. "It's about that time Josh came at you with the shotgun."

"You already apologized, Nick. Enough said."

"No, that's not why. You asked me and Wiley then if we heard shots that morning."

"Did you?"

"Well, yes. That's what's been bothering me. Keeping me up nights, actually. I haven't told anyone."

"Okay. I'm listening."

"There were *two* shots. About a minute apart. Wiley will tell you the same if he can manage to spit it out."

Evan replied, "Thanks, Nick. You've got guts. For now, best keep this to ourselves. I'll know when and how to tell the sheriff."

Nick sounded hurt when he came back, "Evan, did you know he had cancer?"

"He told you?"

"He did."

"When?"

"Does it matter?"

"Maybe not, but did he tell you he was considering suicide?"

Nick was sobbing, probably woozy from the whiskey. And becoming incoherent. He ignored the question and came back with, "Evan, you didn't kill him, did you? I mean, did he *ask* you or something?"

"How can you think that?"

"I don't know. You were his best friend. If he asked you, maybe you'd help him do it."

"Look, Nick. As far as I know, Bob shot himself. And I'm trying to make sure no one helped him. Can you trust me on this?"

"I'll try," he said weakly, and hung up.

Griggs' report said they never found a bullet. Let alone, two.

39

FRIDAY MORNING
BUTLER

Bailey & Associates was located on the second floor of a mini-mall, with a dry cleaner, a convenience store, a branch office of the Department of Motor Vehicles, and the office of B. A. Vasquez, Notary Public, down below. Besides the DMV, if any of those businesses had been successful, there wouldn't have been enough spaces in the parking lot. As it was, Evan had his choice of three.

Jeremy Bailey was young, scrawny, and tall. The proverbial Jack Sprat. Allowing some years for graduate school and maybe a clerking job, he should have been in his mid-twenties. He looked sixteen. Put him in a jersey and he'd be warming his team's bench at basketball games. His wife Marcella also fit the story — she was short and chubby. She more than filled out her wool-tweed twinset, which looked two sizes too small. Her husband's plain gray suit was off-the-rack and two sizes too big, as if he were a larger man's clothes horse. His cheeks were pock-marked, with some residual acne. Her face was round, peaches-and-cream smooth, with deep-set, cheery dimples.

Evan gave his name and repeated he was here to discuss the drafting of a will. "Welcome to our practice, Mr. Wycliff," Marcella beamed sweetly as she offered her soft hand. She must've known the details of

Jeremy's cases because she hastened to add quietly, "I suppose Mr. Taggart referred you to us?"

Overhearing, her husband stepped out of his closet-sized private office and extended a fistful of bony fingers to Evan as he shot her an aside, "You know that's confidential, Marcella."

His wife's voice dropped as she replied meekly, "I'm sure we're all friends here, Jeremy."

Evan shook the lawyer's hand without comment, and the fellow invited him in to sit down.

Taking his seat behind the desk and shooting his cuffs, Jeremy said in a satisfied, lowered voice without prompting, "Title work on the farm's all done. I had to do some convincing there, let me tell you. The rate's no bargain, but I'm sure you understand the necessity. I've got the policy declaration in the file if you want to see it. It has a contingency set-aside for the sinkhole and the access road, so ownership of that plot is severable such that the farm stays free and clear once the government gives us a survey map of their boundary claim. Which eventually I believe the probate court will require them to do. Osceola registered the ex-post-facto property deed with Robert as sole owner, and I've got that also. And, of course, there's always been clear title to those walnut groves. So, I'm really glad to finally meet you, but I expected Bob would be dropping by to help me wrap things up for now. Or do you have another matter to bring us?"

Evan hesitated, then said simply, "Do you know Bob Taggart is dead?"

This obviously came as a shock. Bailey took it in with a gulp, then said, "Why, we finalized the will just a week and a half ago. What was it? Heart attack?"

"From all appearances, he shot himself."

Bailey turned white. Mortal consequences should have been routine in his line of work, but here he was out of his league. "Omigod." Evan let the wheels spin in the guy's head. The young lawyer finally asked, "Did it have anything to do with *this?*"

"I'm afraid it might've," Evan said soberly.

"Omigod."

"There were obits in the Springfield and AC papers, also online. But I take it you were unaware?"

"Totally," Bailey said. "But totally."

Evan thought a moment, then realized he might be the only one to blame. Amid his own difficulties, he'd neglected to phone the Baileys in St. Louis.

There has to be a connection. Clapper's hand is in this.

"Did you know Bob's wife, Edith Taggart?" Evan asked. "Edie?"

Bailey shrugged. "She's mentioned in the will, of course. But, no."

"I had her power of attorney, but I'm not sure where it stands given the changed circumstances. Bob didn't give you any instructions regarding how she'd be informed?"

"Actually, he did," Bailey said, perhaps uncomfortable he might somehow be in error. "Bob specifically warned us against getting in touch with her. He made it clear you would be the executor, and, if anything, her people might be disputing the terms of the will. In the event of his demise, all communications were to be with you. Or the contingent executor, Ms. Angelides."

"It could be I'm the one who dropped the ball here. You see, Bob and Edie hadn't been married very long. Three years. And even though I was his closest friend, we didn't talk that often. So — not only does Edie not know of the new will's existence, but she also doesn't even know *you* exist. She gave me a list of friends and relatives to inform about the memorial service, and on it were Henrietta and Ezra Bailey of St. Louis. I should at least have informed them by now, and I haven't."

"My grandparents," Jeremy said. "My parents moved to Scottsdale years ago. My dad likes the golf, and my mother says the dry air is just the thing for her sinuses. They weren't in touch with Bob either. I didn't know of him until he showed up here a few weeks ago."

"And Angus Clapper was your great-uncle. Did he get you interested in the law?"

"Yeah, did you know him?"

"I met him once at Knox. The day he passed on, actually. I asked him a lot of questions about Molly Redwine's will. That's how I found out about all — or most — of the complications with the Emmett farm. But before he'd tell me anything, Angus insisted we play chess."

"And did he win?"

"Of course."

"Then you're no better than me!" The young fellow laughed. "But he didn't tell me about you. I guess he didn't have the chance. There weren't many people at his funeral. He'd outlived his friends, he was hardly religious, and I guess that's what it takes for a turnout in these parts."

"So Angus referred Bob to you?"

"He did, some time ago, but Bob didn't get around to it. Or he couldn't make up his mind. When he did, he told me he didn't want any of our discussions to get back to Uncle Angus."

"Why?"

Bailey grinned. "He said the old fart was a chatterbox!"

Evan sighed. "Anyhow, Edie made no mention to me of you or Marcella. It didn't occur to Angus either. I didn't manage to send out notices for Bob's memorial. Besides the obit in the newspapers, there was an announcement last Sunday at First Baptist. Edie told me everyone would be local, so I didn't make the rest of it a priority. Then, I got kind of sidetracked. Edie never knew your grandparents, and I'm not even sure she knew they were family. She'd heard of Angus but didn't know how far Bob had gone with him. For sure, she knows nothing of you. Seems like Bob wanted to keep it that way."

"Bob was very cagey about all of it," the young Bailey said. "We offered to have the document witnessed here in the office. Our notary Betty is just downstairs. But Bob said he wanted his own witnesses, and Betty makes house calls, so he did it that way and kept all the copies. Even though it's all fully executed, he gave us the impression he might still want to change his mind. He kept saying he had a lot of decisions to make. Besides the terms we discussed and drafted, I was never sure what other decisions might be troubling him. I believe that's the reason he had the only signed and certified documents. If he changed his mind again, he didn't want other versions floating around."

"Here's what I came to ask you," Evan said. "Does the probate court have a signed copy? If not, how do we register this thing so I'm not the only one running around with it?"

Bailey grew uncomfortable. "Certainly, we have the master file in our computer. But it's not signed. There were two certified originals, and Bob had both of them. You have the one. God knows who has the other."

"He was taking a huge risk. I almost didn't find the one I have."

"He was nervous about all of it," Bailey admitted. "We did everything necessary, down to a gnat's eyelash, but he was still nervous as a jaybird."

"What do we do now?" Evan asked him.

"Bob was sure his wife would contest it. What do you think?"

"I'm certain she will."

"The last thing I told Bob, I advised him to let me submit a certified original to the probate court. That way, the process is started, and it's a matter of official record. No one can dispute the existence of the document, and it's tougher to challenge its authenticity later. Unless, of course, they want to assert he was nuts. Which, given the suicide, they well might. That's a whole other can of worms, but down the line."

"And he failed to do that? File with probate?"

"Actually," Bailey said, "I assumed that's why you came today. But he wanted the title work done and the deed recorded before we presented it to the court."

"So can we do that now?"

"If you trust me with the document, we'll file this afternoon. The probate court is in Osceola, and I'll take it to the clerk's office myself."

Evan thought for a moment. The paranoia kicked in. Then he asked, "Is it at all possible some bad actor could have enough pull with the probate court they could cause a document to get lost? I mean, like someone in law enforcement, or some wheel with political connections?"

Now it was Jeremy Bailey's turn to think for a long moment. Then he asked Evan, "Are you worried Mr. Taggart met with foul play?"

"I am."

"Wow," Bailey muttered. "No wonder he was nervous." Then with a far-off look in his eyes, he demonstrated to Evan why he made the law review in school and how he'd been so crafty with the terms of the will: "The higher legal authorities in this state are the Supreme Court and the Attorney General's office. Now, I don't have any connections either way. And, without proof, which I expect you don't have at this point, you can't just call up the AG and tell them you suspect some cop is crooked. I mean, you can, but you probably won't be taken seriously. But any citizen in the state can call the AG's consumer hotline and register a complaint. Let's say you do that, and your beef is, in my capacity as Mr. Taggart's attorney, I had no business drawing up a will for a plot of land he didn't own. And you submit a certified copy of the will as evidence. Then, just to add another nail to my coffin, you c-c the state bar association. So besides probate, two other official entities in the state will be holding Mr. Taggart's last wishes as a matter of record. The bureaucrats won't pay any attention to it now. It'll be lost in the noise. But someday in the future, any court of competent jurisdiction in the land could subpoena the document. Hard to fuck with that."

"Won't I be casting aspersions on your reputation? Risking your standing and your practice?"

Bailey chuckled like a kid in camp who'd just given you a wedgie. "I told you, no one's going take it seriously at first. And just what reputation would that be? I need business. Like they say in Hollywood, there's no such thing as bad publicity. I mean, whose rep would I rather have as a model? Ruth Bader Ginsberg or Gloria Allred?"

Before Evan left the office, Bailey summoned Betty Vasquez, the visibly pregnant notary, and she certified five more copies of Evan's original so he wouldn't leave empty-handed. (As Cora had, Betty swore Bob never shared the terms of his will with her.) Evan took three of the certified copies, one for himself, one to give to Edie, and one for Josh Emmett. Bailey kept Evan's original, to register with the clerk of the probate court, and two more sets for his "backup plans."

Leaving Marcella to mind the store, Jeremy set out for the courthouse in Osceola, a drive that would take him about an hour and a half.

Two hours later, Evan received a text from Jeremy that Bob's will was now a matter of public record.

EVAN DROVE from Butler to Peculiar, where he checked out of his room at the Ak-Sar-Ben and scarfed down a hearty midmorning breakfast at Merle's. He must have been on okay terms with Mammon, because his credit card still worked.

He'd forgotten he still had Bob's phone in the car. It was plugged into the charger and tucked into the glovebox in the console. He glanced at the phone and saw there were more text messages, all from the same number. Messages about a past-due bill and reminders to pick up a package. He reminded himself those matters could wait until after the memorial.

Should I live so long!

His obligatory move now was to bring it all back to Edie. She'd be sure to inform her co-conspirators he'd checkmated them. Once they all knew the probate court had the will, Evan should no longer be a target. And if he assured her he wasn't into vengeance or retaliation, perhaps they'd let him slip quietly out of their lives and back to Boston. He could fly back from time to time as probate matters came up, but he'd simply be executing Bob's specific instructions. Or, if he judged Cora could be trusted, as Bob must have believed, he could have her do it. He'd had more than enough of St. Clair County.

Go ahead, tell God your plans!

40

FRIDAY EVENING
TAGGART HOUSE

E van chose not to announce his arrival. He found Edie in the kitchen slicing carrots. She was making vegetable stew. She'd responded courteously to his knock and welcomed him in with seeming graciousness. She poured him coffee as he sat at the counter, just as she had before. You'd think his dropping by was a usual and neighborly thing with them. She even remembered he took extra sugar.

She was trying to appear calm. "Come to pay your respects?" she asked, finally turning to face him as she wiped her hands on her apron. And she pointed in the direction of the fireplace. "He's right over there."

There was a gleaming rectangular hardwood case on the mantel.

"He's not in there, you know," he told her. "And I doubt he's hovering around here anywhere."

"Is that what you think?"

"It's what I believe. When we die, we return to God, but not necessarily as individuals. What's in the urn are endlessly borrowed and recycled molecules, shared with billions of other people — and with plants and animals — who came before us. He's in a better place than here, it's joyful. There's nothing to experience and everything to know. I doubt if anyone living can understand what it's like. There's nothing to learn. That's for down here, on Earth, in this world where we've chosen to act out our dramas."

"I don't know about any of that," she said, not admitting to her starring role in this drama. "I just didn't want him in a cardboard box in the basement."

At first, it seemed to Evan she hadn't paid attention to his impromptu sermonette. She went on about the urn and the burial, saying, "Stu says the Masonic rite is usually conducted around the coffin, laying the brother's ceremonial apron on it. There are references to the body in the words they are supposed to say. But these days, so many people opt for cremation, they've started doing it with the urn placed on a table, draping the apron over it."

"I see," Evan said. "I doubt Bob would have objected, if anyone had explained it to him."

She became stiff and defensive as she asked him, "So, Evan. Tell me what you've learned."

"Yes, Bob was stressed to the limit over Molly's will. He made a series of decisions in the weeks before he died, and, as you might not expect, he was surprisingly thorough in attending to the details. With the help of a bright, young attorney named Jeremy Bailey — a relative of Bob's and Angus Clapper's — he wrote a new will and had it duly witnessed and notarized."

Evan summarized the will's terms, which brought a scowl to her face she tried to hide.

"Bob named me as executor, and if I'm unable or unwilling to act, the contingent executor is Coralie Angelides."

"Who is that? I never heard of her."

"She's the counter waitress at the C'mon Inn, where Bob and I often enjoyed sumptuous meals."

"Some tramp?" she sneered.

"No," Evan said. "I wouldn't say that. In her job, as with most bartenders and all shrinks, she listens to a lot of personal storytelling. And she understands it's her duty to maintain the confidentiality of those confessions. In short, besides me, I believe Cora is one of the few people in AC Bob thought he could trust."

"Was she his girlfriend?"

"I have no idea," Evan said truthfully.

Then she announced, striking back, "Stu and I will be married in June."

"I thought he was already married."

"He won't be by then. Ann is in custodial care, and she'll be nicely taken care of."

But perhaps never visited.

"Well, congratulations. I'm sure you two have a lot in common."

I shudder at the irony.

"What about the walnut groves?" she wanted to know.

"All assets except this house and your bank accounts will be held in escrow to pay the Emmetts' legal expenses enforcing their new rights to the farm. If it's a court fight, it might take a long while. But with all that financial backing, I'm sure they'll prevail."

Evan handed her one of the certified copies of the will, informing her, "I'll be keeping a copy for myself, giving another to Josh Emmett. Unless you'd prefer to give it to him yourself. The original is on file with the probate court in Osceola."

"You no longer have my power of attorney," Edie huffed.

"Turns out any interested party can register a will, as long as it's authentic. There's no probate proceeding yet, not until one of us petitions to get it started. Which you'll have to do eventually if you want anything."

"Half of everything should be mine, anyway. And I'll contest it," she said.

"Which you have every right to do. But Missouri isn't a community-property state, and inheritance is usually deemed separate. But if you read his will closely, you'll see Bob has anticipated the possibilities. The Emmetts will win, in the end."

She ran her finger along the edge of the folded paper, as though by doing so she could sense how much money was left in there for her and her hubby-to-be.

"Go ahead and give it to young Emmett," she said. "Precious little I can do about it until we're in court."

"Too bad you don't have the ability to call off the Army to save the farmhouse."

"Yes, too bad. I'll read through this. Then I'll seek Stu's advice. Which is something I believe you neglected to do."

"I'm sure he'll advise you to do the right thing," Evan said, although he was not at all sure, "as I understand he's done concerning the memorial service. And whatever else."

She cleared her throat while she decided what to say next. "I would still want you to deliver the eulogy. It's what people are expecting." She waited for agreement from him, but when he hesitated, she added, "As long as you can leave these earthly matters out of it."

"Jesus said, 'Render to Caesar the things that are Caesar's and to God the things that are God's.'"

"Is that a yes?"

He smiled and replied, "It's the very least I can do."

He was about to go when he turned to her and said, "By the way, there's been a change of plans."

She was coiled and ready to strike. "You're telling me this *now?*"

"Something about the county health inspector and the church kitchen. But all is well. We'll be holding the memorial at the farmhouse."

"That's impossible! It's not acceptable!"

"Like you said — by Sunday, it'll all be over. What's the problem? Some of us are sentimental about the old place. I know Bob was." Then he added, "We're going to delay the service an hour, give the people who show up at the church time to turn around and get there. But a half-hour before, I want to meet with you and the other interested parties — for a more private conversation about earthly matters. Then, I'm sure you'll find my message for the ceremony to be inoffensive and appropriate. But I have a few things to share among ourselves you all need to hear. And don't forget to bring the urn."

He left before she could insist he go.

EVAN DROVE to Reverend Thurston's house. On the way, he phoned Nick Berner and asked him to meet him there.

And he called Josh Emmett to tell him about the change of plans, and Josh's role in it.

41

FRIDAY NIGHT
FIRST BAPTIST PARSONAGE

Thurston didn't like last-minute changes, but he went along with Evan's requests because he knew what was at stake. He and Evan divided up the invitation list and made calls, telling them the service would be held at the farmhouse at eleven o'clock. Thurston talked to the chairwoman of the Loving Embrace reception committee, assuring them the place had a big kitchen, but to bring extra serving items and paper plates from the church's supply. The sexton would help them find things. They asked Birch to post a sign on the church entrance directing people who didn't get the message to proceed to the farmhouse.

And Evan had a long talk with Otis, who scoffed at the plan. But he didn't say no.

Then came a cautious knock at Thurston's front door, and here was Nick. Evan invited him to take off his coat and wet boots, get comfortable, and take a seat with them around the pastor's kitchen table, where there were already three steaming mugs of coffee.

Evan wasn't sure how to ease into it, but he knew when he got started, the floodgates were sure to open. Nick looked nervous but insisted he was anxious to help however he could. Evan briefly proposed how he,

Nick, and Josh would be going out to the farmhouse later tonight, before the midnight deadline, and camping out on the floor of the empty house.

"Like a sit-in?" Nick smiled.

"Exactly right," Evan said. "Holding vigil until our religious service. Then, with luck, and some cooperation from our friends, with any who want to stay, our nonviolent protest could last a while. But no firearms."

"Count me in," Nick said.

Evan drew a breath and stared earnestly into Nick's eyes, which, like one time before, were rimmed with red. The indication his friend had been crying added to Evan's suspicions he was on the right track. "Nick," Evan said softly, "I know you loved Bob, as I did."

Nick started to choke, even then. "Yeah, sure thing. He was solid. Never meant harm to anyone. Awful, just awful, he had to go like that."

Evan went on, "You said you heard *two* shots that morning."

"That's right. I should have told you sooner, and I'm truly sorry."

"You also told me there was about a minute between those two shots."

"Yeah, about that long."

"And you asked if I knew Bob had cancer."

"Helluva thing," Nick said, and he choked again.

"And you asked me then if maybe I *helped* him do it. If perhaps he might have *asked* me to help him."

"Evan, I was out of line. I'm sorry. I didn't mean —"

In a suddenly strident, commanding voice, Evan got in Nick's face and demanded, "He asked *you*, didn't he?"

Nick folded. He broke into heaving sobs. "I, I —"

"Did you *miss* the first time? Then did he plead with you?"

"God forgive me," Nick mumbled.

"We're not here to judge," Thurston assured Nick in a gentle voice as he placed a comforting hand on his arm. "But we need to hear it. All of it. And you know your soul will be in torment — you must be in anguish, I'm sure — until you tell us the whole story, just the way it happened."

Nick sniffled, and Thurston, not having a box of tissues handy, got up and handed the young man a roll of paper towels. Nick blew his nose mightily and began. "I knew what Bob wanted. I'd known for days. And, God help me, I didn't tell anybody. I tried to talk him out of it, but, you know, I didn't have the words. I should have told you, Evan, but I was afraid I'd mess up Bob's plans, whatever they were. He said they were complicated, and he insisted you couldn't know about any of it until it was over. He said it took him a long time to work out. Anyhow, the turkey shoot was just an excuse to get us all there. Wiley was going to be some kind of witness. He'd tell people Bob wanted it that way. We were supposed to do it in the woods. We drove out in Bob's truck together, and that's why it was parked farther off from where you found him. We were arguing and drinking the whole way. We finished the pint he'd brought and we threw the bottle out the window. I was still trying to get him to change his mind, so we were running late, and it got so you'd be showing up soon. You were supposed to be the one to find him, all along. So Bob said we should change the spot so you'd find him on the path on the way into the woods, not so far inside. That way, Wiley wouldn't see it. Bob did change his mind about that."

Nick seemed to lose his will to go on, so Evan coached him, "So you got to the place on the path, in the pasture on the edge of the trees, and Bob got down on his knees..."

Weakly, Nick mumbled, "And he prayed. Me, I wouldn't know how. But Bob asked God to forgive him, to forgive me, to bless each and every one of us he was leaving behind. Then he said he was truly sorry for taking a precious life before its time."

"Did he mean himself?" Thurston asked.

"He must've," Evan said. "And then?"

Nick went on, "I wore a golf glove. Bob told me, no prints on the gun. But my hand was shaking so, and I was crying like a sonofabitch, my eyes were full of water, I couldn't see straight, and of course it was bitchin' cold…"

"And?"

Nick heaved a huge sigh and let out, "And I fired and I missed. It went high over his left shoulder. Maybe I meant to miss. Or some angel jerked my hand. Or I just didn't have the guts."

Evan confirmed, "That was the first shot."

"Yeah. And I dropped that gun and I ran as fast as I could into the woods. I should have kept hold of the gun, should have taken it away from there, thrown it into the woods. But, I dunno, maybe I hoped he could find the courage to do what he had to do? I was gonna find Wiley, maybe we'd think of something. Or I was just chickenshit and I didn't want to be anywhere near what I was afraid would happen next."

Evan asked, "And what did happen next?"

"I was into the trees, I see Wiley, and we hear the second shot."

Evan glanced meaningfully at Thurston, then turned back to Nick and said, "And that's why you asked me if I'd done it. I could have come along, and there Bob would be, still alive and still on his knees, and he could have pleaded with me to finish it."

"Yeah," Nick said. "I had that thought."

"Nick," Evan said. "You know I didn't. I wouldn't. Much as I loved Bob, I cherish all life more. He must have picked up the gun with the hand closest to where you dropped it. Maybe he had to lean over to get it, rolled onto his side. But he didn't hesitate — or he'd have changed his mind again — and as soon as he had his finger on the trigger, he fired down into his heart. And it was done."

It was Thurston's turn to speak again, the voice of both reason and compassion. "Nick, you're going to have to explain all this again to Sheriff Otis. But Evan and I will back you up. I believe your version of it, and so does Evan. And I don't think the sheriff has any intention of reopening the case. Not if you're as honest with him as you've been with us."

"Now," Evan said. "You can help us help Bob — the way he wanted things to turn out."

Nick seemed purged and also relieved. He excused himself to splash some water on his face, then he headed out, promising to show up later that night at the Emmett farm.

∼

WHEN NICK HAD GONE, Evan helped Thurston clean things up in the kitchen. They worked in silence for a few minutes, then the Reverend turned to him and remarked, "You took a chance confronting him like that. It might have gone all the other way. How did you know?"

"There was something in his voice on the phone," Evan said. "He wanted to confess. He asked me if I would have helped Bob if he'd asked. Then he wanted to know if *I'd* done it. He said there were *two* shots. It only made sense if he was confessing to *trying* to help Bob do it, to taking the first shot but not the second. But I wasn't sure until he told us. Do you believe him?"

"I believe him," nodded the pastor. "So what about all those other greedy ones? They had nothing to do with it?"

"Oh, the land grab is a real thing. But Edie's thinking Bob killed himself because he bungled the estate has to be all wrong. He didn't bungle it. In fact, he was rather clever."

"So, why did he do it?"

Evan exhaled a long, exasperated sigh. "I still don't know."

The pastor put a hand on Evan's shoulder and asked, "Do you want to know what I think?"

"When have I not?"

"I think you're a smart guy, Evan. Probably the brightest fellow this little community has ever produced. And you've followed the tangled threads of this thing right down to the cleverest, nastiest knots. But whatever drove Bob to do what he did can't be found in logic. Now, I don't pretend to know what the answer is. But I'm sure it's not about money. Down deep, it's somehow about love."

AFTER HE LEFT THURSTON'S, Evan drove out to the Emmett farm in the rented Subaru. Nick had gone ahead in his own truck. There they met up with Josh Emmett, who'd brought bedrolls for all of them, a kerosene lamp, and a sack of sandwiches Linda had made. They camped out in the barren parlor of the farmhouse after unloading thirty folding chairs from the church van.

42

SATURDAY MORNING
EMMETT FARM

The last big storm to pass through was the blizzard on the night of Evan's luckless effort to retrieve the tin box. On this Saturday morning, the cloudless, sunny skies would persist, and the temperature would climb into the mid-forties. Like stalling the show with a coming attraction at the movies, Nature was taunting the farm folks with a preview of the spring thaw. It was not yet to be (Evan remembered a year when snow fell, however briefly, on the first day in May), but surface water began to trickle its way toward the creeks, and the wind carried the smells of rotting vegetation and last summer's animal dung. Easter and the resurrection of the Earth's flora and fauna were only weeks away.

Just before dawn, two Humvee troop carriers and a command car led a convoy of two bulldozers and a skip loader on flatbeds, along with three triple-trailer, bottom-dump trucks. Riding comfortably in the back of the command car was Col. Sedgewick Pryce, a man on a mission. His job was to flatten everything in sight on the Emmett farm and haul it away by Monday morning. The road graders, cement mixers, and paving crews would be taking over then.

But as the colonel's car pulled off SR P and onto the dirt road to the farm, he was met by a single St. Clair County Sheriff's squad car with its emergency lights flashing. Seeing the approaching vehicles, Sheriff Chet Otis stepped out of the driver's side, and Col. Pryce strode over to meet him. Griggs was noticeably absent.

"What are you doing here, Sheriff?" the military man demanded.

Otis delivered the speech he'd rehearsed, a series of tactics Evan had mapped out for them. The preacher was still holed up with Nick, Wiley, and Josh in the house.

"I'm afraid we've got an impending situation here, sir," Otis informed him.

"I have my orders, if you need to see them," Pryce insisted. "This site was to be vacated by now, and I'll be setting up perimeter control with armed guards to make sure it stays that way."

"We've got squatters in the farmhouse who refuse to leave."

"Are they armed? No matter, I'll pull them out!"

"Not so easy, Colonel. Don't forget a little complication called *posse comitatus*. As I'm sure you know, federal troops don't have powers of arrest on domestic soil."

"Well, you're the sheriff. Saves me a phone call."

"That I am, sir. And, for sure, this is my turf. But, you see, these aren't just any squatters. You've got a man of God in there and two of his loyal followers. They intend to hold a religious observance here mid-morning, a funeral for one of their own who I believe had some Native American ancestry. And I'm not inclined to disrupt a sacred observance."

"Okay, after their mumbo jumbo, you go in at noon, and we'll get done what must be done."

"Not so fast. There's other folks coming in here to join them in the singing and such. Including most of the congregation at First Baptist.

Sympathizers, I take it. We'll have to let them pass. My fear is, knowing what you're about to do here, a lot of them will refuse to leave."

"Don't tell me this is some kind of burial ground."

"They do intend to do a burial. They haven't said where."

"If they refuse to leave, and you can't or won't act, I'll have no alternative but to call in the FBI."

"Waco? Ruby Ridge? Bundy Standoff? Standing Rock? Don't tell me you want a mess like that."

"We don't intend for anyone to get hurt. My guys are engineers, not police."

"I'm not talking about the violence. Although human welfare should certainly be a concern. No, I'm talking about the publicity."

"What do you mean?"

"As I understand it, the government's intentions about this site, whatever they may be, have not been made public, have not had the benefit of public debate about land use, environmental impacts — you know, whatever other nonsense hoops they should make y'all jump through."

The colonel let out a gasp of disgust. "I'll have to call my commanding officer. You don't have any proposed solution, I suppose."

"Actually, sir, I do."

"By all means, spill it."

"The man they're burying might not have owned this exact spot, but for sure he owned the acres adjacent. And one of the fellows inside has inherited it. I'd propose you let this house — *his* house — stand until a court can decide who owns what and what should go where. Give it, I don't know, a couple of months?" Then Otis smiled broadly and added, "Then, however it all plays out, we can both blame it on some *judge!*"

THE FARMHOUSE WAS AN EMPTY NEST. Thanks to the moving crew from the church, every stick of furniture was gone. The living room was bare to its hardwood flooring, and there was an echo in the place. The kitchen crew had brought its own supplies and was already setting up.

Zip Zed was among the first of the invited guests to arrive at the farm-house. He asked Evan, "What's up with the cops and all those camou-flage clowns outside?"

The preacher smiled and replied, "They planned a party and hoped nobody came. But here we are!"

"Your place is still a godawful mess, you know," Zip informed him as he handed over a bundle of clothes, including Evan's sports coat and tie. "You want me to get a cleaning service in there?"

Evan smiled and said, "I need to get my house in order, Zip. And taking care of the housework with my own two hands will be a good way to start."

"What's this confab all about? Are you gonna nail me to the wall? Or someone else?"

All Evan said was, "I'm simply going to tell everyone what I know." Then he added, "So I'm not the only one who knows it. We've got some time before our meeting, and I need to change, so why don't you check with the cooks in the kitchen and see if maybe they haven't already got the coffee pot going?"

Evan ducked into the bathroom to change clothes. He was glad for the indoor plumbing. When this house was built, no doubt it had only an outhouse and a well. He smoothed his thinning hair back in the mirror, and he realized he hadn't shaved in two days.

Ah, well. Stubble is the in-thing these days. But maybe not for a preacher. Besides, my appearance has got to be the least of my worries today.

Evan met up with the arriving Reverend Thurston, dapper in his dark suit, who asked him, "How are you boys holding up?"

Evan replied confidentially, "Nick calmed down. Every dog needs a job, and he's glad he can do his part. He'd bar the door with a loaded weapon, but it mustn't come to that. Wiley's confused, but the sweet guy is always confused. His being here actually helps stabilize Nick. And Josh — his head is spinning about his good fortune. He had no idea Bob held him in such high esteem. I told him it will be a long fight, but with the backing Bob's given him, this will be his farm again, and his title will be ironclad."

Minutes afterward, the usual suspects began to straggle in. They were all present except for Doc Wilmer and Arthur Redwine. The old doctor had either forgotten about the memorial service altogether or judged himself as being above reproach. Redwine probably missed it out of pure cussedness and refusal to leave his house. Evan had been looking forward to seeing Birch again, but the sexton wasn't there. Perhaps he had duties back at the church preparing for services tomorrow. Evan craved the fellow's calmness just now.

Evan had asked Wiley to show any early arrivals who were not among the "interested parties" into the kitchen, offer them coffee, and close the door.

Josh and Linda Emmett sat holding hands on two of the folding chairs. Next to them sat Cora Angelides, surprising Evan by wearing a simple, powder-blue dress rather than her diner uniform. She sat primly with her purse in her lap. Edie, dressed like the clubwoman she no doubt wished to be, must have hated the inconvenience of a metal chair, but she looked more uncomfortable being so close to the Emmetts. Shackleton, Otis, and Griggs sat together, making Evan wonder again how any two of them might have paired up. Thurston presided by the fireplace in the front of the room, and Evan folded his hands and stood off to the side. Wiley's task that morning had been to build and then stoke a roaring fire to take the chill off the room.

On Edie's arrival, Thurston had taken the walnut casket holding the urn from her and placed it reverently on the mantel of the fireplace.

Zip was the last in, stepping from the kitchen and still holding a steaming Styrofoam coffee cup. He remained standing at the back.

Thurston began, "Thank you all for honoring Brother Taggart today. And Edie, may I take this opportunity to extend the condolences of our fellowship. I do believe a sizable number of our congregation will be here this morning, and know we all hold you in our prayers and wish you solace during this difficult time."

Edie was able to say "Thank you" but nothing more.

Thurston continued, "You're all here because I understand Preacher Wycliff has a few sensitive remarks to share with you before the service. Preacher, you have the floor."

Evan surveyed the faces in the room and wondered what each feared he was about to say. He began, "You probably know I was the one who found our brother Bob's body just after dawn on the morning of the twenty-ninth. In a way, I wish I hadn't been the one. In every waking moment afterward, including some sleepless nights, I've been trying to make sense of it. My first question, of course, was why he did it. I've since changed that question to 'How did this happen?' Our sheriff's department soon concluded Bob's wound was self-inflicted. He left a note, after all. There was an autopsy, and it gave no compelling reasons to suspect otherwise. So, days after Bob's death, Sheriff Otis considered the case closed."

Otis nodded and assented, "That's right."

Evan continued, "Now, I'm not an experienced investigator, just an obsessively curious person who has some training in making inferences from evidence. I know Bob was right-handed, but his pistol was found in his left hand. The autopsy found powder residue on that hand, but not on his right. The pistol, a Sig Sauer, is a powerful weapon, and you'd think it would take two hands to steady it and fire. Then again, with its kick I'd expect the gun to fly out of his hand on being fired, but I found him still clutching it. As well, according to the anatomical diagram in the autopsy report, the path of the bullet through the body looks wrong. You'd expect a self-inflicted wound to pass upward, from chest to upper torso, but the angle of this one was slanting downward, from chest to lower back. Cordite residues on his clothing might have yielded helpful information, but apparently, those tests weren't done, and the clothes have been destroyed."

Evan drew a breath and looked around the room. They were all stony-faced. They might be teens in Sunday-school with their eyes glazing over as they lost the thread of his Bible lesson.

Otis piped up, wanting to know, "Preacher, are you going to accuse anyone in this room of anything? Because, if you do, I'd be the one to do something about it, and I've already marked this case closed. If you've got hard evidence, bring it to me. We don't need to concern anyone else here. Seems to me, we owe Bob Taggart a proper sendoff, and you should be about the Heavenly Father's business instead of flapping your gums about a lot of hypotheticals."

Evan had briefed Otis last night during their phone call. The sheriff had agreed, and he did not have the slightest inclination to ask Nick Berner to sign a formal confession to attempted murder. Evidence of intent would be murky, at best, and the only other likely witness, Wiley Krause, hadn't actually seen anything.

Evan went on, "Admittedly it's circumstantial, but there was a lot that didn't add up. Please hear me out. Bob's truck was parked too far from the scene, as though someone took or stopped him there and then marched him out into that field. The knees of his pants were soaking wet, indicating he'd been kneeling long enough to melt the icy ground beneath them. The spent bullet — or bullets — weren't found, which would be consistent with a shot fired in an upward direction, but the path through the body was downward. Nick and Wiley have now admitted they heard *two* shots. So I thought maybe somebody else with another, similar gun, marched Bob into that field and killed him, then fired another round into the air from Bob's gun so analysis would show it had been fired. Deputy Griggs gave me the empty clip, but he kept the live rounds, so only he knows how many shots were left in it."

"Preacher," Griggs interrupted, holding up a cautionary hand, "In real life, a lot of things don't make sense. You talk about the path of the bullet, which hand he used and all, when a man is drunk, which he was, scared, which he most certainly was, and indecisive, which he may well have been. His hands are going to shake. Not to mention how friggin' cold it was out there at six in the morning. Likewise with the path of the bullet and the number of shots. He might be so weak, or like you say the recoil might have been so strong, his first shot went high and wide and didn't hit him. As to the clip, it didn't have to be full to start with. He probably only thought he needed one bullet, after all. So, okay, it took two. Yes, I have a Sig Sauer as my service weapon, and our friend Stu here also owns one. Him and me and Bob all practiced with our guns at the same range. So I can tell you Bob was capable with it. But he was also, I surely believe, one terrified human being, for reasons nobody knows. And, you're right, you're no investigator."

No need to confuse anyone with Nick's version of events. For my part, I had my suspicions, but now these folks will all be convinced I should stick to renegotiating car loans and preaching for pennies.

Griggs may never realize he's just exonerated Nick Berner.

"Deputy Griggs," Evan admitted, "you're absolutely right. I am no professional in these matters, and I've concluded, as you and the sheriff have, that our dear friend Bob took his own life."

And then Evan summarized for them the terms of Bob's amended will — the bottom line being, after what was likely to be an extended court battle — or several battles, including confrontations with the government — Josh and Linda Emmett would end up owning this farmland, as Bob had intended.

Shackleton was visibly agitated, wriggling in his chair as his frustration grew, but so far he hadn't interrupted. Now he blurted out, "That's as may be. But when the dust clears, maybe sooner rather than later, there's nothing to prevent some of us from offering to buy Josh out." Then he turned to Emmett and added, "For a fair price? For a *handsome* price?"

Wisely, Josh just shrugged sheepishly, turned his head, and smiled into Linda's eyes.

"Sure," Evan replied to Shackleton. "But the price will be in line with whatever the community decides — after an open public debate — on how this area is to be developed. If Josh can't farm it and it's to be casinos and such, he'll get enough so he can buy the biggest farm in the county. *And* build a new house."

And the meeting was over. Wiley opened the door to the kitchen, and they waited for the chairs to fill up with the other arriving guests, including the small group of Masons dressed in their business suits and white-leather aprons. They came with two flagpoles — one bearing the Scottish Rite insignia and the other, the Stars and Stripes. Bearers also carried a large, leather-bound Holy Bible, a small pedestal, two foot-long columns, and two metal instruments, the square and the compass.

The Hill and Sons limousine pulled up outside, and they unloaded two large sprays of flowers, which were set in front of the fireplace. The gathering began to look more like a solemn ceremony than a town-hall meeting.

DURING THE MEMORIAL SERVICE, there not being a table in the house, Reverend Thurston placed the urn on a folding chair. In front of the urn, the Masons set the Bible on the pedestal and opened the book to Ecclesiastes 12:1:

> *Remember now thy Creator in the days of thy youth, while the evil days come not, nor the years draw nigh, when thou shalt say, I have no pleasure in them.*

On top of the open Bible, they placed the brick mason's square in the bottom position, the compass spanning it in the top, positioned as they appear in the Masonic emblem, in the third degree, with both points of the compass covering the square. One of the columns, designated the Senior Warden, was placed to the left of the pedestal and standing up like a candlestick. The other column, the Junior Warden, was laid on its side on the right.

No one bothered to explain to the congregation what these symbols meant.

Evan kept his remarks brief. His message was an abbreviated version of "Love Thyself." As he'd preached many times before, if you love and honor yourself, you love and honor God's creation, and you find it easier to love and be generous to your neighbors. He concluded with, "If Bob had known how much God loves him, he might still be with us today."

The Masons performed their ceremony around their arrangement of artifacts, just as if Bob's body were laid out in a casket, draping the walnut box with his own ceremonial apron. Although the Masonic doctrine and ceremony are said to be nondenominational, the references in the text of Stu Shackleton's reading were decidedly Old Testament, as is the verse from Ecclesiastes. No one in the congregation seemed to object, and no one asked questions.

Throughout the ritual, Shackleton stood at the head of his standing rank and file, flanked by the two flag bearers. The tailoring of his pinstriped suit looked immaculate, and his muted-paisley tie was probably the most expensive Italian silk. As he concluded his reading, out of keeping with his lodge's protocol, he added his own impromptu remarks:

"People who aren't familiar with our brotherhood talk about its secrecy, and some might think we're involved in nefarious plots. Shadow government, Deep State, whatever. But our practice, our reason for being, is — we're builders. We get things done, we make things happen, and all for the good of the community. And this means we have to be visionaries. To achieve that shining city on the hill in the world of tomorrow, somebody in the world of today has to look at a barren hill and see the possibilities, draw up the plans, enlist our neighbors in the projects, and then manifest the vision and erect the new city, brick by brick."

He paused, and some would say he was about to shed a tear. Others would say he simply had a canny sense of timing. He went on, "But Masonry, at its core, isn't about community service, even though we do a lot of it. And it's not about having parties or good fellowship, and we surely do plenty of that. No, it's about the personal development of the individual. It's about each of our members following a disciplined path to becoming a better person."

He paused again. This time, the wetness in his eyes seemed real, and his otherwise imperious voice cracked. "I sold Bob Taggart the gun he used on himself. And I practiced alongside him at the shooting range. And I freely admit, I have a sweeping vision about how our beloved corner of Southern Missouri may grow and prosper. And, regrettably, Bob did not share that vision. Neither, I think, do the Emmetts here. I respect their feelings and their views. And events will unfold as they must. But if anything I have ever said or done caused Bob Taggart a moment's grief, even though it's far too late, I sincerely apologize to Bob's spirit and all assembled here. And I humbly beg for the forgiveness and mercy of our Great Architect."

In unison, the Masons pronounced, "So mote it be." And their part was over. They left immediately as a group and without further remarks to anyone else.

Edie, Evan, and Marcus Thurston left the house next, as Edie carried the cremains out to the waiting black stretch limo.

The other congregants then milled around the kitchen, where they enjoyed their sandwiches and coffee.

They noticed on leaving that the Army vehicles had all gone.

43

SUNDAY MORNING
FIRST BAPTIST CHURCH

E van sat in Thurston's office waiting for the pastor to summon him to the sanctuary. Marcus had wanted to indulge in a bit of theatrics. He wouldn't let the congregation know who their guest speaker would be until it was time for Evan to speak.

How about: "God Is All That There Is?"

Bob had been dead for eleven days. During that time, Evan's role in the world had changed from being an itinerant preacher who struggled to hold the attention of his listeners for scarcely an hour, to an obsessively curious investigator who drew more attention than he wanted, and from the wrong people.

And I got wrong as much as I got right.

Naomi had never liked to wear black, even though Evan was sure she'd look stunning in it. She was demure in the pastor's guest chair, dressed in a navy-blue frock made less austere by a row of oversized buttons down the front and set off with two strands of classy pearls around her neck, with matching earrings. She had her hair done up in back, lending her the conservative hauteur of the dutiful wife of a minister.

Naomi glared at him and finally broke the silence by observing, "You know you have a death wish."

Rather than denying the accusation, Evan shot back, "Well, it seems like Bob did. And I'd say volunteering for an assignment in a war zone puts you in the same company."

She said haughtily, "Maybe you'd rather be having these conversations with Bob? You're the living one, the one who can still make choices about your future."

"I wasn't planning on threatening anybody. I was never really in any danger, you know."

"Perhaps some didn't see it that way. They might have wanted you to step out of the movie permanently. If your story were a movie, after the ceremony, Stuart Shackleton would have gotten into a bulldozer and slammed into the house, not realizing the gas lines hadn't been cut off. He'd die horribly in a spectacular ball of fire. Didn't you ever hear, 'The punishment must fit the crime?'"

"'Vengeance is mine, saith the Lord.' And besides, you and I decided years ago we don't buy into the vengeful deity thing." He smiled and spread his hands in a gesture of what he hoped was conciliation. "Besides, we're moving back to Boston. I miss having beer for breakfast and asserting my manhood in the roller derby with other crazed drivers who share my death wish and think a green light is a signal to turn left."

"You can go wherever you want," she said icily. "But what makes you think I'll go with you?"

He looked into her lovely, candy-brown eyes as he asked her, "How could you not?"

"Because," she cooed softly. "If you know what's good for you, sooner or later you'll have to release me. Oh, I'm not asking you to forget. But you shouldn't continue to pretend we talk." Then she added, "That Coralie seems to be a nice person."

"Oh, you're going to play matchmaker for me now? You're some kind of Mensa Yenta?"

She chuckled sadistically. "I didn't say I'd pick you smart ones."

Then her chair was empty.

There's something to be said for having conversations — and relationships — with real people. Provided you have the courage to say goodbye someday.

Evan had been lost in his reverie. He'd lost track of time. But he was pretty sure he still had ten minutes or so before he'd be asked to the pulpit.

Then came a soft knock on the door. The man opened it cautiously, and there stood Fred Birchard. He was holding a cardboard carton about half the size of a shoebox.

He smiled and announced, "I got me a new job!"

"Congratulations, I guess," Evan smiled back.

Birch sat in the guest chair recently vacated by the beautiful image of Naomi.

"Yeah, it's a different kind of hospital," the old fellow said.

"You like it there?"

"Love it. Nice people, doing good work. Kind, compassionate work."

"I hope you're happy there, Birch. But remember, anywhere you are, you'll be the one holding the tentpole. Even if no one else sees it. Now I'd worry about the place you left!" Evan saw the box. "Is that a gift for me?"

"Sad to say, it's the ashes."

"Cremation? Someone we know?"

Who is it now?

"The doctor, my boss, he said bring it to Mrs. Taggart. I thought she went here, as her husband did. But I guess not."

Evan's world tilted. "Why, we buried him yesterday! This has to be a mistake."

"Nossir," Birch said. "Pretty sure this was a *she.* "

"No."

"Name of *Brownie.* "

"Omigod."

"Vet said he left messages on Mr. Bob Taggart's phone. Didn't know how else to reach anybody. He said Mr. Taggart was in some awful distress about it. Brownie's lower back so bad, her back legs wouldn't take her weight, she couldn't walk a step. But Mr. Taggart wasn't sure at all whether to put her down. He finally decide to have it done, two weeks ago. The doc asks him, does he want to hold her? He says no, he can't bear to watch. So he leaves the room, the doc gives the poor dog the shot, and she's gone in the blink of an eye."

"That's sad. I don't blame Bob. He was under a lot of stress. But he loved that dog. I would have thought he'd want to hold her at the last."

"That's just the thing. No sooner it's all done than Mr. Taggart comes racing back in, says he's made a terrible mistake, wants her to live out her life however many days she has left!"

"Oh, my."

"But the doc has to tell him, she's already dead."

Bob and I argued about when to pull the plug. I told him suffering is life. You might think death will end the pain, but a soul without a body can't feel relief, can't feel anything.

Then Evan remembered how Bob had addressed his cryptic suicide note:

My Dearest Ones

ABOUT THE AUTHOR

Gerald Everett Jones is a freelance writer who lives in Santa Monica, California. *Preacher Finds a Corpse* is his eighth novel. He is a member of the Writers Guild of America, the Dramatists Guild, Women's National Book Association, and Film Independent (FIND), as well as a director of the Independent Writers of Southern California (IWOSC). He holds a Bachelor of Arts with Honors from the College of Letters, Wesleyan University, where he studied under novelists Peter Boynton *(Stone Island)*, F.D. Reeve *(The Red Machines)*, and Jerzy Kosinski *(The Painted Bird, Being There)*.

He is the host of the GetPublished! Radio Show (getpublishedradio.com), and his book reviews are published on the Web by *Splash Magazines Worldwide* (splashmagazines.com).

Photo by Gabriella Muttone Photography, Hollywood

ALSO BY GERALD EVERETT JONES

Fiction

Preacher Fakes a Miracle (Evan Wycliff #2)

Clifford's Spiral: A Novel

The Misadventures of Rollo Hemphill (#1 - 3)

My Inflatable Friend

Rubber Babes

Farnsworth's Revenge

Mr. Ballpoint

Christmas Karma

Choke Hold: An Eli Wolff Thriller

Bonfire of the Vanderbilts

Bonfire of the Vanderbilts: Scholar's Edition

Stories and Essay

Boychik Lit

Nonfiction

How to Lie with Charts

The Death of Hypatia and the End of Fate

The Light in His Soul: Lessons from My Brother's Schizophrenia (with
Rebecca Schaper)

Searching for Jonah: Clues in Hebrew and Assyrian History by Don E. Jones
(Afterword)

Made in the USA
Middletown, DE
20 September 2021